Stop All The Clocks

VERONICA ST CLARE

authorHOUSE®

AuthorHouse™ UK Ltd.
500 Avebury Boulevard
Central Milton Keynes, MK9 2BE
www.authorhouse.co.uk
Phone: 08001974150

This book is a work of fiction. People, places, events, and situations are the product of the author's imagination. Any resemblance to actual persons, living or dead, or historical events, is purely coincidental.

© 2009 Veronica St Clare. All rights reserved.

No part of this book may be reproduced, stored in a retrieval system, or transmitted by any means without the written permission of the author.

First published by AuthorHouse 5/5/2009

ISBN: 978-1-4389-7507-8 (sc)

Printed in the United States of America
Bloomington, Indiana

This book is printed on acid-free paper.

To my mother Mai Dunphy of Kilkenny, Ireland for her encouragement over the years when writing the novel.

Thank you to my former husband Finbarr O'Driscoll for proof reading the book and for his support

BOOK 1

PROLOGUE

A man stabbed him. He drew a serrated edge across his face and then dug the knife into the side of his neck. The sounds I heard were a stifled groan, and the horrible sputtering of someone choking in his own congealing blood. As his attacker rained blow after blow down on him I envisaged his outstretched arms being raised in defence, shooting convulsively out, waving grotesque, still fingered hands in the air, desperately trying to save himself. In hacking away at his features the killer sought also to deny his humanity, to destroy the most obvious symbol of his physical identity, his face.

1

29ᵀᴴ Oᴄᴛᴏʙᴇʀ 2004

An Indian summer drifted over the tree-softened avenue like a Mimosa balm from a carefree languid Deity. Sweet silence reigned.

I felt desire clutch at my groin as my partner, Nicholas, stroked my skin and held my breast, rubbing his forefinger over my nipple until it stood erect. The tip of my tongue flickered over my lower lip. Putting his arms around me he pulled me against him. I peered at the clock by the bed. Its feverish little green digits said, 6 a.m. 'Go away, it's too early.' But he persisted.

'Take your night dress off.'

I giggled like a child and then kissed his cheek with a butterfly touch.

He slid the straps down over my shoulders and my eyes opened wide. As the garment slipped down to my hips he cupped his hand over my breast.

'Let me sleep,' I muttered groggily. Determined to take me he ignored my pleas and pulled my nightdress right off, took me into his arms and kissed me.

As my mouth softened under his touch I clutched him eagerly. Tender love making followed.

I was still dozing when he was leaving for the office. He nipped into the bedroom and plopped down on the bed.

'See you tonight, darlin,' I said as he bade me farewell. I looked at him admiring his handsome features. His blue green eyes held dry amusement, his voice, when he spoke, was soft and resonant. Now his black trilby was tilted to one side, so, straightening it and laughingly teasing him, I added, 'Sure, you look like Al Capone with that hat and that large black crombie. Nobody would guess you're a solicitor.' I know he's the one, I thought. Forever!

Before he left he stroked my hair gently with one hand and his lips brushed my forehead. When he tilted my chin and kissed me gently on the mouth it was like nothing I'd ever known before. For a time I lay there reflecting: since he'd distanced himself from his former wife our life had taken on new meaning. Now everything would be perfect. I sighed and muttered, 'La dolce vita.'

Only the faintest wound of the fallen day bled along the horizon as I returned home and climbed the stairs to the study. I clunked the CD button as I twisted towards the phone. Elton John's, 'Candle in the Wind,' filled the void, calming me. I was upset by an event that had occurred at the school where I teach so I picked up the phone and dialled a colleague's number to discuss it. As we connected I heard the front door open. It was Nicholas returning from the office. I continued on speaking.

Five minutes later I heard an incessant buzz of the doorbell. I decided to let Nicholas answer it.

All of a sudden an eerie, ghoulish sound assailed my senses.

Brain in panic mode - slow motion state triggered.
I Listened.
Silence ... a long silence.
All was still.
Must have been Nicholas, knocking something over?
Mental ricochet! - maybe not?
After all that has happened it could…

Then I heard it again.
What was it?
I knew and didn't know.
Something horrific?
That much was clear.
Another unidentifiable sound beset me.
I dropped the receiver.
Left it dangling.
What followed was barely human.
A cry of terror.
Like a tortured animal.
About to die.
Terrified, I raced to the top of the stairs.
I stood, transfixed, and gaped in horror.
'Iosa Criost' - Jesus Christ
Brain back in survival mode.

At the end of the stairs Nicholas was slumped against the balustrade. Blood, great crimson spurts of it, gushed from his mouth. His face was a sickly grey.

Elton's melody interposed. 'And it seems to me you lived your life

Like a candle in the wind.'

Fear snaked up my spine, leaving a chill in its wake.

All of a sudden a tall fair haired figure charged past him. At the front door the stranger twisted round. Momentarily, his ice blue eyes riveted on me, ice blue like glass –sharp glass – vacant and transparent.

EVIL!

Then he darted outside.

My gaze remained fixed on the doorframe but only for a second. I jerked into action and dashed down the stairs.

Deep shock registered in Nicholas's eyes as they met mine. Each feature in his face tore at my heart: indescribable terror, incomprehension, and unimaginable suffering.

The blood was still gushing from his mouth. A shower of red corpuscles drenched my face. As a sickening terror quivered in my chest I grabbed him and helped him back towards the kitchen. When I reached the back of the hall I recoiled in disbelief. Rivulets of blood stained the stone floor and the air held the syrupy smell of fresh blood. Retching, gasping for breath, I stumbled backwards, banging into the wall and loosening my grip on Nicholas. A thick stench of fear, which I had never believed could be so tangible, overwhelmed me. 'A mathair de' - Mother of God. Where's the blood coming from, love?' No reply but his sad green eyes remained focused on mine as if they were trying to tell me something.

Somehow I got him into the kitchen. I flicked the switch. Nothing! 'Damn it,' I muttered. I should have replaced the tube. My mind was a maelstrom as I tried to fathom out where to place him. Wildly I glanced around and opted for the well lit utility room. With difficulty I laid him on the floor, propping him against the washing machine, that way he wouldn't choke to death in his own blood.

By now I was at my wits end. What to do next? Kneeling I cradled his head to my breast. His blood stained jacket lacquered against my cheek. Amateurishly I checked for a pulse but my hand was shaking so much all I managed to achieve was smear blood in a macabre design over his neck and face. What did I know of these things anyhow I was just an ordinary science teacher living an ordinary life. I then pressed my ear to his chest. A faint heartbeat told me he still had a chance. But there was so much blood how could he survive? So...much...blood.

By now the wetness of his body fluids on the floor was soaking through my cream skirt onto my skin. I jumped up, and stared in horror at the bright scarlet stains on the material. As I moved, the new carpet tiles squelched and my shoes made a red footprint on them. Oh, dear God. You won't believe what I did next. Would you do it under the circumstance? Of course not, no one would. Well ... guess what: I took my shoes off. Can you imagine, all this stuff happening and all I could think of was the carpet getting soiled. But I knew Nicholas would be cross - he's so house proud, you know. Anyhow I placed them upside down on the floor.

Not a clever move as you will later learn.

As I turned to Nicholas again my vision tunnelled. All I could see was him, bloodied, terrified, his eyes staring and wide with shock. I felt utterly helpless. Only the ghastly thought that he'd die if I didn't do something jolted me into action. I spoke softly. 'Darling, I'm going for help, be brave.' His eyes sought mine.

Could he hear me? It was only then I noticed the mutilation. I shut my eyes hoping it would erase the vision but the image of his lacerated face seared onto the inside of my eyelids, there for me to see whether I looked or not. I opened them hoping that it was all a nightmare but he was still lying there his eyes still staring. Impulsively I just ran. Ran out the kitchen door, down the hall, a fleeting thought hitting me as I stumbled along; maybe I should have dialled 999. Too late! I was hell bound on getting help close by. Hand to my mouth, I raced past the lounge and exited the house. As I crashed up my neighbour's path and banged on her door stinging surges of adrenalin twitched in my veins, churning through my body as if venom had been pumped into my blood vessels.

'What the hell is going on?' A figure shouted through the stained glass door. Marie appeared and stared at me aghast. 'Alex...'

I pushed her back into the hall screeching, 'For God's sake, dial 999 ... NOW, NOW, Nicholas is bleeding to death. Hurry!'

Marie paused as if trying to absorb the words and then propelled herself towards the 'phone.

Still dazed from the adrenaline shock I staggered back out the door. I heard, 'He's dying.' I froze. Oh my God. Is he dead?

Somehow I got back to Nicholas. He was still in the same position his eyes still staring. Squatting on the floor I cradled his head in my lap, my body in physical shock and the muscles rigid. It was a cold night but I could feel sweat pouring from my pores and streaming down my face like tears. Then I started gibbering, out of my mind, barely able to focus, though still desperate to know what had happened. 'Who ...who ... did this Nicholas?'

His lips moved. Still alive! But no sounds came except the sharp pant of his breathing. Was he going to hyperventilate?

His body gave a sudden violent jerk. His jaws clamped tight. Guttural sounds emerged from his throat.

Oh my God, it's a death throe. The seizure erupted with a frightening intensity, working through him like an electric shock.

My heart started to beat like a fast drum, my breathing a sharp staccato. 'Don't die on me.'

Then with a pitiful gaze Nicholas's eyes met mine. He seemed to plead with me, trusting, begging, 'Help me, you alone can do this.' If only.

'Stay with me love. Stay with me.'

His lips formed the words, 'Help me, help me.' So much pain in so few syllables. But at least his mind was still focused.

I became manic then. The tiny room became a garishly lit stage set and under the glare of the lights the whole bizarre scene was being enacted. Nicholas's slouched body with blood still dripping, like a vampire's, from his mouth was all so extraordinarily surreal.

Then he gave a slight tremor, you know just like when a 'shaky head' among the long grass is about to be picked, and it seems to withdraw and shudder and then yield. It appeared that as the hand of death reached out to claim his soul his body knew and it quivered, yielding and not yielding. He's still clinging to life. Maybe there's hope. In the dark smoky glass of the oven door, I saw the reflection of a face that seemed to be looking out at me from a window in Hell.

'Your candle burned out long before

Your legend ever did.'

Has his candle burned out?

Marie appeared, and knelt beside me.

'The ambulance is on its way.' She cast me a comforting glance. Then Andy, a nurse, arrived from across the road. Hope did a butterfly hop in my heart. He'll save him. I gave a silent thanks to God.

Andy knelt down. 'Alex, I'll take over there's nothing you can do.'

'No I can't leave him,' I sobbed.

'Alex, there's no room for all of us.' He glanced at Marie and twisted his head gunning it towards the door.

Forcibly she led me outside.

Distraught.

Shocked.

Impotent.

We stood.

Waiting for the ambulance.

What else could we do?

I kept my eyes on my watch; the infinitesimal jumps of the thin, delicate sweep of the hands too agonizingly slow. Time seemed to have stopped as I waited knowing that in there his life was ebbing away.

I started to pray again, not that I believed in it anymore. 'Holy Mary Mother of God, let him live.'

Suddenly another horror zapped through me. I shook my head, trying to wipe away the unwelcome thought that started to buzz in my brain. My throat constricted as the dread I had tried to suppress flowed into a full- blown terror. Can you guess what it was? Think before you read on. Write the script with me.

Well turning to Marie I voiced my fear. 'If he dies … they'll think I killed him.'

I bet you got it in one - he's dying and she's only worried about her bloody tiles. Guilty as hell would be your verdict.

And of course Marie asked the obvious. 'Why… would they think that?'

Do you think her words carried a doubt?

I answered. 'Look at me. I'm drenched in his blood.'

Marie put her arm around me then and said. 'Don't worry, it will be alright.'

But would it? With a flash I realised that I'd actually voiced the word 'killed'. Was he dead?

As the terrible reality zeroed in Andy rushed out of the house shouting, 'For God's sake, tell them to hurry, this man hasn't got much time.'

Brain zap. 'Is he… dead, Andy?'

There was a pause then a flash of lightning. Seconds later the drizzle drops gave way to lashing rain. A clap of thunder followed by another streak of lightning gave my words certain omniscience.

He shot me an odd look. Almost inaudibly he whispered, 'Alex, I'm not sure.'

I dived into the house then. Never would I erase the scene from my memory if I were to live for eternity. You won't believe what I had to face.

Nicholas lay on his back.

His eyes wide open.

Twisted backwards.

His face streaked with blood.

Dark and vibrant.

A gash in his neck gaped like a mocking grin while his features were gnarled in shock.

A gargoyle demise.

Murder at its most hideous.

DEAD! DE...AD. Inexplicably Auden's phrase, "Stop all the clocks," sprang to mind. Weird don't you think that at such a time Auden's poignant words could echo so in my consciousness. "Nothing matters now; nothing now can ever come to any good. He is dead." The words were so difficult to understand. I repeated them, 'He is dead,' and tried to grasp their significance, but they eluded me.

Spell bound I stood rooted until the sound of the sirens forced me into an awareness. I hurried outside again, only subliminally aware that the driver of the ambulance was lacking urgency by wasting time trying to park in the crowded street. 'For Christ's sake,' I screamed, 'just double-park, there's a man dying in there.'

Do you know I couldn't admit he was dead. I thought maybe there was a chance they'd revive him and give him back his life. 'Hurry; please, please hurry,' I sobbed as the uniformed staff got out of the vehicle.

All of a sudden the whole place was swarming with black uniformed figures... police and ambulance staff... indistinguishable to me then.

Feeling crushed under an enormous weight I stumbled, in a blind stupor, back into the house. Glancing in the mirror,

I caught a reflection. And guess what? A Banshee, like Kitty the Hair, white-faced, ashen and dark eyed stared back at me. The jet black hair was dishevelled, wild from the wind and matted with blood.

My nostrils then trembled and my mind wandered over the boundary of insanity. All of a sudden figures filled the house swarming everywhere like an army of black ants.

I heard my disembodied voice chant, 'All these ants ... black ants swarming around.

'Black ants, BLACK ANTS ... EVERYWHERE.'

I had gone mad.

Ready for the nut house.

They've come to take me away, ha, ha, to take me away.

Oh God, I'm going crazy.

A sense of unreality had zapped me and I was in a new dimension.

By now crowds from surrounding houses had lined the pavement near the house, but the excitement was muted. A stabbing had occurred; a man had been murdered in this exclusive neighbourhood in the Merseyside. Anxiety was uppermost; what had happened at no 50 could happen at 32 or 39. The world had gone crazy.

A WPC appeared. 'Let's go upstairs while everything is being sorted.' A harsh, hard edge lined the woman's voice. She was thick-waisted, obviously at home in the mannish uniform. Marie she ignored. I had no experience of the police. I might as well have been chitchatting to an alien from the other end of the Milky Way. We mounted the stairs and drifted into the small comfortable study. I sat down on a chaise lounge. A second constable, with doe like eyes, appeared and gave me scalding tea, hot and strong and urged me to drink it. It tasted metallic. How bizarre to notice such trivial details in such an appalling crisis almost as if the mind had to focus on the mundane to remain sane. Suddenly everything seemed distorted as a heightened consciousness pervaded my whole being; my emotions, though swamped were yet sharply focused. I knew I had to talk to someone. How could I acknowledge my terror ... the horror of admitting my man was dead? MURDERED?

And guess what I did next. Would you do it? Would anyone? The need to speak to someone churned round in my mind. I'll 'phone my brother. Can't phone Mam and Dad it would be too much of a shock for them. Even though I guessed that the WPC wouldn't take kindly to me using the phone I, nevertheless, jumped up, pushed past her and grabbed the receiver before she could stop me, after all it was my house. The need to unburden myself, shout it from the roof tops, 'To scribble on the sky the Message, he is dead.' was so critical, almost a 'sine qua non,' because only then, could I actually give credence to it. The policewoman tried to grab the receiver but I snatched it away giving her a scathing look.

'I'm phoning my brother in Ireland,' I said hotly and glared at her. A twitch made her right cheek jump. Her eyes rolled up to mine. But she remained silent. Maybe she knew I'd brook no argument so she allowed me to continue. I dialled.

Diarmuid answered immediately.

My voice sounded strangely calm almost cold. 'Diarmuid... Nicholas...is dead...murdered...stabbed.'

He repeated the words, 'Dead ... Murdered? Stabbed? What happened?'

'He's been brutally killed. Can't talk now. I have to go. Tell Mam and Dad. Tell them the news. He's dead!' I disconnected. My voice broke then, tears so close I had to turn away from the police woman and gather myself together.

'Why don't you sit down and try and relax.' The WPC assumed a hatchet face. She had an exact replica of Stonehenge slotted into her mouth instead of teeth. Her manner was abrupt, accusatory. She stood in front of the phone. It was clear that she wasn't going to let me make another call. I obeyed but her peculiar covert glances worried me. It was then the thought ricocheted into my consciousness. Guess what it was? Exactly. She thinks I killed him. Wouldn't you in the circumstances? She could see I was covered in blood? Domestic violence she'd think! And everyone else.

All of a sudden another horrifying thought struck me as I remembered the threatening note I'd given to Nicholas – telling him he had to choose between me and Zoe. Or else. What a dumb thing to do.

Panic mode again. This is when my mind sticks – like a broken record.

Where is it?

Eyes flickered.

Then I glimpsed it.

On the bureau.

Glowing

I rose.

Sidled over.

My gaze skittered over to the policewoman.

Not looking.

I snatched it.

Shoved it up my sleeve.

A harsh cackle.

'I'll have that.' Her voice was edged like a scythe. Scalpels were not sharper than her eyes.

I flushed as I handed it over sensing the frayed edges of panic.

Her eyes scanned the letter. The woman waited so long I thought she wasn't going to respond. After eons the frosted gaze came up, level and unblinking. A look of smug satisfaction washed over her features. She smiled. You know one of those chilling little smiles.

She now must definitely think that I... She couldn't, could she? Then a hopeless horror enveloped me even further as I recalled taking off my shoes. The police would see it as a sign of guilt. Who in their right mind would worry about a carpet when their partner was dying they'd think. I realised then that the mess I was in had increased ten fold. Horrors were loose in my mind. What would be loose in yours? Well ...

I pictured a prison cell.

I pictured the jury - 'Guilty.'

I pictured the judge - 'Take her down.'

I slumped down, feeling an unruly despair within me, one that walked at the side of fear. But I hadn't killed him. I had seen the guy. I could describe him. The evil Viking eyes, the gaunt face, materialized in my mind's eye. This man had killed my love - a man I had loved extravagantly, fiercely, wildly. It was the passion of a life time. For five years I'd made a feast of love. Though sometimes it was joyful, jolly, solemn, romantic, lascivious fun, it was never banal. On occasions it was as wild and dramatic as a violent hurricane. All my crevices, mind and body were explored, satiated.

I loved him.

With my body!

With my soul!

With my mind!

When I had him, he alone was enough. I remembered that day in a Liverpool office when everything seemed to change. A professional assignation and only there by chance because a senior partner was unable to handle my divorce. In the beginning was the word and so the creation of a new love emerging through negotiations from the dying embers of my failed marriage. Fools rushed in but understandably so. Why wait when you can take a chance and love will find a way

Suddenly I felt a ringing in my ears. I felt as if I might be sick. I wanted this night to have never been. I wanted his love again. A love like that had not come to me early in life. And that stranger had taken it away. Now there was nothing to live for. All of a sudden real hatred welled up inside me for this man. Vengeance would be mine. I didn't allow myself to dwell even for a second on the true nature of revenge, because this wasn't something I was in the slightest bit familiar with. Helping the police bring this man to justice would be my reason d'etre – if they ever believed my story. I now had my doubts.

I began to rock to and forth. And then I knew I was over the edge when I began to hum 'Danny Boy.' The tune transported me back to the dim past. The limpid melody had remained a long while latent in my soul. Now it spoke to me of another time, another place – it was the piece of music he used to play. The delicate air evoked a wilderness of memory. As I hummed I became absorbed in the turbulence of past longings, discord and ambivalent desires. I wondered when everything had gone terribly wrong. Then as I dwelt further on those fragments of my past, it was as if I saw myself in a shattered mirror as the sharp edge of each recollection lacerated my mind.

When had the madness begun? I stopped rocking. January 1999 - that's when it was? That was when David, my second husband, had commenced divorce proceedings. That was when I had engaged Nicholas to act in my interests.

More recollections - disjointed - assailed me. Words his best friend, Pat, had said about him: "I can only describe him as being a stirring presence in any company. You could say his spiritual domain was spacious, and anyone lucky enough to come his way, was warmly invited to share it. He was the quintessential optimist. His eyes never became jaded; his ardour for what was new and alive never diminished. His nature was to be completely in love with life. He was a happy - go lucky, who just loved people. There were always a thousand and one things that he wanted to achieve. He had this great passion for life and such was his charisma that when you met him you not only encountered him, you experienced him."

There it is - the distant past, a chequered existence – another world, a world that spanned just five years. I was unaware then, that out there were those who through sheer coincidence had become destined to weave through each other's lives and mine. I was unaware that those people I had never met would destroy all that I held dear. I was just an innocent in their dark evil world. A Pandora Box had been opened and I'd been drawn into a secret dark web.

I sat for time immemorial and gazed into space. Hatchet face I ignored. I was in another dimension again, lost in a labyrinth of my own restless mind:

He is gone now and my universe is turning black. I see him now, grinning but more often bloodied and faceless as death left him, beckoning me further into hell, beckoning me further into a darkness where love has no place and evil lurks.

I felt disembodied – and observed the first trickle of madness?

Suddenly Marie appeared at the study door and broke me out of my wanderings. 'There's a Detective Inspector Ken Masterson down stairs.' Something flickered in her eyes, shutter - quick - was it fear?

As I left the study I felt that I had stepped into someone else's nightmare. But then it struck me that this was my nightmare and that it was just about to begin.

2

LIVERPOOL January 1999

MUM, David won't change his mind.' Deirdre sat forward in the arm chair her blue eyes flashing.

'But you said… remember, that he might.'

'Mum, get real, that was two weeks ago. Look at him now, relentless. He's determined to divorce you. I'd get legal advice if I were you.'

'I'll be leaving all this,' I replied as I cast my eyes around the spacious lounge. I loved this room. An off white carpet was a perfect canvas for the four plush red armchairs and a matching velvet couch. A large gilt mirror graced one of the walls. The few antique tables dotted here and there plus a collection of gold framed paintings added a touch of luxury to the room. One was an Aubrey Beardsley original. David's purchase of course. Reclining on the couch I sighed.

'Mum, for God's sake. What's more important these possessions or your happiness?' She grimaced.

I leaned forward, rested my elbows on my thighs and said, 'But Deirdre…'

'No buts Mum. Get yourself a solicitor. Anyhow the marriage is on the rocks. You said so yourself. I think you should face reality and think about a future without him.' Her voice had a lucid rawness to it. 'And don't forget you're the one who married an alcoholic.' Her tone was judgmental as usual.

'I thought he was a heavy drinker.' My voice was small, like a little girl's.

'Oh Mum, You're so naïve. We all warned you, me, grandma and even dad. Would you listen? I just hope the next time you get entangled with a man you won't be so rash.'

'The man who makes no mistakes doesn't usually make anything.'

Deirdre rolled her eyes.

'You're talking as if the relationship is already over. What's he said to you?' The conversation was sapping my energy. I slumped back further in the couch.

'Mum, you'll have to discuss it with David. It's not for me to say.'

'He must have said something.' My voice was now tired and low.

'Only that he's going to divorce you. He said he didn't want rows in his marriage.'

I felt a hollow pain in the middle of my stomach. 'But I can't be alone. Sure 'tis a miserable existence.'

'Mum, why do you break into this irritating habit of using Irish colloquiums? It's either that or you speak in Irish.'

'Sure I'm noch.'

'Noch, where's that in the English dictionary? Oh I give up. You know what your problem is, Mum. You've always rushed from one relationship to another. It's your neediness.' She ran her fingers through her long blonde hair. 'Well at least you didn't take up with some Don Corleone when you swanned off to Sicily with Lynda last year. I wouldn't put it past you though.'

'As if I would.'

'Mum, your choice of men is...'

'What?'

'Never mind.' Her voice was softer.

'You don't understand, Deirdre. Being alone is sort of... scary.' My lower lip quivered.

Deirdre cast a comforting glance. 'Sorry Mum. I'm only trying to make you face reality. Not wanting to be alone is natural. They say there's some strange, hidden terror that lives within us that is inherited that makes us crave human contact. Deirdre's blue eyes had softened.

'Oh.' I was dangerously close to tears but I wasn't going to show it. I had my own wisdom. 'They say man loves company if only that of a small burning candle.'

Pursing her lips Deirdre said. 'Where did you get that one Mum? Made it up again?'

'Sure I didn't. It's a quote form George Lichtenberg.'

Deirdre raised her eyes to heaven. 'Never heard of him. You and your sayings Mum I don't know where you get them from.'

It was not lost on me. She thinks just because I'm scatty I haven't got a brain.

'Anyhow to get back to what I was saying about being alone. They say it's a throwback to the times when primitive men huddled together around small fires listening to the distant sounds of a hostile world.'

'Always the psychologist, Deirdre!' My voice was quite grave, quite quiet.

'It's my job, Mum. Look I've got to go. Talk to David perhaps you'll be able to patch things up.' She shrugged her shoulders.

I detected the doubt in her voice.

'Chin up,' Deirdre said, rising from her chair and giving me a hug. 'I just want you to get out of this dysfunctional marriage and start living. And don't forget you'll always have me and Catherine. I better drag her away from 'Dora the Explorer' and go. You look as if you could do with a quiet moment so don't bother to get up.'

I gave a wan smile as my mind's eye focused on my grandchild. Now three, Catherine had an exquisite oval face, with high, prominent cheekbones. Her little teeth were very white against her dark skin. She was very bright for her age; extraordinary articulate and beautiful too, that rare beauty which sometimes comes from being of mixed race. I felt she was a genetic ricochet of her dad.

'Hello.' Deirdre was still standing at the door. 'You're gone again, day dreaming as usual.'

'What is this life, full of care, we have no time to stand and think.'

'You misquoted that one. It's to stand and stare.' She rolled her eyes again. 'Mum you seem to live by these quotes and justify your actions by them. They're like the Bible to you.'

'Sure I don't. And anyhow it fits. I was thinking not staring.'

'See, I told you, you make them up. I don't know what's worse your Malapropisms, your quotes or your mnemonics for remembering things - like KHT. Who ever heard of that?'

'Keys on hall table, it's simple. Wait till you're my age.'

Deirdre shook her head and sighed loudly.

I'll never win with Bossy Boots. 'Before you go tell me how's she getting on at nursery?'

'Can't shut her up. Coming out with all sorts of weird shit. Her latest is f...wanker.'

'Iosa Criost. She learnt that from you.'

'Maybe I should swear in Gaelic like you Mum then no one would understand her.' She grimaced. 'Well we can't all be like you and Daddy.'

'Sure what do you mean?'

'The pair of you. You're so eccentric and allow your life to be ruled by those misquotes of yours. With Daddy's paranoia and your scattiness it's a wonder I turned out normal.'

Normal, she's got to be kidding. 'Sure I'm just a little bit absentminded.' My voice was defensive.

'A little bit. Mum haven't you noticed you've got odd socks on.'

'Noo,' I said looking down. One white and one pink! 'Sure me mind was on a science problem when I was putting them on and I didn't notice.'

'And I suppose you didn't notice the sugar in the fridge either.'

'Sure no, I wondered where it was. I…'

'There, you've proved my point, Mum. You're a successful professional, Head of the Science Department in a private school but half the time you're in the ivory tower of the academic.'

'But…'

'Mum I haven't time to argue. One more thing. I noticed that you've a blue solution in one of those crystal tumblers that I like to use. I hope it's not a chemical?'

'Noo. It's just a blue food dye.'

'Mum I know when you're telling fibs - your eyes open wide. I'm sure it's copper sulphate solution.'

'Copper sulphate?'

'Yes Mum. You'll have us all poisoned if we're not careful. It's well I rinse things before I use them. There's chemicals and science equipment all over the house. Why do you bother to do experiments with your private students? Just stick to the theory.'

I won't let her have the last word. 'Sure they love doing experiments. Anyhow sure everything's a chemical. Oven cleaner is concentrated sodium hydroxide and …'

'Mum I'm off, you're just making excuses. And do your back exercises. Remember what the physiotherapist said.'

I'll wind her up. 'I do them twenty five seven.'

'It's twenty four seven. God!' She grimaced.

'Sure don't I know that but I do them twice on Sunday so it's twenty five.'

Deirdre stared at me, disbelief written on her face, then rolled her eyes horribly and said, 'Mum, if you go around saying such things they'll lock you up. I'm going before I go crackers.'

As she turned to go she glanced at the clock. 'Mum.'

'What.'

'Where did you get that contraption?'

'What contraption?'

'The clock?'

'Oh!'

'Its got no hands and the numbers go backwards.'

'I know, just an experiment, another way of perceiving the universe.'

'Mum you're mad'.

'Just playing with the idea that all is not what it seems.'

'That's it. I knew you were certifiable. I suppose daddy encouraged you, knowing him.'

'Well as a matter of fact he popped in the other day and helped me do the electrics. He thinks it's clever.'

'He would.'

'This time I'm going before I ... Oh I give up.'

Cheek. 'Slan leat' (Good bye), I said as I watched her disappear out the door. Some cause happiness wherever they go; others whenever they go. I hated Deirdre's bossy ways. Maybe she was right about one thing - I did rush from one man to another. I had married young too. Eighteen and pregnant with Deirdre. Over the years my husband Donal and I had drifted apart and after fourteen years we'd divorced. After that I fell in love with every Tom, Dick and Harry until I met the charismatic David at the University staff club. He cut quite a dash with his shock of premature white hair; always something of a weakness with me. Despite our age difference and his heavy drinking I'd married him. And now? I should at least have a chat with a solicitor.

Then I rose and wandered around the room, my shoulders tense, my face a mask of pain. Glancing at the reflection of myself in the mirror I saw childlike features watching me critically. I felt I had the soft face of a younger person. The eyes, a purple shade of blue. I had an even mouth; not over generous but people said I looked pretty when I smiled. Not bad for forty. Then it occurred to me. Will I survive this bad patch? All of a sudden words ricocheted into my consciousness: "Alex reminds me of a phoenix rising from the ashes of ruinous relationships forged stronger than before." This was what my wonderful friend Lynda, had written about me when I'd gone through a bad patch and my self esteem had plummeted. I'd copied it all down into my diary, noting every word. As I stared into the mirror again the remainder of what she had said echoed in my mind.

"She has never minded being the butt of a gentle joke - I say gentle because she engenders in people an urge to protect - never to hurt. She appears a delicate, vulnerable creature. This, however, belies a courage, and a steely determination that has carried her through many hardships."

I felt the tension escape from my body as the memories of her profound words rekindled my spirit. Glancing over at the photo of Lynda and myself taken in happier times I felt an overwhelming rush of affection. In appearance we were so alike but there the similarity ended. Our personalities were polar opposites. I'm messy, Lynda is neat. I eat 5 a day, Lynda has a fag for lunch, I like Mozart, Sibelius, and Strauss, Lynda likes Diana Ross, Elton John.

I loved Lynda more than anybody, more than … Deirdre. Guilt swept through me like a tornado. I loved Deirdre too but I didn't like… didn't like her ways.

Feeling that I was spiralling into despair I rushed to the bureau and extracted my diary. Years ago Lynda had taught me to write down my feelings. "Once you get it down on paper it's out of your mind and you'll feel better," she'd said. "Write each thought on a separate line. It works for me."

I had done so since and found it very therapeutic. I delighted in Lynda's little wisdoms especially the one where she had encouraged me to "hurdle insults when you meet someone who you think is one cell short of an amoeba.' "Not out loud," she'd added. With my convent upbringing I'm still a little uncomfortable with it but I'm getting there.

3

Nicholas Murray tapped his fingers on the desk waiting for Alex Rowe's arrival. He glanced over at the window. Rain was falling outside in a foggy dimness. Instead of working he twisted in his chair, idly fingering the one file that lay on his desk. Then he let his outstretched arm rest on it and continued on sitting motionless with bowed head. Brooding, he dwelt on his situation. He was a tormented man who had been disappointed in life. He thought of his Chinese wife Zoe, and his beloved daughter Elizabeth, now far away in New Zealand. His eyes travelled over to a photograph of Elizabeth on his left. He reached over. His fingers instinctively traced the curves of her smile, traced the dimples that gave her face a happy look. The almond-shaped cheekbones bordered a turned up nose that sloped between a beautiful mouth and large oriental eyes that always seemed full of mischief. Only six he thought. He remembered what Zoe had said, after one of their blazing rows over money.

'I'm leaving.'

'What do you mean, you're leaving, Darling,' he'd said with one of his lopsided grins.

'I'm leaving you and I'm taking Elizabeth with me, back to New Zealand, back to the sun and back to a better lifestyle, back to where I won't feel like E.T. or a second class citizen.'

He'd sighed, and nonchalantly replied, 'You've said that at least a hundred times before and I'm sick of hearing it. You're welcome to leave but you're not taking Elizabeth.'

'I'm not taking Elizabeth? Watch me.'

It was then that his worst fears had come true when Zoe carried out her threat and left with Elizabeth. The life went out of him then.

Now he was financially crippled after to many visits to see his daughter. Then he'd met Danny Delaney, a financial consultant who'd said he'd make him rich. Danny was the solution to his problems or so he thought. Once he was out of debt he'd give him a wide berth. He had to see Elizabeth. She was his reason d'etre.

He rose from his chair, wandered over to the window and peered out, still dwelling on the cost of joining forces with Danny. He didn't like Danny's association with the local Liverpool mob. Not really a man to become entangled with. He strode back to his desk and slumped down. Agonising, he thought again of his daughter. He missed her so much. It was as if his right arm had been amputated. Suddenly a ghost of a smile flickered on his lips as he reminisced again. He closed his eyes for a contemplative moment recalling her droopy slanted eyes, her curved smile, the chipmunk cheeks, the chubby hands that she had as a baby. He recalled how she had started to crawl with the funny to and fro gyrations of infancy all too long ago now. He sighed.

4

'I'm delighted to meet you,' Nicholas said, extending his hand as his secretary showed me into his office. 'My name's Nicholas.'

I shook his hand finding it strong, but with a surprisingly gentle touch. As I sank into a chair I studied him again and drew a sharp breath. He was very handsome in a dark Byronic sort of way. I loved the greeny blue eyes and lashes to die for. Straight away I thought he resembled Hugh Grant only older.

I shifted in my chair and raised my eyes to his face. I felt a strange shiver surge through me, making my scalp tighten and my fingers tingle. I was aware of his wonderful twinkling eyes, warm and soft but full of fun. Though his looks were striking what enthralled me more was his enchanting smile. He's immaculately dressed, I thought as I appraised him. The suit's well cut and the highly polished shoes expensive. The only incongruous part of his attire was the tie with Mickey Mouse patterns on it. Maybe it reveals the playfulness of the man, I reflected.

I glanced around the office. It was dull and tidy; the desk was tidy. Everything was tidy. Just a pristine bareness. Not like my sloppiness. Except for two gigantic plants, a great desk and two leather armchairs, the office said nothing and something about the person who sat there daily. What had my granny said – people who were too tidy had always something to hide.

'My boss Tom Price has filled me in a bit but perhaps you'd like to tell me about yourself. Sorry he's not available to act for you as you requested but he's on vacation.'

For about thirty minutes I rambled on about all the sordid details of my marriage.

Then glancing at me he said, 'Well, now that I've got most of your particulars let's make the next session for Friday next? Will five o'clock suit.'

I nodded.

As he pencilled it into his diary he added, 'Gosh it's almost March already.'

He paused. 'Fancy … a drink in the local bar. I've no one to rush home to now that my wife has left me.' He gave a wan smile.

'A drink,' I said and stared at him. 'Rather unethical don't you think?'

'Sorry. Sometimes a relaxed environment benefits these proceedings. Important items to discuss might spring to mind. But if you'd rather not … it's your choice.' His eyes twinkled.

'Never mix business with pleasure – that's what my granny always said.'

'Well it's up to you. Carpe Diem - that's what I always say.'

'Seize the moment.'

He threw me a surprised glance.

Gone up in his estimation. I smiled and thought; sure there's no harm in having a drink. It might calm my nerves. Besides, who in their right mind would pass up an opportunity like this? Nicholas Murray was drop dead gorgeous.

I nodded. 'Well, okay then, if you insist.' Better not let Deirdre know. I imagined what she'd say. "Mum there you go again jumping in at the deep end."

'Let's go grab that drink then.' Nicholas said raising an eyebrow.

As we strolled to the local wine bar I remained silent, listening to the swish of the icy wind as it came sweeping in from the Irish Sea. I could smell the sharp crisp odour of snow not far away. I stole a glance at Nicholas as we entered the lounge. I liked him. If I was honest it was more that that. You're doing it again Alex, a tiny voice nagged, becoming involved emotionally.

The bar was buzzing. Voices engaged in lively conversation rose and fell, mingled with sudden bursts of laughter. I noticed that it was full of men of all ages attired in the pin stripe professional garb of the legal and business fraternity. Several of them greeted Nicholas. Some of them gave me an appraising glance, one or two raising an eyebrow and then turned away and continued their conversation. One man waved at Nicholas and smirked at me. He was standing at the bar sipping wine with a man I instantly recognised from the media. Icicles of trepidation inched down along my vertebrae. 'Who's that person who waved? He looks like a Godfather with that dark expensive crombie draped around his shoulders.'

'His name's Danny Delaney. I do a bit of business from time to time with him.'

'Isn't that Ron Barry with him? Did you know the tabloids have linked him with the laundering of drug money for a local syndicate? He's just been released from prison.' I was shocked that Nicholas was remotely connected to a mobster. What am I getting myself into? I reddened as I remembered Deirdre's Don Corleone jibe.

A grimace swept over his features. 'Hm … yes! Danny knows people from all walks of life. Come on; forget about him, and let's enjoy that drink.'

I gave him a curious look. His expression had gone cold and closed.

I sensed that further conversation about Danny was taboo. As we moved towards the rear of the lounge I noticed a black and white English Sheep dog lying on the floor beside Danny. 'What a lovely animal.'

'Yes, Danny adores Timmy. Never goes anywhere without him.'

I floated one brow. 'An odd name to give a dog,' I said as we sat in a corner away from too many prying eyes.

Nicholas frowned. 'He called him after his son, Tim.'

'So he's got a son then?'

'Not anymore, he died.'

'Died?'

'From leukaemia at the age of three. He was heartbroken. Shortly after that he got the dog.'

'How sad.' And how odd I thought. What sort of person could substitute a dog for a dead child?

'Right, ice cold champagne?' His voice assumed a compelling softness and before I'd time to reply he continued, 'Bubbly it is then?'

'Hm, yes,' I said; surprised by his lavishness.

As Nicholas disappeared to the bar I stole a glance at Danny. He was about medium height, with broad shoulders and a broad chest. His features were typically Irish. With a name like his he must come from Ireland or be of Irish descent.

Maybe it was telepathy but as I studied him he glanced over and gave me a beaming smile. Quickly I adopted an incurious pose.

Just then Nicholas reappeared with a waiter in tow carrying an ice bucket containing the wine. The waiter poured the wine and withdrew. Nicholas lifted his glass and said, 'Here's to ... us.'

'Tell me about yourself.' Nicholas asked.

Jovially I replied. 'Sure indeed Nicholas it is I who should be asking about you. You've got a file on me. Not much more to add.'

'Oh there's nothing of interest to tell.'

But as he reached for his glass I caught the subtle change in his eyes, an indefinable something that lingered there momentarily. I felt I was encroaching on issues very private and personal.

Reluctantly, he began. As he spoke he seemed to forget my presence. 'I lived in New Zealand for ten years and built up a thriving law practice. When I was forty-four I met a Chinese girl, Zoe. Within six weeks we were married.'

'That was quick!' I gave a half smile.

Draining the rest of his drink he set down the glass and replied, 'Yes, we both wanted children. I was scared that if I postponed it any longer it would be too late. After a year Elizabeth was born. Then things started to spiral. I took too many risks in real estate instead of concentrating on my law practice. When the property crash came I lost everything.' He sighed heavily.

I stared at him. How can anyone be so foolhardy? But what did I know of the world he lived in I thought. I was just an innocent teacher passionate about my work. 'So what happened?'

'Six months after Elizabeth was born I had to do a runner and we came back here.'

'Do a runner. Why?' What next.

He cast his eyes down and said with a sheepish expression, 'When the crash came I lost large sums of clients' money and they wanted their pound ... weren't to happy.'

I glimpsed a fleeting expression of fear cross his face. Unease spread through me. Seems to take high risks.

'Then what?'

'Zoe hated it here. She returned to New Zealand taking Elizabeth with her.' He paused and his eyes watered. 'Honestly Alex, Elizabeth is my life. For her sake I tried to keep the marriage going.' His eyes snapped open and the curtain of his guard was lifted. On the table his fingers closed into such a tight fist that his knuckles turned white. 'God, how I...' he paused in mid sentence and bit his lip, momentarily incapable of continuing. When he did he said, 'Anyhow to cut a long story short, after they left I bumped into Tom, and he offered me a partnership.'

For all his confidence and light heartedness I could see that he couldn't hide the deep hurt within him. His eyes moistened.

'I'm flying over there next week to see her. Of course I'll have to pay for the flight with plastic.'

'Why?'

'I'm broke.'

'How?'

'Trips.'

'Trips where?'

'To New Zealand. Every month.'

Nicholas took another sip of his drink. 'I'm sorry Alex. I didn't mean to burden you with my problems. I got a bit carried away.'

I could see the tears glittering in the corners of his eyes. The pain on his face was raw. Reaching across the table, I gently touched his hand. 'So what now?'

With absolute despair mirrored in his eyes he whispered. 'Nothing. There is no now, there is no after.'

His words sent a shiver through me. What lengths would this man go to too see his daughter? My thoughts skittered back to Godfather and his companion and Nicholas's association with them. Not good.

Suddenly almost as fast as the black mood had descended on him, it lifted. He gave me one of his enchanting smiles. 'Still, as my mother used to say, "battle on". It's bound to come right in the end.'

It was late when we were leaving the wine bar. As we passed Danny I heard his voice. 'Come and join us old boy.' His companion had left.

Inching closer Nicholas replied with a grin. 'Have to rush Danny. I've a train to catch.'

'You're a dark horse, Nicholas, hiding away this lovely lady.'

Grinning again, Nicholas replied. 'Mrs Rowe is a client of mine.'

'Tell me another old boy. Anyhow aren't you going to introduce me?'

Reluctantly Nicholas responded. 'This is Alex...'

'And I'm the man who'll going to make us mega rich,' Danny said effusively his hand grasping mine in a firm handshake. 'You must join me for dinner sometime.'

Mega rich. How? Got to be drugs money? Christ Alex don't go there. Nicholas may be drop dead gorgeous but he's got too much baggage.

'We have to go Danny,' Nicholas said as he edged towards the door.

'I'll give you a bell about that deal first thing tomorrow.'

'Hm… yes,' Nicholas replied as he took me by the elbow and guided me out the door.

'Say goodbye to Nicholas, Danny said twisting towards the dog. Timmy wagged his tail and barked. I watched him as Danny threw a biscuit to him, and saw the devotion in his eyes. It wasn't good to be too fond of animals; they were too easily lost.

As if echoing my thoughts, Danny said, 'If any thing happened to Timmy, I don't know what I'd do. He means the world to me.'

'God, he loves that dog,' I said as we hurried towards the car park.

'Yes. I told you about his son. Come on let's go, it's late.'

Doesn't want to talk about Danny. Odd!

I felt the flakes of snow touch my cheek as we walked. I gazed up and saw over to the west a great white curtain drawn across the sky, a solid wall of snow racing towards us.

As we approached the car park a small child stood, no more than six. The snow was all around her, snowflakes in her eyes and ears and mouth and on her head. She was half frozen. Her cheeks were dead white and blotched with purple. She wore an old anorak, a couple of sizes too small. There were holes in her socks and her jeans were well worn. Her face was pale, skin stretched highly over prominent cheekbones, yet the blue eyes were alert. She gave a ghost of a smile in spite of the fact that her hands, holding a shoebox containing heather posies, were blue with cold.

Traveller's child, I thought as I lingered.

Nicholas paused, nodded, and gazed down into the wan little face. He muttered, 'Only Elizabeth's age.' He reached into his pocket and handed her a ten pound note. Then he gently took the box saying with a twinkle in his eye, 'You can go home now and tell your mother you've sold them all.'

A flicker of understanding washed over her face. She gave him a wide smile muttering, 'Thanks mister,' and skipped away.

I was moved by his gesture. He's broke and yet he gives generously. I mused. Generosity is the flower of justice – Hawthorne. Perhaps my judgement was rather rash. He is a good man.

As we arrived at the car he gave me a peck on the cheek. 'Thanks for listening.' Just then a gust of wind blew my hair across my face. Tenderly he pulled it back, tucking it behind my ear.

I nodded and jumped into my pride and joy, a white Carmen Ghia, an old relic from my first marriage. Swinging round, I said. 'See you next Friday and maybe we can finalize things.'

'Of course.'

As he turned to go, he hesitated, turned back, Columbo – style and said, 'Maybe we could have dinner afterwards?' He raised a questioning eyebrow?

'That's grand, Nicholas. Sure I'd love to.'

It was late when I arrived home. The snow had stopped. I sat for an aeon in the lounge gazing out at the night sky. The stars looked diamond hard and bright in the cloudless sky.

Sipping a glass of red wine I realised, with a flash of wonder, that I'd enjoyed the evening. Nicholas's appearance in my life was the last thing I'd expected. I decided he was the typical gentleman of English loneliness, melancholy and infinite longing, all bubbling away beneath a thin, frigid shell of niceness and reserve.

Abruptly, however my elation was replaced by a sense of unease as I recalled his words, "They wanted their pound of …" what … flesh? And what about this Danny? First of all he reminded me of someone who considered himself to be like Rhett Butler, tall, broad-shoulders with a chortle in his voice, and a twinkle in his eyes. Why was Nicholas mixing with him? Anyone connected with the criminal element had to spell trouble. I remembered my granny's saying, "If you rub to the dirt the dirt will stick to you." Or something like that. And I'd agreed to have dinner with him. Well I wouldn't become too involved, just a bit of fun to get over this bad patch. Better not tell Deirdre. She'd quote her usual; "All solicitors are bent.'

5

EVERYONE SITTING around the table was engrossed as an Oriental fingering his goblet of Cognac, spoke. 'I'm worried about this damn get together in France.' The man's malevolent expression, almost carved into his face, never altered. With steely eyes he continued. 'As you know the Eastern and Colombian 'business' fraternity are meeting to discuss the carving up of Western Europe for drugs, prostitution, etc.'

The men sitting around the table nodded but none spoke. The venue was a pub lounge, a place where the booths were deep and the panels between them were high and the lights dim.

'What's the problem,' a tall fair haired man suddenly spoke.

'We need to make sure we get a fair slice of the action and that's where you come in Luke.'

'So.' Luke shifted in his seat.

'It's essential we stick together here to protect our interests.' He paused, allowing the significance to register.

'You're saying there could be double dealing,' Luke said, sardonically.

'Yes. That's why I want you there, Luke.' He looked at him his eyes now softer. 'So your support, Luke, is vital.'

Luke leaned back in his seat and swallowed half his whiskey. He took his time in answering. He knew he could afford to. The Chinese man needed him - and his syndicate - in on this deal. His voice was quietly authoritative. 'Count us in,' he finally said to the Chinese's man's obvious surprise. Luke liked being unpredictable. It was safer that way.

Luke had shifted slightly in his seat and was now closer to the Oriental. As the shadows from the street light outside fell on the weirdo he seemed almost disembodied, a head that floated in the darkness - a macabre trick. It was the face of an animal, a brute that walked on two legs with small slit eyes, flattened nose and features coarsened by years of debauchery - a gargoyle with a mastermind. Luke had been told that his thin face contrasted strongly with the Oriental's - almost like profiles of Jekyll and Hyde.

'It's a deal then,' the Asian said. A troll's sparkly smile of complicity spread over his face. Luke was being more cooperative than he'd anticipated, although, they both went back a long way and doing business with him had always been profitable. In the underworld certain names resonate for the sheer stunning audacity of their crimes. They win admiration from their peers, and they live on the very edge of an excitingly dangerous world and Luke epitomised this. Quickly he'd become one of the most powerful criminals in Britain always escaping detection. A genius of the underworld, his talents amassed him a fortune and a lifestyle of lavish extravagance.

He continued to dwell on him. Luke came across as a typical prototype of the white Anglo-Saxon persona. On meeting him one would class him as a sophisticated urbane man of the world. Beneath that façade, however, there was a subsurface violence usually under control, but very much alive.

That's Luke, the Oriental thought as he rose. As he took his leave he glanced at the man sequestered in a dark alcove, the light malforming his shadow on the wall. He gave an imperceptible nod. The dark chestnut coloured eyes concealed behind a huge pair of shades seemed to gleam in acknowledgement. Longish dark hair veiled the rest of the man's features. All that remained visible to the onlooker were the cruel thin lips. No one that he knew of had ever seen his face in its entirety. What organisation he was affiliated with was a mystery. He was an enigma and referred to as the 'Ghost' amongst the criminal fraternity - a term he seemed to be fond of. Not a man to cross. He remembered the tale people whispered about him in the back streets of Liverpool:

A small bird was bathing in a water bath. A man approached and stood, silently watching the tiny fledgling. It was too young to have learnt fear. He put his hand out and the little bird placed its head in his palm. He stroked it and it stayed in his grasp. Each day for a week the man repeated this act until the bird was calm in his presence. Then one day after he had gently caressed it he suddenly lifted a mallet and smashed it down on its little body. It shuddered. Before it died its sad doe like eyes fixed on him, mirroring complete incomprehension.

'It's always a pleasure to do business with you guys', the Chinese man said as he twisted away from the gleaming eyes and exited. It was icy cold as he left. Snow covered the ground outside.

6

NEXT DAY Luke Foley sat behind the wheel of his prized possession, a 1925 vintage Rolls Royce. He was on his way to a syndicate meeting. As he approached a warehouse on the waterfront he absorbed the scene. Patrick Street was a narrow brick alley connecting streets built centuries ago. It was no more then a few hundred yards long, frozen in time between the stone walls of waterfront buildings and almost devoid of streetlights. A place that was handy for those who didn't care to be under any scrutiny.

Always a punctual man, Luke was the first to arrive. Inside the seemingly derelict building a swish boardroom was concealed. It was tastefully furnished, with Chesterfield armchairs dotted around. Luke knew he posed a commanding figure as he sat drumming his fingers on the mahogany table as his men began to arrive, each quietly taking a seat. He leaned back in his swivel chair, eyebrows below the fair hair, joined in annoyance. 'What the fuck is keeping Frank?'

His audience flinched.

'I said to stagger your entrance but not by this bloody length. Where the fuck is he?' He sat motionless and malevolently inscrutable as a parrot, his elbows on the table and his head resting on clenched fists that pressed into his face pushing his thin lips into a pout of displeasure. A look of deadly calm registered there but behind the mask, the blood throbbed in the dynamo of his brain, and a thick maggot-like vein in his forehead pulsated angrily. There was deadly silence. Just as it looked as if he was going to explode Frank appeared, glancing warily at him.

'Ah, the prodigal Frank had deigned to grace us with his presence,' and then added in a more menacing tone, 'What time do you call this?'

'Sorry … traffic jam.' Quickly he pulled up a chair and slid down.

Regaining some of his composure Luke said, 'We'll begin then. Frank has a contact who'll launder some dough.'

All eyes riveted on Frank Moran. He leaned back in his chair. 'Our man's Danny Delaney – he's into finance and will invest our money into hedge funding.'

One man, who was doodling, suddenly piped up. 'What, for Jaysis sake is hedge funding?'

Frank gave him a boa constrictor's stare. 'Never fucking mind what it is. What's important is its legal.'

'Sounds too good to be true, it better be safe.' Luke aimed his slim finger straight at Frank's heart, his features remaining impassive but the veiled undertones were obvious.

'Of course,' Frank said, the fear spreading deeply over his face. It's safer than US Bonds and they're the safest. In a nutshell, this is what they're about. Sometimes because of swings in the market bonds can be bought at rock bottom prices and later sold at a much higher value. Vast profits are made.'

Luke leaned forwards in his chair and steepled his gold-ringed fingers in front of his mouth. 'So nothing can go wrong?'

'No. It's a cert.'

'Well.' He paused. We'll consider two million to begin with and see how it goes. And as I said it better be sound otherwise…'

'It's fool proof. You know me; I always do my homework. By the way Luke what the hell is Phil up to? The stuff should have arrived by now?'

Luke studied him with cold, obsidian eyes. 'What Phil does is my concern. But don't worry I'll deal with him.'

It was quiet in the boardroom when everyone had left. Luke was pleased. But he'd every intention of doing his own homework, had every intention of checking out these bonds before he handed over two million quid. That was his reason for his huge success. Never leave anything to chance … never leave anything to chance.

His face suddenly became expressionless, and yet a small muscle twitched in his right cheek, a sure sign of stress. He snatched his mobile from the table and banged out a number.

'Is that you, Luke?'

'Yes Phil'

'I guessed you might call,' he said coughing. 'How's it going Luke?'

'What the fuck is going on, Phil? The boys expected the delivery to be well underway by now.'

'I've had some setbacks Luke. Give me a few days.' He coughed again.

There was an ominous silence.

'We're talking three million Phil. Two days, Phil, otherwise…' An odd finality was in his voice.

The 'phone went dead.

A FEW days later.

'It's too early for this fucking caper,' Luke said to Frank as his Rolls Royce came to a halt. A Mercedes then emerged from the dawn mist and trundled over the worn cobblestones of the waterfront. It stopped outside a derelict building.

Momentarily a patch of perfect blue brightened the greyness of the March day then quickly the blue dulled, turned foul, and spread its malignancy across the skyline as if a foul deed was in the air.

Luke, slumped behind the wheel of the Rolls, turned off the engine, wearily ran a hand through his hair and glanced at Frank beside him. 'Let's get it over and done with,' he said as they excited the vehicle.

Luke stood and watched as the Oriental ordered the couple in the back seat of the vehicle to get out. The two inside remained motionless. The Oriental took a small automatic out of his inside pocket and pointed it at the woman's head. 'Move!'

The man and the woman crept out like frightened animals forced to abandon their last hope and refuge. They stood before their captor who eyed them dispassionately and then glanced callously at the woman sobbing softly on her boyfriend's shoulders. The man tried, unsuccessfully, to catch the slit eyes but he averted them.

The Oriental stepped away from the vehicle and in the car's dark windshield the reflection of the rising sun peered through the buildings on the waterfront. He nodded to Luke. He carried two long pieces of thickened rope slung over his shoulder. 'March!' He stuck the gun deeper into the woman's head forcing her to advance towards the building.

Inside the floor was strewn with wooden crates. 'Up.'

They scrambled onto a few of the crates that were close together. The man threw a pleading glance at Luke but he lowered his gaze. 'Luke please, for old time's sake.'

Luke gazed at him again. Even though Phil had diverted the drugs money into his own coffers it was in his power to save him. Thwarting the Triads, however, was another ball game and they had their ways. He wavered and then decided that there was too much at stake with the other deal he and the weirdo had going. He looked away.

Quickly the Oriental slung the ropes over a beam. With deft fingers he tied them into nooses and slipped one over Phil's head, positioning it around his neck. Phil gasped but before he had time to protest the hard knot of the rope tightened with a faint, peculiar sawing sound as his captor kicked the crate away. His tongue swelled in his mouth and his eyes bulged in their sockets. The woman watched in horror as Phil's face turned blue and his head slumped to one side. Luke felt sick. He never took part in executions. He left that to others.

Luke watched the woman absorbing the hard truth of the moment as she tried to lean towards her man, terror painted on her face, her mouth open but voiceless.

The woman was next. She attempted a scream but quickly the Oriental tightened the knot on her neck. Compulsively her fingers clawed at it as she sought release from the throttling grip. A pair of terrified eyes gazed over in a silent plea for help.

Luke twisted away. He didn't think he could stomach this. He concentrated instead on the silvery swells of the sea and listened to the sounds of the waves splashing against the rocks and tried to let his mind drift. But all he was aware of was the horrible sound of a throat gurgling. He stole a glance at the woman. Her glazed eyes met his, pleading with him to cease the grotesque torture.

He turned away again and dwelt on the gentle lapping of the water against the rocks below and thought of his beloved. His wife wouldn't have approved of this. Maybe he should save her? He looked again. A bright red splurge of blood had stained her white blouse. Killing women was not his game. But he couldn't appear weak in front of the Oriental and tried to listen to the swishing of the waves below. All he could hear was the ghastly choking noise. He gazed across the waters feeling dwarfed by the events he'd set in motion and now had to stick by.

7

'USUAL TABLE sir,' the head waiter asked as we stood waiting to be seated.

'Yes, Henri,' Nicholas replied.

The waiter weaved his way among the tables towards a secluded corner of the restaurant while we traipsed behind him. As we sat down I glanced around the room. Each round table, laced with pure linen tablecloths cascading down to the floor, sat like an exhibit in a museum. The silver service added to the luxury. Shaded red lamps cast an intimate rosy glow over the occupants of the table. The restaurant was full; the diners fully absorbed in the serious business of eating. It all filled me with wonder. But then a bottle of champagne in an ice bucket suddenly appeared. Smiling at him, I said, 'You've thought of everything Nicholas. Is this how you usually entertain your women?' Privately I began to feel that he loved the smell of opulence too much. He's broke and this must be costing a fortune. Unease spread through me.

Motioning to the wine waiter to pour the champagne, he said, 'This is a local haunt of mine since Zoë took off. Anyhow here's to our first dinner together.'

Nicholas, sampling the bubbly, nodded his approval. Filling the fluted glasses to the brim until they frothed over like surf, the man withdrew.

'Good health,' I replied as I studied the a la carte menu and thought that everything was way beyond my budget.

'Have what you like, the food's delicious and Barclay card's paying.'

Barclay card is paying. He's already in debt.

Nicholas's choice was a ballottine of wild salmon that was boned and stuck together again with gelatine and rolled in fragrant herbs. Mine was a saddle of lamb with asparagus and a creamy brown sauce.

8

Nicholas tapped his fingers on the table thinking about Alex as he waited for her to return from the toilet. She seemed to possess vitality, energy that he found refreshingly novel from the conventional English women he mixed with. She had, of course, the sardonic wit of the Irish and had a great capacity for laughing at herself. There was something graceful and mischievous about her, something elegantly unpredictable. Hers was a face you'd notice across a crowded room, the voice you'd try hard to hear, the quiet air of mystery you'd wish to savour.

When he'd seen her he'd felt as if he'd taken a vicious blow to the solar plexus. The shock had dredged up memories and emotions like mud churning up from a river – pain and fear all swirling furiously inside him. The pain he could cope with but not the fear - a fear that he'd lose control again. She had the black hair like Zoe and the same build and the same powers of seduction only she was unaware of it. This was no Zoe bent on getting her own way. And Zoe had hurt him deeply by leaving him and taking his beloved daughter with her. He stared at her as she approached, her red dress hugging her figure, a figure for which Hugh Hefner had spend years searching She's beautiful. His gaze roamed over her face, an angel's face, with its delicate bone structure and liquid eyes. He observed her elegance, noting her choice of colour, red showed a dramatic side to her personality, otherwise hidden by her sad pretty features. Desire twisted inside him. Damn. Don't go there Nicholas. Hand her file over to Tom and get shot of her.

9

THE MOON was veiled in the dark meshes of an old oak tree, the night air heavy with the scent of honeysuckle as we left the restaurant and strolled to the car. It began to rain. 'April showers,' I remarked and then added, 'It's been a wonderful evening.'

'Yes we must do it again.' He arched an eyebrow.

We drove to a detached house in a provincial suburb in Huyton.

He unlocked the door and showed me into a spacious sitting room.

Glancing around I felt everything was too tidy, sterile compared to the clutter of my place. Not my taste. The eerie silence of the green plants added to the starkness of the decor. A patio door led to more luxuriant greenery outside.

My instincts told me I didn't belong.

'What would you like to drink?' he said with a chuckle. 'Vodka, or would you like Sainsbury's best Cava.'

'Cava's fine ... my favourite tipple. Your room's so ...' I paused vacillating for words to describe it ... 'orderly.'

But he'd already disappeared returning almost immediately with a bottle of bubbly immersed in an ice bucket. He poured the drinks into glasses that looked like chalices.

'Let's have some music,' Nicholas said as he led me into another room.

I took a step backwards. A white baby grand bestowed a luxurious touch to the otherwise almost empty lounge. The light from the pink lampshade streamed over the white veneer, making it shimmer in the dimmed glow. I decided again that he was a bit of an enigma. Though broke he pursued a lavish life style.

He mooched over to the piano, lifted the lid and began to play a theme from Sibelius with a sweetness and dignity I'd rarely heard. Then the tempo changed to a wild, frenzied, romantic lyric ending in an exulting crescendo. His small fingers moved across the keyboard with lightening speed.

Motionless, I listened to his playing, becoming fused with the moment, feeling his passion for it. I observed his silhouette half of it in soft light, half in mysterious shadows bending intently over the piano. Outside, in the patio, the long grasses and creepers swayed gently in the light evening air. The sense of peace and the balmy quietness drifted over us with a soothing effect.

Next he played, 'Some Enchanted Evening', his eyes meeting mine as he sang:

> Some enchanted evening
> When you find your true love,
> When you feel her call you
> Across a crowded room,
> Then fly to her side,
> And make her your own
> Or all through your life you
> May dream all alone.

I was transfixed by the lyric. Was he feeling those sentiments for me or was it just the after effects of the wine and the sumptuous food. On his face, fleetingly, there registered a strange emotion. Could he be falling for me? Alex for God's sake stop romanticising. You hardly know each other and you're thinking of love. Just think of this as leading to a quick fuck. Ouch. Swearing again Alex. What would people think and you a product of a convent education? I focused on

Nicholas as he settled the lid of the piano down, noiselessly as if a fledgling's nest lay among the keys. 'It's time we hit the sack,' he said quietly gazing at me in a questioning way. 'I'll show you to the spare room.'

I wandered upstairs, Nicholas following. A door stood ajar and impulsively I wandered in. The walls were white and unadorned except for a large photograph of his daughter. I stared and thought Elizabeth's face, against the white canvas was Nicholas's despair and his hope, his loss and his future. Though oriental in appearance she had his wonderful smile.

'That's my darling.' Sadness suddenly clouded his features.

He's a bit obsessive about his daughter, I mused as I inspected the room. Who could blame him? I adore Catherine.

We both knew what would happen but a sense of propriety made us spend some time on the preliminaries.

10

'STOP! ENOUGH!' Luke tore his eyes away from the splashing of the waves against the rocks and stared at the woman.

Momentarily a flash of incredulity swept over the Oriental's features. He paused, released the tension on the rope, shook his head and strode back to his car. Where women were concerned Luke was soft, but that was his problem. And he knew Luke would make good the drugs money that Phil had diverted for his own gain. Anyhow three million was only peanuts compared to the latest scheme that they were hatching. He recalled Luke's words when they'd discussed it. "Billions, we're talking billions." And now the grand plan had been implemented. Hopefully letting the woman live wouldn't be their undoing. She'd have to be taught a lesson though. Remind her of what would happen if she squealed. He smiled as he dwelt on Luke again. Someone high in the echelons of the Triad organisation had once asked him why he trusted Luke so much. 'I don't,' he replied. "But I know his dark secret and Luke will do anything to keep it hidden. Even kill a woman. Others have been silenced because of it."

Luke climbed into his car with Frank in tow. 'Let's get the hell out of here.' As they drove in silence, Frank's thoughts turned to Luke. He knew all about him. Knew his closely guarded secret, knew what his Irish relatives and the community in Glengarrif, Co Cork thought of him. He'd heard their gossip in the Irish bars. "Sure hasn't your man got it made, all that money, the bespoke tailoring and the looks to go with it." They'd lift their glasses and contemplate, proud of his Irish connections. If a member of the Gardai were present he would agree. There wasn't the slightest suspicion that he was behind the growing drugs trade in the vicinity. Some of the elders remembered his grandmother who'd come from the locality but had left for Liverpool when she was young. He'd also heard the rumours. "Ah now didn't she have the hard life. Would you know looking at him now that his Mam was forced to leave him behind with his drunken bastard of a father and he so young?"

11

Later that day he who called himself the ghost and was named by others as 'psycho' sat, alone, his eyes forever flickering hither and thither. The luxurious drawing room was half in shadow; the only light a shaded lamp in one corner. Some might have termed him insane; others would only see him as evil – the devil incarnate. But nothing touched this man. Some considered him omniscienct in that he knew the underworld's every move. Where he acquired this knowledge and what syndicate he affiliated with was a mystery. He had the habit of speaking aloud to himself, an act that most would perceive as madness but he saw it as part of his genius. Now he sat muttering, his audience the four walls. 'Fools. Luke has botched things again. The bitch should have been annihilated. He'll rue the day he let her live.'

The ghost then glanced at his masterpiece on the wall. He was proud of his artistic creation. It showed a fugitive running, a pack of dogs at his heel, the terror in the poor wretches eyes frozen into place for all infinity. A warm feeling spread through him.

Then the iron mask slipped as fragments of the past lacerated his mind. He wiped his hand across his eyes as if that would erase the horror:

It was eight oclock. The small boy lay in bed in his cubicle staring at the ceiling. The other boy's were at study. He was always excused – by Father Bryne. He hunched himself down in the bed as he waited. Footsteps! He listened as the door creaked open slowly and someone came into the room. The child was terrified. The priest moved towards the bed. The boy felt the warm fetid breath on his face. A rancid miasma of sweat wafted towards him as the clammy hand crept under the bedclothes and began to caress him. He saw in his mind's eye the naked grin stretched humourlessly across the priest's jaw.

'Turn over boy.'

Then he felt the searing pain in his rectum – a sizzling hot poker pain like his insides were being charred. A wave of nausea washed over him. He began to sob quietly. For six years the obscenity continued and then one day...

12

IN THE north east of Scotland there is a house nestling in a valley, hidden away from any prying eyes that might, through chance, pass by. The likelihood of that was remote. No one in his right mind would want to venture into such an isolated spot.

An old woman lay on a couch, the bay window in front of her revealing the early northern snows. Like her hair and her pale wan face, everything outside the glass was white and frozen.

A man entered the room and asked, 'How are you today Gran? You said you wanted to discuss something important.'

'Yes! Let's be honest. With my state of health I could drop dead anytime.'

'Gran, you're fine. The doctor said it's only your angina playing you up.'

'Nevertheless we need to talk, to take steps to insure our secret is safe.'

'You're worrying too much. No one knows.'

'I just want you to be more vigilant. The truth must remain buried forever. I've spent too long now watchful...'

'Don't worry Gran, remember the story you told me about granddad.'

The old woman brought her thin and delicate fingers up to her face, a gesture of quiet reflection. 'Yes.' She cast her mind back to the distant past. Her husband had entered the room and she'd said quietly, almost in a whisper, 'Who is it that knows?'

'Only the old woman in the village.'

As he turned to go she said, "Kill her."

13

THE WORDS 'Degree Nisi,' leapt out at me from the page. So it's finally over I thought as I stared at the document. Nine months to the day since David had filed for divorce.

A week later I viewed an old Victorian house in Crosby and fell instantly in love with it. Three bedrooms and a bathroom up. Kitchen, pantry, sitting room, dining room, conservatory and a glass outhouse off the kitchen. Small garden. More than ample for my needs.

Within two months I moved in and entered a new phase in my life. It was a couple community and I was single and Nicholas lived in Huyton, on the other side of Liverpool.

As the natural rhythm of things brought us closer together Nicholas moved into my house and rented his own out. Deirdre went ballistic.

We embraced the usual routine activities of most couples; theatre, concerts, dining out and entertaining. One evening Nicholas's sister Sheila and her husband, Clive, arrived for dinner. As Sheila, Nicholas and Clive chatted my attention drifted and focused on my choice of décor in the dining room. The room was large with a high Victorian ceiling, and with a carpet so thick and luxurious that it felt as if you were walking on velvet. On one side there was a large mahogany bookcase. Along the opposite wall there rested an antique table with two bronze Spelter figures stylishly positioned. An eighteenth century mahogany table graced the centre. Six chairs, embellished with inlaid mother of pearl, were centred round it.

Then turning around to Sheila, who was still deep in conversation with Nicholas, I appraised her. She was tall, very beautiful and the image of Nicholas.

'You're better, Nicholas? You've lost that haggard look, thank goodness,' I heard her say. Then facing me she added, 'I know we've you to thank for this radical change.'

'I'm always in good humour,' Nicholas interjected brusquely.

'Rubbish, you know perfectly well that you were a mental wreck when Zoe took off with Elizabeth.'

'Shall I make the coffee, Alex?' Nicholas interrupted as he inched out the room.

'Yes, Darling, do.'

'We'll leave you two women to natter,' Clive muttered as he too made a dive for the door.

'Good. We can speak more openly now,' Sheila said surreptitiously. 'We're all delighted you met. Let's hope Zoe doesn't do her usual.'

'What do you mean?' I swallowed the knot of apprehension in my throat, clasping my hands together in front of me like a schoolgirl.

'Return.'

'What?'

'Well, the last time she left him she returned as she couldn't cope with a small child alone.'

Unease spread through me. 'Do you…do you… think she will this time?'

'No, I don't think so she hates England and Elizabeth is seven now and easier to manage. She's the cause of him being broke taking that child so far away and he having to trip over there to see her. And now to make some money he's become mixed up with that Danny Delaney. You know that man went bankrupt last year and was given a suspended prison sentence for setting up in business again. He just uses Nicholas and hasn't paid him a penny for his services.'

'Why does Nicholas act for him then?' I twisted the edge of the lace table cloth wrapping it around my finger.

'Because he's broke and needs the money ... to see Elizabeth.'

'But if Danny doesn't pay him, why work for him?'

She gave a baffled shake of her head. 'Danny's a charmer and good at persuading people to do what he wants by promising the earth. Danny's connection with the criminal element worries me though.'

'Yes, I saw him with one of the Barry's.'

'It's not the Barry's that bothers me. They're small fry. It's his contact with ...Lu...' Then she stopped and glanced at me a concerned look washing over her features.

'Look Alex I'm droning on to much. Enough about Danny. Gosh it midnight, we'll have to get going.'

Alex, get out before it's too late, before it destroys you a little voice plagued as I lounged in my conservatory after they'd gone. I'd doused the lights in the house so the only glow there was came from the solar lamps dotted around my garden. I peered up at an India-ink sky in which stars seemed to drift, seemed to shudder. I shuddered when I dwelt on what Sheila hadn't said. Did she know that Zoe might return? And who was this anonymous person or persons she was about to mention. "It's his contact with Lu... With whom? Was it a syndicate someone like the Kray brothers? I should never have become involved. At my age I hadn't learned. There had been some excuse when I'd met Donal. I was only eighteen and working in the Civil Service in Dublin. I'd ignored the advice of my three flat mates who'd said that fifteen years of an age gap was too much. Then I'd become pregnant, a shot gun wedding followed, and Deirdre was born, but I wasn't happy. Donal was undemonstrative. I was lonely and I craved love, a romantic love that didn't exist in my marriage. After four years I met David, a lecturer in Mathematics, at Liverpool University. What attracted me was his personality. He had a limpid and effervescent intellect that makes engaging connections and lively, challenging assumptions. But more importantly he gave me what I wanted – an undying love. It was what I'd read of in romantic books. I fell deeply in love and ignored the pit falls – the drinking and the seventeen year age gap. Then I'd run, headlong, into another liaison.

And now here I was - still pursuing the ideal. And already there were cracks. Nicholas hadn't declared his love. But in time he would. Once he divorced Zoe he'd be free to love me and we'd be happy. No, not happy - ecstatic. I knew our love would conquer all. What did one of the great philosophers say; "In love, pain and pleasure are always at war?"

14

IT WAS an overcast late October day, the grass spliced by frost, and winter grinning through a break in the clouds like a dreadful joker peering between the curtains before the show begins. Staring out of the bay window from my upstairs living room I dwelt on the events of the past year. It seemed to have been one of those extraordinary idyllic periods when everything was almost perfect - a time of drifting from one lovely day to the next. I sighed and glanced around the room admiring my handiwork. I loved this room. It was almost a direct copy of the lounge in the marital home. An off white carpet was still the perfect canvas for the four plush red armchairs and the matching velvet couch David had relinquished as part of the divorce settlement. Instead of one large gilt mirror gracing one of the walls I had added three. The effect made the room look twice as large. The few antique tables dotted here and there plus a collection of gold framed prints added a touch of luxury to the room. The Aubrey Beardsley original was missing but I'd purchased a print of 'Isolde' from the Victoria and Albert museum when I'd made a trip to London. The extra touch was a forty inch plasma TV screen.

My thoughts drifted back to Nicholas. Life might have been perfect if it was not for the fact that Elizabeth was far away – lost to him.

In spite of everything, a pattern had emerged in our lives. He made frequent visits to New Zealand which irked me since it plunged him deeper into debt. For peace sake I kept my council. Although he returned transformed his happiness was always short lived. I frowned. I hated it when he spiralled into despair. It made me feel that my love was not enough. Will it ever be enough? I pondered.

He'd felt honour bound to tell Zoe there was another woman in his life. Zoe had grabbed the chance - divorce and a large settlement to go with it. Meanwhile affecting anger and bitterness she'd demanded extra maintenance for Elizabeth. Either that or he wouldn't be permitted to see her.

'I can't afford this extra payment, Alex,' Nicholas said one Saturday morning as he strode into the room a letter in his hand. She's demanding more money.

'Say no.'

'If I don't she won't let me speak to Elizabeth. That's her usual trick.' A smile suddenly lit up his face. 'Never mind, Danny's bound to hit the jackpot soon and then all my worries will be history.'

My heart sank. Not Danny again and what was this jackpot? I knew nothing about the schemes he and Nicholas hatched. I gave him a searching glance. 'What will you do if Danny's grandiose idea fails? Whatever it is?'

Nicholas assumed his defensive look. 'It won't. I'm certain of that.'

'How much do you owe on credit cards anyhow. Surely you could economise somehow and pay them off. Then you wouldn't have to bother with Danny.'

'I'd need to cut down drastically to be able to pay off fifty thousand pounds.'

'Fifty thousand! Sweet Jesus, Nicholas, how could you possibly owe that amount?'

'Trips to New Zealand.' His face crumpled.

'You spend money like water.'

'It's the visits that cost the money. The rest is peanuts.'
'You'll have to stop tripping over to see Elizabeth then. And my granny always said, "If you look after the pennies the pounds will look after themselves."'

'Alex, no one will stop me seeing her and for God's sake let's change the record. And I'm sick of your sayings. Most of them are misquoted.' He paused. 'The garden needs weeding.'

Oh dear, I've hit a raw nerve. I frowned. Our relationship was starting to change. Was the honeymoon period over?

15

AS NICHOLAS strode into the silent garden he calmed down as he felt the soft breeze blowing through the lilac and found the scents of jasmine and honey suckle strong in the air. Here, surrounded by nature he was at peace - a peace which eluded him these days.

He castigated himself for blurting out about his debts. Dwelling on his predicament he mused. You should have gone to New Zealand with them. And now it's too late. With these debts to pay off you're trapped unless of course Danny pays up. He frowned. When he'd confronted him about payment for services rendered Danny had said: "Nicholas old boy, it's only a matter of a few weeks and then we'll be rolling in it. Bear with me my friend. You know I won't let you down."

And then there's Danny's involvement with Luke Foley. That worried him. He'd heard from Pat that Luke intended to invest in Danny's hedge funding. If Danny lost Luke's money God's only knows what Luke Foley would do. His reputation went before him. Nicholas shuddered. I'm in quicksand here. If it wasn't for Elizabeth he'd never have become involved with Danny.

It's well Pat, Danny's right hand man keeps me informed about things. Pat and he went back a long way. He smiled as he remembered his primary school years when Pat had always protected him from the bullies in the playground.

Half heartedly he pulled another weed and sighed as his thoughts turned to Alex. He was fond of her. In fact if it wasn't for the family unit he'd be free to love her but - and that was his dilemma - in the eyes of God he was still bound to another. He shouldn't have become so heavily involved. It had all sort of spiralled out of control and now he found he couldn't do without the love and affection she showered on him. Was that love? He didn't know anymore. Nonetheless he was painfully aware that he was unable to sever the ties with Zoë. Still, she was Elizabeth's mother after all.

The weightless dimness of early evening had descended by the time he'd finished gardening. In the field at the back of the house, a small bird chirped, and above him, the first stars of night dotted the sky. It all seems so benign, he thought - a night when one should be at peace with the world.

16

IN A medieval town in France a mix of nationalities and expensive limousines gathered. It was a sunny and silent morning and none of the town's people seem to take any notice of the comings and goings of this group of foreigners. Danny Delaney strolled through the ancient streets on his way to his hotel. A feeling of contentment suffused him as he inhaled the salty air.

Mountains on three sides and the sea on the fourth cocooned the little settlement. Dragonflies hung motionless in the thick air. An old man was sweeping multicoloured leaves. Giant strangler figs formed around the old streets, their roots, as thick columns, sank like claws into the masonry.

An air of peace surrounded the ancient municipality. The rays of the early sun broke through the mists of the eastern sky, lending a glitter to the calm waters of the sea. Danny's thoughts turned to Luke Foley. Tonight he'd meet with him to discuss a deal in bond trading.

Danny was pleased with his success. Some time ago he'd clinched a deal with a Canadian middleman who'd given him entrée into this world of highly lucrative hedge funding investments. With the promise of high returns he was in a position to entice well-heeled investors like Luke.

When Luke had deferred their meeting because of his commitments Danny had assured him that it would be no trouble for him to travel over to France to see him. Luke had agreed, as he was a man who liked things sorted. Life's becoming rosy.

Later that evening Luke Foley stood at the bar of his hotel pondering, as he waited for Danny. He liked the ambience of the place. The interior was elegantly appointed not unlike the London Ritz, though much smaller. Old fashioned but magnificent and glowing like a newly minted gold coin, it was managed with a calm and courteous efficiency that would have put the typical English hotelier to shame. The bedrooms were luxurious; the food superb – the memory of the five-course dinner Luke had enjoyed the night before still remained. From the patio the scene of the haze-softened peaks across the moon lit bay was breathtaking. He only stayed at the best. Just then he spotted a medium sized man, with broad shoulders approaching the bar with the head waiter leading the way.

'Great to meet you at last,' Danny said effusively as he extended his hand at the same time slipping the waiter a tip.

Luke pushed his hand away, shuddering at the texture of skin. He hated skin contact unless, of course, it was with the female gender.

'I've booked a table for nine,' Luke said smiling with his mouth but his eyes held no expression except a piercing hardness. 'I've taken the liberty of ordering a bottle of Veuve Clicquot,' he added congenially.

'An excellent choice,' Danny said as the hovering waiter took his coat. They moved to a table and sat down. Lounging in the soft red velvet armchair and sipping his bubbly Luke began. 'Judging by your enthusiasm on the 'phone your business sounds exciting. And,' he added, 'thanks for including me in your…' he adopted a quivery baritone … 'eh little venture.' He smiled making his eyes exude a certain charm by wrinkling them up.

Danny snapped his expensive pen closed, and seemed to study him. Fiddling with it he explained about hedge funding.

Luke smiled non-commitally. 'What do you say to two?'

'Two million!' Danny exclaimed.

A half smile appeared on Luke's face. Leaning forward he chose his words carefully. 'The organisation is willing to launder two to start with and if all goes well then there'll be more. Of course, my friend, if anything goes wrong you're dead meat,' Luke said as his eyes rested incuriously on Danny. His voice had changed and his expression. His eyes had become urgent, commanding. Then they became expressionless except for the same piercing hardness as he continued, 'We won't tolerate screw ups.'

Danny paled and said in a subdued voice, 'Nothing will go wrong. I'll stake my mother's life on it.'

Luke's face froze, the amiable façade gone. 'I hope not or otherwise it will be your own life you'll be staking.' He smiled again but his eyes were about zero degrees Celsius.

'I must visit the little boy's room,' Danny said his voice quavering as he stared into the manic face before him.

Luke glanced around the lounge as he waited for Danny watching the group of 'business' men at the bar. The Turkish gangsters were rubbing shoulders with the triad groups, the Gambinos, the American based Mafia group and the New Russian Mafia. Also among these immaculately dressed gangsters were the notorious Colombian Cartels from Medellin who flood Europe with hundreds of tons of cocaine a year.

As Danny returned and sat down Luke remarked, gesturing at the 'business men,' 'They're here to discuss the carving up of Western Europe for drugs, prostitution, and smuggling and extortion rackets. In a nutshell the crime economy has become global. I'm here to make sure that we get a fair slice of the action. No one messes with the Foley's.'

After Danny's departure Luke sat sipping a brandy engrossed in thoughts about him. He'd made sure to find out everything about him before he'd committed himself. Danny, he now knew, was a man who dreamed of making it big at the corporate front but never quite managed to. He'd acquired the whole trick bag of company finance - the easy smile, the firm handshake, the gaze: steady, concerned. It was a gaze that conveyed reliability and trustworthiness.

He knew Danny always had some business venture up his sleeve but was shrewd enough to allow others to take the risk. Although some of his endeavours failed most of them were quite successful. This was the reason he managed to crawl back up after going bankrupt. He had the power to charm men and the manic drive to bend their wills into saying yes to schemes they did not want, did not need and never dreamt of before. Luke had also checked out hedge funding. Bond trading had become the hottest area of the finance industry, a business that the toughest, most steel-nerved traders wanted to be in.

17

AFTER LEAVING Luke, Danny emerged into a warm evening on his way to his less salubrious hotel. Beyond the mountains the sky was sapphire and blue, a golden glow spreading across the night sky. Danny was elated. His dream was becoming a reality. All of a sudden he felt a quickening of his heart and he began to feel uneasy. The whole scene tonight had unnerved him. These gangsters would pierce your heart with a stiletto as quick as they'd look at you. He had noticed that the yakuza were present - the underground gangs who claimed to be descendants of the samurai tradition. They were some of the most feared and violent men in Asia. He had noted the pair of shiny snakeskin shoes and the odd tattoo that gave them a sinister look. And yet Luke Foley could take them on. He shivered again as he though of the consequences if anything went wrong. Luke's warning was still fresh in his mind.

Not only that recently the Nixer Barry had read out the gory details from some newspaper cutting to him:

"The corpse was dangling from the ceiling, the face swelled and puffed and purple and his mouth open. One eye was still staring out. A look of absolute terror registered on his face. Flies had gorged on the open wound in his neck laying eggs there so that parts of the lower face seemed to give tic like quivers as if the muscles were still functioning. Some carrion creature had pecked the other eye ball out and all that remained was a mass of wriggling maggots, some bulging out and spilling down his right cheek. A few had started to crawl into his gaping mouth."

Snap out of it Danny boy. Nothing can go wrong. Hedge funding is a cert.

Of course he'd have to find other entrepreneurs who'd invest their money in his project. As he approached his rather run down hotel he smiled and thought, soon, I'll be only staying at the best.

His thoughts drifted back to Luke again. The Barry's had also told him about Luke. Told him about his mother abandoning him and that without the love and warmth of his beloved mother, and in the company of an alcoholic father Luke had become a loner. Maybe it was this deprivation that enabled him to turn it into an inner strength, and hone in himself a core of steel. But he wasn't without guidance. His maternal grandmother invested in his upbringing. Hawk-like she watched over him. She too had been married to a syndicate man and was inured to the gangster way of life, accepting its evilness without question. She respected their ways and had handed them down to Luke. When he passed his eleven plus she saw to it that he attended the local grammar school.

With a background such as Luke's it was no small wonder that he'd wavered from the straight and narrow but what contributed to him being a hardened criminal was the death of his young wife. Deeply in love, she was everything to him. Then, one night, as they left a local pub someone with a grudge, emerged from the darkness brandishing a knife, and took a swing at him. As the blade neared its target Luke stepped to one side. Unfortunately it pierced his wife's heart and killed her instantly. Danny sighed. And then there was Luke's association with this man who was known as the Ghost. He'd heard terrible rumours about him. Some said Luke was close to him. Once he'd got himself straight financially he'd give Luke a wide berth. Some investors had become millionaires over night and now he was in. All he had to do was sit tight and wait for the profits to come rolling in.

18

'BE JAYSIS, they sure take care of ye here,' Devlin said, as he chewed on a piece of duck.

Karl, gingerly cut his portion and politely lifted a small piece to his mouth, as he replied, 'Hm, Ja.' He glanced at Devlin in trepidation.

'Why can't you pick the fuckin' leg up instead of being all high and mighty eatin like tha?' Devlin said a hint of malice in his blue eyes. He took another bite of the fowl letting orange sauce drip down his white T- shirt. Brushing it off with his sleeve and taking another slug of wine, he belched. 'Well now, Baron, it's time you and I had a little chat.' He sat there smiling at him – an oily smile that dripped from his face.

Karl Von Lichtenhof, a member of a German Dynasty family, had been seated in a quiet area in Wilde's club for a while now having lunch with Michael Devlin. It was clear that Devlin was an unwelcome guest as Karl, ill at ease, nervously drummed his fingers on the armrest.

Karl was an unprepossessing, man in his early fifties, with an aristocratic demeanour. He was dressed in a German hunting jacket; cavalry twill trousers and brown leather shoes.

Normally Karl enjoyed the club's atmosphere. Its rooms still held the elegance of time, with Victorian ceilings and antique furniture. Heavy mahogany doors guarded the entrance and apart from members and their guests, few people gained admission. Its atmosphere reflected its members, stiff, ageing and masculine. It smelt of pipe tobacco, cigar smoke and Baltan Sobranne cigarettes. He loved this setting and the life he led but if he wasn't careful all that he valued would be destroyed. Better treat this low life delicately. He then studied Devlin and thought how much he looked out of place for this peaceful, moneyed atmosphere. The orange red splash on the T shirt was almost obscene, certainly bizarre. It seemed as if he'd taken a bullet. Devlin had insisted on having lunch in the club, a perverse way, perhaps, of showing that he was in control.

Karl replied nervously, 'I told you I'm vorking it out, Mr Devlin but I need more time.'

'The gaff is gettin tired of waitin.' He said this as he lit up a cigarette. Then dropping the glowing match on the back of Karl's hand he took a puff.

Karl became even paler as he snatched his hand away, rubbing it where the match had burnt his skin.

Devlin leered and said menacingly, 'Just a little taster. Believe me my gaff is not nice when you mess with him.'

'I can't get hold of that amount of money right now.'

Sniggering, Devlin replied, 'Codology, sure you're part of a grand German family and from what I hear they're filthy rich. You've one of dem big baronry manors here in Liverpool, and a fine flat in that Bel gravy place in London. You're not exactly broke are ye?'

Karl's face reddened. 'I take it you mean Belgravia and I am broke. I haf a diplomat's salary but that only covers my expenses. I haf no real money...'

'You're jokin. Your father, I hear has plenty. I'm sure he can help out in an emergency and your wife, Yvonne, drives a Porsche.'

At the mention of Yvonne, Karl became even redder, horror registering on his face. How did this piece of scum know her name? He thought of her now as he had left her that morning asleep, in the nude, her soft curvaceous body lying half exposed as she curled up inside the duvet.

It escaped his memory that she, with her reckless spending habits, was responsible for his present predicament and the low life he was sharing lunch with.

Yvonne had been working in the Dorchester as a waitress when he'd first met her. She was young, stunning, and vivacious and within months he'd proposed.

And then the blow came. When his father heard that he'd married a waitress he cut him off without a penny. With Yvonne's mounting debts he was forced to borrow from loan sharks. They had said, "There's no hurry to pay it off."

Now six months later they were pressing him for the money. Worse still, they hadn't told him the exorbitant interest they charged. Now he found himself with this terrible man, having to swallow his pride and plead for more time to pay off some of the interest.

'The money, Baron,' startled him.

'Ja… my father disinherited me when I married Yvonne. She was a waitress and not a suitable wife in his eyes.' He hated to have to grovel to this scum of the earth and reveal private personal details.

'Enough of the sob story Baron. Have the reddies soon or else. My gaff can't let this go on any longer. It looks bad for his business.'

'But I've already paid back nearly as much as I've borrowed. He can't…'

Devlin's face went red with anger and he had flecks of spittle at the corners of his mouth. 'Cut the crap that was just a bit of the interest. You still owe a hundred grand.'

'It's day light robbery,' Karl retorted, raising his voice. 'Tell him to go to hell.'

Michael's eyes darkened and his ruddy Irish face turned apoplectic. He cackled, a grating phlegmy cackle that warned Karl that he was not amused. 'I'll give the gaff your message.' He stood up.

Realising his error Karl pleaded. 'Please. Sit down.'

Slowly Michael resumed his seat. 'I wouldn't use words like tha' if I were you.'

'I'll think of something. Give me a few days.'

'Alrigh', three fuckin days or else. Wouldn't want anything to happen to that pretty wife of yours.

It was a few days later when the call came through to Wilde's club. 'A call for you Baron,' said the waiter.

Karl's stomach clenched into a ball and the taste in the back of his mouth was acid as he hurried to a private booth and picked up the 'phone.

'Baron.'

'Ja.'

'Michael Devlin.'

Karl started to perspire. 'Good afternoon.'

'I'm 'phonin' to collect.'

Karl began to sweat even more. 'I told you I haf not the money yet. You gave me a few days.' He licked his lips.

'You've had them. So stop stallin.'

'I promise you I'm not.'

'I'll be around to your house tomorrow. So you better have the dosh, otherwise...'

'Listen vait,' but the 'phone went dead.

Karl stood there now drenched in perspiration - desperate. It was only last week that he'd read about some gang disfiguring a debtor with acid. God only knows what might happen to him or to Yvonne if he didn't pay up. He shuddered. Somehow he had to get out of this terrible dilemma he was in. It was then that he thought of Danny Delaney and his proposal. He was his last resort.

19

AS I pottered in my spacious kitchen I looked around my favourite room. An antique pine table stood in the middle of the room with four matching chairs placed around it. I liked the colour scheme I had chosen. Interior design was one of my passions and friends told me that I had excellent taste. A dresser, handmade from old pine, graced one of the walls. Full of bric-a brac, blue delph and old oil lamps, it drove Nicholas mad but so far I'd resisted his efforts to relegate my bits and pieces to the attic. Just as I glanced at my watch and clocked six, I heard the key in the door. 'Had a good day, Darling,' I asked earnestly as Nicholas slouched in. One glance was enough to tell me that something was up. My stomach clenched.

'I heard from Zoe today,' Nicholas said miserably.

'Oh,' I replied, my voice suddenly flat. 'And?'

'She's just up and moved to Christ Church.'

'Well, sure what's wrong with that? From your demeanour I thought something dreadful had happened.'

'It has.'

'What …but… she's only moved to…'

'Without Lassie?'

'She left the dog behind?'

'Yes, with a damn neighbour. Elizabeth was in tears on the 'phone saying, "Daddy, if you love me send Mummy a thousand dollars to have Lassie flown down. I really miss her."

'A thousand dollars?'

'Yes, Zoe said that's what it will cost. I don't know why she didn't take the animal with her in the car. It's her bloody way of extracting more money out of me.'

'Are you … going to pay?' I said, apprehensively.

He looked at me coldly. 'No, I'm not going to submit to Zoe's blackmail. She can go to hell.' With that he shuffled into the sitting room and began to play the piano non-stop as if the music was his only refuge.

The following evening Nicholas returned from the office. My heart skipped a beat when I saw the dejected state he was in. 'What' wrong?' I asked tentatively.

'What's wrong? You ask me this knowing I'm going through hell.'

'What do you mean, what has …?'

'Zoe won't let me speak to Elizabeth. She's unplugged the 'phone.'

As each day passed he became haggard, his appetite went; he lost weight, lost his sense of humour and retreated slowly into his own lost world.

Then one day he arrived home drunk - not angry drunk, he wasn't like that. Not silly drunk, or aggressive or maudlin. He was just courteously drunk. His face was a damp mess, running with tears. He said nothing just walked into the down stairs sitting room and began to pound the piano. His fingers careering over the notes evoked a sound that was at once terrible in its sadness and exquisite in its beauty.

From the shadows of the dimly lit room I watched him. I'd never seen him like this, drunk and unkempt. He must have fallen on the way home.

When he saw me he gave out a choked sob and with one hand on the piano for support, rose unsteadily to his feet. He gazed at me with a face of such piteous misery that my heart was ripped wide open by it.

'I can't stand it anymore. I'm going to send Zoe the money.' His voice had a broken edge and his eyes were windows to a haunted place.

I stared at him and as he slumped down on the Chesterfield I said quietly, 'Do what your heart tells you.'

A day later, he returned from work. As the key turned in the door I heard, 'Hello darling. What's for dinner?' His voice was animated and as he strolled into the kitchen he had a grin on his face and his eyes sparkled.

'I spoke to Elizabeth today,' he said cheerfully.

'Oh,' was all I could muster.

'Yes and Zoë is having Lassie flown down this weekend.

I didn't reply. Would this obsession with his daughter ever end?

20

'THAT'S DRAMATIC,' Lynda said as she scrutinized my white linen suit. 'I suppose you bought that outfit in 'Help the Aged'.'

'Of course! There are great bargains to be had. You should pop in sometime.'

'Me. Alex you know I wouldn't wear cast offs. You don't know where they've been.'

'Haven't you ever heard of H2 0?'

'Alex forget it.'

We were both out for the night and to add a theatrical vein to my garb I'd draped a long red silk scarf around my neck that trailed all the way down to my ankles.

'You better watch out, remember what happened to Isadora Duncan,' Lynda said laughing.

I raised an eyebrow. 'What?'

'Her scarf got wrapped around the wheel of some Ferrari and that was the end of her.'

'Lynda, are you trying to tell me something?'

'Alex, you act just like her sometimes, sort of eccentric. It's the thespian in you. And let's face it you're rather risqué. They say red is for danger.'

'I wonder how that cliché originated.'

'No idea. I suppose red is synonymous with blood. That's why I won't wear it. Tempts fate too much.'

'Do you think I tempt fate?' I said giving her a quizzical look.

'It's second nature to you, love. Look at the way you're with Nicholas.'

'I need to talk to you about him.' I started to feel desperate.

'Later in the pub love. I want to concentrate on driving.'

Pulling into the traffic, Lynda began to tease. 'Suppose you meet some Don Juan tonight would you give Nicholas the push?' Her blue eyes flashed as she glanced quickly at me.

'I would not. Sure ye know it as well as I do myself.' I looked out the window. Didn't she know I loved him?

'Do you realise you always slips into your phoney Irish when you're upset, or when you're trying to be funny, or when you've had a glass too many.'

'Sure it's the language we laugh in. Don't you think it validates the ties between us Lynda? Ye know I trust you. You're about the only person I can be myself with.'

"I'm myself with you.' Lynda had a twinkle in her eyes.

'Yes, except I think I'd turn to you if I was in real trouble. I think it's the same for you. You think me and Nicholas aren't right together. He's the love of my life, Lynda.' I sighed deeply.

Lynda nodded. 'You know it's not just your good looks which made you drop dead gorgeous. You're scatty, witty and intelligent but somehow utterly vulnerable. That's the key to your attractiveness and the potential source of your unhappiness.'

'How am I vulnerable?'

'He's married. All that baggage! Look I'm struggling with this tail back. Let's talk more when we get to the Swan. At this rate the music will be over.'

'I hope not. I love the folk scene. Deirdre was only saying the other day that I'm a philistine when it came to my taste in music.'

'Well we all know what Deirdre thinks. You shouldn't let her boss you so much. And she's always dumping Catherine on you when it suits her. She exploits you Alex.'

Lynda doesn't like Deirdre much. 'Sure she means well.' I hope.

The traffic was getting worse. 'I hate scrushes.'

'What's a scrush?'

'You know, a crush, a jam.'

'Where do you get them?'

'I make them up. Some day they'll be in Chambers.' I smiled. My mood was lifting. Lynda and I always managed to cheer each other up. We'd known each other since our daughters started infant school. Almost thirty years and we're still close. If anything happened to her I'd die. Funny I'm closer to her than Deirdre. Deirdre's too … controlling. Despite the traffic it wasn't too late when we arrived at the Swan. Inside the lounge was warm and cosy, lit by a flickering fire in an immense stone hearth. 'Annie's Song' was belting out as we ambled across the room.

'It's our tune,' I said eagerly as we grabbed two comfortable arm chairs and plopped down. At least that was one thing Lynda and I had in common, we both loved folk music. I started to hum and Lynda started to sing:

> You fill up my senses
> Like a night in the forest
> Like a mountain in springtime
> Like a storm in the desert...
> I croaked in;
> Let me die in your arms.

'Sure 'tis beautiful. I love the words, "Let me die in your arms." 'Sure I could die in Nicholas's arms.'

'Alex, I wish you'd slow down a bit with this romance.' She made a face.

'Hm. What's your opinion of him?'

'A bit complex! You're as simple as the winds that blow over Ireland.'

'Lynda, this is bugging me what are you trying to say?'

'I feel Nicholas was born of a line of men who spend their leisure time spinning dreams that leave them out of touch with reality. He seems to move in a private world that is more alluring then the real world and he comes back to it with reluctance.'

'You have him well taped.'

'Taped?'

'It's an Irish phrase. You know, you've sized him up.'

'Alex, you and your Irishisms,' Lynda said affectionately.

I laughed.

'His obsession with his daughter worries me though. When do you draw the line between obsession and love?'

I shivered. Sheila had called it a sublime love, some might call it an irrational love, others, like Lynda, called it an obsessive love but to those close to him it was a love that turned the lives of those he loved upside down.

'I'll tell you something. If it's a choice between that little girl and you she'll win hands down.'

'Oh God, Lynda, what am I going to do.'

'Alex, enjoy his company but try not to get to involved. It will only bring heartbreak.

'Do you know what my new philosophy is going to be?'

'The mind boggles.'

'I'm going to dread one day at a time.' I smiled. 'Only kidding.'

'Break, break, break,
On thy cold grey stones, O Sea!'
And I would that my tongue could utter
The thoughts that arise in me.'

'You're drunk Alex'

'Sure I'm noch.'

'You are and you're melancholic.'

'Stop the car and let's enjoy the ocean.'

'Are you mad? It's midnight and we've work in the morning. Anyhow it's dangerous.'

'Sure you're right Lynda, you're right. Why do you put up with me?'

'Till death us do part, love.'

'We get on well don't we? If anything happened to you I don't think I'd want to live.'

'Alex you're being melancholic again.'

> "Break, break, break
> At the foot of thy crags , O Sea!
> But the tender grace of a day that is dead
> Will never come back to me."

'Sure I love that poem. Think of it Lynda. The tender grace of a day that is dead will never come back to me. That's how I feel about you and me. We'll never have this moment again. We must cherish it.'

'Stop bull shitting. I better get you home.'

I detected the tremor in her voice. 'I love you Lynda.'

"You're drunk Alex.' This time her voice was thick with emotion. Why do our generation find it so hard to express our feelings?

'You're a great friend.' Silence. Nothing is often a good thing to say, and always a clever thing to say. But I caught her, caught her wiping a tear away.

21

'TO GET these guys off your back I've a friend who can lend you fifty grand to pay off part of the loan.' Danny's voice was conversational, as if they were old friends.

'Fifty grand? That's not enough. I owe nearly twice that.'

'Hold your horses, Karl. If you borrow a second fifty and invest in the scheme I was telling you about within six months you'll have doubled your money and be in a position to pay the rest off.' He paused, taking in the moneyed atmosphere. Perhaps he too would become a member of Wilde's club once the dollars came rolling in.

'Is the scheme safe?' Karl coughed nervously as he twirled his wine glass round and round. A tic pulsated on his cheek.

'Karl, my friend, you know I only deal in the best. Trust me.' His voice had become low and conspiratorial again, as if he was his dearest and oldest friend.

'Ya.' The tic throbbed even more.

'The bonds are worth a lot more then their trading value.'

He sat straight in his chair. 'How does their value drop in the first place?'

'Panic among investors. There's this man Meriwether who has the knack of knowing their worth so he buys millions of dollars worth. Then, when the market stabilises he sells. To prove it I'll show you the figures. Nothing can go wrong, old boy. I've even invested my mother's money.' Danny's face never altered as he told his little white lie. A man had to make a living.

Karl's eyes lightened. 'Your mother's money? They must be safe then.'

'Of course! Would I risk my old lady's money?'

The call came a day later. 'Well, Baron, have you the dosh.'

'I'll haf the money tomorrow for definite.' Sweat poured from his forehead, every pore in his body seemed to be erupting; his breath came in short bursts as his chest heaved. He gripped the receiver. In his world Karl had never had to deal with something like this.

'Cut the crap Baron. Tonight or else!' The 'phone was disconnected.

Karl stood there sweating. He thought about what he'd read in the Telegraph about money lenders. One had smashed a lead pipe into a man's face and then he'd brought the implement down on the man's shin breaking his femur. Karl shivered. It was time to go along with Danny's plan.

22

AS I SAT on a pale-yellow, almost white beach in New Zealand. I watched the breakers run up on the sand, watched a man and a child splash at each other near the waters edge. The man's face registered pure joy.

What a peaceful place, I thought as I gazed again at the palms with their little green leafy hats dotted along the sands. The man and the girl had moved nearer, so close I could see her clearly now. Her long flowing jet black hair shone like ebony in the golden sunlight. Dark slanting eyes, which held a hint of naughtiness just like her fathers, sparkled. Two people totally engrossed in each other. This was my only chance to see her –from a distance.

I glanced again. They'd moved under the shade of a great tangle of dark-green trees just a few metres away. I could just about make out what they were saying. Nicholas was burying Elizabeth in the sand; she was laughing and saying, 'Dad, I'm not a little girl any more. I'm nearly ten.'

'You'll always be by little girl. Maybe if I clinch this deal with Danny we can be together…forever and we'll be happy. We'll have a garden and you can chase butterflies like you used to when you lived in England.'

'Dad, I'm not a little girl anymore. Anyhow,' her voice became animated, 'soon, Mummy says, I can go to the school disco with my friends and then …' she looked at him under her long lashes, 'I'll be able to meet boys.'

Nicholas's face darkened. He stopped pouring the silver sand over her and with eyes downcast seemed to vaguely listen to her chatter as one listens to the rustle of the wind in the trees, immersed in his own deep musings.

Elizabeth, obviously noticing his withdrawal said, 'It's okay Dad, you're my best boyfriend...'

'We used to be so close.' he muttered. Like an adult she gently stroked his face, and softly said, 'I'll love you for ever, Dad.'

Then Nicholas grinned and said. 'Tell your mum I said you're too young for boys. Then in a more serious tone he said, 'You're growing up too fast, without me by your side. 'It's four years since your mother took you from me. '

All of a sudden, jumping up, she clasped her arms around his waist and squealed excitedly, her eyes popping out of her head, 'Dad you stay with us and don't go back to England. Just the three.'

Nicholas dropped his eyes leaned his head upon his hand and gave out a small moan. A whiff of pathos emanated from him. After a moment, he lifted his face and in the sunlight, his eyes were shining brightly. He began to speak in a halting tone; his voice, catching, had a haunted quality about it that would soften a stone. 'If only.'

'But you said...'

We'll have to wait and see. With Danny it could be all pie in the sky.'

'Never mind Dad I'll say a prayer tonight and ask Jesus to find a way that we can be together ... for ever. And Mummy says that Jesus always grants children their wishes.'

I was staggered. So Nicholas wasn't absolutely sure of Danny. Something must be up. And Nicholas hadn't said an iota.

Later that night Nicholas sat in Elizabeth's bedroom. His eyes were pools of misery as he gazed at the sleeping figure and thought of his imminent separation from her. This was their last evening together. The night was close and sultry and she'd kicked off the blanket, which lay twisted round her legs. Suddenly his love for her welled up within him with such intensity that he felt the tears starting in his eyes. He sighed deeply. He knew that Elizabeth loved him with all the passion of which a young girl was capable. He sat there for time immemorial in his desperate loneliness, head bowed. Suddenly he found himself fumbling in his pocket, extracting a pen and scribbling words on a scrap of paper, lots of words as if they'd no order, until he read them:

> Tears roll down my cheeks
> As I look at your picture, oh so sweet
> I hear you whisper, Daddy dear,
> Please, keep me here,
> That cry will stay with me in my heart
> Till only death us do part.
> Till only death us do part.

He placed the poem on her pillow and quietly left the room thinking about his situation. His heart yearned for Elizabeth. He'd never known a love like this before. Not even for Zoe not even for Alex. Up to the age of forty-four, when he had married Zoe, he had been a lusty, charismatic philander with a down-to-earth sexuality. Most women found him irresistible and fell over him and after the romantic interlude was over he'd saunter out of their lives, the rakish grin intact, and his heart unsullied except for once or twice when he felt his heart was broken. And now…?

Maybe he could do a runner, leave his debts behind. Then he'd have Elizabeth in his life forever. He and Zoe would have to make a go of it for Elizabeth's sake. Or he could live near them. But that would mean leaving Alex. As he weighed up the pro's and cons he instinctively knew the answer. His heart was with his family. Who could blame him? All he'd ever wanted was the family unit. Then maybe

Zoë and he could get back together. But…he knew he had a more peaceful life with Alex. And she was mad about him. He could love her if he didn't have this moral dilemma. In the eyes of God he was married to another. He stared out the window. The late-autumn stars were as icy as those of an artic winter, and it seemed to him that then as in all the seasons, the sky was not deep but lifeless, flat, and frozen.

Next morning Nicholas stood at the front door saying goodbye to Elizabeth. He pulled her close to him and held her tight, his own tears scalding his eyes. 'I love you Elizabeth. Don't worry I'll find a way for us to be together.'

'Promise, Dad, promise.' Her voice was muffled against his chest.

'I promise,' Nicholas muttered, his throat throbbing, the pledge he didn't know he could keep.

Father and daughter stood, for time immemorial and cried. Then he gently pushed her back from him and whispered, 'I have to go.'

'Please Daddy. Don't go. I can't bear it.' She clung to him sobbing. Gently disentangling her from him he whispered, 'I have to …' As he walked down the path he thought; there are some deep sadness's that stay in one's heart no matter how much you try and expunge them. And this was one of them- parting from Elizabeth.

23

KARL VON Lichtenhof lay with his wife, a rare occurrence lately. This occasion had come about because she wanted him to pay for a little black number she'd seen. The phone suddenly rang. An uneasy feeling swept through him as he padded across the cream carpet to a white French dressing table. Picking up the receiver he said, 'Karl Von Lichtenhof speaking.'

'We want the rest of the dosh, Baron. Remember you only paid the interest and a bit of the capital off.'

'Look, Devlin, this isn't a good time can I call you back later?'

'Look, either you cough up or we'll be paying a visit to your wifey.'

'I told you I'll get it for you soon,' Karl said, his voice raised.

'We're calling in the rest of the loan.'

The 'phone went dead.

Danny had promised him that his money would double quickly and that was nine months ago. He'd have to contact him and demand it. He knew these low lives meant business.

Next morning Karl rang Danny's office. 'It's me, Karl. I need ze money urgently.'

'Look, I told you I'll have it for you in a few weeks.'

'I can't vait Danny. They've threatened Yvonne.'

'The middleman is away on business but I'll see what I can do. Trust me.'

Danny's hand trembled as he replaced the receiver and stared out through the open window distracted. Outside the spring afternoon air was lemony yellow with slanted sunshine that would lift ones spirits. But not Danny's. He'd already been in touch with the Canadian and knew that he was stalling for some devious reason. He could handle Karl but Luke was demanding his money. He was not a man to be trifled with. Danny thought of the hanging corpse and felt sick. He reached for his glass of whiskey and slumped back in his chair. If he didn't get the cash soon God knows what Luke would do. He shivered.

THE GHOST SAT QUIETLY IN HIS SITTING ROOM LISTENING TO HIS FAVOURITE MUSIC. IT WAS A PIECE FROM WAGNER, A COMPOSER HE GREATLY ADMIRED JUST AS HITLER HIS HERO HAD. HE LIKED TO COMPARE HIMSELF TO HIS IDOL WHO, HE FELT, WAS A PSYCHO JUST LIKE HIM. HE LIKED TO THINK OF HIMSELF THAT WAY AS TO HIM IT NOT ONLY EPITOMISED THE DARKNESS WITHIN HIM BUT IT WAS SYNONOMOUS WITH HIS GENUIS.

PICKING UP A FILE, HE GLANCED AT THE NAME 'DANNY' AND FLICKED IT OPEN. HE LIKED KEEPING FILES; FILES OF PEOPLE WHO HAD TO BE DEALT WITH. HE WHISPERED, 'DANNY MY BOY, YOU BETTER PLAY BALL OR ELSE!' HE REPLACED THE FILE ON HIS SHELF GLANCING AT HIS COLLECTION OF VIDEOS - ALL ABOUT DEATH. HE SELECTED ONE WITH THE TITLE 'THE MANY FACES OF DEATH' AND PLACED IT ON THE COFFEE TABLE, SOMETHING TO WATCH BEFORE HE RETIRED TO BED. HE GLANCED AT THE PHOTOGRAPH HE'D TAKEN

OF A MAN HALF IMMERSED IN A HUGE FISH TANK. THE TANK WAS FULL OF ACID AND FROM HIS WAIST DOWNWARDS HIS ENTRAILS HAD STARTED TO FLOAT IN THE LIQUID. HIS LOWER BODY HAD ALREADY BEEN EATEN AWAY BY THE ACID, EVEN THE BONES. EXCRUTIATING PAIN WAS PAINTED ON THE POOR WRETCHES FACE. HE SMILED, AN EVIL NASTY SMILE. 'YES DANNY YOU BETTER WATCH OUT.'

24

PAT MORGAN lingered at the bar of the Hyatt waiting. Danny, Nicholas and Alex were due to arrive for dinner and Danny was picking up the tab. His thoughts turned to Danny as he sipped his beer. When Pat was seventeen he'd joined the army for three years. It was there that he'd met Danny. He remembered the incident as vividly as if it was yesterday and the impact it made on him. He was at the bar in the mess and had asked for a pint.

'With that accent you've got to be Welsh.'

Pat pivoted around to look at the speaker.

The stranger was a medium sized man, his body lean and hard looking. He had black hair combed back to reveal a widows peak. His eyes were the colour of a green black stormy sea. What struck Pat at once was that it was a face extraordinarily alive and animated so that you felt that he was ready to laugh, to smile, or scowl. Pat had never met any one quite like him. His dark eyes sparkled with enthusiasm as he spoke, blazing with an overpowering irresistible vitality. Pat was captivated by him then and found him open, warm and alive, enjoying life and making sure that everyone around him enjoyed it also. Quickly they became buddies.

Only another soldier can comprehend the satisfaction that army comradeship gives. From the start of their friendship Pat had been in awe of Danny, in awe of his daring escapades, in awe of his charisma. Soldiers together they shared their joys, their sorrows, their loves, their hates. They shared the same women, got drunk together, shat and pissed together. And then, something happened while they were posted abroad that heightened Pat's adoration. While out patrolling one night in a small garrison town Danny lunged at Pat knocking him to the ground. Suddenly rifle shots rang out. A slug missed Pat, penetrating Danny's arm. Pat fired back but the sniper disappeared into the night.

Later in the hospital Danny told him how he'd seen a glint of metal flashing in the darkness and had acted without thought.

In Pat's mind Danny had taken a bullet for him. This episode cemented a lifetime bond. But it was more than that. Pat had always been aware of his own homosexual tendencies. Years ago he'd decided that marriage and children was the moral route. He suspected that Danny knew his secret.

When he eventually joined Danny in business he quickly found that he was a man who demanded unquestionable loyalty. As the years passed their friendship grew. Danny became his Svengali. Now there was nothing Pat wouldn't do for him. He loved him.

'HI PAT,' suddenly made him jump. Nicholas was standing close by, grinning.

'Nicholas, I didn't see you arrive,' Pat said, returning the grin.

So this is Alex,' Pat asked as he stood up and shook hands with me.

'And this is Danny's shadow,' Nicholas said with a smile.

'Great to meet you at last,' Pat interjected. 'I've heard so much about you.'

'I didn't know Nicholas was singing my praises,' I replied, laughingly, at the same time studying the man facing me. His age was difficult to determine. He might have been twenty or forty but not fifty or seventy. He was small in stature, fat with a receding hairline.

'It's not Nicholas whose been singing your praises. It's our Danny. He said you were beautiful and he's right.'

I blushed at this unexpected compliment and was just about to reply when we spotted Danny arriving with Timmy at his heels.

As the dog reached Pat he leapt up on him, licking his face, while furiously wagging his tail.

Turning to me, Danny said, 'Wonderful to see you again Alex. It's about time Nicholas showed you off.'

Twisting back to Pat, Danny added. 'Pat, be a brick and take Timmy to the night porter.' Then he addressed me again. 'In case you're wondering, the secret is to tip the hotel staff generously if you want good service. Money buys everything, doesn't it,' Danny said then, looking at both Nicholas and Pat, 'except of course loyalty.'

'And you certainly didn't have to buy mine, Danny. It's always been there. You should know that by now.'

'Indeed, I do, Pat. Indeed I do.'

'Slainte.'

The four of us sat in the bar making a toast with champagne.

Danny Delaney definitely has charisma, I thought as we clinked our glasses together. I noticed that when he looked at a person he could make them feel as if there was no one else in the world and he used this to his advantage. I studied him observing an open face that made people trust him implicitly; his dark eyes and black hair with attractive streaks of grey at the sides gave him a somewhat debonair appearance. 'How did you two meet?'

Danny answered in a warm tone, 'Pat was singing Nicholas's praises; telling me what an asset he'd be to the business. So one night we got chatting over a meal and…the rest is history.'

'Oh,' It's a pity you ever met.

'I'm trying to persuade Nicholas to give up working for Tom and join forces. We're going to hit gold soon.'

'Really?' Nicholas had kept that to himself. I'll tackle him later.

'Yes,' said Danny, ' I've something new in the pipeline that's going to put us on the millionaire list.

He sounds so convincing. Does he really mean it or is he a charlatan? And is this some other deal or the same one Nicholas has being going on about?

I watched him as he held out an attractive case containing cigars. His dress too spoke affluence, and a ring glittered on his finger as he tore off a tiny match from a book of matches bearing the name of the Hyatt. He's a poser. He exudes confidence but yet it's as if he has something to hide. I'd noticed how his eyes were always on the move and only too ready to take refuge beneath those heavy eyelids.

As we strolled into the dining room the headwaiter hurried towards us. 'It's a pleasure to have you in our restaurant again, Mr Delaney. A little crowded tonight but I've a secluded spot for you.' He weaved his way between the diners to a quiet corner. Pulling out four chairs he snapped his fingers for the maitre d'hotel and the wine waiter and placed four menus in front of us 'I wish you and your guests an enjoyable evening.' Then he disappeared.

He certainly does things in style, I thought. Judging by the way he was received by the staff here it's obviously a frequent haunt of his.

I found I was warming to Danny as I listened to his friendly banter. He's likeable, I thought. I understood why Nicholas was so smitten.

Later I sat, sipping my coffee and looking around the spectacular dining room, impressed by the splendour of the wood panelling and the glittering chandeliers. The food had been excellent. I wondered where the money had come from to pay for it all as Sheila had told me that Danny had gone bankrupt.

'Another bottle of champers everyone?' Danny said jovially as he drained the last drop from the bottle.

'Well…yes…that's very generous of you Danny.'

Noticing my hesitation Danny added, 'Forget the expense, Alex; we'll be rolling in it soon. Isn't that right Nicholas,' giving him a wink.

Nicholas gave a hesitant smile, avoiding my stare as they both stood up and headed for the bar. Must have something private to discuss - and not for my ears.

He's like a godfather, I thought as I observed him from a distance his hand draped over Nicholas's shoulder. It was obvious they were deep in conversation about business.

'You and Nicholas seem happy?' Pat said, interrupting my train of thought.

'Yes, everything would be perfect if it wasn't for his family problems. Still not to worry. What is it that Dryden said? "They can conquer who believe they can."'

He gave me quizzical look as if the quote was too profound to understand. 'I hope so. But be careful. He's obsessed with Elizabeth. I know if he'd got the money he'd be off like a shot.'

'What…'

'Sorry Alex, I didn't mean to say that. Anyhow it will never happen. He's broke. So don't worry he's stuck here.'

Stuck here! Is that all our relationship meant? Just as I was about to reply Danny and Nicholas appeared. 'We'll chat again Alex,' Pat said, as Danny began replenishing everyone's glass.

The soft sounds of a piano being played floated in from a nearby lounge. The rich melody did nothing to diminish my melancholy as I tried to process what Pat had just said. What if this deal was a success then he'd have enough money to join Zoe and Elizabeth - permanently. This evening is becoming a nightmare. I mustn't think about it. What is it my father always said? "Nothing is neither bad nor good but thinking makes it so." I'll be like Scarlet O'Hara and think about it tomorrow.

25

'BECOMING INVOLVED in corporate law is the only way I'm going to make money,' Nicholas said as we sat eating dinner in the dining room.

I eyed him critically. 'Darlin', I wish you'd concentrate on what you're good at, and not dabble in things you know so little about.'

Nicholas smiled decadently. 'It's exciting.'

I raised an eyebrow. 'Don't forget what you told me; you spend years looking over your shoulder.'

'Alex, your trouble is you're afraid to take risks. Typical teacher.'

'I'd rather know I wasn't going to end up in some dark alley, with my throat slit.'

'Oh, come on, you're paranoid.'

'They said world war two would never happen. Nicholas, these people are far more street wise than you and are only using you to further their own ends.'

He stared at me defencelessly. 'Danny will deliver soon.'

I let things percolate a moment in my head. 'When did he tell you this?'

'Today actually.' A muscle tensed, then loosened in his jaw.

I gave him a probing look. His expression had gone cold and closed. Was it curtains for me? I chewed my bottom lip. Would he go back to New Zealand when he was in the money? I toyed with my wineglass, twirling the stem between my fingers, watching the light refracting through the red liquid on the white linen tablecloth. 'What exactly is this deal?'

'I'm not at liberty to say. When it's all done and dusted you'll see.'

I frowned. More questions bumper-car-ed through my brain. 'What's the nature of Danny's business anyhow? I get the impression that it's not all legit.'

'Rubbish. For God's sake is this 'the weakest link?'

I gave him with a steely look. 'Anyone who starts up in business so soon after going bankrupt must have been into something dodgy.'

He shrugged. 'Danny knows how to find loopholes in the law.'

I threw him one of my haughty ice-princess looks. 'You mean you do.'

He ignored my remark and continued explaining. 'Part of it is money lending.'

'Not this loan sharking business?'

'No… of course not. To give you an example; recently a couple wanted to buy a nursing home. The building society had promised them a mortgage but it wouldn't be released until underpinning on the property was completed and the work passed by a surveyor. To secure the deal the couple had to take out a bridging loan.'

'How much?'

'A hundred … grand.'

I noticed his face become grim. Did he think he was revealing too much.

'A hundred grand?'

'Let me try and enlighten you. Danny provides the capital. When the underpinning is complete the mortgage company will hand over the money. It's a short-term loan but Danny receives about ten grand for his trouble.'

'So where does Danny get the cash?'

'Well.' He paused, and looked at me worriedly. 'Danny gets it from a client.'

'Who?'

'An Italian.'

'An Italian?'

'Well Turkish - Italian. His name's Bruno Rosso.'

'Where does he get the funds?'

'It's tax avoidance. By investing with Rosso they avoid it. He gives them twenty five percent interest and no questions asked.'

'You mean the interest is not declared?'

'Yes.'

'That's against the law. You could be struck off if the law society gets wind of it.'

He looked past me, as if I had ceased to exist, his face a stony mask and muttered, 'If it weren't for Elizabeth I wouldn't touch him with a barge pole. Anyhow I only sign a few papers for him. Let's have an early night. I'm sick of this interrogation.'

I felt hurt. This wasn't the old Nicholas I had first met - a time of drifting from one lovely day to the next together. Now ... he was defensive, secretive and antagonistic. There's a lot he isn't telling me. I felt all the breezy eccentricity and liveliness in my manner had dissipated. I reached for my glass of wine and noticed that my hand shook slightly.

That night as I lay in bed wide awake my mind was turning in circles, my thoughts drifting away on different tangents as I tried to grapple with what we'd discussed. Who was this mysterious Italian, Bruno Rosso, Nicholas had mentioned? Gradually, it seems, the darker elements in Nicholas's life were being slowly uncovered. But a tiny voice at the back of my mind sought to contradict me. Nicholas is an upright man look at how he was towards that traveller child. I recalled Wordsworth's words: "That best portion of a good man's life, his little, nameless, unremembered acts of kindness."

26

THE LATE afternoon sun was a ball of flame, its rays bouncing off the waters of the estuary. The crowds sauntering in the street squinted as they went along the ancient cobblestones, grateful for the October sun. Too often the month brought fog and rain; it was not the case that day and everyone seemed elated by the clear biting air tinged with the warmth from above.

Danny was not elated. His eyes were tired, the hollows beneath dark and stretched, the result of too little sleep for too many reasons. He'd been in touch with the Canadian several times and he'd been fobbed off. Anytime now Luke would be on the phone demanding his investment. He dreaded to think what would happen when he found out he hadn't got it. A shiver shot through him as he recalled the mental picture he had of Phil's body hanging from the rope. He turned away from the office window, sat down at the antique desk, and poured a whiskey. Might steady his nerves. Timmy, lying under the desk gave a little whine as if sensing that something was wrong.

All of a sudden the 'phone rang. 'Yes,' Danny croaked.

A voice said, 'They're here.' It was Pat from the lobby down stairs. His words had a grim inevitability about them

Danny started to sweat. 'Send them up,' he said, his voice quaking.

'Do you want me to join you?'

'No, I'll handle it.' His limbs felt like jelly and his stomach was quivering.

'Be wary.'

Seconds later there was a knock on the door and it swung open before Danny got to it.

Luke strode in with Frank in his wake.

'How's it going Luke?' Danny said nervously.

Timmy sprang up with a blood-curdling growl, the hairs rising on his neck.

'Down Timmy,' Danny said as he pushed the dog onto the carpet.

Timmy continued to growl.

'Your dog doesn't like me,' Luke said, with a harsh laugh. 'Can't say I blame him. They say animals sense the evil in the air.' He gave another harsh laugh.

Frank was silent.

'Things are looking bad, Danny.' Luke had a grin, or the beginning of one, on his face, but his eyes were not laughing.

'Sit, down, sit down Danny said anxiously, waving him to an armchair. 'Like a whiskey,' he said in a tone, which began with a lilt of levity and then swooned into a quiver, as he rushed to the drinks cabinet.

'No drinks, Danny.' Then Luke's face grew as hard and serious as Danny had ever seen it. 'Just the money.' He smiled then, obviously aware of the effect of his smile. To Danny it was chilling in that there was no apparent menace. He smiled as if there was some private joke only he himself appreciated. But since he smiled like that when he'd only deadly things to attend to and since his eyes didn't smile and since his whole manner was usually pleasant, the sudden revelation of this side of him struck more terror into him.

Danny coughed. 'I've been in touch with my business partner.' Best to let him think we're on good terms. 'The dough will be here in a week. You know how things are.' He gave a sickly grin.

Luke's brow darkened with a depth of fury that made his previous expression seem benign. 'Cut the crap, Danny.'

Danny grew pale. 'No problem Luke. I promise you it will be here soon.'

'No good Danny. We've come to collect – NOW. I warned you there would be consequences. You should have listened.' A vein in his temple was doing a river dance.

Danny grew paler. Timmy growled once more.

'Lovely dog Danny, lovely colouring,' Luke said, bending as if to stroke the animal. Like lightening Luke's right hand whipped a knife from his pocket and in one swipe he slashed the dog's neck. Blood gushed forth like a jet, spilling out over the cream carpet. Luke stepped to one side. Almost at once, as if on cue, a great shaft of sunlight, vibrating with dust particles, streamed down from the window and lit up the ghastly scene.

Transfixed Danny gaped in horror. Timmy gave a shudder and whimpered. A yawning grimace of agony seemed to spread over his face. The dog was looking up at him, his eyes cold and bright through a dripping mass of blood. His jaw moved, but no sound emerged. Before it expired its sad eyes fixed on him, mirroring complete incomprehension.

'Think yourself lucky. Next time it will be you, Danny.' Luke said, softly, almost purring, as he made his exit with Frank in tow, whose face, as always impassive, except for the jagged scar on his jawbone that throbbed in such a way one would think there was a gigantic worm beneath the skin.

Danny wondered was this a sign of his innate horror of what had happened or perhaps Luke's actions had aroused the sadist in him. As he knelt beside Timmy his head, like the consciousness of the insane might be, was filled with the shrieking of ravens. A shuddering groan escaped him. In the awful heavy silence of the office as he slumped impotently on the floor with his arms around Timmy he could still hear the sweet, evil laugh of Luke echoing in the corridor. With his hands on Timmy's blood soaked lifeless head he sobbed chokingly. He remained there, for what seems ages, covered in blood, his voice now almost like a whimper, just like Timmy's had been. Finally he rose and pressed the buzzer, a signal to Pat down stairs that he was needed.

When Pat entered the room he recoiled in horror as he spotted the red stained carpet and then the dog.
Danny was sitting at his desk, a drink in his hand, his whole body shaking as he stared at Pat.
'What happened?'
'Luke…the money.' His voice was listless. His complexion was a horrid, pasty white, darkening to deep shadows under eyes that seemed overlarge and hectic.
'My God, the man's depraved.'
'Said it would be me next time…'

As Pat bent down beside Timmy, a scream rose from his throat but he choked it unvoiced. He must stay strong for Danny's sake. He stroked the dog and then, heavy limbed, stood up and reached out with trembling fingers for Danny's hand and took it in his own. Pat's mouth was pinched with pleading and denial. His eyes, round with hurt were haunted by a horror that both men seemed to share.
Danny began to cry, a high piercing crying that was tinged with mania.
He was still in tears as Pat wrapped the dog in his anorak.
'I'll take him down stairs,' Pat said gazing at Danny. His voice broke then and he lowered his gaze and could no longer look at his friend. He compressed his lips, which had begun to tremble. His eyes opened wide, and when he closed

them again, they were brimming with tears, which rolled down his cheeks. He covered his face with his hands so that Danny didn't see the tears. Tears for Timmy, tears for what had happened, but above all tears for Danny, a man he loved and had given his soul to. Quickly he made his exit, angry that he'd failed to have the foresight to follow Luke upstairs. Maybe he could have prevented what had happened. Such feebleness in life-and death events in evil matters, always spawns tragedy.

Upstairs, as the enormity of it all sank in, Danny began to despair. He could feel a strange wave spreading through his central nervous system and he could hear a sound like a rushing stream inside his head almost like the rush of madness, this incorrigible madness he found himself in. He knew if he didn't return Luke's investment something far worse would happen. What could he do to stall him? Suddenly an idea ricocheted into his consciousness. His spirits lifted. Why didn't he think of it sooner? At least it will keep them off his back for a while until I sort out this whole mess, Danny thought as he poured himself another Bushmills.

LATER THE GHOST SAT ALONE. SILENCE POOLED IN THE APARTMENT, AND NOT A SOUND ASCENDED FROM THE LIVING QUARTERS BELOW OR FROM THE DARK DEPTHS OF THE STREET. 'ANOTHER BLUNDER. IT SHOULD HAVE BEEN YOU DANNY. TAKE CARE MY FRIEND TIME IS RUNNING OUT.' HIS HEAD TURNED WITH CROCODILIAN MENACE, EYES COLD WITH A CRUELTY AS OLD AS TIME.

SUDDENLY THE MEMORIES STARTED TO ASSAIL HIM AGAIN. HE TRIED TO BLOCK THEM

OUT. THE SIZZLING HOT POKER PAIN SEARED THROUGH HIS RECTUM. HIS INSIDES WERE BEING CHARRED. BLOCK IT OUT, BLOCK IT OUT.

THEN THE BRAINWAVE. EXCUTED MARVELLOUSLY. THE GARDEN SHED. THE PRIEST'S SORDID SECRETS. MAGAZINES. PICTURES. LITTLE BOYS.

IN HIS MIND'S EYE HE WATCHED THROUGH THE WINDOW AS THE PRIEST POURED OVER THE MAGAZINES. SOON THE LOOK OF ECSTACY WOULD BE WIPED FROM THE PERVERT'S FACE. THE DOOR WAS ALREADY LOCKED BY THE PRIEST'S OWN FINGERS. THE BOY TIPPED THE COLOURLESS LIQUID UNDER THE DOOR. HE HAD ALREADY SATURATED THE ARMCHAIR AND THE OLD COATS WITH THE SPIRIT. THE PRIEST HADN'T NOTICED. TOO BUSY WITH HIS FILTHY HABIT. HE WAS MASTURBATING NOW, HIS PENIS DISTENDED. THE ELEVEN YEAR OLD PICKED UP THE BOX OF MATCHES AND LIT ONE. A TINY BLUE FLAME LICKED ITS WAY UNDER THE DOOR. HE WATCHED FROM THE WINDOW. A GUMMY BURNING SMELL EXUDED FROM THE CHAIR THE PRIEST WAS SITTING ON. THE PRIEST LOOKED STARTLED. HIS CLOTHES STARTED TO BURN, FIRST HIS TROUSERS. THEN, ALL AT ONCE, THE CHAIR WAS AN INFERNO. WITH HIS HEAD GLUED TO THE WINDOW THE BOY WATCHED AS THE BLAZE STOOD UP AND STUMBLED TOWARDS THE DOOR. HIS BRIGHT ARMS STRETCHED IN FRONT OF HIM, BLUE-YELLOW TONGUES OF FIRE SEETHING OFF HIS FINGERS. A TWISTER

OF BLOOD-RED FIRE WHIRLED IN HIS OPEN MOUTH, DRAGON FIRE SPURTED FROM HIS NOSTRILS, HIS FACE DISAPPEARED BEHIND AN ORANGE MASK OF FLAMES AND YET HE CAME ONWARD. AN ALMIGHTY ROAR EMANATED FROM THE FIERY TORSO. THE SCORCHING SHAPE FELL TO THE FLOOR. AS THE FLAMES DIED DOWN A BLACK INCINERATED BODY WAS REVEALED. ONE OF HIS SCORCHED CLAWS OF A HAND STILL GRIPPED THE KEY.

THE WHINE OF THE FIRE ENGINES JOLTED HIM. THE PRIEST WAS DEAD. THE CHILD MERGED INTO THE SHADOWS OF THE TREES AND MADE HIS WAY BACK TO HIS ROOM.

27

'I'VE A bit of bad news,' Nicholas announced as he strode into the kitchen after a day at the office.

'Oh, has someone died.'

'Well ...' he averted his eyes.

I froze. What now?

'Danny's dog is dead.' His face twisted in grief.

A chill raced over my flesh, settling into my arms and legs in trembling pools. 'How?

'He was slain.' His face became more anguished.

'I don't understand. How was he killed?' My voice was almost a whisper.

'His throat was slit.' The pain was now raw on his face.

'Who did this, Nicholas?'

'Someone Danny owed money to. When he didn't return it they paid him a visit and killed the dog.'

'Who are these people for Christ's sake?'

'Just someone Danny knows. I don't know who they are.'

His voice hasn't a ring of truth. What's he hiding?

'These men are dangerous. It could be Danny next or even you.'

'I've got nothing to do with these people.'

'You don't know what sort of trouble Danny might drag you into.

'Here we go again always the same record. I've had enough. I'm out of here.' And with that he disappeared into the garden.'

I sat there feeling emotionally fatigued. Suddenly an unruly despair welled up within me. There was so much going on in his life that I didn't know about.

I sighed heavily and caught sight of myself in the mirror. I looked haggard and drawn. All this was taking its toll. Perhaps Lynda was right. Keep it light. I realized with a terrible crystal-clear clarity that I'd fallen deeply in love with him. The thought hit me with a violent jolt every time it came. And yet it didn't make me happy. Anyone with any strength would have backed away long ago. But this was my failing. Where men were concerned I was weak. Too weak.

28

THE FOLLOWING morning I rose after a fitful night. The death of Danny's dog bothered me. Was the dog's death a warning I thought as I strode down the stairs? Sunlight streamed through the stained glass panel, catching motes of dust as they danced in the air. As I opened the porch door to get the milk I spotted a letter on the mat. Strange the postman hadn't been yet. Must have been hand delivered. As I picked it up my heart skipped a beat. Someone had stuck my name on the envelope with letters cut out of a newspaper - like on a ransom note. I stared my mind racing:

Alex CLARE R0WE

Few people knew my middle name but, additionally, hardly anyone would know that I spelt it as Clare and not Claire. I tore open the envelope and withdrew a sheet of paper again with letters randomly strewn over it. I read only the first two lines:

Danny betTer get his aCt together or else - NeXt TiMe IT wILL BE CLoSER TO HoME.

I stumbled back up to my study, slumped down at my desk and spread the sheet out in front of me. I'd never felt fear so acutely. Now, this new dry, acid taste in my mouth was as unwanted to me as the rapid beating of my heart. I took a few moments to try and calm the turbulence within me. Then I read on, pausing over each sentence, allowing dread and disquiet to take root within me.

Not a g0od idEa to Mess with US. NiChoLaS should TaKe this aS a warNing.

I shifted uncomfortably in my chair. I could feel a wave of heat rippling up from the page in front of me, like energy from a bonfire caressing my body. My lips were dry, and I fruitlessly ran my tongue over them.

I began to pace around, assessing the letter. A tiny voice within me wanted to be dismissive, to shrug the entire warning off, too deem it an exaggeration without any basis in reality but I found that I was unable to. I tried to tell myself, empathetically, that it was all a charade but I knew that wasn't the case. The killing of the dog told me so. I passed my hand over my forehead. I'd the beginnings of a migraine coming on.

I sat down again and tried to think tangentially. I didn't think of myself as very qualified to be my own detective. But then I shook my head, rationalising that, in a unique way, that was untrue. For years I'd been a sort of detective. That was what science and maths was all about.. I picked up a pencil and began to scribble, thinking in a logical, mathematical way, applying a simultaneous equation method to give me answers :

The person knows my middle name - X.

It had to be someone close to Nicholas - Y

$X+Y = Pat$

Would he have this information? Maybe from Danny.

Something twanged at the back of my mind.

He'd helped me mortgage my house.

I chewed my pencil. Rippity zip - too many electric impulses coursing through my motor neurons. I took a rain check and stared out of the window, my eyes following raindrops as they slid sluggishly down the glass. Rolling my theories around in my head I concluded:

Danny must have my details.

A neurone whimpered.

Did he give my details to the person who killed the dog.?

If so why send me a letter?

The dog's death had got to be pivotal in all of this?

But what had it got to do with Nicholas. Perhaps they thought Nicholas had it. But he was broke.

Impasse.

I screwed the paper up and tossed it in the bin. My heart sank as I realised I knew absolutely next to nothing about crime or criminals. After all I was just a science teacher grappling with something far beyond the norm.

After that my entire day seemed to fall together in routine normalcy. I drove to school, delivered my lessons, ordered equipment for experiments for the following day.

29

'Guess what I did today?' Nicholas had just arrived home from work and had strolled into the kitchen.

'Not Danny again. You've got to keep away from him, Nicholas. What if these men that killed the dog come after you? Promise!'

'What's got into you all of a sudden Darling. You revelled in Danny's company at the Hyatt.'

'Yes...' I paused. 'Danny is very charismatic and likeable.'

'There you go.'

'I still think you should distance yourself from him before it's too late.'

'Do you know something I don't?'

'Of course not! I'm just concerned.'

'Well I'm glad you brought it up. I've decided to give Danny a wide birth for a while.'

'Oh.' Thank God for that. Could I believe him though? He loves Danny's and Pat's company.

'This scheme of his hasn't delivered yet and I'm not waiting around any longer. Instead of spending valuable time toeing and froing to Danny's office I've decided to concentrate on personal injury.'

'I told you that's what you're good at.'

'If I double my efforts with Tom I'll make enough money to pay off my debts in no time. So Danny's past tense.'

'Oh Darling I'm so pleased.' I ran to him and threw my arms around his neck and kissed him.

'Steady on. I haven't told you the other news yet.'

Still smiling I said laughingly, 'Go on tell me. You've won the pools?'

'I booked my flight to New Zealand for the end of September.'

I slumped down on the nearest chair. 'You what?'

'You heard what I said,' he replied, an edge of resentment appearing in his voice.

'For God's sake Nicholas you haven't got the money. Surely you didn't pay with plastic?' My voice was high and breathless now.

Looking rather sheepish he said, 'Oh, a thousand pounds came my way.'

'Just like that?'

'From Danny.'

'My God Nicholas I thought you said he's past tense.'

'Let me explain.'

'Go on.'

I told him I wasn't prepared to act for him any longer as he hadn't paid me and that I intended to concentrate on personal injury.'

'What did he say?'

'The usual promises - soon we'd be rolling in it and all that nonsense. And then he wrote a cheque for a thousand pounds for services rendered and said that there more would follow.'

'That was just a bribe Nicholas to get you to reconsider.'

'I know, that's why I stuck to my guns.'

'So how did you leave it?'

'Just that I was prepared to re-evaluate things if his plan materialized whenever that would be...today, tomorrow, whenever.'

At least Danny and Pat are out of the picture. Maybe when the anonymous writer discovers this he'll back off. I sighed. There's no need to mention the note. I ran my fingers through my hair. I seemed to be jumping from one crisis to another. Suddenly I started to cry, a silent tearless crying that was all the more powerful because it was so deadly quiet.

30

ALMOST EXACTLY forty-eight hours later, Nicholas flew to New Zealand. For the first week he rang me every day. Then the 'phone calls stopped.

Disappointment.

Then the usual mental gymnastics.

You really expected him to phone.

He's back with her.

They're an item again.

Were they eating out together.

Window shop while strolling along, hand in hand.

I drove myself mad listing all the possible things they could be up to.

Then just before he was due back my cell warbled. I answered. It was Nicholas. 'What's wrong, you didn't ring.'

'Nothing, I...'

'Nothing. Nicholas, I know something's wrong. Tell me.'

'I wish it wasn't so difficult.'

I let things percolate a moment in my head. 'What's difficult?'

'I can't speak about it over the 'phone. I have to go, Alex,' he said in a distant voice. 'Good-bye, see you Sunday. There's a letter in the post for you.'

'A letter...?' The 'phone went quiet. Silence! I just slumped there - numb.

After what seems an eternity I stirred, put my coat and scarf on and exited the house. Aimlessly I just walked. Morbid musings, like a dirge overwhelmed me:

I know it's over.
Grey sea, grey clouds, grey roads.
Oh no, not grey; grey is a colour.
There is no colour.
Colour means hope.
There is no hope.
Just blackness, the blackness of despair, of desolation of loneliness, of grey sorrow, of weariness.
So weary, to struggle on, no, too weary.
I am lost, my indomitable will, my ever-ebullient spirit is no more; My soul is DEAD.
I succumb to oblivion.
I am no more.
He is gone.
How far can the human spirit sink - until no reserves are left?
And when there are none left, and no way out, around or through, then what?
Alone, alone again.
Desolation
Hope, even a glimmer, like a fragile sunbeam.
Grasp it.
It eludes me.
No more resistance - give in.
The effort is too great.
The spirit is broken.
Sleep; doze, perchance to dream.
Perchance to escape.
It comes in spasms now; the suffering.
Around me the desolate landscape; the trees are leafless; black ravens soar over the grey skeletons of the silent oaks.
Black and grey, grey and black.
When does human endurance reach its limit?

Now, here in England, I witness the death of the soul, my soul.

Lifeless I stare round.

The letter was there, waiting...waiting to destroy me when I got home. I picked it up and cried, cried before I opened it for I knew the contents. It's over; it's over.

Night-time!

The letter remained unread. I put the tear soaked envelope on the bed, turned the side lamp on and with a feigned calmness took off my coat and hung it up. I took off my scarf and threw it on the bed. Next I took off my boots and put my slippers on. Then I began to shake because I'd forgotten in my distress where I'd put the letter. I found it on the bed. Before opening it I dried the envelope with a tissue, taking care not to smear the ink.

I opened it. I absorbed the contents as if it was my executioner. I sprawled back on the bed and digested it again, reading it through as quickly as I could. I laid it, folded, on the table in the light shed by the angle-poise lamp. I undressed and turned out the light, and lay still, my head supported by my pillow. I read it again, this time monosyllable by monosyllable, examining each one so that none of the letter's hidden intentions would be concealed from me. Then I read it repeatedly, until I was so full of the words that they began to become meaningless. Finally I placed it on the table and lay on my back with my hands by my side. I didn't close my eyes; I just lay there hardly daring to breathe. Dawn came. I got up and made myself some tea and sat again and reread the letter. Then I lay back again and adopted the pose of a reclining marble statue, moving from time to time to sip my tea. Finally as dawn broke I read it one more time:

Dear Alex,

Our life together is over. Something drastic has occurred. It has far reaching consequences for us both. So sorry! See you on Sunday.

Nicholas.

NO kisses, no endearments – nothing. In the distance I heard the toll of a church bell. Seven o'clock. Whose demise was it heralding?

31

LATER THAT morning, at about eleven, Nicholas arrived home.

'You're back then,' I said as I answered the door.

Unshaven, haggard and drawn he stood there.

I waited for him to speak, fear clutching at my heart, unable to face what was about to transpire.

'Yes, and I'm too tired to be plied with questions,' he said, giving me a sideways glance. 'I want to go to bed.'

'I want to know what's gone on.'

'Can't it wait? Anyhow there's nothing to tell.'

I turned my head sharply, without subtlety and glared at him. My legs felt like jelly as I strode into the kitchen. I made tea in an effort to distract myself. 'I want to bloody well know what's going on?'

He dropped his eyes and murmured, 'Nothing.'

'I don't believe you. You can't even look me in the eye.'

He flopped down on the chair, silent, a pained expression on his face. Intuitively I sensed that what he was going to reveal was not going to be pleasant- far from it. I gave him a desperate look and demanded, 'Tell me?'

'Look, it will be all right in a day or two. We'll get back too normal." He spoke very slowly, and the words seemed wrung out of him.

A glimmer of hope penetrated my consciousness – "We'll get back to normal". Maybe there's a chance. Aloud I said, 'So, something has happened?'

'Yes,' he said, avoiding my stare. 'When I arrived there,' he paused and looked at me beseechingly, 'I had no intention of allowing it to happen; it all got out of hand.'

'What got out of hand?' My voice was unusually harsh but God hadn't I a right to know.

Nicholas stared at me again. 'You're like an inquisitor.'

'Go on,' I said, narrowing my eyes, lifting my chin and putting on the grimace that signifies tolerance stretched to its limit.

'Well, Elizabeth started to put the pressure on me.' He dug out a letter from his pocket and handed it to me. The childish handwriting said:

Dear Dad,
I love you very much. Please, please remarry Mummy. I love you lots and lots.
To the best Dad in the world.
Elizabeth. xxx

"Please remarry Mummy." like bullets, pierced my heart. 'Remarry Zoe?' My voice was suddenly flat and pained.

'Yes.'

'And Zoe?'

'She wanted it.'

'She would,' I interrupted him with anger in my voice.

Ignoring me he continued in a hurt voice. 'She fixed up for us to get married.'

'Get married?' My heart sank. 'How could you Nicholas,' I said, with anguish in my voice.

He continued, barely audible now. 'We set the wedding for last Thursday morning.'

'Thursday morning?'

'Yes, that's what I said, Thursday morning.'

I eyed him even more intently. 'And,' I said, tonelessly, 'you married her.'

'No.'

'No?'

'Jesus Christ, Alex, are you deaf?'

'Oh, so you didn't marry her,' I said sarcastically but I breathed a sigh of relief. 'Why the change of heart?' I continued in a biting tone.

'Alex, don't go on.'

'Don't go on, for Christ's sake, who wouldn't in the circumstances?'

'I'm tired. Try and understand why it happened.'

'What did happen? Maybe then I might begin to grasp it,' I said, with hot tears streaming down my face. How could he betray me like this?

'I couldn't go through with it. I got so depressed when Zoe arranged it all.'

'So you backed out. Why?' I heard a chilling bleakness in my voice.

'Maybe it was because of you. I don't know. I thought of you and how I... lo... cared for you. But this week Zoe was so nice. We were a family again.'

I sat, stunned. Here was this man I'd given all my love to telling me that he'd almost remarried his former wife. Swallowing hard I said, 'Since you didn't marry her, what's going to happen now?'

'Alex, please. No more questions. I beg you...' He paused and in that spell of silence I became conscious of his tenseness and the startled sad expression that lingered on his face.

After a while he continued. 'Can this wait until tomorrow?'

Still he couldn't make eye contact. I sensed then that something ominous was about to be revealed.

'Nicholas, I know there's something you're not telling me.'

'I wish you wouldn't persist. I'm weary and need to rest.' He sat with his shoulders hunched. His face held a deep despair.

'Nicholas, you're selfish. I haven't slept for a week.' There was animosity again in my voice

Guiltily he looked at me. 'I promised …'

Just then the 'phone rang. Grabbing the receiver I said crossly, 'Yes.' Wrong fucking number.

Nicholas availed of the opportunity and hurried upstairs to bed.

I sat in a daze. My hands were shaking and my head felt as if it was going to explode.

The hours went by. Frequent pacing. Futile activity. Dishes. Ironing. Biting my nails. Over in my mind the phrase 'I promised to...' kept repeating itself. What did he promise? Night had fallen. At around eight I heard movement upstairs. I would tackle him now. I'll put the kettle on, be ready for him.

Nicholas entered the kitchen.

Toast.

He nodded.

I popped two pieces in the toaster.

Took flora pro-active from the fridge.

Got mugs.

Tea -spoons.

Back to fridge for milk.

Back to drawer for knives.

Back to the cupboard for plates.

'No more questions.'

I eyed him with a reproachful look. 'No Nicholas, I want to know now.' My voice could have flash-frozen petite - pois.

He slid down on the chair.

'What did you promise Zoe?'

'You'll never give me any peace until you've wormed it out of me.'

'So tell me then.'

'Oh God, give me strength. I promised...' he stopped obviously unable to go on.

'You promised her what?'

'I would… return in December.'

'You did what!'

It was then he threw the hand grenade. 'I promised her that we'd remarry. Then she and Elizabeth will return to England.'

For that second I thought I'd go bonkers. I was unable to speak. Shaking I turned to the sink and filled the kettle. I must do something, anything; move, scream.

'For God's sake, say something.'

I gazed at him abstractly then in deep shock. I walked away from the sink, moving like a sleepwalker, my face blank. I was angry but the shaking had ceased. I glanced in the mirror. My eyes were flat and dulled; my face ashen. I sat down on the chair with a shocked bump. I clunked the mugs down and poured the tea. My voice was calm and strong again as I spoke. 'And are you going to marry her?' I said it in such a remote and cold way that he winced.

He looked at me. 'I don't know. I feel it's my duty if she's willing to come back to this country; it's for Elizabeth's sake,' he said with despair in his eyes. 'Elizabeth needs a father and a mother and that's all that matters to me.'

'But Nicholas, what happens if the abuse starts again?'

'She's promised that it won't.'

'Leopards never change their spots. Within months you'll be at loggerheads.' I took a sip of my tea.

'I couldn't stand it again, Alex, I'd just walk out. However I must give it a go.'

'So you've made your mind up?'

'No.'

I paused, my mug halfway to my lips. 'No?'

'It's so difficult. Just when I decide that the best thing to do is to go, a black despair descends on me when I contemplate life without you.'

'You better make your bloody mind up Nicholas; I'm not going to let you mess me about.' My mug clunked the table.

'I can't. I …love you. But I love being with them also. I don't know what to do.'

I was dumbfounded. This was the first time he'd mentioned love. But I was in no mood to acknowledge it. 'You've betrayed me, Nicholas,' I said in a low quiet voice.

My calm indictment goaded him as he blazed back. 'What would you do if your daughter was twelve thousand miles away? This is my only chance to get her back.' Then defensively he said, 'I didn't mean it to happen. I'm so sorry Alex.'

I looked down at the back of my hands, spread on the table. I hesitated a moment, then said, 'You've behaved in a contemptible way, Nicholas.'

'You don't understand,' he replied angrily. 'You don't understand anything.'

'I have a child also Nicholas and a grandchild that I adore,' I replied.

'I'm sorry I've put you through all of this. I don't expect you to forgive me.'

I glanced in the kitchen mirror again. I was shocked by my appearance. My face now held a deep sadness. I looked haggard and drawn. The delicate bones of my face were prominent now. I was thin, and pale. My eyes, usually bright, were clouded with suffering. I turned back to him. My gaze fixed on his face; even when I raised the cup of tea to my lips my eyes never wavered, never left his. After some time I spoke, 'I know you didn't do this on purpose. I know what Elizabeth means to you.'

'I'll leave now if you wish.'

'Where will you go, Nicholas? Your house is rented out,' the studiously imperturbable voice said. Inside I was far from being controlled.

He shrugged and spread his arms in a small despair. 'I don't know. I'm so sorry for what I've done to you. I wrote you a second letter and tried to explain everything but I never posted it. He handed it to me and strode out into the garden:

Dearest Alex,

By the time you get this letter it will be too late for both of us. You may never realise this but to have a child is the most exquisite kind of happiness. Then she was taken from me and it broke my heart. And then you came into my life. The support that you gave me in your fragility, which hides your strength, kept me going and now I must hurt you greatly and leave you because just as you gave me all of those things so did Elizabeth equally and more, that warmth that only a child can give, that serenity, that joy. No longer can I be parted from her and though I love you tenderly I must perform my duty and be a father to her. I hope you will, in time understand the anguish I am going through and that in time you will forgive me.

I will always love you, until my dying day.

All my love
Nicholas. x

A strange sadness washed over me. In my heart of hearts I knew that I should let him go but … If I let him stay for a while maybe he'd change his mind. Pigs might fly.

32

'WHAT'S THE matter Nicholas?' I said as I noticed conflicting emotions spread over his features as he read his mail. It was Saturday and we were having breakfast in the kitchen

'She's changed her mind,' Nicholas said as he continued to read.

'Who?'

'Zoe, she's not coming back.'

'Why, for God's sake?

'She doesn't want to live in England again.'

Not coming back. My heart did a little butterfly hop.

Nicholas sat and read bits of the letter out to me.

Interrupting him I said, 'You must return then. It's the only way to be with Elizabeth - permanently.' Inside my heart was breaking.

Nicholas's face darkened and a determined look swept over his features. His voice was clipped as he replied. 'No. Zoe promised she'd live here.'

There was a different man now, hackles up nerves extended. The hardness was in his eyes. But I remained silent - waiting.

'She knows I can't go back. She even said so herself. "There's no work here for you. Solicitors are two a penny."

'And, furthermore, I've a good position here. Anyhow if I returned I'd have to do a runner and leave my debts behind. I can't understand her. She desperately wanted us to be together, for Elizabeth's sake.'

'Maybe when she thought about it she just couldn't go through with it. Remember she detested England and was miserable here. I'm so sorry Nicholas,' I said as I placed my hand on his cheek. When I looked his eyes were full of the circles of fright.

Nicholas and I tried to settle back into our life together. But in no time there was a sudden precipitous collapse into the blackest melancholy. I'd had enough. It was time for action so I tackled him one night. 'Nicholas I can't stand your moodiness any longer. It's getting me down. It's not that I'm not sympathetic ... but there's only so much one can take. Perhaps now that your house is vacant it would be a good idea for you to spend some time there ... to sort out your feelings.'

"My minds sorted? I can't leave I need you.'

'Neither can you live like this, Nicholas. Anyhow ... it's not just your moods...' Should I dare mention it. 'I ... still feel that if Danny hits the jackpot you'll be off.' I remembered Pat's words.

'Don't be daft I've made up my mind to stay. Anyhow my mood has nothing to do with Elizabeth. I've got some business problems at the office. So forget about me leaving. Let's watch the news.'

He never listens, I thought as he stormed out of the kitchen. God I hate confrontation, hate letting him see how upset he's making me. I'll put it in black and white. Maybe then he'll take notice. I scrabbled in the kitchen drawer for a pen and scribbled down the first thing that came into my head. I read the contents.

Dear Nicholas,

I feel that as soon as Zoe finds herself a job you'll go back to her. From what you say she wants you with her. It's with great sadness that I ask you to leave. At least then I can have some peace of mind. The uncertainty is driving me to distraction. If you remain here any longer I feel I won't be responsible for my actions. You've driven me beyond all rational thought.

Alex.

Not a clever move I was later to learn.

The letter shocked Nicholas. He promised to change. 'Besides, Elizabeth will be twelve soon. She'll be old enough to fly over to see me,' he said optimistically, 'and her mother won't be able to stop her.'

To my relief the arguments began to vanish as our old relationship was re-established. Nicholas's friends were telling me how much he had changed for the better and there was all the time in the world for us to share our love.

33

I ROSE early and padded down to my conservatory. I glanced out. It was a beautiful morning. The sky was smoke blue, faintly glazed with gold. The sun was up and making diamonds over the fish pond. Maybe we'll have an Indian summer I thought as I stepped out into the chilly air. I tipped my face to the sky and drew in a deep, invigorating breath. At least I have my teaching, I thought as I dwelt on all that had happened.

Going back into the kitchen I sat down. Just then my mobile began to vibrate on the table. 'Hello, the Milky Way.'

'You are funny, Alex. Can I pop round?'

'Course you can, Lynda. I'll put the kettle on.'

A few minutes later Lynda was on my door step. She strode into the hall a look of consternation on her face.

'What's up Batman?'

'Disaster has befallen me,' she said as she followed me into the kitchen and plopped down on the nearest chair.

'Join the club.'

'Bloody bats!'

'Those lovely creatures.' Lynda gave me a dirty look.

'I knew you'd say something like that. Lovely creatures my a... They're not staying in my attic. Have you got the yellow pages? I threw mine out. And they haven't delivered the latest edition yet.'

I smiled. That's where Lynda and I differed. She hated clutter.

'Sure the bats eat up all the mozzies and insects. Anyhow you can't move them.'

'Why.'

'They're a protected species.'

'Christ Alex there's droppings all over the attic.' She rolled her eyes.

'Sure they're only tiny poo's.' Lynda screwed up her face.

'Rat's droppings are worse. Look they'll leave to hibernate soon so leave them.'

'But they're attracting bloody cats.'

I opened my eyes wide, feigning innocence and said, 'Since when did cats fly?'

'It's a pity they can't, and then my problem would be solved. Are you sure they'll go?'

'Yes.'

'But they might come back.'

I floated one brow. 'Sure if they do they're harmless.'

'Christ Alex, you and your laissez faire attitude. It's easy know you're Irish. Brew me a chamomile for Christ's sake.'

'Ugh. Lynda chill out. I'll stick two bags in,' I said as I went to brew the tea.

'Did you go to watch the game last night?'

'Me watch football are you kidding. Sure I heard it was like the River Dance with all that rain anyhow. Did you?'

'Yes, You know I always watch Liverpool playing. Bye the way how are things?' Lynda said, as she flicked through the yellow pages.

'Well… not to good.' I related all that had happened since Nicholas's trip, the cryptic note, everything.'

'God Alex and here I am worrying about a few bats.'

She stood up and put her arm around me.

I sighed. 'I've an uneasy feeling about things — as if something terrible is going to happen.'

'Of course it won't Alex.' She took a deep breath obviously trying to sound reassuring. It was only the flickering pulse in her neck that told me she too was concerned.

I bit my lips. 'I had this dream about a bush covered in white roses its spiky twigs covered in thorns and twisting inwards. Within the entrapment that they formed a white dove flapped and screeched, as it struggled. Red blood stained the white roses until they appeared variegated - red with white, white with red.'

She cast me a concerned glance. 'Alex it's only a dream. Maybe you should get away for the weekend, have a change of scene.'

'Yes, your right.'

'Look I must go. I'll jot this number down first.'

'They won't touch them, Lynda.'

'At least I can try. See you soon love. Keep your pecker up.'

34

YVONNE VON LICHTENHOF relaxed in the restaurant of Harvey Nichols having afternoon tea. As she sat sipping Earl Grey tea she noticed a man sitting at the next table. He seemed to be scrutinising her. He was squat but what he lacked in size he made up for in magnitude. Broad and massive, he'd the huge arms, shoulders and barrel chest of a wrestler. His forehead was high and out of proportion for the rest of his face. It was a brutalized face with a thin cruel mouth, porcine eyes and a scar, which ran from the left eyebrow to left chin - a freakish face, startling in its deformity.

Realising he was being observed the squat man gave a shrug, his thick lips twisted in a mocking leer.

Yvonne tried to avoid his gaze as his tiny eyes met hers and widened fractionally. He knows who I am, she though, horrified.

She began to feel uneasy and on an impulse called for the bill. Looking over her shoulder, as she made her exit she saw, to her dismay, that he was following her. Hurrying towards the exit she paused. 'No, I'll nip into the loo; he'll never follow me in there.

The toilets were empty. She was beginning to regret her decision. At least in front of all those diners she'd have been safe. I'll return there, she thought as she opened the toilet door that led to a passage way. Suddenly she went limp and began to sweat. Facing her was the little man, a menacing stare on his face. His mouth was twisted into a sneer. 'Mrs Von Lichtenhof I've been dying to meet you and unfortunately, up to now, I haven't had the pleasure. I was told you were beautiful but I never dreamed someone could be so ravishing.' Then he took a step nearer and muttered, 'It would be a pity to spoil such beauty.' His smile spread so far she could have counted his teeth. But his eyes were full of malice. They contracted into little frozen balls.

Yvonne stood, aghast, horror written all over her face.

Then he leaned even closer to her, until his face and his milky eyes and his hideously benign smile were barely a few inches away. He had a cigar perched at the side of his mouth. Taking a deep puff he snatched it, grabbed hold of her and held the burning cigar close to her temple. 'Tell your husband that he'd better pay up or else,' he said in a soft, almost sugary voice, ramming the Havana into her temple.

She could smell her hair scorching as an intense burning sensation enveloped her. She stared at him, paralysed, and then screamed, putting her hand up to the side of her face. Dazed, she stood there in shock as the squat man turned on his heels and charged out the door.

When Karl Von Lichtenhof heard about the incident murder was in his heart. He knew that at all costs he had to get the money from Danny or maybe his solicitor, Nicholas Murray had it in a client account.

BOOK 2

35

29ᵀᴴ October 2004

'KEN WE'VE got ourselves a murder - 50 Coombe Road. Fancy it?' Peter Gibson's voice heard over Detective Superintendent Ken Masterson's mobile sounded as cocky as ever. Ken could feel his hackles rising as the old resentment towards his boss surfaced. 'I think you'll find it a clear cut case. Sounds like domestic violence to me so it won't take long to wrap it up.' Ken hadn't missed the veiled undertones. Shit and he wanted an early night. After mentally noting the details he switched off 'Talk Sport' and swore under his breath. He gunned his vehicle in the direction of Crosby.

Ken surveyed the murder scene. In the hall there was blood everywhere. Everywhere! Not just on the tiled floor but on the wallpaper. He craned his neck to look at the long spray marks all over the walls. He imagined the blood flying off the knife, as maybe the victim's neck was ripped open. Ideas jumped from synapse to synapse. Blood pumps at high pressure through a person's arteries. It doesn't just simply drip when one of those vessels is cut. Already before he'd even seen the body he knew that a main artery had been severed. Arterial splatter patterns on the wall would indicate that the stab wound to the throat or other parts of the body severed a major vessel and occurred while the victim was standing and still had a blood pressure.

He dragged his attention away from the gory sight and turned to the policeman who had emerged from the kitchen. 'What have you got?'

'We're doing fingerprints and forensics right now. The ambulance is here to pick up the body and take it away for autopsy. We wanted you to look at it first.'

'Where is it?'

'In the utility room, off the kitchen.'

Ken took a deep breath and entered. He looked once, and turned away in impotent horror. And then he twisted around again. The victim was sprawled on his back. His eyes had remained open, and now they stared out with macabre intensity. Not only that but both eyes bulged slightly in their sockets. The right one was askew as if in life the victim had had a cast eye. A scarlet mist of blood had painted the white of the washing machine, and deep, dark blood was seeping from a gaping wound in his neck, staining his white shirt. He noted the multiple lacerations on the face. He tries to imagine the victims face as it might have been when he was alive. He shuddered. Why carve up a face? The blood has spurted out and gushed all over the carpet tiles. It squelched under Ken's feet as he stepped back from the corpse.

'Not an attractive sight,' the policeman said.

'No,' Ken said as he looked again. He'd seen it all before. The man had a sort of profound look on his face as if he knew death was imminent. With death so unexpected, every human being is reduced to horror and longing – the longing to live and the indescribable torment that she or he wouldn't. No one could die with dignity in these circumstances. And this person before him certainty didn't.

He retreated into the hall. That was the part he hated, looking at the gory details. He'd never hardened to it.

Two women had just come down the stairs. The dark haired girl was soaked through with blood. The deep red stain on her cream skirt seemed obscene somehow.

'This is Alex Rowe, partner of the man who's been stabbed,' the other woman said. I'm Marie a neighbour from next door.'

A pair of terrified grey blue eyes looked into his.

Ken gave her a quick once over. Her eyes were stained dark pink from crying. Black mascara was streaked across her cheeks.

Cutting across he said to Marie, 'If you pop back home and put the kettle on we'll take her into you in a minute.'

36

I FELT ignored…like a child is talked about but I did as I was told. The thought, this is a ploy to split us up didn't occur. What did I know of police methodology? When Marie left, Ken said, 'We need to take you to the police station.'

In other circumstances I'd have laughed. 'Go to the police station, why?' It sounded like something tragically comic that one would see on TV but this was not just some burlesque play act; this was for real; a murder had been committed and it was becoming more obvious that I was the prime suspect.

Ken, breaking me out of my thoughts said rather brusquely, 'We want you to make a statement.'

'Why?' A terrible fear seized me I began to shake. I wanted to voice my qualms, to get reassurance, but I mustn't let him know that I was afraid. Could he possibly think I murdered him? Oh my God will this nightmare ever end? 'Could…' My voice faltered; I was unable to utter a sound.

I finally managed to gasp, 'Could Lynda Hughes accompany me? She only lives down the road?'

He paused. Studied me and then said, 'OK. We'll pick her up on the way.'

Stumbling down the path to the police car I suddenly froze. 'I must see him.' Before he could stop me I rushed back inside and entered the kitchen and then froze. Horror shot through me as I tried to absorb the bizarre scene before me.

Nicholas was still on his back but now his eyes had been closed. His Saville Row pin striped suit had jagged tears and his silk tie was still in place except for a ragged rip in the middle of it near to his heart. A dried red round stain about three inches in diameter covered the Mickey Mouse patterns of the tie. The black leather shoes still gleamed through cakes of blood spattered over them.

I looked at his face again. Lacerated with cuts, it was almost as if someone had drawn a serrated edge across his face. He lay there, mutilated, his humanity destroyed by the pouring out of his blood, his life, his dignity, even his identity. Blood was now everywhere. I felt then that I too was being swamped in it as if it oozed into my every aperture, my eyes, my mouth; my nose.

A police photographer had arrived on the scene and, vulture like, was circling the body, taking shots.

I stood enraged. Suddenly I made a lunge.

Fortunately, at that moment Ken entered the room and dragged me away. 'We must go.'

'Please just a few more minutes with him,' I begged, and then, unrestrainedly, threw myself on the body. I guess I had a wild look then. My black hair was damp on my forehead. I kept shaking my head and moaning. 'Oh no, oh no.'

The pathologist appeared and tried to cover Nicholas's body with a sheet but I cried, 'Oh, Jesus, no, he won't be able to breathe. Oh God do something; don't let him die.'

Gently Ken took me by the arm and led me out. 'He's dead Alex, he's dead. There's nothing we can do.'

Wrenching my arm free I ran out and vomited in the front garden. A terrible coldness was seizing me again. My teeth began to chatter so much that I thought they'd leave my mouth and terror was gaining an increasing hold.

'Come on Alex. We've got to go.'

'Detective sergeant Bill Cummings will take you both to the station. I need to have a word with the pathologist,' Ken said as he walked me to an unmarked police car.

37

ON THE way to the police station DS Cummings picked Lynda up. As she crawled into the back seat of the car I could see her face was ashen and she was shaking. She threw her arms around me and held me.

'Oh my poor love I'm so sorry,' she muttered. I clung to her and sobbed uncontrollably as the police car gunned in the direction of the police station.

'What's happened Alex?'

Struggling to stem the flow of tears I whispered. 'He was stabbed. Lynda, they think I did it.'

'Did you? Oh God Alex what am I saying. Of course you didn't. You're too gentle.'

From the lonely glow of a street lamp I could see a shadow of concern wash over her features.

'How can you think such a thing about me, Lynda?'

'Alex, I'm so sorry for even thinking it but if it was me in your shoes I might have been driven to a crime of passion. I mean Nicholas has put you through the mill in the last couple of months. That business with his ex and his daughter would have driven me over the top but you're so tolerant you put up with it.'

'If it's crossed your mind that I might have done it and you're my closest friend, then what do you think the police are thinking. They don't know me like you do,' I whispered. I felt the clawing talons of hysteria envelop me. Got to stay calm.

'If you didn't do it you've got nothing to fear. Just tell the truth.'

I didn't miss the concerned tone in Lynda's voice. The primeval fear returned. Then an idea struck me. Maybe I did do it. Maybe I'm blocking it all out. I remembered what I'd written in the letter when our life had been in turmoil.' "I feel I won't be responsible for my actions. You've driven me beyond all rational thought." Had I had murder in mind? Could I be capable of such an act? I shuddered. No never! I'd never kill him. I'd adored him.

38

FIVE MINUTES later Ken was on his way to the station. As he drove he thought about what the pathologist had said. It had been a frenzied stabbing and the deceased had sustained about fifteen stab wounds. The mortal blow had severed an artery in his neck. And the partner is covered in blood. It was a sad fact, Ken knew, that in cases of domestic murder the person most likely to have committed the crime was the spouse. Peter was right as always. Ken dwelt on Alex. Everything about her, her general demeanour, her quivering, her indecisive speech, her gaze, her silence, her every movement expressed one impulse, terror. Had she killed him? Was she putting on an act? He'd a job to do. After all she'd been alone in the house with her lover, the murdered man. Chances were she was guilty.

He'd noticed that as they'd walked down the path, her face had been turned to his, her terrified features caught in the street lamp. Her wild eyes were two dark orbs reflecting primordial fear, her tear stained skin taut and pale. She was genuine in her grief he saw, no psychopath, but he'd met murderers before who had acted on impulse. Uncontrolled! She had been definitely out of control then.

39

EVERYTHING ABOUT the world I entered that night was foreign to me. Lynda was asked to remain at reception as a WPC escorted me down a corridor.

The sights, sounds and the smells of the central police station seemed to me to represent an aperture on the city that I'd never before peered through. Being just a teacher I was vaguely aware that such places existed. My nose tingled as the faint aroma of urine and vomit hit me. A cacophony of sounds reached my ears as I passed a man shouting unintelligible phrases and then a telephone blaring somewhere from a nearby desk.

We entered a small room. It was a vault of monotony, windowless, airless and poorly lit. 'Take a seat Alex,' DS Cummings said as he sat down at a desk and gestured to a seat opposite him. Another WPC brought in three mugs of tea, and milk and sugar on a tray. Just then DI Masterson arrived and quickly sat down beside DS Cummings. DI switched on a tape recorder.

'Your statement is vital,' he said. 'We need to know as much about you and your friends in order to establish a motive for the murder. Maybe a jealous lover ... or a former friend killed him. It's imperative that no detail is omitted, however small.'

I nodded. I could see that Ken was cool and efficient and good at his job. Fear crawled up my back. I stole a glance at DS Cummings. It was then I noticed his lovely kind brown eyes and his pleasant smile. Maybe he'll believe me even if this DI Masterson doesn't.

DI asked, 'Do you want a solicitor?'

'No…'

'Are you sure? It's your right.'

'Why should I, I'm innocent.' The trained eyes on me exchanged glances.

As I told my story question after question were hurdled at me: Was there a lover or a friend in my past that held a grudge? Could either of my former husbands' David or Donal have been jealous enough to commit such an act? I'd wanted to scream, 'No, no, no, you've got it all wrong. It's not them. Instead I said, 'It's Danny Delaney you should be looking at.'

Four eyes zoomed in on me like a camera lens again.

'Who's Danny?' Deadpan again.

'Nicholas's friend. He's got connections in the underworld. He's into all sorts of dicey deals.' Already the idea had formed in my mind that Danny was in some way linked to the murder.

Their two faces were trained on me again. I read disbelief on DI's. DS's face was softer, more kindly. Maybe I had an ally here.

'We'll investigate him. Tell us about the shoes. Why did you take them DI.'

I tried to explain that I felt Nicholas would be annoyed about the blood stained carpet. I wasn't to know that he'd die. I knew then, by their expressions, that the two faces scrutinizing me didn't believe a word I'd said. They obviously saw the incident as cold-blooded, and an indication of my guilt. Who would blame them? Who would, in their right mind, worry about a carpet when one's love was bleeding to death? But I hadn't been in my right mind and I didn't know he'd die.

The inquisition seemed never ending. I delivered my replies abruptly and jerkily without letting my eyes waver from DI's gaze, answering his questions with a fixed stare.

Sometimes DI would, repeat a question: 'Why did you take your shoes off?' At one time I angrily replied, 'You've asked me that question five minutes ago, are you trying to catch me out? You think I did it, don't you?'

A silence lasted five seconds, during which time eyes roamed other eyes, throats were cleared and no one moved in their chair. Then DI'S studiously imperturbable voice merely said. 'We're only trying to get at the truth.'

'I'm telling the truth,' I screamed. I was starting to crack and understood why prisoners confessed to crimes they had not committed. I'd given a description of the man I'd seen running out the door umpteen times but still they queried it. I was beginning to wonder had I ever seen him; was it my mind playing tricks.

Ken gave me an odd look and then glanced at Bill.

40

BILL GAVE a slight nod. He knew what Ken was thinking. He and Ken went back a long time. Ken was forty, of medium height and over weight. He had thick black hair and wore glasses with rectangular titanium frames, not the typical tall, handsome, brash type one envisages for a detective. Bill knew that to anyone meeting him for the first time he came across as being pleasant and cheerful. Had it not been for the expression in his eyes one would have believed that he was a cool character. Those who were on familiar terms with him knew that behind those eyes there was a fanatical look. He was not only an ambitious man but became obsessive when he got his teeth into a murder investigation. Most detectives forgot about the case when it was closed but not him. He pursued things to the bitter end often putting him at odds with his superiors.

His father had been Detective Chief Superintendent in the Liverpool constabulary. Known as Big Dan, tall, handsome, ruthless and shrewd, he'd risen to the top quickly after he'd solved a serial killer murder when everyone had given up on it. 'Caught the perp', they'd said, 'single-handed.'

He knew Ken had always regarded his father as a domineering character but he did admire him. He believed in justice just as strongly as his father did, but he also believed that civilisation depended on respect for the law. He knew that sometimes it irked him that he always had to live up to his father's image, particularly in the police force where his superiors were always comparing him to the great man. The innuendo was there but unspoken - never be as good as Big Dan. That was Ken he thought as he refocused on the woman sitting before him.

41

'WE'D LIKE to take your finger prints.

'Take my finger prints? What for?' Terror was taking hold again.

'That way we can eliminate you from the list of suspects when we find the knife. It's bound to have fingerprints on it,' Ken said quietly but with a look that said it all. A sense of horror enveloped me as I interpreted his look. By now he'd decided I was guilty, maybe not of a cold-blooded murder but of a crime of passion.

Feeling completely helpless I muttered, 'Oh God, help me.' I was the accused, accused of Nicholas's murder. The words hadn't been voiced yet. But worse now a dark, tormenting thought was mounting inside me - the idea that I was going insane and that I wasn't at that moment in a position to protect myself. I should have had a solicitor; murder had been committed and I was the accused.

Something else added to my ordeal. I'd been told that my first husband Donal and Deirdre were in the building. They'd been denied contact with me.

Finally when my fingerprints were taken I was escorted to an equally windowless room where Deirdre, Donal and Lynda were waiting. It was an emotional time. Deirdre clung to me and wept.

I managed to gasp, 'Deirdre they're trying to stitch me up,' before I were whisked away and driven to Lynda's house as I'd no where else to go. On the way DI explained that my house was cordoned off.

'It's now a murder scene and our men are sifting through the evidence. Maybe you could stay with Donal? And tomorrow we can continue with our little chat.' A rictus like smile appeared.

'Little chat.' The tri syllable was a drop of blood. So they were going to continue their interrogation until I'd crack. Tonight was only a taste of what was to come and that had taken six hours. And then they'd charge me. A new thrill of terror washed over me.

Seven o'clock, the street was stirring with the clang of waking life. Light was beginning to twinkle through the grey clouds. A bird flew to the glistening roof singing a sweet melody but I walked up the path to Donal's flat, my heart a piece of stone. Just up the road a murder had been committed and it was clear I was the accused.

WHY? One person sprung to mind - Danny. And Nicholas? I knew every one lives two lives: our real life and our secret life.

42

A QUIET professional, I'd never confronted the media. But the following morning they were camped on Donal's door step. Someone had tipped them off about my whereabouts. 'What can I do,' I wailed.

'You're not princess Diana,' Donal reassured. Give them a few words and you'll be yesterday's news. In the end he had to write them down for me.

'I can't do it, I can't do it.'

'I'll stand with you,' offered Lynda who had just popped in via the back door.'

As I opened the door I was momentarily blinded by the flash of lights as camera's clicked into action. A barrage of questions was hurled at me. Holding Lynda's hand tightly I focused on Donal's scrawl and read:

'I saw a man with intense blue eyes run out my door the night of the murder. I'm sure I can identify him and I'll leave no stone unturned until I bring him to justice.' I choked on tears and withdrew as further questions were barked at me.

Next day headlines were emblazoned across the front page of the Liverpool Mercury:

'I CAN IDENTIFY THE REAL KILLER,' SAYS CHIEF MURDER SUSPECT.

Later that afternoon I was asked to drop into the police station to give an artist's impression of the man I'd seen. The following day it appeared in the front page of all the national newspapers.

Months later I wrote in my diary: Could I have stopped the whole awful circus in its earliest tracks - avoided the media, kept a low profile? I didn't and so set my destiny in motion.

THE GHOST SAT READING THE DAILY TELEGRAPH STARING AT THE ARTIST'S IMPRESSION ALEX HAD GIVEN. HIS BROWN EYES FLICKERED BACK AND FORTH TO THE DRAWING. WITH A FROWN ON HIS FACE. HE PICKED UP HIS MOBILE AND BANGED A NUMBER OUT. HE GLARED AGAIN AT THE PAPER, HIS EYES ROLLING HORRIBLY, AND WHEN HE SPOKE HIS VOICE WAS THE MEREST WHISPER. 'TRACK HER' AND THEN PUT THE HANDSET DOWN. HELL CAN TAKE MANY FORMS. THINK OF ME AS MERELY ONE OF THEM, ALEX. WITH A SMILE ON HIS FACE HE PRESSED A REMOTE CONTROL. A WAGNERARIAN PIECE BOOMED LOUDLY.

43

AS I locked my front door on my way to the police station I glanced across the road. A man, partly hidden by the shadow of an old oak tree, stood under it. He was tall, thin and dressed in an old jacket and a wide brimmed hat. His face was his most extraordinary feature. One eye had a squint and the mouth was like a knife-slash. It was a face as repulsively fascinating as a medieval gargoyle. What was he doing here? I shivered. As I dashed to my car he quickly merged into the thick mist and disappeared. Was he watching me or just some crazy man with nothing better to do but stand around good citizens streets staring at people? Alex you're being paranoid. Dismiss him from your mind. But I couldn't - the pocket of fear

As I drove I thought of the incident about the murder weapon. When DI Masterson had shown us the knife that had been found under a bush in the next street, Deirdre had blurted out, "Mum, that's your knife."

I'd shouted, 'Deirdre, for God's sake, its not.'

Quick to grasp an opportunity the DI had rejoined. 'How do you know Alex? It matches the set you've got in the kitchen. And there's one missing.'

'It's not I tell you.' I paused. 'Maybe... the killer grabbed my knife and stabbed Nicholas.'

Ken had given me an odd look. Oh God I'm making it worse, I'd thought.

Murky rain drifted across the square as my stilettos clattered down the steps. I crossed over to the police station. DI had asked me to drop in for a friendly chat. I shivered as the billowing grey murk closed in around me, enveloping me in its icy embrace. Tugging my coat tightly around me, I pulled the collar lapels over my mouth and hurried into the building.

A constable escorted me into an office. To my surprise a stranger ambled towards me.

'I'm Detective Superintendent Peter Gibson.'

I studied Peter Gibson and reckoned that he was about forty-five. He was of medium height and overweight. His large head was bald. His face, though bloated, exuded a vivacity that I found disconcerting. What impressed me most were his eyes. They were the most profound blue I'd ever seen but cold and irresistible in a way that made you uneasy when you looked at him. They also held an extraordinary expression of power. Looking into them I fully grasped the situation. I was going to be the murderer. It was there in his gaze. His eyes seemed to look right through me and beyond, as if I were not there at all. The kind of eyes a German SS officer had had in a film I'd seen about a concentration camp during the war. At times the man was gently compassionate, other times he smoked a cigarette without turning a hair, while a prisoner was beaten to death.

I shuddered as I looked again at Gibson.

'Alex, it's nice to meet you. First of all may I offer my condolences at your tragic loss? I don't know how you're managing to bear up under the strain.' He said all this as he extended his flabby hand in a friendly pleasant way while ushering me into his office that was plush compared to the airless room where I'd spent my first night of interrogation. Strange that it's not the usual type of interview room, I thought as I glanced around. It was large, containing an antique desk. Along one wall there was an ox-blood Chesterfield. In one of the bay windows there stood an old fashioned mahogany bureau. Two easy chairs were positioned at each side of the desk.

I stood beside the chair and examined myself in the huge mirror that hung opposite me. My face was drawn, the eyes dark pools set too far back in their sockets.

'It's good of you to agree to this meeting, Alex. I wish everyone was as cooperative as you are.'

What if I'd refused to attend? My unease increased. Maybe I should have engaged a solicitor to protect my interests. But why? I wasn't guilty. Surely he'd soon see this.

'I must apologize, my colleague, who should be here, is unavoidably delayed so I hope you won't mind if we proceed without her.'

Is this legal?

'May I take your coat,' Peter said, with a beaming smile.

'Yes,' I said hesitantly. He's too friendly. He also has that calm deference; that look of pleased attentive interest in listening to a female.

I sat in the armchair near his desk.

'Come and sit here,' Peter said, indicating a space next to him on the Chesterfield.

Immediately I was on my guard wondering why he was being so gracious. To disarm me? I stared at him but he avoided my gaze. I didn't move.

Peter, placing his lighted cigarette on an ash tray, crossed quickly to a mahogany cabinet, opened it, and extracted a bottle of brandy and two glasses. He poured the drinks, his podgy hands moving slowly, in counterpoint to his walk. He handed one to me. He smiled faintly. 'You look terrible Alex. Have a drink. I know it's early but it will make you more relaxed.'

Unwillingly I accepted. I coughed as the liquid caught the back of my throat.

'Dull days like this get to me,' he said still avoiding my gaze as he ambled over to the window and looked out.

Plump as he was I noticed again that his movements were astonishingly light and easy. Then he strolled over to his desk and sat on the edge directly facing me. He was now on a much higher level and I felt at a disadvantage.

I sat there treating his every move with suspicion. Had he manoeuvred this little ruse? Yes, he's playing a cat and mouse game. Well, I'd be as smart.

'Do you smoke' he said offering me a Benson and Hedges.

'No.' Fecking stupid question to ask.

'You don't' mind if I do?' The voice was pleasant, the mood tranquil, but I was beginning to recognise the technique and I grudgingly, admitted that a professional was in action.

Suddenly I heard a squawk. A cage, containing a colourful parrot stood at the far corner of the room.

'Naughty, naughty,' it said.

'You haven't met Polly,' Peter said as he ambled over and opened the cage door. The creature flew out and perched fearlessly on his hand hopping from one finger to the next of his outstretched fat hand as he muttered, 'Who's a pretty Polly then.' It screeched again. Then he put it back in its cage.

It unnerved me. Next time you might be reincarnated as a human.

'Clever isn't it?' He had one of his smiles. He coasted back to his chair.

I nodded, thinking what peculiar traits he had.

As if reading my mind, he said, 'I suppose you think I'm peculiar.' Then he said, 'Do you like the décor,' waving an arm at the furniture. I always think antique furniture adds a touch of class to a room, especially the Chesterfield. I was particularly impressed with your sitting room. Pity about the carpet, you know, covered in blood,' he said casting an enigmatic glance. Something flickered behind the man's eyes and there was the merest hesitation. But it was enough to alert me. He took a Benson and Hedges out of the packet and lit it. He squinted at me through the smoke and steepled his fingers obviously waiting for a reaction.

So he's been to the house. The mention of my decor told me where the line of questioning was leading. It was about the removal of the shoes again. Act dumb. His eyes seemed to lock with mine. I stared back unintimidated.

'I can understand why you removed your shoes. Who in their right mind would want to spoil new carpets?'

I stared at him in surprise. He's on my side. But his next statement dispelled the illusion.

'Strange though, most people would think that your mind would have been on other things, like your partner dying. Probably think it was a bit of a callous act, but I understand, I understand perfectly why you acted so.' Peter folded his chubby hands like some kind of passive Guru.

Wildly staring at him I said, fingering my glass nervously, 'Mr Gibson, at the time I didn't want to cover the carpets in blood stains. Nicholas is very house proud ... and ... anyhow I didn't know he was going to die.'

'Of course, my dear, and please call me Peter. How could you possibly know that he was mortally wounded, even with all that blood around?' He paused, 'Must have been about six pints.' He threw me a glance.' His voice had dipped an octave and the intonation of each word gained a razor-sharp edge. 'Terrible way to die' He unfolded his hands, still retaining the Guru pose.

I knew then. Knew he was watching me. Watching for signs of guilt or innocence or outrage or despair – for signs of something anyhow – and watching me in vain for I was innocent. The very essence of me revolted.

'Of course most people would say that you knew he was dying with all that blood around but not me. I understand. It just didn't sink in did it?' He looked squarely at me.

I gaped at him. Looked at his small eyes, his poker face and his despicable leer. I knew what he was implying. In his eyes I was guilty.

'Mr Gibson, we both know why I'm here and I'd be grateful if you'd get to the point instead of beating about the bush. I know you think I murdered Nicholas so stop trying to trip me up and either charge me or let me go.'

'My dear,' Peter said, looking a bit askance at my outburst. 'I only want to put you at ease and certainly I'm not insinuating anything by my simple observations.'

Just as I was about to reply he rose and began to pace back and forth, a bemused look on his face, his arms behind his back at the same time throwing me quizzical glances. Then he stopped in front of me and assumed an isosceles stance, his arms crossed behind his back.

I watched him as intently. For a second a flash of pure malice registered on his face. I knew then that he intended to pin the murder on me. 'Detective superintendent...'

'Please, Alex, I beg of you; call me Peter, it's much more convivial.'

Reluctantly I began again, 'Peter...' but the name stuck in my throat. Suddenly I hated him, hated him with a strength that momentarily overpowered my fear. 'I know you think I'm guilty. You've all the evidence. I was alone with Nicholas, covered in blood, his blood. Then there's the kitchen knife; Deirdre said it was mine. But most of all, the letter is an indictment. With such circumstantial evidence any jury would convict me. So charge me?'

'My dear I asked you in here to establish the truth. Once you've provided me with satisfactory explanations about the points I'm making then I can eliminate you from my list of suspects and get on with catching the real killer.'

He smiled - a nasty cold smile that had nothing to do with humour. 'I can see that this is very distressing for you.

Tell you what to show that I'm a considerate man we'll call it a day. When you are feeling less distraught we'll continue.' The smile on his face assumed a distinctly sardonic twist.

As I walked through the park to my car the burst of sunshine and the languor of the early winter day helped me to relax and for a moment I almost forgot my ordeal. Then a thought struck me, would I be able, this time next year, to enjoy the freedom of strolling in the park. It was obvious to me that by postponing the interview Peter was allowing me time to think, time to get anxious, time to get confused. Then like a cat about to catch his prey he would pounce. A chill, inched up my spine

Later inside his study Peter Gibson sat, his hands clasped in his lap. He sat, quite motionless, his grey matter working overtime. He pushed himself out of the armchair and traipsed over to the cage. 'She's guilty, Polly. There's no doubt about it.'

'Guilty, guilty!'

'So you agree with me Polly. Who's a clever bird then?' The whole set up had served him well. The nice room, the parrot, his informal tactics; it all helped to get a conviction. None of the airless police rooms for him. I do things my way and up to now have got away with it. And he had Robert Cooper's approval. He and the boss did things their way. A thin flicker of excitement moved coldly in his stomach as he rose and exited the room.

44

A DAY later I waited anxiously at the police station for Peter Gibson to appear. Fifteen minutes had passed. I glanced worriedly at my watch. Was this delay a ploy to unnerve me? My eyes flickered over to the duty policeman at the reception desk. He was probably in his early forties. He sat there engrossed in some report or other and was almost oblivious to my existence. Or was he? I wasn't convinced. Maybe he'd been told to keep me under surveillance. Nevertheless I deliberately made a great effort to stop biting my nails. I realised that I was also shaking and that it was due to an innate mistrust of Peter.

Just then Peter appeared and said, 'Alex, sorry to have kept you waiting.' He didn't offer an explanation. Ushering me into his office he waved me to the sofa. I glanced in the gilt mirror behind him as I sat down. I'd a figure to be proud of given two children and pushing fifty. Now I wasn't slim, just skinny. I can't see my eyes because of the bags under them. Was I up to this?

Sitting beside me Peter began, 'You mustn't think I'm trying to pin this crime on you.'

Shifting away from him I thought - fibber.

'Alex it was you who rolled off the list of reasons as to why you might be charged with the murder. And as for my reference to the blood stained carpet it started off as a discussion about how tasteful your décor is. Bringing up the topic wasn't deliberate.'

I glared at him. May the fleas of a thousand cats infest your armpits.

He ignored my glare. 'But come to think of it, my dear, you hit it on the nail when you said that all the evidence was against you. I was just considering that myself.'

I suddenly noticed that his voice had a metallic, tinny sound to it, making it seem nearly mechanical.

'Because viewing it in pure hypothetical terms, we've a suspected murderer, she turns her shoes upside down on the carpet and when questioned about it says she didn't want to spoil the furnishings. Peculiar!' His lugubrious face was set in the same incredulous sneer, his mouth round and open like a cannon muzzle. I stared at him aghast. He'd let it slip - a suspected murderer. The fear that ricocheted within me was almost tangible and it left my mouth dry and a bitter taste on my tongue.

Suddenly he jumped up and paced up and down. 'I know if my nearest and dearest was dying I wouldn't be worried about a silly carpet. Would you my dear?' He shot the question straight at me like a bolt out of the skies and before I'd time to think I responded.

'No.' Oh my God, what am I saying.

'Exactly! Even you agree with me my dear.'

'No.' The parrot squawked.

'See, even Polly agrees with us.'

My lips quivered, my eyes glazed and my voice that before then had been modulated and calm became high pitched and hostile. 'I won't permit you to play with my emotions. Do you hear me?'

'Loud and clear, Alex and what's more the whole building must hear you. Look, calm down and I'll fetch you a cup of tea.'

'I don't want tea and I am calm.' Anger swept through me like a Tsunami.

'Guilty, guilty,' shrieked the bird.

'For God's sake shut that blasted thing up.' I was out of control.

He shot me a sly pleased smirk. 'Alex, you're becoming hysterical. Polly's a harmless parrot. I think under the circumstance we should postpone our little chat, yet again.' Satisfaction seemed to sweep through him like a neural wave.

As I drove home I began to cry suddenly; a haemorrhage of tears that threatened to extinguish the explosive anger that nestled in my stomach as I'd fled Peter's office. I knew that it was only a matter of time before Peter would charge me for the murder and then …

45

IT WAS my third meeting with Peter Gibson. I sat in my usual seat waiting for him to speak. The absent colleague had not appeared. Very irregular! Still Peter Gibson was a law on to himself and since I hadn't complained he was getting away with it. And protesting might imply guilt. I feigned calmness. He couldn't see the two or three drops of hot sweat that had left my armpits and were crawling, like fat insects, down my breast. He attempted to light his pipe.

For Christ's sake, say something.

'I'm trying to give up,' Peter said at last. 'The doctor said smoking will be the death of me. Cancer, of course, cures smoking.' Then he roared with laughter at his pathetic joke.

I glared at him and thought. He's like a spider, slow, but not lazy, endlessly patient, seductive. He could weave a web so subtle, so fine, that the victim would never see or feel it until it was too late.

But Peter wasn't put off by my mordant contempt. He was obviously used to this game. He sat opposite me; smoke curling up from his pipe. 'Tell me again, Alex, why you and Nicholas were, to coin a phrase, estranged.'

'We weren't estranged. We were happy just before he died.'

'Alex, judging by the letter you wrote to him a few weeks ago it doesn't appear so.'

'But we sorted it out and then we were ... okay.'

'Tell us anyhow why you asked him to leave.'

I related all that had happened after Nicholas's visit to New Zealand.

Peter took a puff and smiled - a smile that was broad but his eyes were new slits. A tic at the left corner of his mouth suggested that the eyes more truly revealed his calculating mind than did his smile. What was coming next?

'Alex, you must have been in a very unstable state when you wrote that note. So unstable that maybe you'd decided that if he didn't commit himself to you, you'd make sure he couldn't return to New Zealand. Then in a moment of uncontrolled passion you stabbed him with your kitchen knife. Or maybe you hired someone to do it?'

Should he be doing this? But this is his swansong in his role of a hangman, a truth he himself seems to recognise, I thought as I watched him grimacing and tugging at his ear and very nearly looked apologetic.

I slipped my right hand over my left wrist, gripping it, my fingers pressed into my flesh with such pressure I thought my skin might tear. I had to say something - reclaim my innocence, anything. I only knew I couldn't take anymore. 'I didn't murder him,' I whispered.

Gently he said, 'Who did you get to do it? Alex, the courts will be lenient with you when they learn that you were under a terrible strain. You performed this act when the balance of your mind was unhinged.'

I looked at him aghast and shook my head. 'I …did… not… kill… Nicholas. I loved him.'

'We know you loved him,' Peter said. 'It was your passionate love for him that drove you to this. When you realised that he might get back with his former wife you lost it.'

'I didn't kill him.'

He plodded over to the cage again and opened it.

I became more edgy as I watched him distrustfully.

Peter was stroking the parrot. Suddenly it flew across the room and landed on the desk. Then it hopped up and down screeching, 'Killed him, killed him.'

I flashed him a look of scorn. I understood his little game perfectly. It was a ploy to demoralize me, a psychological strategy to break me down. I should complain about his tactics but that might make matters worse. No. The truth will out – it had to - and then everyone will know that I'm innocent.

'Polly, come here. Naughty Polly,' Peter said as it flew to him. Placing it back in the cage he covered it with a cloth. 'There's no need to be alarmed, Alex. It's only a parrot. It picks up all sorts of jargon in this place.'

I looked at him not only as if he were repulsive but also as if he had a room to let upstairs. 'You did that on purpose. You trained it to say those things.'

'Alex, you're paranoid. How could I? Parrots only repeat things that are drilled into them.'

46

ON THE Thursday of that week Nicholas's sister, Sheila, arrived for the grim task of identifying the body. Sheila, Deirdre and I met up at the police station. Sheila's features were impassive. Tight lipped, she embraced me and Deirdre. 'Hello Alex, how are you bearing up?'

I shook with emotion. The resemblance between the siblings was striking and it induced a pang of deep longing within me. But she remained composed. I stood alone in my misery.

DI and Gibson drove us to the morgue. With Deirdre holding my hand we were led to what was our last sight of Nicholas. I stood, silently, looking at his frozen beauty. Lily-like, white as snow he lay there.

I lunged forward to kiss his lips but I was dragged back.

'You can't touch the body,' someone muttered.

I looked again and thought how death almost became him. The wounds on his face were well camouflaged and he had a peaceful repose. His pallor and his curly hair, his sculptured features, were now like the marble head of a young Caesar. He was handsome even in death: his manly face, so short a time ago filled with power and with irresistible fascination for all women, was still striking.

Just then I glanced over at Peter Gibson. He was staring at me watching my reactions. I shuddered.

47

IN THE background Peter Gibson had Alex under intense scrutiny, watching her demeanour for any traces of guilt or shame or regret that she might reveal. Zilch. He had to admit that she was putting on a good act. But he knew of course that she was guilty. And the evidence was there - the letter being the most condemning. He had his ways. He was familiar with this game and had never failed. With yet another solved murder under his belt it would pave the way for him becoming assistant chief constable and eventually chief constable itself an ambition he'd always nurtured since he'd joined the police force. He imagined it now emblazoned in all the broad sheets and tabloids.

DETECTIVE CHIEF INSPECTOR SOLVES YET ANOTHER MURDER.

The anticipation made his heart leap up with joy. Fame at last.

As a child he'd a permanent fear of dying. He'd lie in bed quavering; realising that adulthood would only bring him closer to death and with it oblivion. His mother had the answer. He remembered her words vividly now: "There's only one way to go – make your mark." And that had been his ambition – recognition so that in a hundred years or so he'd go down in the annals of history as someone who'd made a difference. He never thought that would be easy. Hard work was the only solution. And so he'd become driven. Obtaining justice for all these victims was imperative.

Yes he'd get a conviction and soon. It wouldn't be difficult to break her down. She was of the vulnerable type and would definitely crack under his expert techniques. His glance over at Alex was malevolent. He'd get her; she was a murderess after all.

48

"COMMON LAW WIFE KILLS IN A FIT OF JEALOUSY WHILE THE BALANCE OF HER MIND IS DISTURBED."

In my mind's eye the headline mocked me as I imagined the taunting caption across the tabloids I'd see in tomorrow's papers. As I strode, yet again, through the park on my way to the police station and inhaled the freshness of the earth, wet after heavy rain, I wondered why everything couldn't be simple. Three days of interrogation and each time I left the police station it was on an ever-growing question mark. I knew I was cracking up. I had decided to confess - today. Then I would gain a measure of peace. Already I'd retreated deep inside myself to some far off horizon, removed mentally from all that was going on around me. I could always retract it later after I had a rest.

I faced Peter, who sat chain smoking. This time there was a woman present.

Nods. 'Alex Rowe. Sinead Moore – Alex Rowe.'

Must be Irish with such a name. Maybe she might be more sympathetic.

She nodded. 'Pleased to meet you Alex.' No hand shake.

I could feel the tightness of my skin across my cheekbones and the backs of my eyes filled with black fear. The tea, the secretary had made for me spilt as my hands shook.

'Well Alex, have you thought about what we've discussed? If you plead guilty to murder your lawyer can ask for a plea of non compis mentis. The judge will view your case with leniency.'

I paused. 'Yes… I'll give you a statement. Anything to stop this torture!' I was aware that my voice now sounded desperate. Many people who plead guilty to things in life are not guilty at all, but seek some relief from intolerable strain.

Their two faces were trained on me like cameras one to either side of me just like DI and DS's had been.

'We only want the truth, Alex. Did you stab Nicholas?' It was Sinead this time. The voice had a harried urgency to it and she had a zealot's stare. There was no doubt in my mind that she considered me guilty.

'Yes, I did.' I said my head bowed. 'Can I go now?'

A sly smirk appeared on Peter's face. 'I'm sorry, Alex, we must take a written statement.' His eyes gleamed - at last a conviction.

'Can I go home then?' I glanced again at the huge mirror. A stoical immobility had settled over my face. I wouldn't show fear.

Peter cast his eyes down.

I knew then, knew that I'd be taken to the magistrates court and then to Risley. There was a strange taste in my mouth, fear - bone dry, metallic, like powered rust in my throat.

'We'll see.' As Peter reached for the 'phone it rang. He picked it up. 'Detective Superintendent Gibson speaking.' As he listened his eyes flickered in my direction. 'Really, when did you find this out?'

I was too exhausted to listen. All I wanted was to fall into the oblivion of sleep. My head nodded forward and I started to sink, sink, and then the sentinel, somewhere deep in my brain, would jerk me back into consciousness.

49

I STARED at the prison officer in horror as she spoke.

'Some of you are going to be here for quite a while. You can do your remand the hard way or the easy way. You'll follow orders, when to eat when to work, when to go to the bog. You step out of line and you'll wish you were never born. We don't want any trouble here.'

Her eyes flickered over to me obviously knowing why I was there. Murder! A hideous attack, she would think.

'You'll be taken for a physical, then a shower and then you'll be assigned a cell.'

I pushed my hair from my eyes and settled it behind my ear.

It was a graceful unconscious gesture and it made the prison officer's cheek twitch.

'So you think you're a cut above the rest. Well a few months here will knock the high and mighty way out of you.'

I shuddered.

A slight young girl close to me said, 'Do you mind if…'

The prison officer whirled around, her pockmarked face filled with fury. 'How dare you. You only speak when you're spoken to. And that goes for all of you.'

I was shocked and reached for words to say. Just then I felt someone shaking me.

'Alex, wake up.' I stared in horror, but it was not the prison officer, it was Peter peering down at me. Sinead had disappeared. I must have nodded off. As the nightmare assaulted my senses I shuddered. Maybe soon it would become a reality. I knew by his expression that he had something ominous to tell me.

'Alex, I've got some information.'

I paled. 'Imformation …?'

'Yes.' There was new electricity in his eyes.

Suddenly the door barged open. I sat up straight in my chair.

'The boss wants to see you immediately. It's urgent.' The secretary looked flustered.

'I'll be there in a minute and knock next time.' His eyes were zero Kelvin.

'This will have to wait. Can't keep the chief waiting.'

50

'CHAMBERS OF horror,' Ken said to Bill as they walked into the morgue. 'These places always look the same,' Ken said as he glanced around the place. Like police interrogation rooms they're vaults of monotony, airless and windowless.

'The stink, too, is conspicuous to anyone who walks in from the fresh air outside, but barely discernible to the medical examiners that spend their day carving up corpses for autopsy.'

Ken raised an eyebrow. 'That's a mouthful for you, Bill.'

'Just read it in some novel.'

'Hmm. I'll do the talking,' Ken added as they entered the room where the pathologist was working. The pathologist was a tallish man with black hair and dark eyes. He was wearing a bloodstained white smock and rubber gloves, and handling a heart. A stain in the centre mimicked the shape of a heart. Bizzare!

He immediately plonked the organ into a glass bowl and yanked off his gloves.

'You'll want to know the cause of death,' he said as he approached Ken and Bill.'

'You got my message, then?' Ken said raising an eyebrow.

'Yes. Death was caused by the right carotid artery being severed in the neck.'

'Have you worked out what may have been the sequence of events?'

'A frenzied stabbing.'

'How do you know?'

'To stab someone fifteen times is overkill and must have been prompted by some incident that enraged the killer enough to stab him repeatedly.'

'What are your assumptions?'

'First I think they taunted him.'

'How do you know?'

'The cuts on his face were jagged. It shows that either a serrated edged knife was drawn across his face or he may have been prodded with the point of the knife.'

'And then?'

'Then for some reason it spiralled out of control.'

'One thing puzzles me. Why didn't he call out? Alex, his partner, says she heard no voices.'

'He couldn't call out.'

'Why.'

'Bruising was found on his neck. The voice box had been pushed backwards from the force of an arm around the neck. I would say that whoever got a stranglehold on him was an expert in the martial arts.'

'How come?'

'Only a pro would know how to inactivate the voice box.'

'So it's watertight. Someone held him.'

'Yes. The right wrist showed marks to the skin caused by pressure gripping.'

'So one person restrained him while the other stabbed him?'

'Yes, but it was a tall man who wielded the knife.'

'A tall man?' Ken shuddered.

'The angle of the stabbing had to come from above, from someone much taller that the deceased, about six foot.'

'Is it possible that only one man carried out the deed'?

'Not in my opinion.'

'Why?'

'There were no defence cuts to the victim's arms.'

Ken nodded in agreement. 'If someone attacks you with a knife you instinctively put up your hands in defence.'

'Precisely.'

'Maybe you're right,' Ken said, fingering his chin. 'Alex said that at first she heard a noise as if some thing had fallen and then after about a minute there was an enormous clatter. One more question do you think a woman could have done it?'

'She'd have to be very strong to have held a man such as the deceased. Doubtful but who knows. By the way the victim could have known his attacker.'

'How come?'

'Stabbing someone fifteen times is very personal. With cases like this we routinely assume that the victim and assailant knew each other.'

'Jesus. Look, I won't take up anymore of your time. We'll be in touch if we've anymore questions.'

As Bill and Ken walked from the morgue Ken was deep in thought. If there were two men then that made their hunt even more difficult. And it looks like Alex could be off the hook. Of course she could have hired them to do the deed. If she' guilty she's putting on a good act. It's hard to be genuinely as grief stricken as she appeared to be.

'Penny for them?' Bill said interrupting his train of thought.

'I was just thinking that Alex might be innocent unless of course she hired someone to kill him.'

'That's exactly what I was thinking.'

'So let's say, for the sake of argument that she's telling the truth when she says a white guy ran out the door.'

'Well we'll find out soon enough. Knowing Peter's perverse methods he's bound to break her soon.'

'Let's hope she doesn't confess under duress if she's innocent. It's happened before. Peter's psychological tactics would break anybody. Even that parrot unnerves me. Cooper allows it but of course Peter and the chief are bed mates.'

Bill levelled his dark gaze on him. 'Yes. That's what worries me. It's always difficult in a case like this to tread the tightrope between suspicion and sympathy.'

'I agree.'

51

'SOMEONE HAS been arrested for Nicholas's murder.'

It had taken Peter twenty minutes to return. Now he sat facing me.

'Arrested for his murder?' I made an inarticulate little sound.

'Yes.' He cast his eyes down. 'Honestly Alex I didn't know that this man was a suspect. Sometimes these things take time to filter through from others in the team.'

I noticed that for the first time the cool, imperious calm was gone, and in its place was the cold presence of fear.

'You mean somebody cocked up.' I glared at him. 'Who's this man?'

'His name's Bruno Rosso. He's thirty-three; of Italian extraction and a client of Nicholas's. We had to be sure, Alex. Lots of people came under suspicion even Donal and David.'

I felt broken. 'Tell me about this Bruno Rosso.'

'Yesterday the local squad finally established that a man fitting the description of Bruno Rosso was involved in the murder. The CCTV footage picked up an image of him wearing a baseball cap in the foyer of Tom Prices offices. He'd been lurking there – waiting for Nicholas. Ten minutes later he was seen on the CCTV footage at the train station following Nicholas as he got on the train for Crosby.'

'But how did you catch him?'

'The morning after the murder Rosso phoned Tom Price's firm and asked to speak to Nicholas. When one of our boys told him that Nicholas was dead Rosso disconnected.

He must have thought that we'd check him out so a day later he went voluntarily to a local police station. He told the constable at reception that he was the person who'd rung the office that morning.'

'Why would he do that?'

'Obviously to throw us off the scent just in case we checked up. Maybe he figured that in telling us this it would show he'd nothing to hide. He approached us before he was even in our scope.'

'I see.'

'Of course he wasn't to know that we had him on the CCTV footage. Anyhow to cut the story short our man at reception thought there was something odd about it all. He took his name and address and later alerted us and gave us a description of Rosso. He's the same man we saw on the CCTV footage. His baseball cap was found at the back of your hall.'

'But the man I saw running out the door was Caucasian not dark skinned.'

'Yes, so you said.'

I gave him a fixed stare. 'I did see a white man.'

Peter nodded, 'I believe you. No doubt with Rosso in custody he can tell us who this man is. By the way have you ever heard his name before?'

'Yes, I do remember Nicholas mentioning an Italian who was involved with Danny in money lending. I think he said his name was Bruno Rosso.'

'Did you?' Peter said, scratching his chin. 'Interesting!'

'So what happens now?'

'You're free to go.'

'Really.' I felt as if the sun had come through a dark cloud.

'He told the team that you had nothing to do with the murder.'

'Why was Nicholas killed then?'
'Ken will fill you in.'
'There's a lot of money missing. Millions!' He cocked a questioning eyebrow.

Oh fecking hell he thinks I have it. I'm not off the hook yet.

I lay wide awake in the darkness for hours before giving up the unequal struggle against insomnia. Fatigue was in every bone. At three a.m. I got out of bed, stumbled to the kitchen and put the kettle on.

As I waited for the kettle to boil I began to doodle. As the grey matter cranked up I began to jot points down on a scrap of paper.

Two did the deed.
One Caucasian.
One mixed race.
Known to Nicholas and Danny.
And Pat? Maybe.
Something to do with the pot of gold.
What happened?
Turned out to be base metal.
My next move?
Contact Pat - ASAP.
Wheedle info out of him.

And the money? Did Nicholas have it? No. Had to borrow from me before he died.

I read over my points. I didn't know how the professionals worked it all out but I felt my skills as an amateur detective were improving.

52

AT THE church Pat paid tribute to Nicholas: "Ships that pass in the night, and speak to each other in passing: Only a signal shown and a distant voice in the darkness; So on the ocean of life we pass and speak to each other; only a look and a voice; then darkness again and a silence." And then Pat added, 'With Nicholas's death had come that infinite darkness. We were a single soul dwelling in two bodies.'

The day of the funeral had arrived. Friends, relatives and neighbours were there. It was almost as if they had climbed out of the woodwork. The whole community had turned up to pay their last respects to this lovely man.

Now seated in the church I was listening to Pat. "We were a single soul dwelling in two bodies. We were a single soul dwelling in two bodies," echoed like pearls round my mind. What a beautiful friend. Tears flowed then. Lynda held my hand tightly.

After the cremation an unusual mixture of mourners returned to my house. As well as friends, family and colleagues the police were there in force. After all the victim had been a solicitor. To my surprise Danny and his wife had turned up. I wondered how he dared show his face. I'd already decided he was connected to the murder. At the church he'd quickly offered his condolences and then skulked away as if he'd something to hide.

The house was packed. Danny and his wife huddled in a corner in the kitchen chatting. Donal, Deirdre and Lynda were busy in the dining room seeing to the buffet. Pat approached, put his hand on my shoulder, and said, 'I'm so very sorry Alex. It's tragic.'

Trying to keep my emotions tightly in check I replied, 'It's so terribly difficult Pat. He was young; only fifty- four.'

'Alex, ultimately, it's not about how short a life is; it's what that life did for people. Certainly, during his years on this earth he was very inspirational to so many people.'

My tears flowed then. Pat produced a white handkerchief from his pocket. Gently he wiped my tears away and said softly, 'Anytime you want to talk about Nicholas I'm only a 'phone call away.'

As we spoke I spotted Danny glancing in our direction. He appeared to cast an inquiring look towards Pat. Maybe he thinks we're discussing the case.

As if on cue Pat said, nonchalantly, 'Have the police come up with any clues?'

'You know as much as I do. It's been in all the papers. Now that they've nabbed Rosso I'm sure we'll find out who the white guy is.' Is he delving? Does he know Rosso?

As if reading my thoughts, he immediately replied, 'Alex, I know you feel that I'm Danny's right hand man and that I might be, in some way, covering for him. Danny had absolutely nothing to do with the murder.'

'Why do you think I suspect him?'

'Detective Inspector Masterson let it slip. Apparently you told him that Danny and Rosso did business together. Danny and Nicholas were close; he'd do nothing to harm him. And I'm Nicholas's closest friend, so of course I'm interested.'

I gave a shrug, and then added. 'Look Pat, I intend to find Nicholas's killer if it's the last thing I do. It's going to be my mission.'

'I'd leave it to the police if I were you. You might get more than you bargained for.'

'Is that a threat?'

'Of course not. What do you take me for? You're dealing with vicious killers.'

Is he trying to warn me? An icy chill crept through my veins. He's hiding something. Now's not the time to tackle him, Alex. Wait a few days. Deep down I knew that what he said was true – Nicholas's murder, the cryptic note and the slaying of Danny's dog told me that these men were vicious killers. Perhaps if I'd put Nicholas in the picture he'd be alive today. This was getting all too much for me.

'I must be alone.' As I dashed from the room I glanced in Danny's direction again. His wife Sarah, standing near him was nearly a size zero. Dark circles under her eyes gave her an exhausted look. She looks as if she has been through the mill. The last time I'd rung her she had said that Danny hadn't slept since the murder. Was it guilt? Fear! Fear of what? Sarah had said that Nicholas's death had devastated him. There was so much I didn't know? But I'd find out.

As I made my exit the muted babble of whispers hushed suddenly. Their gossip is not for my ears.

I wandered into the garden and stared at the bleak wilderness surrounding me. I'm living in a world of deepest loss. I stood alone:

"Sometimes when I stand there feeling like the last man in the world I don't feel so good. When I look out into the bushes and frozen ponds I have the feeling that it's going to get colder and colder until everything I can see is going to be covered with a thousand miles of ice, all the earth, right up to the sky, and over every bit of land and sea."

In some weird way the Alan Stillgoe's quotation, 'But I'm not the last one in the world,' perversely gave me some hope.

During that week I received hundreds of condolence letters - even some from complete strangers. The one communication that intrigued me most came from a priest in New Zealand:

Dear Alex,

It is with great sadness that I write this letter of sympathy to you. I have been a friend of Nicholas's for the last fifteen years. I met him in Christ Church when he first arrived from England. One Sunday he attended mass here in St. Mary's. Afterwards he approached me and informed me that he would be part of my parish. As time passed I found in Nicholas a gentle soul, one of the gentlest.

I find it hard to comprehend that this dear man is dead and will no longer be with us.

I will be in England soon as I am en route to Ireland to my hometown in Sligo. This is a sort of a sabbatical year for me, a year out to see my family, especially my mother who is alone now, God Bless her, since my father died.

My brief is to attach myself to a parish in Liverpool while I am there and then in my own time visit the old country.

Though I have never met you I feel I know you well. In his letters Nicholas spoke about you often. Alex, I would very much like to call on you and offer my condolences in person.

I will 'phone you when I get to England,
                Yours,
                      In Jesus Christ.
                          Father Patrick O'Malley.

I sighed as I placed the letter on the bureau. What beautiful sentiments. Nicholas indeed had many friends, people who valued him. Strange though, he had never mentioned Father O'Malley even though he'd obviously kept up contact. But that was Nicholas. Some things he kept close to his chest.

Next day I opened another envelope expecting a sympathy card to drop out. Instead it was a note. My eyes widened as I read the content:

I was dumfounded. How dare he write to me. But had the letter a ring of truth? He said he was innocent.

That week I sent Nicholas's ashes to Elizabeth. A week later I received a letter from one of Nicholas's friends. A little cameo for you he had said:

It is a small garden of remembrance overlooking the bay where he used to live and where he used to run a tall reed of a twelve years old, heartbreakingly beautiful, kneels at a small grave The sky is the colour of tarnished pewter, and the air is heavy with rain. Her skin is lustrous, glowing with an iridescent dark sheen, her enormous eyes glistening, as she places the urn containing her father's ashes in the opening.

The wind that was faint grows in strength, gathering up bits and pieces of the old dead leaves and twigs, swirling them about in eddies, adding to the sombre atmosphere of the place. As she throws a handful of earth into the tiny grave the sounds that emanated from that sad soul were heart rendering. It was like the death cries of some one who had endured unbearable suffering.

Nearby, under the shade of a darkened yew a beautiful woman with long flowing hair stood, her eyes almost obscured by sunglasses. But if you looked closely you could see the darkest of eyes, opaque, dead, revealing only sorrow and pain.

53

'THE ONLY way to get it out of your system is to talk. Anything that comes into your head let it out,' the priest said.

I studied the priest as he sat at my kitchen table speaking. He was a black haired man with streaks of grey in it. Must be about fifty five? He wore the garb of the cleric; a dog collar and a black suit. His face was full of strength, ascetic and touched with a tranquillity that I found completely reassuring. He had the moving gift of speaking so kindly he could almost illicit tears.

I had been unburdening myself to Father O'Malley for almost an hour and found him a compassionate listener.

Patrick rested a hand on my shoulder briefly and said softly,

'They say confession is good for the soul.'

I broke then, my head slipping forward in a rare show of self-pity. Harsh sobs racked my body. As my crying subsided I began. 'It's like as if a haze has fallen over me, enclosing me in a dismal solitude. Over and over I recall down to the last detail, all that occurred that night. Slowly I understood that what has happened is terrifying and that it is beyond the realms of anything I have ever experienced.

I looked at his face as I spoke and, feeling comforted by the serenity of his features, continued. 'For weeks, here alone, I have been almost catatonic.' I paused and gazed at him again to seek encouragement.

He nodded, a slight smile appearing on his face. 'Alex you're permitted to have these feelings. Go on.'

'In this depressed state I question, look for answers to life's great absolutes. Where is he now? I deliberate, and write, 'If he's somewhere, he must be with God.'

'He's with God, Believe me Alex, he's with God.'

'I yearn for him. My body feels empty, barren,' and then I blushed, 'devoid of sexuality. And so I sit and grieve, why were we so unlucky in being ripped apart from each other. He's dead. I repeat it out loud 'HE IS DEAD.' I paused momentarily. The priest had a glazed look on his face as if he was either concentrating on my every word or he wasn't listening. I decided he was concentrating on my every word.

He took my hand then in his huge one and said gently. 'Don't worry Alex you'll get through this.'

I stood up then, and pacing the kitchen floor, continued in a loud voice oblivious to the priest, oblivious of everything around me, aware only of my crushing grief. Louder and louder my words became until I was shouting them. 'HE'S DEAD.' I stopped and looked at him but by now I had entered my own sad world, almost like an actress on a stage, playing my last role.

He smiled patiently.

Dramatically, my arms uplifted. I continued. 'Now I know that behind every exquisite thing that existed, there is something tragic, like thorns amongst the most delicate of roses. I know that worlds have to be in turmoil, so that an insignificant flower might blossom. Would we have ventured into our tryst when we first met on that fateful day in his Liverpool office if we had known that both of us were on the verge of a terrible crisis and that exquisite joy and acute sorrow would be ours?'

I began to wring my hands. 'I try to bring him back; to keep alive the essence of him; to breathe his sweat, this unique odour that was all I had left of him.' Suddenly without warning I rushed up to the priest sitting there and grabbed at his sweater. 'I wore his unwashed jumper; wrapping it around me, inhaling his aroma, becoming a prisoner of my emotions, sitting, caressing the softness of the garment to capture his presence. Then one day Deirdre took it away from me, and feeling treated like a child I parted with it. She put it in the washing machine and the Persil did the rest. It eliminated all living traces of him. It was like having him die all over again, acute, more painful. I knew then that I would never experience him again.'

All the time the priest sat quietly a strange look registered on his face. It was as if he couldn't understand my words. It seems as if it was he who was grappling with one great dilemma, unique to his own existence.

I stared at him again my eyes seeming almost to recognise him. Then I looked away, into a far off distance. 'During all this time I was not alone. Donal, my first husband, had moved in and though there he wasn't intrusive, not that I noticed his presence much anyway. I lived in a world far from reality. But I haven't forgotten his devotion to me during those weeks.

By now the priest had his elbows on the table and was leaning forward, an utterly rapt expression on his face or so it seemed?

Mornings would come and Donal would make a plate of toast, boil an egg, and squeeze fresh orange juice, cutting the bread into thin soldiers. Then he'd say, 'Eat your gooey egg.'

'I'd bring my distant gaze away from the window and look at the egg without interest. And then say, 'Thank you...' and my voice would be listless and without emotion. I'd look at him and then at the plate. Sometimes I'd pick at a few crumbs and eat them and once I actually took a bite but I couldn't swallow it; the 'gooey egg' I ignored. Each morning the ritual was repeated; day after day the plate of toast and the 'googy egg' appeared and then one day he noticed a space where the thinnest soldier had been. The next day, two spaces; by the end of the week there were only spaces; I had eaten all two slices; but the 'gooey egg' was untouched.'

The priest put on a dead-serious look.

'He watched me from a distance ... he had triumphed ... I had eaten; the weeks of sitting there watching and waiting were over. I had worked through my colossal grief and now my mind seems to have accepted reality.

Donal didn't know that I was preoccupied with unsolved riddles, and the time I didn't stare into space was dedicated to finding answers in books. I would ponder on what I had read, analysing the material.'

'And the 'gooey egg?''

He knows my story, knows it as if it has been already written in the wind. Exalted I continued. 'A week after eating the toast I ate his 'gooey egg.' His mission completed, Donal moved out. I was ready to start life again. Something had snapped me out of my pathological state; this Donal knew. "What it was," he told Deirdre, "I will never know."

I was in a trance now; the priest, the stranger who'd walked in out of the night, walked in out of the storm, no longer existed for me. I was alone on my stage acting out my sorrow, shouting it to the rooftops. Nothing, nobody could take this away from me. And certainly the priest didn't. 'I sought solace in the bible; read it from page to page, devouring it like a hermit. Old and new, I inspected it from page to page, writing down so very carefully all the evidence. I found no signs, no simple explanations. Then I'd go to Plato, Aristotle, Russell, Sartre. Lining them up, I'd say, 'Give me your wisdom.' Silence; they gave no answers.

In all my reflections my greatest need was to know that Nicholas existed in some form. This was as crucial to me as only then could I begin to live my life more freely. Then one day I found the answer that satisfied my craving. It was when I read Hess's 'Steppenwolf'. In it he describes how the hero Harry Haller, while on one of his ramblings through the less salubrious parts of Paris, hears a piece of music. This sound in this less than tranquil part of Paris was so exquisite and heavenly that it ravished his senses. As he listened he was bereft of thought, no longer conscious of the drab darkness of the streets but of a greater cosmic glory. He didn't know whether this ecstasy had lasted an hour or a minute so exquisite was the strain. What had he heard that enveloped him in such an ecstasy? It was a concert of old exquisite music. Suddenly 'after two or three notes of the piano the door was opened all of a sudden to the other world. I sped through heaven and saw God at work.'

Haller had in that moment found a 'track of the divine in the midst of this life we lead.'

Now for the first time since the murder my soul is quieted. This Maestro, this God has for me a form. He is the Author of such exquisite sounds. From then on I believed that Nicholas was with his Master.

I stopped then and slumped into the kitchen chair exhausted, but feeling I had expunged my terrible pain. Slowly I regained my composure and in a small, embarrassed voice said, 'I've only just met you and you've listened to my monologue, heard my grief.'

'Don't apologise, Alex. This is my vocation; this is what I do. A priest's role is to administer, give help where it is needed but above all, be a good listener.' Then he moved towards me and with all the tenderness one human being can give to another he gently folded me in his arms and laying my head on his chest he caressed me like a baby, stroking my hair, my forehead, my temple. He did this until I was completely calm and then gingerly, as if I was a porcelain doll he took my hand and lead me upstairs to the bedroom. Gently he laid me on the bed and covered me with the duvet. Kissing me on the forehead he said, 'You rest there a while Alex.' Quietly he left the room as I drifted off into my first peaceful sleep since the murder.

54

AFTER MY session with the priest I began to pick up the threads of my life. I even found myself attracted and intrigued by the books in Waterstone's. I'd select a title from among the philosophers but feel that I wasn't intelligent enough to read them. To be able to read Kant, Descartes, Aristotle, Plato the way people read thrillers that would be a feat. I browsed and tried to absorb them and stood in an obscure corner devouring them. Reading became an insatiable vice. The more I kept trying the more I was forced to weigh each paragraph, each word, each sentence. I gave myself up to the pages of the philosophers. I nearly died with the desire to become intelligent; to read their works. I resolved to have an inner life of the mind, to contemplate, to juggle and become a trapeze artiste in the world of concepts, the realms of ideas, what an accomplishment - to be clever like David; to understand. I dwelt upon the agonising penury of my mind and was determined to make it rich. Words flitted in and out again like moths. I would read, forget and read again. My objective was to debate, to exchange views, to have opinions. My feat was to juggle with words so that I would dazzle and impress people. I strove to use an original expression, an original concept. I realised that a literary creation would be my salvation.

'I shall write,' I said in my diary. I read and I wrote. I wrote about the murder, etching syllable after syllable onto the page. I saw the appearance of a woman embracing a new literary world, beginning to succeed. I read avidly and in my reading began to learn how to write. It was through my own efforts that I altered the course of my existence and expunged my grief.

In writing my book I would write about my life and reveal a life ruled by emotion and by a past that is ever present; my dependency in adult life, my yearning to be looked after, to need and be needed; my feelings of loss and insecurity. My life would reveal an eccentric streak but I would eventually, against all odds, show that I could take control over it.

When I couldn't sleep writers like Tolstoy and Dostoyevsky became the companions of my sleepless hours. I lived in their worlds, colluded with their characters. I swallowed them down because the more I read the hungrier I became.

I wrote in my diary.

Ken keeps popping in.
We're on Christian names now.
Maybe he has an ulterior motive?
Sometimes I stand in the garden and watch.
Trees shimmer in the cool evening air.
Not a blade of grass, not a leaf stir, and no bird sings.
Autumn flowers have lost their dazzling colours.
The garden is slowly turning black.
The shrubs are black.
The foliage is black.
He is gone now and my universe is turning black.
He appears to me in my dreams still.
Grinning.
Bloodied.
Faceless.
Beckoning me into hell.
Beckoning me into a darkness.
Then the black mood descends.
Like the black dog.

55

WE SAT facing each other across the kitchen table sipping tea.

'How's it going?'

'Well, it's a struggle but I'm surviving.' Looking at him searchingly I added, trying to keep my features immobile.' I'm sure this isn't just a social call Ken, What's new?'

'Nothing.'

Sensing his caginess I said, 'Come on Ken, spill it.'

'Well,' he said, giving me a hesitant glance. 'I could get the sack if Gibson finds out that I've been discussing the case with you but you're the only person who might be able to provide us with some answers.'

'Feck Peter Gibson, Ken, what's going on?'

Ken raised an eyebrow. 'You and your Irish swearing.'

'Soz.'

'We paid Rosso a visit the other day and you'd never believe the latest wind up.'

'Wind up?'

'Rosso's a pathological liar. He changes his story every time we visit him.'

'Spit it out then.'

'Alex you surprise me sometimes with your choice of words.'

'I surprise me. I do it for effect. Something a dear friend taught me.'

'You are funny Alex. There's more to you than meets the eye. I think the Mother Teresa facade is a cover. You actually possess unique survival strategies. You'd have to, I suppose, to survive Gibson's

M 0.'

'Glad someone agrees and that parrot ...'

'Tell me another – but the boss, Robert Cooper goes along with it.'

I sensed Ken wasn't a fan of either of them. Should I tell him about Rosso's letter? Later perhaps?

'So out with it.'

'You know Rosso started, what can be termed his 'scam', in 1999. Clients were persuaded to invest small sums of money in his various projects. When they learnt of the high interest they'd receive they started to put in larger amounts.'

I could hear the tension in his voice as he spoke. I raised a sculptured eyebrow. 'What did he do with the money?'

'He's a money lender.'

'Nicholas did mention his name once and sort of said he was into financing.'

'Did he by golly? We call it money lending, Alex.'

'It all fits. This is where Danny is connected.'

'We've turned Danny's office over. There's nothing to tie him to anything. He admits that he knows Rosso, through Nicholas, but says that it was Nicholas who was involved in the money lending with Rosso and not him.'

'Danny's lying, Ken.' I proceeded to tell him about the underpinning and that it was Rosso who lent Danny the hundred grand for the bridging loan.

'So Danny's not giving us the whole picture. I thought so. Unfortunately we can't prove anything. Anyhow to get back to his scam, we know from a man called Mullins, a local face, that Rosso had five hundred grand from him and never returned it.'

'Go on,' I said with a shudder. 'I'll pour another cuppa.'

'When Rosso didn't pay up, Mullins hired two men to kill him.'

I was pouring the tea, clutching the teapot in both hands, one for the pot, one to keep the lid from falling off. I lurched forward and dropped it. 'Iosa Criost!'

'My sentiments to,' he said as he raised an eyebrow and retrieved the lid. 'Rosso got a tip off and fled to Italy. Mullins sent two thugs over who ordered Rosso back to Britain. He was told that if he didn't repay the money he was a dead man. It was then, we feel, he started his scam up again, persuading people to part with money so he could repay Mullins.'

'And did he repay him.'

'I don't think so and that's why Mullin's may have killed Nicholas.

"But why Nicholas?'

'Rosso says that he gave Nicholas the five hundred grand to hold in his client account. We think he told Mullins that. So one version of events could be that Mullins, or one of his minions and Rosso went to the house. Things got out of hand and Nicholas ended up dead.'

'Gosh.'

'We know from the pathologist that two men held Nicholas. Rosso's base ball cap was found at the back of your hall and you saw a white guy.'

'So that proves that Rosso was here. Now all you need to do is find out the identity of the other one.'

'It's not as simple as that Alex. As well as claiming he's as innocent as Little Bo Peep he also denies being here and gave us this cock and bull story about how the cap happened to end up in the hall.'

'What does he say?'

'Alex, I'm not permitted to say. I've said too much already. It will all come out at the trial.'

'To get back to the five hundred grand, is there proof Nicholas ever had it?'

'No. We only have Rosso's word for it. The question is did he give it to him and if he did whom did Nicholas pass it on to? Was it to Danny for that underpinning or to invest else where?'

'Maybe…maybe, just hear this out Ken. Maybe Danny could have lost the money in one of his risky schemes.'

'We don't know Alex. For the moment one of my hunches is that it's Mullins. He wanted his money back and no one messes with him.'

'So he targeted Nicholas?'

'Possibly … but…'

'What?'

'A client, named Hart told us that Nicholas denied ever receiving money from Rosso.'

'So you're not sure?'

'At this stage in a murder inquiry everything is just pure speculation. We have to examine every angle.'

'You must have some idea?'

'It's a difficult one. It could have been Rosso himself. By killing Nicholas he could then say to his clients; "My solicitor has the money and he's dead." On the other hand it could be Mullins or one of Rosso's clients.'

'I see.'

'Hart told us that he'd been putting pressure on Rosso to return his investment. He was desperate to get his money back. It ruined him financially. He's a suspect, but the only flaw is he doesn't fit your description of the guy you saw.' He scratched his head, paused and added, 'Others have come forward.'

'How many?'

'About eight. They said Rosso conned them out of large sums of money. Some gave their life's savings and one man took a hundred grand out of his pension fund to invest.'

'But why kill Nicholas?'

'If you'd that many people pressurising you what would you do? As I said Nicholas told Hart that he didn't get any money from Rosso. Maybe, to prevent Nicholas from telling this to others, he decided to kill him.' He paused, and with one of his dead pan expressions, added, 'Dead men tell no tales.'

'Is this what you believe?'

'Don't know yet.' He sipped his tea.

'It's hard to accept that he'd commit such a cold-blooded act. After all he just owed money to these people. It's not as if his life was in danger.'

'We know from Rosso that some heavies from the Moss side in Manchester were threatening him.'

I stared at Ken intently. "If he did carry out the deed he wasn't very professional. Nicholas was still standing when Rosso and the white guy left. If they'd intended to kill him they'd have finished him off there and then and maybe me too.'

'I agree. That's what keeps puzzling me, that, and the taunting. In some ways it looks like they tried to make him talk.'

'Maybe Nicholas did have the money.'

'Yes possibly but where is it? Not in any of his bank accounts.'

'So Mullins and Rosso are at the top of your list for now?' I felt I was listening to a literary expert going over the blurred complexities of a dark Shakespearian tragedy, patiently clarifying each twist of an essentially inexplicable plot. 'I still feel Danny is behind it all.'

'So Rosso claims. He says that all roads lead back to him.'

'Danny was acquainted with people in the underworld.'

'That doesn't make him the perp. Alex. There's no evidence.'

'Maybe someone out there thinks I may the money.' Then I put my hand to my mouth. 'Oh my God maybe my life's in danger!'

'Don't be silly, Alex. Why should they think you've got it? Anyhow they'd have got to you before now if they suspected that.'

With a crystal stare, I riveted on Ken. 'Would they? Maybe they're waiting for the dust to settle before they make their move.' He cast his eyes down looking uncomfortable. He's worried. I shuddered.

Just then the doorbell rang. I was taken aback when I saw Father 0'Malley on the doorstep. This was his third visit this week.

'I was just on my way to the church and thought I'd pop in to see how you are, Alex.'

'You're a glutton for punishment Father. Come in and have a cuppa,' I said as I ambled back into the kitchen. 'Or maybe you'd like something stronger. A whisky perhaps? By the way this is Detective Inspector Ken Masterson. He's been assigned to the case.'

'Pleased to meet you, detective,' the priest said and shook his hand.

'You two chat while I get the drinks,' and then added, 'Ken you'll join us in one. After all you're off duty now, I hope.'

'Well if you insist.'

As I busied myself fixing the drinks Ken turned and addressed the priest. 'You're a friend of Alex's?'

'Only just. I knew Nicholas well. He was in my parish.'

'So you know all about the murder then,' Ken asked in his usual dead-pan way.

'Yes, Alex filled me in on all the horrendous details. It was a terrible thing to happen. He was the gentlest of persons.'

'So you were in Christ Church the same time as Nicholas. You must have met his ex wife, Zoe, and his daughter Elizabeth?'

'Actually I didn't. He mentioned about them many times though.'

'Oh.' Ken said and took a sip of his drink.

A long silence intervened – so long that it became a matter of suspense to see who would break it first. I felt that Ken was scrutinising the priest. Then I remembered that was the way he was with me at first, always suspicious. It was the pro in him.

'What did you say the name of your parish was in Christchurch,' Ken said, studying him as he took another sip of his Bushmills.

'I didn't.'

'I only ask because I spent a few months there during my student years.'

He's still studying him...still studying him. Then he broke eye contact and put on his self-effacing smile again.

'It's St. Mary's in the centre of the city.'

'I know it's on top of the hill. Has an unusual spire. It seems to stretch into the sky.'

'Yes, that's the church. Look I must be going I promised the local parish priest I'd pop in to the hospice and chat to the patients.' Draining the rest of his drink he stood up and gave my arm a squeeze.

Escorting him to the front door I said, 'Janey Mack Father that was a grilling Ken put you through.' Noticing his blank expression I added, '**Sure** father they must use that expression up in Sligo. Have you forgotten?'

Begorrah I haven't, sure you know that yourself. It's not part of a dialect you'd hear much up in Sligo though.'

Odd I thought as he disappeared into the night.

'I thought you were going to give poor Father O'Malley the third degree there, Ken.'

'Well you know me by now Alex. Always suspicious.'

'I hope he passed the test then,' I said smiling.

'With flying colours, Alex, with flying colours.'

'Ken I've something to tell you that you're not going to like.'

'Try me.'

'I had a letter from Rosso and I wrote back to him.'

'Letter from Rosso? Bloody hell! What did he have to say?'

'He says he's innocent.'

'Alex I can't believe you wrote to Rosso. He's dangerous.'

'Well if you read his letter you'd have doubts.'

'Alex, for God's sake, he's a pathological liar. You're so naïve. Here we are trying to protect you and you go and do this.'

'But the letter sounded so genuine.'

'Why are you willing to trust people you don't even know? These people you have calling, that Pat and that priest. You don't need these people around you.'

'Ken they were friends of Nicholas's.'

'Don't forget one thing Alex; they all have their own agenda's. If what you say is true about Danny then Pat could be just popping in trying to get information out of you. And as for that priest, I can't believe his motives are genuine. After all you're a woman alone.'

'Ken he's a priest.'

'That doesn't stop them.'

'You're so distrustful, Ken.'

'It's my job. Suspect everyone, that's my motto.'

After Ken had gone I let things percolate around in my head. I decided to pay Rosso a visit. That way I might learn more.

Then my thoughts turned to the priest. What a God send he was to me in my hour of need. I'd ignore Ken's intolerance, I needed someone like Father O'Malley in my life to help me get through this.

56

THE BUZZ of the doorbell jolted me out of a day dream. I peered out the glass panel as I swung the front door open. Pat.

'Hello Alex. I thought I'd pop in.'

'Tea?' I said as he followed me into the kitchen.

'Yes please. How's it going?'

'I can't believe he's gone,' I said as I busied myself filling the kettle. My voice had a lucid rawness to it.

'I know, Alex. I feel the same.'

As I sat down I said, 'Pat, do you think he knew he was going to die?'

'I don't know, Alex.'

'I wonder. Something I haven't told you, something the milkman said. It puzzles me. Apparently a few weeks before he died Nicholas asked him had he seen anyone watching the house. He told him to report it to the police if he did see anyone. So Nicholas was scared of someone.'

'I'm sure there's nothing in it. Maybe he was afraid of a break in. Remember you told me that someone broke in when you were away one weekend.'

'That was about two years ago.'

'Let's get off the murder topic, it's getting me down.'

'Sorry. Anyhow to change the subject guess who wrote to me?'

'Who?'

'Bruno Rosso.'

'Rosso wrote to you?'

'What does he ... want?'

I thought I detected a flash of fear in his eyes. Could be my imagination. 'He said he was innocent and that he'd explain everything if I wrote back to him.'

'I hope you didn't, Alex.'

'I did.'

'Alex, for God's sake don't you know you're inviting trouble having anything to do with a murderer?'

'If you read his letter you'd be convinced he's innocent.'

'Alex, the man is a pathological liar.' He bit on his bottom lip. His pupils were like pinpoints in the harsh light of the room.

He's scared. 'He wasn't the only one at the scene of the crime.'

'Alex, take my advice and leave well alone. Rosso is a murderer.'

'He said in his letter he'd give me names, names of people who know things.'

Pat stood there, face expressionless, and yet a small muscle twitched in his right cheek, a sure sign of stress.

Finally he spoke. 'Knew…things…like what?'

I handed him the cup of tea. 'Like who's responsible for Nicholas's murder, plus the identity of the white guy.' I eyed him. His face had paled. I was lying, but I wanted to draw him out. I looked at him - the nerve jumping in his cheek, and the way his hands shook. Now the tea cup rattled in the saucer? He knows something.

'Look I have to go, Alex.' He stood up unsteadily his face a mask of fear.

'You haven't finished your tea.'

'I haven't time. Sorry about this I just remembered I've got to meet someone.'

Later as I put the kettle on to make another cuppa, I mused. I had seen the fear on his face. And his abrupt departure showed something was amiss. It was as if he needed time to recover from what I'd said. It's got to be something to do with Danny. I was even more determined to visit Rosso in prison but not till after the trial.

57

THE FOLLOWING day while shopping in Liverpool I saw a gypsy caravan parked in the precinct in the city centre. A sign outside read:

GYPSY ROSE READS THE TAROT CARDS.

On impulse I stopped at the door of the caravan. I opened the door and stepped inside.

The woman sitting wore a long cotton black skirt and a red scarf around her head. Golden ear rings dangled from her ear lobes. 'You'll be wantin' your future told,' she said as she indicated a seat. I sat down. She started to deal some cards. Suddenly as she looked at them her eyes filled with horror. She made the sign of the cross and said in a high-pitched voice. 'Go please. Only evil and death lurks in these cards. I cannot read anymore. You'll bring bad luck to me.' As I scurried outside I heard, 'Remember, friend is foe and foe is friend.'

That night Lynda popped in. As we sat at the kitchen table I told her about the gypsy. 'The old crone. I'm sure she was making it all up. She must have noticed the sad expression on my face and knew instinctively that something tragic had happened in my life. Or she recognised me from the media coverage.'

Lynda looked at me and said, 'I don't know Alex sometimes I feel that they can see into the future.'

'Lynda I'm frightened. What terrible things are in store for me?'

'Nothing is going to happen.' She cast me a concerned glance, reached for my hand and gently stroked it.

I watched as she fingered my hand tenderly. The sight deeply affected me.

I suddenly said, 'I'm glad I gave you to me.'

Lynda raised an eyebrow. 'What?'

'Robert Louis Stevenson – "A friend is a gift you give yourself."

'You and your sayings Alex. I know what you mean though. Well I have one for you:

"A friend is a person with whom I may be sincere. Before him I may think aloud."

'Who said that?'

'Emerson.'

'He's right. I always think aloud with you. You know my innermost secrets.' I laughed.

'To change the subject do you know what my view was about Nicholas.'

'What.'

'Though he was a quiet shy man, ethereal, gentle and a gentleman yet…'

'Go on …'

'Juxtaposed with these same excellent qualities there lurked a complexity so enormous that it seemed unbelievable. He was a man who was drawn to the obsessional and the bizarre.

I nodded.

'He was a man in shadows, his women in unending tunnels of fear.'

She's right.

'Gosh it's eleven o'clock. I must be going and get some shut eye. I've to organise a buffet tomorrow. There's a board meeting scheduled .'

I made a face. 'Rather you than me. You're so methodical unlike me.'

'The joys of being a PA love. By the way did you know that Yasir Arafat died today.'

'No, I've don't read the papers if I can help it. What's today's date anyhow?'

'The eleventh.'

'Gosh it's November already.'

'Got to go.' She gave me a peck on the cheek and then she was gone.

Later as I lay in bed I couldn't forget the gypsy's words. The phrase, 'friend is foe and foe is friend', echoed and re-echoed in my mind. Who amongst my friends was a Judas?

At 2.a.m. the phone rang. I answered it. Nobody! Silence! The caller didn't respond even when I said 'hello' again. Then a soft replacement at the ghostly other end. I recalled Lynda's word's, "Women in unending tunnels of fear." My mind clicked. What terror was about to begin. No sleep again, a twisting night. Questions crowded my mind. Was the phone call a wrong number? Or perhaps it was someone trying to frighten me. But why? I didn't know anything. Except of course I could identify the white guy and they knew that. I shuddered.

58

'THAT GAME'S done me in Dennis I think I'll have an early night. Gosh, it's ten thirty already,' I said, looking at my watch.

'Okay, Alex, see you next week for a game, and practice that backhander.'

I was in a buoyant mood as I left. The exercise had restored my equilibrium. No streetlamps brightened the night, but the moon silvered the leaves as I walked to my vehicle.

Making my exit from the car park I drove very slowly in the dark drizzly evening. In the fitful breeze, a funnel of golden oak leaves spun along the mews. I zoomed through them, crisp autumn scraping across the windshield. Just as I turned right I noticed a dark Four by Four parked on the left. The car, without lights, started up as I passed, its wheels fighting for grip on the wet road. I took little notice of it but as I reached the island, about twenty yards on, I glanced in my mirror again and saw that the car was still behind me. The headlights were now on. Was it following me? Turning left I peered again in my reflector. I froze. It was still there. Zoom

Stopping at the lights, I looked again. It was dark and the glass in the car was tinted. I wasn't certain whether there was someone sitting in the passenger seat or not. Were they following me? Stop it Alex, you're being paranoid, nevertheless I checked to see had I locked the door. Turning right I stole a quick glance again. This time my heart leapt up in fear. They were still behind me. The falling rain made it difficult to see the number plate. God, what do I do? I daren't go home. I'd be an easy target for them. Oh, if only I had my mobile. Then I had an idea. I'll drive to my friend Liz's house.

This was the acid test. I'd know for certain then if I was being followed. I slammed the gearbox into reverse and the car shot backwards. I did a three point turn and headed in the opposite direction.

Close behind me a single pair of headlights was approaching quickly. I took the first turning left; swinging the wheel so sharply that I didn't think I'd make it. The back of the Carmen Ghia slid on the wet tarmac and the rear wheel on the passenger side smashed against the kerb, jarring me in my seat. 'Feck!' I changed down into second with difficulty and brought the car under control and slammed my foot to the floor.

At that moment the petrol guzzler loomed up behind me, its headlights blinding me. Five metres separated us. My car shot forward, gathering speed, its engine beginning to squeal as the rev counter almost hit maximum. I rammed into third. The guzzler accelerated even faster. Now it was centimetres away from the rear bumper. I knew they were going to ram me. I kept my foot to the floor even though the engine protested with a whine. Too late I saw that I was heading for a wrought iron gate. I slammed my foot on the brakes and did an emergency stop. The tyres screeched as I went into a zig - zag skid. Just as I recovered from the skid the pursuing car smashed into the back. I careered forward and my forehead hit the windscreen. The steering wheel and seat belt prevented me from crashing through the glass. I tried to control the car but all I could see ahead was the gate. Seacht meadaracht, se, cuig, ceathair, tri... (7metres, 6, 5, 4, 3,) I swung the steering wheel round and tensed as I hit the gate side on. The other car had also come to a halt when it was knocked sideways. As I watched, the driver's door opened and a black-clad figure appeared in the opening. He had a gun in his hand and he was aiming it straight at my heart.

Like a demon out of hell I shot the car forward and accelerated through the gears until I was in fourth. I glanced in my mirror and saw that I had lost them. I veered up a side street and peered in the mirror. Immediately they were in pursuit. They were close now, only a car length away. Petrified, I maintained an even pace keeping an eye in my rear view mirror. They were still behind me. Ahead I could see the sign, showing the end of the thirty-mile an hour zone. Once beyond that point I was done for. Was this how I was going to end up my days? Murdered! The moonless night seemed to have become even darker as the headlights of the vehicle flared out over the line of trees on either side of the road. There was no sign of any other vehicles.

A few more yards and I would pass the sign. I must do something, anything. Could I jump out of the car and make a run for it? Too late for that, they'd catch me before I got very far. I pressed my foot down on the accelerator and swung round a sharp bend far too fast and for a brief period I left the vehicle behind.

Quickly the pursuing vehicle caught up. I skidded around the next bend, regained control, and kept my foot down to the floor. Watching in the rear-view mirror I could now vaguely make out a second man. He wore dark glasses and a peaked hat.

The car tried to overtake. Risking more speed, I swung round another bend. The gap had widened, but only briefly. The guzzler was again roaring down on me. My headlights swung round yet another sharp bend. I gunned past a cottage and a farm making sharp ascents and sudden descents that make my stomach plunge.

I turned into a poorly surfaced road, taking the tyres at speeds they weren't meant for. The mixture of the uneven surfaces and the car's overstrained suspension system caused the car to shudder and jolt. Once I could hear the car's chassis scrape loudly against a hump in the pavement, and I saw sparks in the rear view mirror. I was driving recklessly, my growing terror overcoming anything like caution.

I sped over an old stone bridge so narrow that there was barely room for traffic in either direction. But I couldn't shake off the other car.

What could I do? All of a sudden I saw headlights in front of me. An idea, conceived out of desperation, began to form. Without warning I swung my car out in front of an approaching Volvo and did a U turn. The driver braked, sounded the horn and flashed the lights. Keep flashing, keep flashing - anything to attract attention. I put my foot down. I glanced in my mirror and saw that the Guzzler was now behind the other car. But I was far from safe. I still had to get home, a journey of eight miles.

I suddenly noticed that I was in a built up area. People were coming out of a pub. That's it. I'll stop at the 'Black Dog' further on.

I glanced at the digital. Ten past eleven. The way seemed interminable and the streets were like the black web of some sprawling spider. The cold rain continued to fall and the blurred streetlights appeared deathly in the dripping mist. As it thickened I felt even more terrified. A dog barked and far away in the darkness a night owl cried. The mist became lighter and the lights of The Black Dog in the distance seem to beckon to me. There was a crowd outside chatting. Maybe there's a chance yet. I planned my next manoeuvre.

I twisted the steering wheel and headed for the mass of people on the pavement. As I mounted it a man jumped out of the way. I headed for the wall. There was a screeching as I braked. I jumped out of the car. By now the man who had leaped out of the way started to scream. 'You fucking maniac.'

I almost fell to the ground. Yelling at those standing around I shouted, 'For God's sake call the police, I'm being followed.'

They looked at me as if I had two heads.

'Dial 999,' I screamed again.

My legs gave way and as I slumped to the wet pavement a man caught me. Shouting, he said, 'For God's sake help me, this woman's in a bad state.'

'You're not making sense,' he said as he assisted me.

'I'm being followed, that's the Four by Four. Get the number.' I watched as the car, like a phantom, disappeared into the darkness.

After being helped to a chair in the lounge, I sat trembling. Someone forced me to take a sip of brandy. The rough taste shocked me but I swallowed it. Then I heard the sirens. A few minutes later a policeman approached me.

In faltering words I related all that had happened.

'But why should they follow you?'

Quickly I told them about Nicholas and the fear that my life might be in danger. 'Ring Detective Ken Masterson he knows all about it.' I mumbled the number. He left me alone. In the background I could hear him on his mobile.

'We have her here now. She told us this cock and bull story about her life being in danger. "Oh" ... I heard him say, and then a pause... "So it's true, I didn't know. No, she's OK, but she's hysterical. I'll put her on for a moment.' Turning to me he said, 'It's Ken, he wants a word.'

In a shaky voice I said, 'Ken, it's you. Thank God. I don't think they believed me.'

'What's happened Alex?'

'I was followed by this Four by Four. There were two of them.'

"Are you sure they were following you?'

'Of course I'm sure Ken.' Briefly I told him the tale.

'We'll be over shortly. Try and keep calm.'

A member of staff said, 'Perhaps a hot cup of tea would be in order. 'Mick, could you ask the landlord to make a strong brew,' the man shouted.

'You'll be okay, don't worry,' he said gently, as he stood holding me.

By now I was shaking like a leaf.

'It's delayed reaction.'

Someone handed me a mug of tea. Just like the last time, it was hot and metallic. I gulped it down at once.

A large moth hummed round me landing on the table. I watched it with that strange interest in the trivia of life we try to develop when things of frightening significance make us fearful. After a while it flew away.

Ten minutes later Ken and two of his colleagues arrived. Ken sat beside me. 'Did you manage to get the number?'

'No, Ken, I couldn't see, it was too dark but it was a Four by Four.'

'What make was it.'

'Make? Haven't a clue. As if I'd know that.'

'And you're quite certain they were following you?'

'Of course I am. One of them had a gun and he was aiming it at me. They even slowed down as I mounted the pavement and then they took off.'

Ken stared at me, a brooding expression on his face. 'Maybe it's Mullins's gang.'

'Are you going to arrest them?'

"We'll have to prove it. Don't worry our men will keep a watch on your house.'

I stared at Ken, total fear now on my face. 'They could strike anytime, anywhere.'

Ken looked at me with concern. 'Alex, I don't know what to say. Why this should happen after this length I don't understand. Either they suspect that you know something or they think you have the money.'

'God, Ken, how can I live like this? '

'We'll be watching the house and you for a long time to come; they daren't make a move.'

'But you can't guard me forever, Ken. Surely you can pin something on them?'

'Let's hope so.'

I gave a little moan. 'Ken, tonight I could have been a goner. The next time I mightn't be so lucky.'

'Look, Alex, I'm going to get one of the boys to take you home and he'll sleep in the house for a few nights.'

'Ken, this sort of thing happens only in banana republics, tin pot dictatorships and totalitarian states, not in England.'

'It's happening all the time Alex, only we don't notice it until it's on our doorstep.'

As I drove home I started to cry. Suddenly I was plunged into an eye-stinging blur of anger, anger against the men who had followed me and anger against Nicholas. His shadowy past was now putting my life in danger. I felt betrayed. I hurriedly pulled into a lay by and switched off the engine. Wrapping my arms around the steering wheel, I dropped my head in my arms and wept.

The next day I didn't leave the house, and spent most of the time upstairs, ill with a savage and wild horror of dying. The consciousness of being hunted, snared, tracked down, began to dominate my mind. When I closed my eyes I saw again the dark figures of the unknown men peering at me. Horror seemed to lay its grisly hands on my heart.

The constable remained in the house for three days.

I felt that from this moment on every shadow would be malignant; every sudden sound a death knell and knew that until my foe was revealed, my life would be at risk.

After a week I ventured out. There was something in the clear, foliage-scented air that seemed to bring back my courage and my zeal for life. I looked around at the milling crowd in the High street, walking slowly along. I wondered which, if any, was concerned with me - the pocket of fear.

59

NEXT DAY I returned to the house after shopping. I entered, closed the door and frantically twisted the locks double locking the entrance. Perspiration stung my eyes and flashes of heat, like hot flushes, suffused my body. I backed away from the front door, twisting to survey the interior. A single dim overhead bulb in the porch threw odd shadows into the corner of my sitting room. The door to the room I taught my pupils in was open, yawning darkly.

I was abruptly overcome by the feeling that when I'd gone shopping that morning I'd closed that door behind me as was my usual routine. A rough-edged sense of angst clawed within me filling me with doubts. I gaped at the open door, trying desperately to recollect my exact movements when I'd left.

A group of memory cells offered a collage of images. I could visualize myself donning my jacket and placing my house keys in my handbag. I remembered thinking KHT. I saw myself stepping over the threshold and pulling the front door behind me. All this was in my mind's eye. It was a ritual I had repeated hundreds of times since Nicholas had died.

Now I'd returned and things didn't seem as they should be. A little voice asked: Did you close the study door. I bit my lower lip in frustration, trying to remember the sensation of the door handle in my hand, the sound of the PVC shutting behind me. The memory eluded me and I felt thwarted by my inability to remember such a simple every day act. Deirdre is right. I'm getting very absentminded. I shrugged and reassured myself: You must have left it ajar – an oversight.

Still I didn't venture further. The darkness seemed to tease me. The passage was shadowy except at the far end where a thin wedge of light stabbed in from an aperture somewhere. I listened trying to penetrate the gloom. No one in there I told myself. To make sure I shouted, 'Anyone there.' Don't be fecking stupid, the person is hardly going to reply. No sound - obviously. I inched forward, trying to calm myself. My hand reached for the light switch. I clicked it on. Nothing happened just darkness remained. Trying to adjust my eyes to the dimness, I moved slowly into the room, my ears pricked for any minute sound that would alert me to danger. I moved towards my bureau keeping my arms outstretched so I didn't trip over something. I felt the cold surface of the brass lamp. I sighed deeply and uttered a mantra. I fumbled for the switch and pressed it. Nothing - not a glimmer. To much of a coincidence I reminded myself to have two bulbs not working. Maybe there's a power cut but a glance at the red glow from my computer winking at me was enough. The power was on. I groped around for my office chair and plopped down. Motionless, I tried to arrive at some obvious explanation for why none of the lights in my study operated. They were functioning this morning. My nerve ends were on edge, my hearing sharpened in an effort to determine whether I was alone or not.

I tried to remember where I'd put the torch that I used to demonstrate light forming shadows to my pupils. In the desk drawer silly. I stepped gingerly into the centre of the room keeping my hands out in front of me again. I was half way across the room when my mobile warbled. Fumbling for it in my pocket I turned it on. 'Hello' No answer. 'Feck.' It rang again. 'What the bloody hell do you want?' Silence. I threw the phone on the desk. It rang again. 'What the…'

Someone disconnected. Gobshite.

I reached out with my right hand and feeling the base of the lamp I traced the cord down to the plug socket and felt with my fingers. The lamp was plugged in. Nothing untoward there. I retraced my steps making sure I didn't trip over something. Then I checked under the stairs where the fuse box was situated. One of the buttons was depressed. I banged it in. The house burst with light.

I breathed in sharply. Am I being watched? Has someone been in my house? Is it someone I know? Someone close? Some one who knows where everything is. Or is it someone trying to warn me, to back off, not become involved in finding the other killer. Or maybe it just my imagination. It's easy to trip the fuse switch. Something could have fallen against it. I lifted a hand to my forehead feeling suddenly feverish. Someone was targeting me but why? Was it those who had followed me the other night – Mullen's gang? Must ring Ken. I made a dive for my mobile, banged out his number. Within seconds I was through to him. Haphazardly I related all that had happened.

'Alex we've checked Mullins out. He's not responsible. His gang have cast-iron alibis.'

'Who's this person then that's stalking me? Ken.'

There was a silence and then Ken said, 'Alex we'll station a couple of men in an unmarked car near your house for a few weeks. If there's any activity at all they'll be on to it.'

To me however his words were hollow. I'd have to make my own move. Find out who my adversary was. I forced myself to bring my mind back from the shadowy hollows it had wandered into. Suddenly I sobbed unexpectedly, once, then twice. I held my breath and closed my eyes, the third sob lodged deep in my throat.

60

THE EARLY morning sunlight filtered though the blinds, casting shadows across the entire office. Chief inspector Robert Cooper met me at the door and greeted me. As he waved me to an armchair he rang for tea. I studied him as he sat down. Robert Cooper was tall; a powerfully built man in his late forties. He had a bull neck and a massive head. His grey eyes had a challenging expression.

What struck me, though, was that his dress bespoke wealth. Strange – and he on a copper's salary.

I studied again. He radiated physical energy and his manner was aggressive. He drummed the knuckles of his left hand on the leather-covered desk, his mind obviously on some problem. He smiled; not a pleasant one as his secretary entered and placed a tea tray on his desk. The woman shuddered and made a quick exit. He's got out of the wrong side of the cage this morning.

He rose and circled his desk and perched himself on the edge. Interrogation tactic: height advantage.

'About the murder, Alex,'

I flinched.' I feel we should discuss the case in more detail. See what we can come up with.' There was a pause as we both looked away.

As he poured the tea and sugared and milked it, he remained silent. Interrogation tactic: silence. After what seemed an aeon he spoke. 'I'll get straight to the point, Alex. The question is … where's the money? It's much more than what we thought.'

He thinks I have it. That's why I'm here. I stared into the manic face before me and felt real fear forming in my intestines. I closed my eyes for a few seconds, hoping to take away the throbbing behind them. 'I haven't got a clue.' The police searched the house. They must think Nicholas had the money. Therefore this horrible man must also think this. And Ken keeps popping in obviously hoping I'd let something slip. I shivered.

Cooper studied me intently. 'Have you any idea what Nicholas would do with the money if he had it?'

'No.' I'm damned if I'm going to cooperate.

Lighting one of his cigarettes, he coughed loudly, a phlegm-ridden, hacking cough that made my stomach turn. He took a deep drag and spoke. 'Is there a bank in New Zealand where he might have deposited any large sums?'

'No,' and then I reluctantly offered, 'He was very friendly with a bank manager there. They always kept in touch.'

'Hm, what's the name of the town?' Cooper said in a syrupy baritone.

'I've no idea. The only person who can tell you that is Zoe and she's moved and no one seems to know where she is.' My headache was worse now, a migraine in the making. 'Anyhow you've got all his bank statements. You can contact the bank.' The headache was off the Richter.

'Yes of course.' He stared into my face, his eyes bright with malice.

One thing was clear Robert Cooper suspected that I had the money and he wasn't going to let me off the hook. God knows what he had up his sleeve.

'Alex I'm sorry I had to bother you with all this but you must agree with me that the missing money is a huge mystery...'

'It's quite simple really Mr Cooper. Nicholas didn't have any money.' My voice was clipped now and hard.

'We can't be sure of that Alex.' His eyes appeared to narrow just slightly. Why is he so interested? My brain cells threw out a thought. Maybe he's in cahoots with these people who ever they are - on the take. Wants to get their money back for them. It's not unknown for the police to take bribes. I appraised him again. His dress was definitely too up market for a detective. I decided he was a baddie.

'Well, I am. Why would he borrow a pittance from me a couple of nights before he was murdered and ask me to pay the phone bill that was in his name if he had millions stashed away? And furthermore he owed at least fifty grand. If he had the money surely he'd have paid his debts off.' I impaled him with a glare.

He compressed his thin lips in a small moue of annoyance. Was it for me or Ken.

'Oh. That's news to me. Why didn't you tell Ken all of this?'

'I did.' I bet your brain feels as good as new, seeing that you've never used it.

Anger clamped itself across his face like a death mask. 'You did, did you? I must have a word with Ken.'

'Mr Cooper I've nothing to hide.' The migraine was intense now, jagged and penetrating.

'We'll call it a day then Alex. We'll keep in touch though.' The hint of malice was back in his eyes.

'P-og mhoin.' (Kiss my arse)
'What does that mean?'
'An Irish goodbye.' He arched an eyebrow.

Robert Cooper sat in his office brooding. Then he grabbed the receiver and buzzed Peter.
'She's just gone.'
'So, what did she have to say?'

'She's adamant that Nicholas didn't have the money. He related all she had told him. She's appears so fucking naïve you'd think she didn't know her arse from her elbow. I'm not so sure of her innocent little stance.'

'What next?'

'I want you to put the word out that we suspect that Nicholas had the money and that Alex might have it or know where it is. If this gets round the under world it might draw them out in the open.'

'Don't you think this might be dangerous for Alex?' Peter said.

'Well if she's in on it serves her right.'

'But we don't know that yet.'

'We will soon. I want her bank details. So get cracking on that.'

'What about Ken.'

'Say nothing. He's gone soft. He thinks she's Mother Teresa and Princess Diana rolled up in one. Let it drop that we think she has the money. And Peter keep this under wraps.'

'Of course.'

'Yes, and maybe the trial will throw up something. It starts next week.'

BOOK 3

61

THE TRIAL

Day 1: September 5,

The weekend came and went. I tried to busy myself with mundane tasks but when night came, so did the terrors. I slept fitfully and was haunted by monsters and Gremlins tapping at my window. Madness beckoned from a doorway in my mind like a familiar friend. Friends called to wish me well and offer me roses when all I saw was thorns. Words of comfort but only pain is perceived.

I thought of Nicholas how we had thrown in our lot to make a life together - taken a chance. Then with Zoe it burned into fury and hell knew no bounds. Our love became a tug-of-war, harm emerging...actions deeply wounding leaving scars old and new lining up like soldiers on a battlefield.

Now twelve months on and the drama has faded. Only the pain, dark and deep remains. No solution because love seems to be on trial and the stench of fear permeates what once was pure and good.

Even after Nicholas's death Zoe is still relentless. Elizabeth's little letter to Daddy tears at me. 'Please re-marry my Mummy.'

Sifting through the treacle I see the sticky fingers of love scrabbling at last year's dreams. The man offers long distance support ... torn in two. Meanwhile our new found happiness is threatened. He flies to New Zealand in an attempt to restore order to chaos. The volatile Zoe will have none of it. She scoffs and screams REJECTION and then invites him to be her husband. It's all she knows. Damaged and brutalised she cannot see there's a flower in the dung heap. The father of the child has a sad look. Now he has found his peace. And me – I was desperately in love with him in a blind first love way.

The clock mocks my impatience as I attempt to eat a healthy breakfast. The muesli sticks in my throat as I fight back the tears. Reality beckons and I grab a suit and attempt to 'look the business' as Nicholas used to say. 'Battle on,' his teasing voice would reassure! Somehow, I don't feel so alone. How will I face those prying eyes, the crowded courtroom? The police have been great. God knows we've seen enough of each other.

A quick glance at the clock. I stare in the mirror, surprised to see that the bright expression belies the sadness within.

Another cup of tea and soon the police will arrive, my escorts Ken and Bill. The first day of many more to come. No time to think. The doorbell rings and I head out to the waiting car. It was good to see familiar faces and I climbed in giving them a wry smile. We drove in companionable silence.

How does one even begin to think about having to go through what must be the most harrowing experience of such a tragedy after the tragedy itself.

I clocked my surroundings as I strode into the building. It was all new to me. The county court was a modern brick building four storeys in height. Visitors were funnelled through electronic security checkpoints. The courtroom where Rosso would be tried for murder was situated on the second floor.

Ken had briefed me as to the layout of the courtroom; told me that I must face the judge when I gave my responses.

The court usher seemed miraculously to appear from nowhere.

'It's time to go in,' she whispered.

As I entered the courtroom she motioned me to a seat reserved for the defendant and victim's families. The judge's bench stood against the front wall. To the right of the bench was the jury bench, and in the centre of the room were several rows of tables. One was for the Queen's council and the other for the defence barrister. It was then I saw Bruno Rosso. He stood in the dock, flanked by two prison officers. For a brief instant our eyes riveted on each other. A look of surprise swept over his countenance and some vestige of emotion registered fleetingly.

Bruno Rosso looked Italian. His dress, a dark well-tailored suit, was also sombre, befitting the occasion.

I was glad that now at last; confronted with Nicholas's murderer I could release my pent-up anguish. But no, I felt nothing, or maybe my anger was buried to deeply within me or was I beginning to doubt his guilt.

I had been told that the Queen's Council, Mr White, had the sharpest brain in the legal profession. As I watched I noticed that he had the habit of scratching his head as if he wasn't sure of what he was going to say next which gave him an air of vague bewilderment. He reminded me of the actor, Charles Laughton.

Rosso's defence barrister, Mr Bailey was young, slightly built with a rather non-descript appearance.

The courtroom was packed with reporters and the type of spectators attracted to murder trials. As murder trials went this was a spectacular one.

There was a hushed silence in the courtroom as the QC awkwardly gathered his papers as he prepared to make his opening speech. I stared, aghast, as he tried to put some order to them. No one could possibly take him seriously. How was this man going to find Rosso guilty? Slowly he approached the jury bench tripping over the leg of a table.

In a soft voice he began, looking directly at the jury, 'Ladies and gentlemen I'm grateful to you for your presence. I'm aware of the tremendous sacrifice some of you have to make to be here. Thank you.'

He's not such as clown as I first thought. Judging by the faces of the jurors he'd already got them on his side.

Continuing, Mr White said, 'However, I won't be taking up much of your time, as this case is so obviously open and shut. Bruno Rosso here,' as he spoke he turned and looked straight at him, 'is accused of murdering Nicholas Murray in cold blood. There's no doubt that he did it. The evidence against him is overwhelming.'

Mr. White walked past, pausing to look at each one. 'To reiterate, this case will not take long. Why? The defendant standing over there,' he paused, turned around and waved an arm in Rosso's direction, 'murdered an innocent man. His baseball cap was found at the scene of the crime. Here we have a man, a crooked financial consultant who killed Mr Murray when he feared that a money scam he'd carried out would be discovered. The taking of the life of another human being for money is the worst kind of crime and to do it to save his own skin is despicable.'

I watched the faces of the jurors and felt they were already convinced of Rosso's guilt.

'Rosso's aim was to persuade clients to invest in his business by promising them a high interest on their investment. Of course, attracted by such high returns they reinvested the profits and capital. But Bruno was clever. He always returned the investment and interest within weeks, which guaranteed the utmost confidence in his scheme. By 2000 Rosso had received up to two million pounds.' Mr White paused, scratched his chin again, and looked over at Rosso and then at the jury. 'Two ... million ... pounds.' He paused.

'But he had a little problem, didn't he. Gradually he found he was unable to continue paying such high returns. His clients, alarmed at not receiving their dues, demanded their capital back. Of course Rosso fobbed them off, telling them that he'd given the money to his solicitor and that it was he who was stalling.' Swinging round, in a thundering voice he shouted, 'Rosso used Mr Murray as a scapegoat to keep his clients at bay. And then...' His voice lowered until it was almost inaudible, 'we find there's a fly in the ointment ... Mr Hart, one of his clients. His interest on his £100 000 hadn't been returned so he panicked and demanded his capital back. He rang Nicholas who told him that Rosso hadn't passed any monies to him. What was he to believe?' Mr White said, addressing his question to the jury with a quizzical expression, 'Mr Rosso or Mr Murray, a respected solicitor, the man now deceased.'

The jurors looked at Rosso with contempt written on their faces.

'So what does Rosso do? He spins Hart a yarn telling him he would be meeting Nicholas Murray at 4.30 pm. on 29th October at a hotel and that Nicholas would be handing over a large cheque.' Mr White then turned his thumbs in the top part of his waist coat, and glared at the prisoner. In a loud voice he said, 'So, to stop Nicholas Murray from blowing the whistle on him, he followed him home, accompanied by an accomplice, forced their way inside as Mr Murray opened the door and stabbed him fifteen times.'

The jury seemed transfixed.

'And after this cold-blooded attack our Mr Rosso then has the gall to telephone Mr Hart and say, "The bastard hasn't turned up."

Mr. White continued. 'Then next day Rosso, knowing that he had taken part in stabbing Mr Murray to death had the temerity to telephone Price's office and ask to speak to the deceased. This ladies and gentlemen is the true account of what happened. And here I rest my case. It is your business to find the defendant guilty or not of these charges. It is my job as Queen's Council to prove beyond a reasonable doubt that Bruno Rosso murdered Nicholas. Then Mr White turned to the judge. 'If it pleases your honour I would like to call Alex Rowe as the crown's first witness'

I gave a concise account of what had happened. It was all over in ten minutes. I had waited a year for this. Dazed I stumbled back to my seat.

It was twelve o'clock and the jurors looked weary. Glancing at the clock the judge said. 'Perhaps this is an appropriate time to adjourn.'

62

IN THE afternoon Mr White called the pathologist to the stand.

The pathologist gave the same story as he had given to the police reiterating that it was two men who were involved in the stabbing.

Next the defence barrister stood up and walked towards the dock.

'I…' He paused. Suddenly he threw a hand grenade. 'In your opinion could the attack have been carried out by one person?'

'Objection, your honour,' the QC said, 'it's already been established that it was a two man attack.'

'Overruled. Council is entitled to ask this question.'

The pathologist looked perplexed. 'Well, I suppose so, but it would be very difficult and it's most unlikely'.

'Please answer the question.   Yes or no?'

'Yes, but…'

'No more questions.'

He had scored one over White.

Next, David Hart, who had invested money with Rosso, took the stand.

He was a tall man with receding hair. He had a gaunt pinched face, with thin lips. His nervousness showed as his eyes kept darting here and there.

The QC walked nearer to the witness box.

'Your name is David Joseph Hart.'

'Yes.' The muscle in his left cheek gave an involuntary twitch.

'Mr. Hart, are you acquainted with the defendant, Bruno Rosso?'

'Yes.' His eyes automatically went to where the defendant was standing.

'We did business together.'

'When did you start?'

'In June 1999.' The muscle in his cheek started to twitch more rapidly.

'Could you explain the nature of your business?'

'First I invested a grand and after two weeks I received twenty five percent interest. Pleased, I reinvested this sum. I was impressed with the way Rosso worked and decided to invest £100,000.'

'Were there any records of these transactions?'

'The amount was just entered into a journal but no receipt was ever handed over.'

'After investing that large sum what happened?'

'Things started to go wrong. I wasn't receiving my interest so I demanded my capital back.'

'Did you get it?'

'No. I began to get desperate and threatened to go to the police. Rosso then told me that the money had been used for a bridging loan for a property in Liverpool and that a consortium of people was buying it. However to purchase it they needed cash, as the mortgage lenders would not lend the money until the underpinning was completed. He claimed that although the work had been done the surveyors had not given the okay. He promised that once the job was passed the money would be released by the building society and passed to Mr Murray as he'd arranged the loan.'

'So to sum up you invested money with Rosso and you never got it back.'

'Yes.'

'That will be all.'

About six witnesses in all took the stand. All of them had a similar tale to tell.

That night the trial was emblazoned all over the front page. There was a small paragraph devoted to Hurricane Katrina been declared a Category 5 storm. Almost a year since he died I thought as I copped the date Tuesday 29th 2005.

63

'MR ROSSO, can you relate to the jury the events of the 29th October leading up to the murder of Nicholas Murray.' It was the second week of the trial and Mr White had called Bruno Rosso to the stand.

In a nervous voice Rosso began. 'Three men confronted me in the gym car park around 8.45 a.m. One of them put a gun to my head.'

'What was their business?'

'They wanted me to follow my solicitor to find out where he lived. I decided to pretend to play ball. So that evening I lurked in a doorway as Nicholas left the office. It was five o'clock. He went to the station.'

'And?'

'I followed him. We both got on the train and got off at Crosby.'

I followed him and as we turned right up a hill towards the bridge in Oak Tree road a man got out of a blue car and said, "Bruno stop where you are." The man frisked me and took my baseball cap off. He never gave it back to me. That's how the cap got to be in the house. He ordered me to continue following my solicitor.'

'And did you?'

'I felt I'd done enough to appease the people so I retraced my steps, walking back to the station and decided to return home.'

'LIAR!' Mr White said in a thundering voice.

I nearly jumped out of my skin.

'MR WHITE,' the judge said sternly, 'This is not a circus, and I don't intend to let you turn it into one. How dare you tell the defendant that he's a liar when you've no evidence.'

'I'm sorry your honour but I have proof that Mr Rosso is lying under oath.'

'Mr White, this is a very serious allegation. Any more outbursts like this and I'll hold you in contempt.'

Mr White faced Rosso. 'Perhaps you'd be good enough to tell us what really happened.'

'I'm ... telling the truth.'

'Then, why is it that your watch was found at the scene of the crime?' This time Mr White spoke very softly.

'My...watch,' Rosso said, his voice quavering, and a look of fear spreading over his face. 'That's not possible. I have my watch.'

'You have your watch,' Mr White said. Giving him a fixed stare he ordered the court usher to pass something over to him.

Everybody leaned over to get a closer look.

'Is that it?' Mr White said quietly.

'No.'

'Where is it then? Are you wearing it?'

'No. I lost it.'

'Have a closer look,' Mr White said as he walked towards the defendant.

'Is it yours?'

'No.'

'Can you explain then, Mr Rosso, how your fingerprints cam to be on it?'

Just then the briefing solicitor raked through a huge bundle of papers and passed one to the defence barrister. The defence barrister glanced at it, with a look of intense annoyance, stood up and said, 'Your honour, in view of the circumstances I would like to request a short recess.'

The judge glanced at the courtroom clock. It was five minutes to twelve.

'This is unusual but in view of the circumstances and the time factor I will order a recess until 2 p.m.'

With that she stood up and swept out looking annoyed.

64

MY MOUTH was dry but I felt elated. Mr White was running rings around Rosso. I scooted to the canteen for a cup of tea and a piece of fruitcake. As I sat, sipping my beverage, I spotted Pat pushing his tray to the check out.

'Hello. What do you think of that fiasco then,' Pat said as he approached my table and sat down. 'Clearly he's as guilty as hell. Nothing will save him now.'

'The QC is brill, isn't he?'

'Yes, fancy misplacing the evidence about the watch.'

As we chatted a man sat down at an adjoining table and begun to read the Daily Telegraph. I noticed he had large hands and on one of his huge hands there was a signet ring. As I glanced over I caught him staring at me.

I turned to Pat and then glanced surreptitiously again. He was glaring. Quickly he averted his eyes.

'Do you see that man at the next table?'

Pat twisted around. 'What about him?'

'He's watching us. Do you know him?'

'He's a client of Danny's. His name's Karl Von Lichtenhof.'

'What's he doing here at the trial?'

'He's probably interested, like me, like everyone else.'

I looked over again. His eyes were still riveted on me but this time I glimpsed a hint of malevolence sweeping over his features.

'Did you see that look of hatred on his face?'

'Alex, there you go again, imagining things.'

'I'm not. Honest. If looks could kill I'd be dead.'

Just then Ken appeared. 'It's time to go in Alex.'

As I passed Von Lichtenhof's table he avoided my stare.

This time I sat next to Ken and Bill near the front of the gallery.

As the judge made her entrance Ken turned to me and whispered. 'Alex, I want you to turn around and see do you recognise anyone in the back row.'

I swung round. Two strangers, a Laurel and Hardy were sitting there. Turning back I whispered, 'Never seen them in my life.'

'Henchmen,' he whispered. 'I thought the skinny one might be the one you saw the night of the murder.'

"No! What are they doing here?'

'Who knows? Maybe they're here to make sure Bruno doesn't squeal.'

Just then Rosso took the witness stand. You could hear a pin drop as Mr. White begun. 'Well, Mr Rosso, would you like to tell us what really happened?'

Rosso shifted from one leg to the other and started to speak. 'This man put a gun to my head. He tells me to follow my solicitor. I start off in the direction Nicholas has gone. I walk in the direction I am told until we come to 50, Coombe Road.'

'Indeed.'

'He then tells me to ring the doorbell. As the door opens, I'm pushed aside. The man enters the house. I stand, semi shocked, near to the front door. This man grabs Nicholas around the neck and has him pinned against the wall. I see him raise a knife. He holds it against Nicholas's face as he threatens him. Then I move towards this man who has his back to me. I stretch and grab his right arm that has the knife in it. I swear at his man as we three struggled. The knife drops to the floor. Then the three of us fall to the floor me behind the other guy, Nicholas facing him and obviously him in the middle. It's at this point and only this point that my watch and cap came to be at the scene as they came off during the struggle.'

'Now maybe we are getting nearer to the truth.' Mr White said quietly.

For me some of it began to make sense. It told me that the first noise I'd heard was the three of them falling to the ground.

'We get to our feet. The white man has the gun pointed at Nicholas and me. I'm nearer the front door. The man says, "Keep the fuck out of this; it's not your beef. I panic and I decamp from the house.'

'So you left Nicholas to face an armed man with a gun and a knife?'

'Yes. I know it was cowardly but the man had the gun trained at me. Nicholas was alive and standing when I left the house. I rang Hart and told him that Nicholas didn't turn up for the meeting. I was going to tell him the truth but decided against it and lied to him just to stall him until the next day as I should be getting paid and I didn't want him getting the police involved.'

'I decided to try to get a bus to Liverpool and pick up my car from the fitness centre. I rang my ex girlfriend, Janet whom I was still good friends with. And told her what had happened. She even said I should have a bath at hers.'

"Why? To get rid of the evidence?'

'It was me who showed Janet the bit of blood on my left hand sleeve. I asked her to get me a black bin liner. I put a tracksuit on and put my clothes apart from my jacket in the sports bag. I put my jacket in the bin liner and went home. Next day Hart rang me. His exact words were "Nicholas has topped himself." 'He'd rung Nicholas's office and had been told. I didn't believe him. We met at TGI Fridays. He told me to call Nicholas's office. I did so. I spoke to DI. Warner. He informed me Nicholas had been murdered. I said I had business with Nicholas and I gave him my home number and my name and address.'

'What was your reaction?'

'I was totally shocked. I did get one 'phone call early that morning from an unknown man stating if the police got them they'd get me.'

The QC glanced at his watch it was nearly 4 p.m.

As if on cue the judge interjected.' I feel this is a good time to conclude the proceedings today.' Everyone stood up as she swept out.

65

IT WAS the last day of the trial. I arrived just as Mr White was saying, 'Ladies and gentlemen of the jury it is your duty to bring in a verdict. There I rest my case.'

I decided not to stay to hear what the defence barrister had to say so I headed for the canteen and waited. Two hours later I watched intently as the jury filed back in. The judge asked the foreman of the jury to read out the verdict.

The foreman stood up. 'We the jury find the defendant guilty.'

The judge rose to pronounce the sentence. 'Stand up Rosso.' In a harsh tone she addressed him, 'You've committed a brutal crime and I sentence you to life imprisonment. I recommend that you serve a minimum of eighteen years for this heinous crime.'

The crowd stood up as the judge made her exit.

Outside the court, the media homed in on me as I tried to make a dash for my car.

Questions like, "Are you pleased with the ruling," were hurled at me. I felt that I had to give some response. 'Yes but the second killer is still free. I know what he looks like and I intend to hunt him down.' What a statement to make in front of millions of viewers and the killer. But I couldn't retract it. I didn't know then it was to have far reaching consequences for me.

'FOOL.' THE GUTTURAL WHISPER CAME FROM HIS LIPS INVOLUNTARILY, CAME FROM THE DIM SHADOWS OF THE ROOM, AND CAME FROM A VOICE WHOSE SINISTER UNDERTONES

PERMEATED THE SILENCE LIKE A SINGLE SHOT FROM A GUN. IT WAS ALL THERE LOOMING BEFORE HIM, THE COURT STEPS, THE WOMAN, TV CAMERAS, HER WORDS, 'I KNOW WHAT HE LOOKS LIKE" HE PICKED UP THE RECEIVER AND BANGED OUT A NUMBER. 'FIND OUT WHAT SHE KNOWS.'

'DONE.'

A THIN FLICKER OF EXCITEMENT MOVED COLDLY IN HIS STOMACH AS HE REPLACED THE HANDSET. HE SAT DOWN. NOW A DULL FIRE BURNED IN HIS BROWN EYES AND THERE WAS A TOUCH OF EXTRA COLOUR IN HIS PALE CHEEKS. HE WAS NOW CALM, RELAXED, AND PROFOUNDLY CERTAIN OF THE OUTCOME. HE WOULD BE TRIUMPHANT.

66

THE WEIGHTLESS dark of early evening had descended by the time I returned to the house.

That night I deliberated, writing bullet points in my diary to try and make sense of it all:

- Why kill Nicholas if he had had the money.
- That way they'd never get it back.
- If they'd wanted him dead then they'd have remained, and finished Nicholas off and then me.
- But they'd fled leaving Nicholas alive to tell the tale or so they thought.
- Did they know that a fatal stab wound had severed an artery?
- It all looked like an interrogation gone wrong.
- And who was this man I'd seen?
- The murder didn't seem to be planned.
- Why kill him in the house where they risked been seen.

I paced up and down the sitting room trying to focusing on the points I'd made but to no avail. Better make a brew and clear my head.

As I circled the room I peered out the bay window into the tree-lined avenue. All was quiet, not a soul stirred. Just as I twisted away my attention was drawn to a person standing near the oak tree. It was a bag lady. A woollen hat was pulled down over her ears and forehead. What looked like an old mohair coat was pulled tightly around her with cord, the long brown skirt beneath reached to the ankles. There was something about her, the set expression of her face, the eyes that darted from side to side that I found strange. She stood, momentarily, now in the light of the street lamp, staring across at my house; then quickly slipped back into the shadows.

Odd! Was I under surveillance? Don't be silly Alex she's just some fruitcake with nothing better to do but to stand around doing nothing. I quickly drew the curtains and switched on the light. I tried to watch CSI Miami but I was over the edge again. Rushing sounds like a cascading waterfall filled my skull like a surge of madness, this incorrigible madness I found myself in. I shivered feeling the cold talons of evil throttling me. Then I knew I had to visit Rosso. I had to move things forward.

67

'I'M REALLY grateful that you have actually taken the trouble to come and see me, especially under the circumstances.' Bruno Rosso said with a nervous smile.

I was sitting in a prison hall speaking to Rosso. The room was like a large church hall. Thirty or so melamine-covered tables were spaced evenly apart with chairs around each one. It was full of wives and some children. Near the entrance there was a dais where three prison guards lounged at a table chatting. They seemed relaxed.

My attention refocused on the man sitting opposite me. This was beyond surreal. Here I am sitting opposite Nicholas's murderer. I stared at his hands mesmerized by the large knuckles and long fingers, nails bitten to the quick. The fingers twisted –no, strangled the corner of the sleeve of his sweater. I imagined those same hands catching Nicholas around his throat in a vice grip as the second attacker rained blow after blow down on him.

I continued to study him. Bruno Rosso was medium sized with a body of a trained athlete. His eyes were sultry brown, slanting downwards, giving him a slightly oriental appearance.

Leaning towards him I blurted out over the tightness in my throat. 'Did you kill Nicholas?'

'You're like the rest of them.' The low guttural accusation came from somewhere deep and dead. 'You want me to confess to something I didn't do.' His hands tore a hole in the sleeve of the jumper. 'I was there but I didn't kill Nicholas. Somewhere out there, Alex, there's an ogre. He's evil personified – the devil incarnate himself.'

Could I believe him? I stared and said, 'Well let's hear your side of the story then.'

He unravelled the hem of his sweater wrapping the thread around his little finger, pulling it so tight that the tip bulged red.

Is that how he held Nicholas? Until his eyes bulged.

He spoke softly then as he stared into the distance past. 'It all began when I was first introduced to Danny. I would guess it was in 1998.'

He paused. 'I was buying and selling bankrupt stock. Danny set up his own company. He said he could pass on business to me. Danny impressed me.'

And Nicholas and me.

'Anyhow, to continue, I became involved too much in Danny's business and neglected my own. Nicholas's role there was to be their solicitor. I loaned Nicholas ten grand in 1998. He told me he was setting up an import-export company to buy and sell antique jewellery.'

I froze. It was I who had set up this and funded it. He had lied to Rosso. I wonder what he did with the money.

'He said he might have clients who needed cash. He asked me not to tell Danny or anyone else about our business together.'

Dark horse!

'It was now approximately end of 1998. Things were going wrong. I was losing clients' money from making some bad decisions.'

There was a silence. So maybe this is how he lost client's investments risking them in dicey deals.

'Go on.'

'I distanced myself from Danny and Nicholas early in 1999. My other business had been greatly affected and I tried to get things back in order.' There was a quickening in his voice as he continued. 'I'm quite sure I'd no contact with Nicholas or Danny in the year of 1999. Slowly I started trying to arrange loans by being a broker working from home and things started to improve.'

'So when did you get in touch with Nicholas again?'

'I think 2003. Nicholas asked me over to his office to have a chat. He told me he was into something that would bring in vast sums of money.'

The deal that was going to make them all rich.

'We decided to lay down some ground rules. Firstly we decided to handle only cash. Also he said he'd only deal with me and not my clients. He insisted on keeping our business strictly private. I asked Nicholas for his phone number but he wouldn't give it. I now know why. It was your number. He said I could always call him at the office. He didn't want to have business calls at home.'

So this is why I never knew about Nicholas's shady deals with Rosso.

'This leads me to April when I invested with Nicholas £200,000. I think reading between the lines, Nicholas invested it with Danny.'

'In other words through Danny?'

Just then the bell rang announcing the end of visiting hours. 'I'll have to go,' I said.

'I'll write to you and tell you the rest of the story.' Rosso said and then added, 'I hope all this gives you a little more insight into how certain matters worked.'

Driving out the prison gates I though deeply about my conversation with Rosso. I sensed a lot of what he said was true but knew, from Ken, that he twisted the truth when it suited him. One thing I did know. Nicholas's death had exposed a dark grisly secret as if there was a grotesque deformity that previously lay hidden on the body of our relationship.

The man in the Mercedes punched out a number on his cell phone.

After a few pulses of the ringing tones, a voice answered.

'Yes.'

'She's just left the prison.'

'Interesting!'

'Do I do anything?'

'No. I'll contact our man. He knows the score.'

'What if she finds out?'

'She won't. Remember no one knows.'

'Okay'.

He pressed the OFF button on his mobile - his face a mask of pure, mind-less evil.

68

TWO DAYS later I received a letter from Bruno Rosso thanking me for my visit.

I read and reread the letter. He's so convincing, I mused, but could I believe anything he said? But I knew some of the things he'd mentioned were true. Was what the QC said, true? I wasn't sure anymore. The attack was amateurish and a frenzied one. Surely if Rosso had planned to murder Nicholas he'd have carried out the deed in some alleyway. After all, Ken had told me that he had a black belt in karate. None of it made sense.

I made three more visits to see Rosso. On one occasion I was accompanied by Rosso's solicitor Jane Archer. As I drove she had suddenly said: 'I've dealt with one hundred and fifty lifers and Bruno is the only one who has convinced me of his innocence. I believe him when he says he wasn't involved in the stabbing itself.'

I sighed 'Why doesn't he tell us who the white guy is?'

Her voice was quiet as she answered. 'Either he doesn't know or he's afraid. Then she added, 'There's one person though who might be able to provide some answers.'

My heart beat quickened. 'Who.'

She frowned, raking her fingers through her blonde hair and said, 'I'm not happy with you pursuing this on your own. Don't you think you should leave it to the police?'

I shrugged. 'As far as the police are concerned they've got their man and are happy to close the case. But not me. I'll pursue this to the bitter end.' My voice was hard now.

'I can see you're determined. I think I'd be if I were in your shoes. Anyhow I suggest you have a chat with Geoff

Baker. He's a barrister and knows a lot about what's going on in the street. He, like me, believes Bruno is innocent. This is his number,' she said handing me a card.

Jane sighed. 'Well good luck and let me know what you find out.'

69

KEN LEANED back in the chair. 'Alex, I can't believe you visited Rosso in prison.'

'Well, I did,' I said defensively as I circled the kitchen to the sink and filled the kettle to make tea.

'Can't you see you're only inviting trouble? He's a murderer and he's only using you to get out.' He frowned and shook his head.

'Do you really believe he killed Nicholas? I'm not so sure any more.' My voice was small like a child's.

'Alex you're so naive. You worry me sometimes. I've no doubt what so ever that he did it.' He took off his spectacles and rubbed his eyes before putting them back on.

Mustn't tell him about the lead I've got. 'But it doesn't make sense. It was so amateurish, killing him in the house. Why not in a dark alleyway?'

'Christ Alex, a jury found him guilty. He grimaced. 'What did he have to say anyhow?'

I gave him a gist of what we'd discussed. 'He's very convincing you know. Read one of his letters and you'll see.' I fished out the letter from a nearby drawer and handed it to Ken.

As Ken read the letter I busied myself making tea.

'Well what do you think?'

He leaned forward. 'Alex, I have to admit he's very persuasive and maybe he wasn't the one who wielded the knife but he was there.' He shrugged.

'But he says that he'd left the house when Nicholas received the fatal blow.'

'He was part of a conspiracy to harm Nicholas so therefore by law he's guilty. And I don't believe he doesn't know who the other guy is. I'm afraid Alex as far as I'm concerned he's guilty either of the actual murder or he's an accessory. If on the other hand he tells us who the other man is and where the money is, then we might be prepared to look into his case again.'

'He said he gave most of that money back to his clients. He says they're lying.'

'All eight can't be telling porkies. Look, I have to go. Just then the doorbell rang. 'It's your priest friend again,' Ken said with a deadpan expression.

I arched an eyebrow. 'How do you know? It could be Donal, anyone.'

'Just a hunch, Alex, that's all. Bet I'm right though.'

'You're impossible,' I said laughingly as I strolled out to answer the door. 'So it's you, father,' I said as I opened it.

'Oh, sorry, Alex. Am I intruding?'

I laughed. 'Not at all, father. It's just that Ken said that it might be you and he was right.'

'So Ken's here then? I'll only stay a few minutes.'

I noticed an unease sweep across his features. He doesn't like Ken, that's for sure.

'A pleasure to meet you again, Ken,' Patrick said as he entered the kitchen.

'Likewise,' Ken replied, sardonically, remaining seated. 'It looks like we all take turns seeing Alex is okay,' Ken said, pokerfaced.

'I only popped in for a sec to check on her.' Anger seems to make two bright red spots appear on his cheeks. God what is it between those two?

'It's good to know that Alex has such caring friends,' Ken said woodenly.

What's with the attitude? I'll tackle him later about it.

'I'm off, Alex. Something's come up about the murder. I need to check it out.'

'Anything interesting,' Father O'Malley asked casually.

'Yes, as a matter of fact, but as you know I'm not allowed to discuss the case with the general public.'

'Come on detective you surely don't consider me as part of the general milieu. I'm a man of the cloth remember.'

'So you are, so you are,' Ken replied. 'I must bear that in mind.'

I was taken aback. Ken was deliberately being rude to Patrick.

The next day Ken rang up on some pretext. 'By the way Ken I've a bone to pick with you.'

'I think I know who the bone is.'

'Yes, it's about Patrick. You don't like him do you?'

'No.'

'Why?'

'Just a hunch Alex.'

'There you go again, Ken with one of your hunches.'

'I don't like these men you're surrounding yourself with. One of them could be connected to the killers. A spy in the camp so to speak.'

Unfazed I answered him. 'You're mad Ken. These people are my friends. What have you to go on anyhow?'

'Nothing, but take Pat for instance. We both know that he's besotted with Danny. If I didn't know otherwise I'd say they were an item.'

'It's obvious that Danny's not gay,' I replied bitingly. 'Not with his reputation with women.'

'Yes, but Pat's another kettle of fish. There's something strange about him. Anyhow Alex I really feel you should be more careful whom you allow into your house.'

'Ken you're so suspicious and illogical. So who else is on your list?'

'Anyone who comes within ten yards of you. Got to go Alex. Got to go. He disconnected.'

After Ken rang off, I reflected on his words. Should I heed his warning and distance myself from Pat and the priest. I thought of Pat and his words, 'We were a single soul dwelling in two bodies.' No. Pat's kosher. Then I thought about the priest, his patience, about the gooey- egg and his tenderness. He understood me, understood my grief. He's a true friend as a man of God should be. I'm damned if I'm going to be dictated to by Ken. But if I'm to take Ken's advice then I should be including him in the scenario. After all Ken could be on the take. It's been known to happen.

70

THE NEXT morning was serene, with a sunrise of warm purple mixed with rose. I breakfasted early and decided to go shopping. The street was crowded as I walked along immersed in my own musings. A gaggle of hoodies stood at a street corner. I suddenly thought I heard my name. Alex - a single, long drawn out sound that soared on a soft breeze lingering in the rooftops. I froze and then pivoted round. No one! I scanned the buildings and then looked up and down the busy bustling street craning my neck but the source of the sound had gone. I saw a stranger in a peaked cap and wondered had it been him. I told myself that I'd imagined it, that I'd been mistaken. Or maybe it was another woman called Alex walking along. What was happening in my life had put me on edge and I'd imagined it all. But a tiny voice prodded – no Alex its you. Was I being stalked?

71

A DAY later Lynda rang me and announced, 'I'm having my entire house redecorated so I'll have to find somewhere to live for a few months. Any chance I could stay with you love. I'll be a paying guest.'

'I'd love you to stay, Lynda.'

Two days later Lynda moved in.

That night we sat chatting at the kitchen table. I regaled her with tales of the parties I'd been to. 'Guess what happened last week when I went to that cocktail party?'

Lynda cast me an affectionate glance. 'Knowing you my love it could be anything.'

'The hostess is stinking rich and owns a string of hotels in Liverpool.'

'So, come on, tell me, what did you do?' Lynda said affectionately.

'Well, when I was in the loo my beady eye spotted a bottle of Christian Dior on the table. Rushing out, I had forgotten to wear some so guess what I did?'

'Go on, shock me.'

'Well I opened the bottle and inadvertently poured about half the contents down the inside of my dress.'

'You didn't?'

I smiled wickedly. 'Yes, but that's not all. The stuff was more powerful than I imagined. Smelling like a great perfumed cloud, I wondered how I'd disguise the odour.'

'So what happened?'

'Coming out, I saw a couple of women wrinkle their noses as I wafted by them. Then the hostess looked at me suspiciously and narrowed her eyes. I could tell what she was thinking: You come to my house, bring a cheap bottle of plonk and then help yourself to my expensive perfume.'

Lynda laughed, her blue eyes crinkled at the side as she responded to my humour. 'Alex how could you do it. I'd be mortified.'

'How did I know that the stuff was going to spill all over me? I meant to try only a little bit. Anyhow, I tried to behave myself for the rest of the night and make up for the 'faux pas' by being the model guest.

Lynda gazed at her and shaking her head said, 'I shouldn't think you'll be invited there again.

'How's the job going?'

'Half the personnel are fossils, the other half are too hassled to notice there's a life out there.'

'I know what you mean.'

'To change the subject do you fancy a power walk in the park tomorrow? Alex? I've the day off work.'

'What time?'

'Around ten.'

'By the way, Alex I didn't want to tell you this in case I'd scare you but I feel you ought to know.' A look of concern flashed over her countenance.

My heart skipped a beat.

'There was a woman by the oak tree last night. She appeared to be watching the house.'

'What did she look like?'

'A sort of derelict. She had a threadbare overcoat tied around the waist with cord.'

'Probably some homeless person with nothing better to do.' I didn't want to tell Lynda I'd seen her. It might scare her too.

'That's a nice photo of Catherine,' Lynda suddenly said. Maybe she was trying to change the subject. I looked over to the photo of Catherine attached to the fridge by a magnet. In it Catherine was a toddler and naked on the lawn drenching me with the water hose and laughing into the camera.

I smiled. 'You know, she's the most precious thing in my life. I couldn't bear it if anything happened to her.'

'Don't be silly, Alex. Nothing will.'

'Of course not.' But my thoughts turned to the gargoyle.

'I dig the shades and the sun hat,' Lynda said as we exited the house the following morning.

'Stops the UV rays from burning my skin.'

As Lynda and I crossed the road the bag lady was standing in the shadows of the oak tree. 'There she is again.'

'What's she up to?' Lynda frowned.

'Don't know that's why I want to get a good look at her this time. When we pass I'm deliberately going to bump into her. See what her reaction is.'

'Good thinking Batman. I'll try and get a closer look too.' She gave me the thumbs up.

As I hurried past the woman I pretended to stumble knocking her bag sideways.

'Watch what you're doing,' a gruff voice said. The face was now contorted, a mass of twisted fury, the eyes squinting, the mouth open, sucking air, baring white teeth that took on the appearance of an animal.

I rushed past feeling a single nightmarish jolt of shock that almost froze me to the spot.

'That's not a woman, Alex.' Lynda looked shaken.

'I know. It's a man's voice.' The fear was inside me again like a cancer.

Lynda was white.

'Did you see the shoes? They're men's. I'm positive it's a man. Another thing, when I stared down at his hands I felt I had seen them before and somewhere recently.'

'His hands? What was so unusual about them?

'Well, they're very sinewy and large.'

'Why do you think he's hanging around here?' Lynda bit her lower lip.

'I don't know. Maybe it's something to do with the murder.'

'I should tell the police if I were you, Alex. Better be safe than sorry. And I've a feeling you won't see him again.'

'Why?'

'Didn't you notice that flash of fear and then fury that registered on his face when you bumped into him? He wasn't expecting it so, without thought, he spoke and gave the game away.'

'I wish I could recall where I saw those hands before.' My brow furrowed.

'It will come to you Alex when you least expect it. Try not to worry.'

But fear had already kicked in, that intense terror that starts in the pit of your stomach and tears through you like a jet until it infects every part and is ready to develop into outright panic.

72

'THERE SHE IS.'

There were two of them. No less sinister than their size and muscular build was their stealthy progress through that shadowed world. They were like phantoms in human clothing.

The two men following the woman wore anoraks with hoods pulled over their heads partially obscuring their features. The rain slashed incessantly into their faces as they stalked her.

The woman wore a windcheater and was almost completely hidden by the large black umbrella she was carrying. A cold November night, the gales had blown all day and now the rain added to the chaos. Branches of trees lay strewn along the path and made progress difficult.

'Are you sure it's her?' one of them asked as they trailed soundlessly in the drenching deluge.

'Of course I'm fucking sure. You know 'who', pointed her out the other night. She's got jet black hair and blue eyes.'

'This is the plan then. We tail her to the house and when she goes in we wait a few minutes. We'll go around the back and get in through the dining room window. I've sussed the joint out and that's the best room to break into as it's quite far back. No one will hear us.'

'Let's hope there're no hitches,' the taller of the two said.

Impatiently the small man looked at the other and said, 'What do you take me for, an amateur?'

'OK. Have the blade ready; rough her up if necessary to get her to talk.'

The woman in front turned left into Coombe Road, walked fifty yards and then turned into number 50, unlocked the door and entered.

'Ready,' the small one said as he lit a cigarette.

'For fuck sake put that fag out. Do you want to draw attention to yourself?' the tall man said in a whisper. 'I hope our look out is near the house. We'll have to make a quick get-a-way.'

'There he is, parked on the other side.'

The two men walked silently along. No one in sight the tall one thought. The street was empty, not a soul stirred. The rain was easing off now but the wind seemed to be whipping up to another gale as it blew around the chimneys of the old Victorian houses.

Stealthily they trailed through the alleyway to the back gate. In a second the taller one was over it and the other one followed. Moving to the rear of the house they came to the dining room window. They paused. Nimbly the tall one took the cutter from its pouch, and quickly cut the glass. Silently he placed the glass against the fence. Nodding, he motioned for the small one to follow. They climbed through the gap.

The tall one moved steadily towards the door. He stood listening. There was the sound of the television coming from upstairs. He gave the door of the dining room a gentle kick with his foot. It yielded, soundlessly, opening a little wider. He paused and then shoved it again. The anticipated sound of a creaking door didn't come and now it was open enough for him to pass. In the hallway there stood a large bookcase, which impaired his passage. In his effort to get past without undue noise he accidentally knocked a heavy book which was jutting out. It fell to the floor making an almighty crash. He froze; unable to move so great was his terror. The sound was frightening and in that instant he felt that the book had become endowed with its own personality alerting the woman upstairs to the impending danger. He paused, trembling; feeling the blood thundering through his veins while the sound of his breathing was like the breaking of a cold grey sea on stones. He was shit scared. He'd never been involved in anything like this before.

Someone was moving about. A door suddenly opened.

Furtively, he darted back into the dining room. He stayed, stationary, not daring to move a muscle. Already he felt he was fucking it up. Footsteps! Someone was descending the stairs. He glanced behind him. Naked fear registered on the small man's face. The tall man, regaining his calm demeanour, steadily moved towards the front of the hall. The other one followed. The tall one's face was a mask, except for a look of utter concentration. Slowly he produced a pistol from his inside pocket. Both men remained motionless, pinning themselves against the wall as a figure appeared.

It was she all right. No one could mistake the black hair and the blue eyes. She's heading for the kitchen, the tall man thought. Slowly, silently, he moved behind her, and whispered, as he put his hand over her mouth. 'Say one word and you're dead.'

The woman moved her head violently, but immediately the tall man dug the barrel of the pistol into the side of her head. There was a look of intense fear in her eyes. Her nostrils quivered, and some unknown nerve shook her lips, and left them trembling. He moved in front of her and pushed the woman up against the wall and digging the muzzle of the gun deeper into the side of her head. 'I'm going to remove my hand from your mouth; scream and you're a goner.' He did so slowly.

Terrified the woman, stood there. By now her face was ashen. She tried to mutter something but the point of the gun was pushed further into her temple.

'Right, you're going to tell us where the money is. One false move and you get this.' Like lightning he took from his pocket a six-inch sharp knife and with his left hand put it to her throat. 'I don't want to have to rough up that pretty face of yours but if you don't tell us where the money is I'm afraid your beauty will be a thing of the past.'

Her face registered sheer horror and bewilderment.

'Come on, we haven't all night. Where is it?' the tall one said as he put the knife to her cheek. His face was contorted with rage.

Suddenly the woman lunged at him.

Momentarily startled by the distraction, the tall man said, viciously, 'What the fuck do you think you're playing at.'

Taking him unawares, the woman was able to dodge to one side and ran down the hall, screaming. She tried to run towards the door. Like lightning, the tall man was on her. With a vicious tug to her hair he dragged her towards him and put the gun to her head but she fought back.

With blinding fury he growled, 'You fucking bitch,' and hit her a blow that sent her reeling, but she managed to stay on her feet as she lunged towards him again.

'Come on, you bloody vixen,' the tall man said, waving the gun at her, 'I'm going to let you have it.'

A shout from behind him made him twist around.

'For God's sake leave her, we've fucked up.' It was the smaller one. 'Let's get out of here before it is too late.' He opened the door and ran.

She darted forward again and the tall man pointed the gun at her and fired. Then, turning on his heels, he surged through the door.

She fell to the floor, blood pouring from her head. She lay there the blood still spurting from a deep wound on her temple. She stirred slightly. Slowly with a gigantic effort she dragged herself to the front door and crawled towards the gate. But she couldn't make it. She was falling...falling under the pitch-black sky. And then the falling stopped, everything stopped, and there was stillness. She could hear her own breathing. And footsteps, she could hear footsteps... a dog barking and the sound of a door closing followed by the rolling, disruptive noise beneath her, in front of her... somewhere. There was a dull pain in the side of her head and it began to radiate over her face. She opened her mouth to shout for help, but she couldn't utter a sound. A warm red stream began to pour out from the side of her head and stained the green grass of the lawn a bright scarlet. She lay there, her breathing now becoming slow and laboured as her life's blood flowed out of her.

The wind had mellowed to a breeze and the softened rain fell on her. No one had heard the disturbance; all was still, silent.

73

OUT OF the dark night came a figure walking his dog. The animal stopped at the gate and growled, sensing danger.

'Come on Rex,' the man said, tugging at the dog's lead but the animal wouldn't budge and growled again baring his teeth. It was then the stranger noticed the figure lying motionless on the sodden pathway. Quickly he bent down and shook her. 'Are you okay?' he asked as he turned her on her side. A look of horror washed over his face when he saw the blood stained face, white and totally still. She looked dead. On further examination he saw that her eyes were half open, with a faint glimmer still glowing in them. Her jaw had fallen loose and her sprawled legs were spread across the path with one arm flung out sideways while her pink fingers curled upwards as if she was appealing to someone.

Swiftly he stood up and dashed across the road to his house and pressed the bell several times.

'What the hell is going on?' his wife shouted, as she flung the door wide open.

'For God's sake, love, call the police. There's a woman half dead over there. I think she's been shot.' He swivelled and dashed back across the road.

A look of incredulity washed over her face for an instant and then she ran to the 'phone and, grabbing it, dialled 999.

'Operator, there's been a shooting, at 50 Coombe Road. Get an ambulance and the police straight away. Hurry, please hurry!' Banging the phone down, she exited the house and rushed across the road to help.

The husband was checking the woman's pulse and turning to his wife he said, 'Get some help.'

As she raced in to the middle of the avenue a car careered around the corner and almost collided with her.

'Stop, stop', she shouted banging, on the bonnet of the slowing car as she hopped out of the way.

A man jumped out, anger registered on his face. 'What the hell, are you nuts or something, I could have run you over?'

'There's been a shooting,' she shouted, grabbing the man's arm.

Alerted to the danger the man jogged towards the house and recoiled as he saw the body. 'Oh, Jesus Christ, ' he said, putting his hand to his mouth as he looked down at the woman. 'Is she dead?'

'No, there's a flicker of life there yet but if the ambulance doesn't get here quickly it will be too late. The driver of the car bent and tried the woman's pulse. 'It's weak. I'm a vet,' he said as he gingerly examined the gunshot wound in her head. 'I'll try and stem the flow of blood until help arrives but I daren't move her, it could be fatal.'

The sirens could be heard above the rooftops.

A crowd had gathered. Someone said, 'Its close.'

'Do you know her?' the vet asked the husband as they stood anxiously waiting.

'I've just moved in across the road. I think it's the house owner. I've seen her entering the house a few times.'

'I'm not from around here myself.'

An ambulance screamed to a stop. Light pulsated, turning the avenue into a flashing vortex of blue and red. Two paramedics, jumped out, one quickly checked her pulse and said in a low voice, 'It's faint. Let's go.' Within seconds she was on a stretcher, and into the ambulance and gone.'

As the ambulance drove off, sirens blazing, a police car screamed to a halt. Four policemen leapt out. An unmarked then drew up. Ken jumped out, charged up the path and grabbed the neighbour by the coat.

'What's happened?' It isn't...'and he stopped, feeling choked, and then continued, 'Is it Alex, the woman of the house?'

'Yes,' the neighbour replied,' the ambulance has just taken her away.'

'Oh God, when will this ever end?' Tears started to roll down his face. He had let her down again. The last five minutes had been the worst he'd ever experienced. He felt responsible and knew that if she died he could never forgive himself. He felt he should have done more to protect her.

The husband broke him out of his abstraction said, 'She's been shot, but she's not dead.'

Another unmarked car pulled up. Peter Gibson hopped out and made a beeline for Ken. His features were tight and drawn. In a quavering voice, he said, 'Is it Alex?'

'Yes.'

'I should have kept up the surveillance on the house and never have become complacent.'

'It's not your fault Ken; we weren't to know.'

Ken stood on the pavement, dazed. His body, inside his grey suit, looked limp, and his arms hung straight down from the shoulders as if his brain had forgotten they were there. His eyes were stark with shock and disillusionment.

By now scenes of crime officers were already busy cordoning off the area.

Ken, slowly, like a man in a trance, looked at his watch. 8.0 o'clock. He said to his boss, 'A bit like the last time only now it's Alex. Let's hope she doesn't die.' The thought sent a terrible shudder down his spine.

74

IT WAS 8.0 p.m. as Donal climbed into his car. The chill wind of autumn blew a multi coloured medley of fallen leaves around, and oppressive scurrying clouds threatened another downpour of rain.

It was then he heard them, Police sirens screaming out over the city. Hm, the mating call of the panda cars. He was on his way to play his harmonica at a local pub. Alex had told him she'd be there. It had become a habit of hers, dropping in every Tuesday night now after her Singles Club and staying until closing time. She seems happy enough, he thought as he drove. Still, after all these years, he still felt deeply about her. As he glanced at the petrol gauge he saw the tank was nearly empty. He pulled into the local petrol station, filled up and strolled to the kiosk to pay. Just as he got to window he spotted an ambulance with its blue turret lights revolving inauspicious as it drove like blazes on its mercy dash.

'Hello dere,' he said in his best Irish accent. 'It's a bad night, tonight?'

'Yes and a bad night for another murder!'

'What do you mean?' Donal said, staring at the attendant. He'd known Fred for about twenty years now and they were on the best of terms always joking and laughing together.

'Someone's been in and said there's been a shooting or something in Coombe Avenue.'

Donal's heart skipped a beat.

'Alex. It can't … be her.'

'Got to go,' he shouted as he hurried to his car. He jumped in and headed for Alex's house. Horrifying thoughts ran through his mind. Had anything happened to her? His hands started to tremble and he gripped the steering wheel harder to steady himself, all the time muttering, 'It can't be her.' She said she was going to the singles club.

As he got to the road a crowd had gathered. Just like when Nicholas was murdered, he thought. His mouth was dry and he could feel the fear in his throat. He parked at the end of the road, jumped out of the car, pushed through the crowd and addressed a stranger, 'What's going on?'

'There's been a shooting at number 50,' the stranger said. 'A woman's been shot.'

Donal didn't wait to hear the rest. He let out a roar and charged up the road like a bull, 'Alex, Alex,' he shouted as he dashed up the path. A policeman tried to stop him but he pushed him roughly to one side. It was then he came face to face with Ken.

Something was burning deep inside him. Rage aimed at Masterson and Gibson - the whole fucking world. The words would not come out, he stood there staring, trying to say something. An overwhelming grief came over him. He couldn't face what he was about to find out, the knowledge that she might be dead.

Ken put his hand out and touched his sleeve gently and attempted to say something but Donal was overwrought and lunged at him.

'Why didn't you protect her you bastard?'

Startled Ken drew back as two policemen caught hold of Donal. 'She's still alive Donal,' he said urgently. 'But we don't know if she'll make it.'

'If she dies I'll hold you personally responsible.'

Ken remained silent. Just then his mobile rang.

Pressing a button he listened. His face froze. A look of absolute grief washed over his face. 'Five minutes ago.'

Donal stared at him his face crumbling.

'She's dead,' Ken whispered, tears escaping and rolling down his cheeks.

'Dead, she can't be,' Donal said his face a puckered wreck of grief.

He put his head in his hands and wept.

75

MEANWHILE A National News flash at nine o'clock, told the story.

'A woman has been shot in the area of Crosby in Liverpool at the same house where Nicholas Murray was murdered a few years ago. Details are slowly emerging but it's not known yet whether the woman is dead or not. The identity of the woman is not yet known but it appears that she fits the description of the partner of the solicitor, Nicholas Murray.'

'Oh my God, Oh my God!' Deirdre stood staring at the TV and started to scream. 'Mum, Mum, it can't be you.' She rushed to the phone and dialled 999.

Yelling down the phone she demanded, 'I want to fucking know who the person is that was shot in Crosby in Liverpool.'

The operator was startled and tried to calm her down. 'Look I don't know; you'll have to ring Crosby police station.'

Slamming the receiver down, Deirdre screamed. 'Oh, it's horrible; please God don't let it be Mum, don't let her be dead.'

Just then a tall figure entered the room.

Deirdre shouted. 'Jim, get the mobile and dial the police. Mum's been shot. There was a news flash on the TV.'

Deirdre watched as she waited for him to connect?

In a calm but broken voice he said. 'There's been a shooting in Crosby in Liverpool. It was on the news. Could you find out how the person is?'

They waited. It seems like an eternity before the policeman got back to them.

'The woman is still alive. She's in the operating theatre. They're still fighting for her life. That's all we know.'

Catherine emerged from her bedroom. 'What's the matter Mummy? I heard you say Moddy's hurt.'

'It's Moddy; we think she's been shot.'

'Is she dead?' Catherine said, her little girl's face all puckered up and she started to cry. 'Dear Jesus don't let Moddy be dead,' she said, as she put her two little hands together in a prayer motion.

Just then the background noise from the TV impinged on Deirdre's consciousness.

'We interrupt this programme to give you the latest news on Alex Rowe. The partner of Nicholas Murray was shot in her home in Crosby earlier tonight. Our news correspondent has just rung in from the hospital. Alex Rowe died five minutes ago on the operating theatre. The police are at the crime scene and are treating the death as a murder case. An update will be given on 'New at Ten.'

Deirdre stared at the screen in horror and crumpled to the floor.

Next morning Ken walked into the hospital. Ten o'clock. He had been up all night. A massive murder hunt for Alex's killer had been launched. It wasn't only tiredness that made him drag his feet as he headed for the morgue. It was his last memory of her and then his guilt. He'd grown very fond of her over the years. He strode into the morgue and found the pathologist there.

Looking at Ken he said, 'I suppose you're here to see the body?

'Yes,' Ken said. Despite all his years as a policeman he balked at the prospect of seeing Alex's body laid out before him - a corpse.

The man pulled out the trolley. A sheet covered the body.

Ken stood his face pale as the pathologist pulled back the covering. He recklessly took in the rest: her black hair plastered to her skull. Her cheeks puffed out like a cherub's. Her eyes closed and eyebrows raised and mouth open in lolling disbelief, dark blood still caked inside as if she'd had all her teeth pulled. His faced registered a strange emotion. The pathologist looked at him intently. By now Ken's face was one of disbelief. He opened his mouth to say something but no syllable was uttered. He felt he was going mad. A wave of blackness enveloped him. As he stared again at the body he felt himself go dizzy as shock waves ripped through his body. He slumped to the ground unconscious a man finally overcome by deep emotion.

76

DEIRDRE, JIM and Catherine arrived from the far side of Liverpool to stay with Donal. He was busy making tea for everyone. It was almost a 'de ja vu ' situation. Here they were two years later but this time it's Alex who had been murdered, he thought as he mooched about the tiny cluttered sitting room.

Deirdre's eyes were red from weeping. Catherine sat on the floor crying and clutching her Dora the Explorer doll. The only one who was dry eyed was Donal. He had to stay strong for the family. Later he too would succumb to his private grief.

The 'phone rang. 'Ignore it. It's probably the press.' Donal said, stonily.

'Could be the police. I'll answer it.' Deirdre said, always the practical one.

'413874,' she said in a subdued quavering tone.

'Deirdre, it's you. What are you doing at Dad's? You didn't say you were coming over.'

'Who are you?' Deirdre shouted as grief spilt over into sheer anger.

'Deirdre, who do you think it is? I've run out of petrol.'

Deirdre dropped the receiver. Her face was pale with a look of absolute bewilderment and disbelief on her face.

'Who the hell is that?' Donal said, aware that something strange was happening as he grabbed the receiver.

'It's me. I've run out of petrol on the motorway. I'm stranded. What on earth has got in to Deirdre? She sounded as if she'd spoken to a ghost.'

He dropped the 'phone. 'It's Alex.'

Catherine picked it up. In a grown up voice she said, 'Hello, is that Moddy?'

Donal, Deirdre and Jim just stared.

'Of course it's Moddy. Tell Popi I've broken down. I ran out of petrol on the motorway.'

Catherine, with extreme poise turned to the three people facing her. 'It's Moddy; she's run out of petrol on the motorway...AGAIN. She wants to know if someone will pick her up.' Obviously Catherine had grasped that her Grandmother, for some bizarre reason, was alive.

Then it was like as if all hell broke loose Deirdre picked the 'phone up and said in a very restrained voice. 'Mum, is that … you?'

'Of course, who do you think it is? Look I've run out of petrol coming back from Liz's. Can anyone pick me up or talk a bit of sense or is the world going mad? '

Deirdre turned to Donal. 'She's run out of petrol and wants to know if you will pick her up?' The conversation was becoming surreal.

Slowly it was dawning on them that Alex was alive; had actually spoken to them on the 'phone.

Donal snatched the receiver again. 'Alex, it's really you.'

'Donal, is this one of your sick jokes? What's going on?'

By now the significance of the uncanny chain of events was beginning to dawn on him as he began to piece the jigsaw together. 'Alex, be prepared for a shock. You've been reported as being shot, murdered in your home last night. We were just on our way to the morgue to identify your body.'

'You're joking. It can't be me I'm here. Shot murdered. But Liz and I went on a pub crawl last night in Liverpool.'

Donal sighed. She was alive and that was all he cared about. Questions would come later.

All four of them set off to pick up Alex. The scene was something of indescribable pathos.

Catherine just placed her little hand in her grandmother's and said 'Moddy you're always running out of petrol.'

Deirdre was laughing and crying at the same time as she hugged her mother. 'It's the best news we've ever heard Mum.'

Donal had recovered and was his usual self again, giving orders and nagging. 'Deirdre you drive Mum's car home after I've filled it up.'

Back in Donal's flat everyone sat around. Things are getting back to normal or as normal as thing could ever be in the circumstance, Donal thought.

'The phone was still off the hook.

'But if it's not you Alex who … is it?' Donal said but then paused as slowly the penny dropped. He looked over at Alex. It was then it dawned on him. Alex – Lynda, long black hair, blue eyes, fair skin, slim, same height. One could mistake one for the other if you didn't know them well

The doorbell interrupted the conversation. Donal strode out and answered it. Bill and three uniformed police were standing there. Bill glanced at Alex as she appeared in the hall. He glanced away, and then did a sudden double take, his pale face whipping back to stare at her. He tugged on an officer's arm. 'Alex,' is that really you. You're not dead then.'

Another police officer went absolutely still and then reached over and touched her. 'You're not a ghost then.'

'No.' She rolled her eyes.

Bill's face looked shell shocked. He turned to Donal and said, 'We wanted you to identify the body. But I can see there's no need. We better go and tell Ken.'

'I should bloody hope so,' Donal said and shut the door.

Alex stared at Donal. 'If it's not me then…it can only be…' she paused unable to continue. 'Lynda! She whispered the word. Her face puckered and tears started to flow. 'Oh no, oh no.' Her legs gave out and Donal grabbed her. Alex's world swirled into darkness. Donal moved her towards a chair and sat her down. Recovering slightly she put her head in her hands and sobbed. 'Why, why Lynda.' Her brain echoed with questions. How can Lynda be connected with these people. Then it obviously dawned on her. 'They were targeting me.' Her world twisted. 'It should be me lying on that marble slab, not Lynda. It's my fault. I put her life in danger by continuing to investigate Nicholas's murder.'

'I think you should try and rest a bit,' Donal said gently and led the distraught Alex to the spare bedroom.

I lay there, thinking. This beautiful girl, this dear heart, would never see her grandchild that was about to be born. Only the other day she'd clasped his photo scan to her breast and had said, 'I can't wait to see him.' Now she never would. Life had not been a bed of roses for Lynda but having grandchildren was going to be the fulfilment of life for her. 'I love you Lynda. I love you.'

77

ON A sunny autumn afternoon in Eastern Green, near where our children had grown up and attended school together, we said goodbye to Lynda. The ancient church in Farm Lane, next to the infant school where our girls attended, was packed with family, friends and colleagues.

I'd said farewell to people I cherished before but I never felt so empty or numb as I did then.

We took our seat and waited for the service to begin. Immediately I felt a rush of emotions. The sombre whirr of the organ. The scent of incense mingling with the sweet fragrance of flora. The sunshine filtering through stained glass panels. I was transported back to Nicholas's pine coffin. I took a deep breath. Focused on the music. Chopin's 'Funeral March'. Suddenly the sounds of a melody echoed through the small church. A woman was singing a hauntingly beautiful version of 'Annie's Song':

> 'You fill up my senses
> Like a night in the forest
> Like a mountain in spring time,'
> echoed through the tiny church.

How many times we used to sing that song, meeting after work at the Royal Oak, straining in wine drenched harmony. Memories; memories of our times together flooded back to me. I cried then as if my heart would break.

What happened next was incredible. Almost from the skies a voice echoed through the eves. In a clear voice, almost as if she was up there looking down on us, Lynda's taped voice recited an elegy.

> I care and love people.
> It is something to treasure.
> In the images of life mine has been special,
> Enchanted, hanging in the balance of yesterday,
> Today, forever.
> You can reach high into the sky and touch
> Eternity.
> Peace.
> God will be with me.
> Sing gentle soul, the way is calling
> My love goes with you.

I felt my cheeks jerk, and my heart went hollow. Grief shuddered through on a Richter scale of ten. I put my head in my hands and wept, wept uncontrollably, wept until my whole body juddered and when I couldn't weep anymore I gazed at Deirdre with such abject misery that she had to look away.

As Lynda spoke the final line the pallbearers picked up the casket, and we all rose to follow.

Grief stricken I slowly drifted after the coffin. I whispered, 'I'll get the bastard, Lynda. Don't worry. Farewell my lovely friend. Rest in peace.'

Afterwards her daughter, Melanie told me that Lynda had planned her funeral when she'd been very ill with a collapsed lung two years previously. She hadn't expected to survive so she'd put her affairs in order.

'I never knew,' I said.

It was early evening. The red autumn sun was setting and to the west the sky was deep gold and crimson. Ragged chimney swifts flew to their nests. Now and then there was the smell of wood smoke drifting on the fragrant air. I sat outside close to the conservatory trying to elicit solace from the tranquil ambience of my surroundings but to no avail. The difficulty was accepting the reality of Lynda's death. It seemed to remain fixed somewhere in the surreal. How could I endure this? I'd endured events no contemporary friend or acquaintance of mine had ever been asked to experience. Not only had I endured them, but I'd done so without the chance to relish the fact that I'd done so. Just as Nicholas's death was beginning to find a place to rest within me, just as the grief and the rage were coalescing into something controllable along had to come this unspeakable savagery.

A deep, unnameable sadness overpowered me. All of a sudden an ethereal being seem to hover before me in a catatonic stillness, staring, lost in the profound desolate contemplation of a being who'd known suffering. I froze, terrified. I suddenly realised it was my reflection in the glass.

Darkness fell but I remained immobile, locked within an impregnable grief. A bank of cloud rolled away from the moon and the garden was bathed in a stark white light. The night sky was incredibly beautiful with stars strung away to the east. Suddenly a resolve started to kick in. I was the intended victim. OK. Well I might well end up that way but not without a fight.

78

'ANOTHER SENSELESS killing. I'll tell you something, Bill I don't believe in coincidences. There must be a connection between the Nicholas's death and Lynda and Alex being followed.' Ken said grimly. He was alone with Bill in the large nondescript office they shared. He started to pace slowly round the room.

'You're right Ken,' Bill said.

'I'd like to know if the killers were trying to liquidate her or…'

'They were only trying to prise information out of her.'

'Precisely! Ken smiled. He and Bill had worked together for so many years that they were rather like an old married couple. They frequently finished each others sentences. It was almost like a double act.

'Who are these killers?'

Silence.

'What's the matter, Bill, you've gone very quiet?'

'Nothing.'

'Come on Bill. I know that look. What are you hiding?'

Bill cast his eyes down.

'Bill, you know something I don't. Spill it.'

'It's best you don't know.' He looked sheepish.

'Bill, cut the crap.'

'Okay but mum's the word.'

'Spill it.'

'The word is on the street that Alex has the money.'

'What. How? Not Peter?'

'Yes.'

'The bastard.'

'Orders from above.'

'Cooper.'

'Yes.'

'Jesus!' Ken drew a sharp breath.

'He wanted to draw the killers out. His words were, 'She's red meat. Put her on a hook and see what the dogs do.'

'I can't believe it.'

'It's true.'

'How do you know all this?'

'Well… it could cost me my job if I tell you.'

'Scout's honour Bill, I won't breathe a word.'

'I was in Peter's office the other day. He'd summoned me and then popped out to have a word with his secretary. There was a memo on the desk with the words: Re: Alex Rowe. It was from Cooper. Of course I read further then. The rest I wormed out of his secretary.'

Ken raked his fingers through his hair. 'Bloody hell ! I thought we were a team. The bastard I'll get him.'

'Forget it for now; let's concentrate on Lynda's murder.'

'It could be someone that owes Rosso money,' Ken said fingering his chin.'

'Yes, maybe.'

'And is it the same person who killed Nicholas?'

'I have a feeling it's not.' Bill said.

'Do you know something that I don't or is this one of your sixth senses again?'

'Just intuition, not based on anything. Though this second killing is amateurish like the first I don't think it's the same killer.'

'You must have some basis for saying this, Bill.'

'Well if it was the same person who killed Nicholas would you be so dumb as to mess up again. Surely you'd make sure you had the right target.'

'Yes, I see what you mean.'

'Maybe Alex can shed some light on it when we speak to her again. She might have noticed someone hanging around near the house.'

'Yes and that's a task I'm not looking forward to, seeing her. She'll blame me for Lynda's death.'

'Alex is not like that Ken. She's very fair-minded.'

79

KARL VON LICHTENHOF sat on a red antique couch drinking a Scotch. It was two a.m. Yvonne had not returned home. He suspected the worst but there wasn't much he could do about it.

Sipping his drink, he heard her footsteps in the hall. He kept swigging his beverage until she entered the room and stood staring at him.

'Still up, Karl,' Yvonne said as she slipped out of her shoes.

'Where have you been Yvonne?' He gazed drunkenly at her, still fascinated by her beauty. She was so very lovely, the angelic face, soulful blue eyes, the fragile but perfectly formed body still affected him.

'I told you Karl, out with the girls clubbing.' Her tone of voice was all too flippant. 'Where do you expect me to get my kicks? Not from you surely? You can't even get it up.'

He sprang from the couch and grabbing her by the hair swung her towards him. But close up to her beautiful face he became helpless. He turned away. She had got him into the fix he was in and yet before her magical beauty he was powerless.

'Poor Karl, you're such a fool. And don't think I'm going to stay around if the dough isn't flowing.' Then she strode out and up the stairs.

Karl poured another whiskey into his crystal glass and took a long gulp. He sat brooding. It was all her fault. Never in his entire life had he been in such deep water, deep slime, deep merd. He'd have to think of a way of stopping all this, of stopping her leaving him.

80

A FEW nights later Yvonne Von Lichtenhof arrived home late again. As she exited the car a figure loomed out of the shadows and stood in front of her. The squat man smiled at her. 'Remember me.'

She gasped in fear and froze

What a pity, he thought. The lady had long blonde hair and deep blue eyes and a deep suntan. She was wearing a little black number with a white wrap draped around her shoulders. Perfect harmony, he thought with a tinge of regret as he took in the high cheekbones, eyes slanting up from them fiercely blue against the tan, slightly up turned nose gently pulling the upper lip away from partially exposed even pearl teeth. Her dress swelled over breasts firm without a bra, the silk cinched tightly at her waist. A slit in the skirt revealed a beautifully shaped thigh as she turned more fully toward him. He had never seen a more beautiful woman in his life. Putting his face close to hers he said menacingly. 'So we meet again. What beauty. What a pity.' He smiled grotesquely.

With a gleaming smile of wolfish satisfaction he lifted his hand and threw the contents of a vial into her face. She twisted her head away but it was too late.

She let out a piercing scream as the caustic liquid burned into her skin. Tearing at it she screamed again. She lurched towards the door and pressed the bell as she fumbled in her handbag for her keys. The man merged into the darkness and disappeared.

81

AT THAT moment Karl happened to glance out the window and almost immediately came a sound he'd never forget as long as he lived. It uncoiled through the garden like a whip. Yvonne was screaming, a terrible penetrating sound that raced around the garden and wedged in his chest. He clamped his hands over his ears; shuddering, unable to listen so great was the terror within it. His eyes watered with fear. Still Yvonne's screeches crescendoed, echoing into the night bouncing off the window panes. Sweating, trembling uncontrollably he wrenched the door open and stared in horror at her.

Yvonne shrieked again as Karl focused on her features. The sight of her beautiful face disintegrating before him struck terror into him. Her tanned skin was peeling before his eyes. A piece of flesh dropped from her cheekbones on to her white wrap exposing the bone structure of her cheek. At first he stood mesmerised, in shock, unable to move. Then with lightening alacrity he caught hold of her, dragged her into the hall toilet, turned the tap on and pushed her face under it, shouting, 'Keep your face under it while I dial 999.'

Next morning Karl was in the hospital at his wife's bedside. She was swathed in bandages and sedated. 'What's my face like,' Yvonne said, in an almost inaudible voice.

Karl cast his eyes down and muttered. 'Don't worry liebschen with a bit of plastic surgery you'll be your beautiful self again' He didn't tell her that it was acid that had been thrown into her face. The surgeon, who had attended to her, had said that she'd suffered first-degree burns and that she'd be badly disfigured down one side of her face. 'The other side is still perfect,' he had said. 'With a wig and plastic surgery she won't look too bad,' he'd added, trying to give some encouragement.

After the incident a neighbour, hearing the screams, had phoned the police. Karl had told the police the attack was out of the blue. He hadn't mentioned a word about the moneylenders. He'd have to keep that a secret. He didn't want the police to investigate in case they found out more.

'Karl will I be okay?'

'Yes of course my dear. Anyhow you have me to look after you.' But there was a strange gleam in his eyes.

As Yvonne dozed he recalled the incident that had occurred a few days previously. As he was exiting his club, Michael Devlin had approached him.

'Count Von Lichtenhof.'

'What do you want?'

'You know. I'm here to collect.' His eyes gleamed.

'Go to hell.' Karl had said.

'Go to hell. That's not a nice thing to say. My boss won't like it.'

'I don't care. He's not getting another penny from me'

'Not getting another penny. We'll see about that. Maybe a visit to your wife again will settle the matter.'

'You're not going to blackmail me any longer. There's nothing more you can do to me. I'm ruined.'

'Not interested in the sob story.'

'Go to hell.'

'Right. But it's your wife who will be going there.'

Deep down Karl had known that they intended to harm Yvonne.

And now that they had there was a strange sense of relief.

82

A FEW weeks later Karl and Yvonne sat in a darkened room in their apartment in Belgravia. She couldn't bear to have anyone look at her not even Karl. It was not much of a consolation that only one side of her face was deformed. The other side was perfect and still beautiful. He'd bought her a long flowing wig to help camouflage her disfigurement. Now she sat, sipping Chardonnay, the shattered side of her face obscured by the coils of hair.

'You know Yvonne I'll have to give up diplomatic service and move to Germany...'

'Germany?'

'I've made up my mind and have made the necessary arrangements. He wasn't going to tell her why he needed to flee the country. 'There I can look after you properly.'

Her face held an expression of perplexity. 'Karl, why did they attack me? Surely you could have stalled them by giving them more money. You did the last time that hideous squat man attacked me with that burning cigar.'

'Ja, I could have. But Yvonne don't you see if I continued to pay them they'd demand more and more interest.'

'But you must have known that they'd do something.'

'They threatened but I didn't think they vould carry it out.'

'But you knew what kind of men you were dealing with. You put me in danger.'

'Yvonne. There was nothing I could do. It's you who ran up all these debts and I couldn't be forever in their grasp. Now I'm free. Now they'll leave us alone. Yvonne, you've got me, just the two of us now. You'll see life will take on a new meaning when ve move to my estate in Germany. Ve can take long walks go shooting and enjoy the estate. I hav rented out most of the lands attached to it including the big house. Ve'll live in the cottage.'

'Live in the cottage.'

Yes, Yvonne. And maybe ve can have a child,' he said looking longingly at her.

A feeling of revulsion swept over her.

He had moved into her bed and started his sexual advances again. There was nothing she could do. She was deformed, disfigured, could not face people and only had Karl to rely on.

83

'TRY AND think, Alex where you might have seen the hands before.' Ken said as he leaned back in his office chair. Bill was busy surfing the net at the other side of the office.

'I don't know Ken. I've racked my brain a thousand times. I just can't place where I've seen them. I only know it was recent, since the trial.' I'd been filling Ken in about the bag lady.

'Or maybe during the trial, someone you met there? Remember some one who lent Rosso money is bound to have been in the courtroom. Someone who knows you've got the money.'

'But I haven't the money so how could anybody know I have it.'

He cast his eyes down but not before I caught the strange look that flickered over his face.

'Ken, what do you know? What are you not telling me?'

He sighed and said. 'I suppose I owe it to you to put you in the picture.'

'Tell me Ken,' I said, fear clutching at my heart.

'The word is out that you have the money.'

'Out where?'

'In the underworld.'

'In the underworld? Jesus. How do you know?'

'We have our sources.'

'The bag lady, who ever he was, was definitely up to no good Alex.'

'I know.'

'So you see Alex why it's vital you remember where you saw those hands. We've got to catch him before he strikes again. I don't want to alarm you but…'

'But why kill Lynda? If it is him that did it. He didn't achieve anything.'

'For what it's worth I think her killer or killers were hired by the man with the large hands. These men obviously mistook Lynda for you and I think they panicked. As you said, why kill her? I think they only meant to question you… her. Getting back to the hands. Do you think it could have been during the trial that you saw this man?'

'Could have been.'

'Think Alex. Where? Someone sitting beside you or near you or someone in the canteen?'

'The canteen? Yes Hm.'

'Maybe someone sipping tea or something?'

'I don't' know Ken. I was in the canteen nearly every day of the trial. How can I remember when it was and who it was?'

'But you remembered the hands Alex. Maybe you saw someone looking at you and then noticed his hands. Sometimes it's when someone does something that attracts your attention you then notice the small details about them.'

'Wait a minute. When I was sitting with Pat one afternoon I noticed … yes …this man was glaring at me. I even mentioned it to Pat. He told me not to be so paranoid. Yes …'

'Go on Alex.'

'He was holding the Telegraph and I remember his huge sinewy hands, almost a deformity. Now I remember. He had a signet ring on.'

'Do you know who he is Alex,' Ken said. His face became animated.

'Of course! His name's Karl Von Lichtenhof. Pat told me, told me that he was a client of Danny's. Told me that he was involved in some money deal with Danny '

'Bull's-eye! Do you hear that Bill,' Ken said, jumping up and planting a big kiss on my cheek. You're an angel, Alex.'

'Maybe we've got our man,' Bill called from across the room.

84

NEXT DAY I was sitting in my kitchen when the door bell buzzed. It's Pat, Ken, Patrick or Donal I mused as I strolled out to open the door.

I stood there transfixed. 'You!'

'Can I come in Alex? We need to talk.'

'We've nothing to say to each other. You're dead as far as I'm concerned.'

'Please, Alex, I just want to put things straight.'

'You can never put things right. So go away. I don't ever want to see you again.' I made an attempt to close the door but he jammed his foot in it.

'Please, Alex I have some information which will be of interest to you. Vital information!'

My curiosity was aroused 'Oh come in for Gods sake.' I strode into the kitchen and stood facing him.

'I've come to warn you, Alex. It's for your own sake. You'll end up dead if you don't stop investigating Nicholas's murder.'

'So this is a ploy to stop me getting near the truth, stop me from finding out the real murderers. I know you had something to do with it. Just get out now.'

'Look Alex I can explain everything if you'd only listen.'

Just then the doorbell rang. Peering out from the kitchen door I could see that it was Father O'Malley. I felt relieved, as I didn't want to be alone with Danny.

'Come in Father,' I said as I opened the door.

As he followed me into the kitchen he paused. His mouth opened and shut. He stared at Danny as if he was an alien. Then I noticed the look of horror on Danny's face. Something was very wrong here.   'Sure you'll have a Bushmills father,' I said lightly hoping to diffuse the situation, whatever it was. 'By the way this is Danny Delaney.'

'Pleased to meet you Danny,' Father O'Malley said as he shook his hand.

Danny went a shade paler as the priest gripped his hand. Wrenching his hand away and in a shaky voice he said, 'I must be going, Alex. We'll speak again.' With that he staggered out the door.

'Something's got into him,' I said. 'It's as if he's seen a ghost.'

'Maybe he thinks that you've filled me in on the details about Nicholas's murder and your suspicions about him being involved. From what you told me Alex, I'm surprised that you even allowed him over the threshold.'

'He said that he'd vital information.'

'Did he indeed? More like phoney lies. He's obviously trying to stop you investigating him."

'That's what I told him.'

'Good girl. You don't owe people like him anything. It appears I arrived in time to prevent him spinning you yarns. What did he say anyhow?'

'He never got to tell me. Just as he started to you rang the bell.'

'Oh.' A frown appeared on his face.

'Forget about him. I'll let Ken deal with it. Look I've a little gift for you Father,' I said as I handed him the leather bound bible I'd purchased in a charity shop.

'A bible!' A strange look washed over his face for a second and then he said, 'You shouldn't waste money on presents for me, Alex. It's very kind of you though. I'll treasure it forever. You know the bible is a way of life for me. I've read it from cover to cover and when I need an answer to one of life's great mysteries I'll always reach for it.'

'Let's drink to that,' I said reaching for the bottle of wine. I poured a glass for the priest but as I was about to pour a second one I found that it was almost empty.

'Silly me, I'm out of wine. Well father it looks like you'll have to perform the same miracle as Jesus did,' I said laughing.

A frown appeared on the priest's forehead momentarily and then hesitantly he said, 'What miracle.'

'Ah gwan dere father. Sure you're the one who says he knows the bible backwards. Surely you haven't forgotten the parable of Jesus changing the water into wine at the marriage feast of Cana?'

'Yes, of course. It's old age creeping over me. I seem to forget so many things these days. Anyhow Alex, I just popped in to check on you. See if you're okay. I'll just finish this and be on my way.'

'It's very kind of you Father to keep calling.'

'It's the least I can do. And Nicholas would want it. See you soon Alex.' And with that he was gone, gone out into the night.

Afterwards as I was busy tidying in the kitchen I reflected. Its strange Patrick couldn't remember that miracle. Well maybe it's as he says, he's getting forgetful in his old age. My mind clicked. But he's only about fifty.

85

THE FOLLOWING day I took Catherine to the park. The gale had been frisky when I'd left home, tickling leaves from trees and swirling them across parklands and paths.

'Moddy can I pay on the slide.' Moddy is her nickname for me.

'Of course my princess.'

I watched lovingly as Catherine slid down a blue slide. I adore that child I thought as I stood keeping an eye on her. She waved at me as she reached the bottom. The park was full of people exercising. I twisted round as a phalanx of joggers passed by.

Then I immediately zoomed back to the slide. The blood thundered in my brain as I stared. Catherine was nowhere to be seen. All I could see was a sea of mothers and children. This was my worst nightmare I thought as I envisaged Catherine been snatched by some paedophile who'd abuse her and kill her. I should never have taken my eyes off of her. My hands started to quiver, my face flushed red, and a thin line of sweat broke out on my forehead. 'Oh my God,' where is she,' I shouted, my voice an anguished howl as I charged over to the slide. 'She's gone. Someone has taken her,' I screamed.

It suddenly dawned on one mother that something was up. 'She was there a minute ago,' she garbled. 'She can't have gone far.'

I screeched then. 'Catherine, Catherine. Oh God please don't let her be gone.' My whole body seemed to sag. A black mix of gloom, helplessness and terror filled my entrails, its weight crushing me. Not my granddaughter. Not the most precious innocent person in my life. Suddenly from the surrounding trees a tall black haired man emerged. He had Catherine by the hand. 'You nutter,' I screamed as I stumbled towards them.

'She wandered off. Didn't you notice? You should be more vigilant and not get distracted by other things. Granddaughters are so precious. You wouldn't want anything to happen to her,' he said as he strode away through the trees. I gaped at his back in horror. How did he know she was my granddaughter? The blood seemed to freeze in my veins. I grabbed Catherine and held her close. Then turning I ran to the car with her in my arms, unlocked it, placed Catherine in the back, jumped in, stuck the key in the lock, switched on the engine and took off down the street. Louise Hamilton had nothing on me. When I arrived at my house I stopped the car and put my head down on the steering wheel. My spirits plummeted then. My heart was cold with despair and a rage surfaced within me. I could feel heat glowing at the back of my neck, in my arm pits and down my oesophagus. It was like a hot flush only ten times worse. I was a pliant, begging wreck, which is I guess is exactly what they must have been banking on – whoever they were. I knew then I was being stalked, knew my family were being stalked and knew that the man in the park had given me a warning – a warning to leave well alone. The message was: We can do whatever we want when we want. Danny was right. I should have listened to him. Maybe he really had something vital to reveal. And now they were targeting the most precious thing in the world to me. I didn't understand the rules of this sinister game and couldn't know how these people defined winning. It was then I decided to back away from it all. Little did I realise that it was too late. I was in too deep.

86

LATER THAT night I knelt in the basement sifting through six plastic bags of Nicholas's papers that the police had returned to me hoping that I might retrieve some scrap of evidence that they'd missed. When I moved, I carried shadows with me, streaking grotesquely through the dark and damp subterranean space. Should have put it all in the bin, I thought as I glanced at my watch. Two and a half hours and so far nothing. I tossed the contents of the last bag on the floor scattering the documents everywhere. I'd drawn a blank. My back had stiffened. I had not eaten and was starving. I'd the beginnings of a migraine. I rubbed a hand through my hair, and then stroked my eyes. The air was dusty, clogging my nostrils, and smelt strongly of brick dust. Might as well call it a day. I gathered up the papers. Suddenly, at the bottom of the pile I spotted a file marked CONFIDENTIAL. My curiosity got the better of me. I opened it and with the aid of my torch I began to read the contents. The first page was headed 'NAZA GROUP'. It soon became obvious to me that it was a contract of some description and as I perused it I became even more intrigued. On the top left hand corner the words 'WORLD TRADE' were typed.

It looks like it was a Currency Exchange Agreement. Slowly I read the words: A currency Exchange Agreement for Japanese Yen and United States dollars Between Albert(Andy) Anzuldua, President of Intercontinental Commerce, Inc., supplier of U.S.. Dollars as 'Buyers and Wonfix Investment Ltd., Hong Kong. It went on to say that 'a copy of said Agreement for exchange of Japanese Yen for U.S. Dollar was attached hereto.' A sensation of confusion slid through me. I didn't understand any of this. I read on:

The exclusive purpose of this Assignment is because, Tempest, and Kane, plc as Account Holder (S) at (100% Exchange: ALGEMENE BANK NEDERLAND HOLLANDSCHE BANKintends to use its authority to provide US Dollars for the aforementioned "Agreement" and further by acceptance of this agreement agrees to act through its designated Prime bank as a subsidiary in fulfilling the terms and conditions of the agreement. :

Provide:

a) Rime Bank W?
b) Good, clean, clear US dollars for exchange.
c) Bank Account for (100%) exchange.
d) Bank Account for (2%) Bonus.

The bonus will be (1.35%). to benefit TTK plc and b) 0.65%) of two percent to Intercontinental Commerce, Inc. as its President Albert (Andy) Anzaldua.

Glancing at the end of the agreement I shuddered. The agreement was signed by Danny Delaney and something - Foley but I couldn't make out the initial. Must be Luke Foley? But it didn't look like an L, more like an M, I thought as I scrutinised it. Then I sucked my breath in and opened my eyes wide. The words, 'acknowledged by Nicholas Murray of Philip Price and Co' with his scrawl underneath, hit me like a bolt of lightening.

My hands trembling, I studied the document further. The agreement was between Danny Delaney of TTK, PLC referred to as the first party and Mr Brian Mandel President Data Jet Ltd referred to as the second party.

I paused. That was the company that Danny liquidated. I read further:

Whereas the first party warrants that they are in a position to supply good, clean, clear, and freely transferable and legitimately earned Japanese Yen for good, clean, clear, freely transferable and legitimately earned United States dollar.

And whereas, the second party warrants that they are in a position to exchange good, clean, freely transferable, legitimately earned United States dollars for good, clear, clean, freely transferable and legitimately earned Japanese yen, paying immediately upon exchange a bonus as hereinafter appears. The first party agrees to transfer Japanese yen to the second party the equivalent of one hundred billion US dollars and the second party agrees to transfer United States dollars to the first party equivalent to the amount of Japanese yen received as per the following transfer schedule until yen or dollars are exhausted. I sucked in my breath again.

Day 1	One hundred million U.S dollars.
Day 2.	One hundred million U.S dollars.
Day 3	One hundred million U.S dollars.
Day 4	One hundred million U.S dollars.
Day 5	One hundred million U.S dollars.
Day 6 - 11	Two hundred fifty million U.S dollars.

Thereafter, the amount up to five hundred million U.S dollars or more shall be exchanged per day, four days per week (Monday through Thursday except Bank and or public holidays in Tokyo/ Hong Kong.)

My head spun. Was this the deal Danny was talking about - the deal that would make them all rich? The interest they would get on that amount of money would be phenomenal. No wonder Nicholas wanted to remain close to Danny. Obviously the police had missed this vital document. It showed that Danny was in cahoots with Luke Foley. Need to speak to Pat about it. He'd know. I dialled his number but got no reply. I left him a message explaining what I'd discovered.

87

IT WAS midnight. Marbella was a beautiful town. Latecomers from the bars picked their way home as he walked along.

Robert Cooper took no notice of all of this, intent as he was on his mission. A passing man made a joke of the weather, but he did not reply. He had no mind for anything but for the tall figure a hundred paces ahead of him who hurried down the almost deserted street.

The dark had made no ritual of coming, nor the hot day of leaving, and the night was sultry with the whiff of summer in the air. The eyes of the smaller man straining ahead of him never wavered from the man in front.

The street curved, taking them past a church. Next to the church there was an old yew tree its foliage glittering in a fragmented canopy of dark green. The men strode on, neither faster nor slower, the one in front busily as if in a hurry. As he walked he swung his arms at his sides. Did he know he was being followed?

The tall man in front entered a narrow alley; the air was filled with the smells of spicy food. Here for the first time the echo of their footsteps mingled in unmistakeable challenge: here for the first time the man ahead seemed to become more alert, more aware, sensing the danger behind him. It was not more then a slight change in his walk that made the man behind recognize that the one in front realized he was being followed. He moved more into the light away from the darkness of the walk.

A taxi drove past. A church bell began its monotonous chime. They walked on, closer together, but still the man in front did not look back. They rounded another bend. The man in front paused, leaned forward as if to admire something in the window, glanced up and down the road, and in that moment the light from the window, shone upon his face. The other man rushed forward; stood; went forward again. It was too late.

An Audi had drawn up, driven by a man hidden behind the tinted glass. The back door opened and closed, and gathered speed, oblivious of the cry of anger from the pursuer who stood gaping after the vehicle. Robert Cooper had lost his prey.

88

AS I reading the Daily Telegraph my heart skipped a beat as I read the Headlines:

NO HIDING PLACE

Phillip Williams's girlfriend identifies Luke Foley as one of her boyfriend's alleged killers.

I carried on reading: Britain's top crime buster gave a warning to the nation's 200 most evil crooks, "You've no hiding place." Super cop Robert Cooper heads a new team dedicated to bringing to justice villains like the murder suspect of Philip Williams, Luke Foley. Mr Cooper said yesterday: We'll be targeting criminals who are the most difficult, the most prolific and the greediest. The unit will pursue underworld chiefs such as drug racketeers, money launderers, counterfeiters and arms' traffickers – even if they have fled overseas.

Fugitive Foley, forty-nine – reckoned to be Britain's wealthiest crook vanished one year ago after Philip Williams's body was found hanging.

Tales of Luke Foley's exploits give rise to images of a world filled with violence, fast cars and fast women. These facts about Foley indicate that he is a frightening man, a psychopath, a man who kills at a whim. He has built his own world, one in which he is the leader and brains behind one of the biggest crime syndicates in Britain.

To his new friends at the bar overlooking the bay in Fort Lauderdale he was known as the jolly Englishman, well tanned and always unfailingly polite when he met any of his neighbours.

He appeared to everyone in the small community as the perfect English gent.

In truth, however, he was Luke Foley, Britain's most wanted man. He was a man who was known to have underworld contacts in Miami, Mafia friends in New York, contacts with North London gangsters who were involved in illegal activities including drugs and racketeering.

Now he's behind bars again after his easy-going lifestyle ended face down on a pavement outside one of the area's finest seafood restaurants.

That was where the FBI and the English police headed by Robert Cooper threw him before handcuffing and bungling him into an unmarked car to face extradition to the UK over the murder of a colleague of his after his girlfriend had given evidence against him.

It was the dramatic end to a manhunt that began more than one year ago and spanned much of Europe, Africa and America.

Philip Williams was found hanging. Foley became the prime suspect after Williams's girlfriend fingered him. It was then that Foley disappeared and in the following months sightings of him were reported in Russia, Canada and the United States.

It was believed he was tracked down after he was recognised by an English Tourist who'd strayed from the usual holiday spots. Prior to this Robert Cooper of M15 had tracked him to Marbella in Spain but had lost him. Now after frustrating weeks of searching they struck lucky when a tourist reported having seen him in Fort Lauderdale.

As I poured over the telegraph spread out on the kitchen table I glanced at Luke Foley's photograph. My breath left me.

Staring at me was the man 'd seen running out my front door the night of the murder. That it could be him was incredible. But there was no doubt about it. It was a face forever etched in my memory - the deep glassy blue eyes gaping at me just as they had the night of the murder. Must get in contact with Ken.

THE GHOST'S MOUTH PUCKERED INTO AN UNCONTROLLABLE MOVEMENT. 'YOU FUCKING BITCH. LUKE SHOULD NEVER HAVE LET YOU LIVE. THE DAILY TELEGRAPH WAS SPREAD OUT IN FRONT OF HIM AND HE WAS STARING AT THE HEADLINES.
'I TOLD YOU WOMEN WOULD BE YOUR UNDOING, LUKE. AND THE ALEX BITCH SHE WILL HAVE TO BE TAKEN CARE OF BEFORE SHE DESTROYS US ALL.'

89

DEAR ALEX,

Bruno Rosso's solicitor, Jane, asked me to write to you concerning Nicholas's death.

There are many reasons why Nicholas may have been murdered. Firstly Nicholas was looking after funds not just for Bruno but for others as well. A Liverpool 'consortium' would lend money to people for various business ventures such as Night Clubs and so forth. They gave some to Rosso. I don't know what Bruno told the consortium the money was wanted for but clearly Bruno would have had to come up with a good business plan.

At the same time Nicholas was working with Danny Delaney. From what I know of Danny and subsequent events, I believe that he gave some inducement to Nicholas to part with a large sum of money. Danny could be very plausible and I take the view that he would have told Nicholas that the money could be doubled in a very short space of time. I know all of this, as I too, worked for Danny so I have it from the horse's mouth.

I have some vital piece of information concerning the identity of the man behind Nicholas's murder. I feel we should meet and discuss everything as it's difficult to put all the facts down on paper; also it could be dangerous. The letter could get into the wrong hands. Perhaps you could 'phone me and we can arrange to meet up.

Yours sincerely,
Geoff Baker.

I arrived at the pub at five to eight. It was a small old-fashioned place near the city centre. The interior was threadbare with a worn-out blue carpet peppered with cigarette burns. I sat down at one of the pine tables and waited for Geoff Baker to arrive.

As I glanced in the direction of the door. A tall thin man fitting the description Geoff had given me of himself pushed open the door and glanced around.

'Thanks for coming,' I said as he drew closer.

'It's a pleasure, Alex,' he said as his outstretched hand grasped mine firmly and his brown eyes crinkled up as he gave me a stare and sat down.

After ordering coffee from a hovering waiter Geoff looked at me, and took out his pipe. 'Do you mind? It helps me to think,' he said slowly puffing at it as he searched for words that would put me in the picture.

"You'll want to know the whole story? That's why we're here.'

I nodded.

'To put it in a nutshell I'm afraid Danny was very involved with people in the underworld.'

'I know that. I saw him drinking with one of the Barry's one night.'

'To name but a few.'

'What do you mean?'

'It's a long story. Danny strove to get in on hedge funding for years. He knew he could double his money quickly provided he had the large capital to invest.'

'What's hedge funding?'

'Bond trading. It is supposed to be legal and above board but of course where there's money to be made there are always dubious people around.'

'So what happened?'

'As I said Danny was desperate to get in on the act. Eventually he met a middleman who said he would be his agent. You never get close to the people at the top. This man promised to invest a few million for him. Danny was determined to invest as much as he could into it. Of course the question was from whom he would get such large sums.'

'How do you know all this?'

'I found out about it was because a colleague who worked for Danny was in deep trouble. Danny had persuaded him to take funds from the firm's insolvency account and give it to him to invest in the bonds. He swore blind that the money would be back in the account in six months and that there would be a fat profit for him.'

'So what happened?'

'Danny invested it with this middleman in Canada.'

'And?'

'The money went missing which is why I, as his barrister, was involved in the unenviable task of having to defend my colleague before his professional body. Unfortunately he's been struck off and now has been arrested and charged with embezzlement.'

'Will he go to prison?'

'Probably! Both he and Danny have been arrested but it will take a while to come to trial.'

'So what went wrong?'

'Well, as I said where there are huge stakes there are some corrupt people. The middleman had some pet projects in operation that needed funding. One was a stretch limousine business that was failing and he was pouring the money Danny was giving him into it.'

'So you mean to say that Danny was duped?'

'Yes. Danny was promised that the money would be doubled. He believed this, he had seen the figures.'

'So where did Danny get the money to invest?'

'I have it from the horse's mouth that Danny had two million quid from Luke Foley a man who heads a Liverpool syndicate.'

My eyes opened wide. Better not say anything about my suspicions about Foley being Nicholas's killer.

'Yes, and you know who Luke Foley is?'

'Vaguely. But what has Luke Foley got to do with Nicholas,' I said trying to keep my voice steady.

'The story in the street is that the syndicate came after Danny for the money. Danny, of course hadn't got it so he lied by involving Nicholas.'

'What do you mean?'

'He told Foley that Nicholas held the funds for him in a client account.'

'And they believed him?'

'One thing about Danny is he always manages to sound convincing. God knows what sort of a cock and bull story he fobbed Foley off with but he obviously believed him as they went after Nicholas and you know the rest.'

'You said in your letter that Bruno Rosso gave money belonging to a Liverpool consortium to Nicholas to hold.'

'Yes, and I believe that Nicholas gave it to Danny for his hedge funding scheme.'

'So Rosso too had a reason to go after Nicholas, a reason to kill him - he wanted his money back.'

'So did others, so did others. It's a huge melting pot, Alex. There's wheeling and dealing and along the way someone gets hurt. For what's it worth I'd say that Bruno too wanted his money back and he willingly or unwillingly went to the house that night with his partner in crime to try and persuade Nicholas to talk. In this circle everyone knows everyone else so it's unlikely that he doesn't know who the other guy is. But he's not saying anything because he's afraid. I don't believe for one moment Rosso is a murderer. He wouldn't hurt Nicholas. They were good buddies. No, I think it all got out of hand. I believe Bruno when he says he tried to save Nicholas.' He paused. 'Fancy a glass of wine.'

'Hmm...yes.'

While Geoff was at the bar I slumped back in my chair unable to take in all in. Suddenly it all started to make sense; the reason for Nicholas's murder, Danny's involvement; the unmistakeable face I'd seen on the night. Now I knew definitely that it was Luke Foley that I'd seen. Involuntarily I shivered. And Lynda's murder. Had Danny invested money belonging to Karl Von Lichtenhof? Was it he who had been watching the house and mistakenly killed Lynda? Ken still hadn't made any headway there. I mulled all this over as I waited for Geoff.

'Well Alex, you know it all now,' Geoff said as he returned carrying two Sauvignon's.

'Yes, so Luke Foley was the white guy that I saw the night of the murder.'

'No Alex, It wasn't Luke. He always got someone else to do his dirty work but he's behind it all.'

'But he must have been, because ...' And then I stopped myself. This was dangerous information I possessed. And how did I know I could trust Geoff.

'You were going to say, Alex.'

'Only that it it's got to be Luke.'

'No, Alex definitely not.'

'How can you be so sure?'

'I'm not but I bet you he has a cast iron alibi.'

'Look I can give you a contact. There's this Al. You'll find him a pub in the city centre. I've forgotten the name but I'll draw you a map. He knows what goes on in the street. He's certain to know about Lynda's murder. Have to grease his palm of course; at least a grand. Information like this doesn't come cheap. I'll get in contact with him. Tell him you'll be in.'

'How does he know so much?'

'He's an informer. Need I say more?'

After finishing my drink I thanked Geoff for his information and said my goodbyes. As I drove home I mulled the conversation over in my head. I was certain the white man was Luke. I wouldn't rest until I'd found out the truth. But a warning voice told me. Leave well alone. You're getting too close. I couldn't forget the day in the park with Catherine.

90

IT WAS six o'clock in the evening and the day had been a dreary one. Dense drizzly fog lay low on the city. Grey coloured misty blotches of diffused light threw a feeble glimmer on the muddy pavement. The yellowish glare from the shop-windows streamed out into the damp air and threw a murky, shifting shimmer across the bustling street. There was something ghostly in the end-less procession of bodies which darted across these thin bars of light – sad and happy faces. Like my mind they flitted from the gloom into the light and back into the gloom once more. The dull evening seemed to combine to make me melancholy and fearful – fearful of my imminent meeting with Al and what he might reveal.

The front entrance to the building opened onto a flight of stairs that led down to a bar. My stilettos clattered as I made my way downwards. At the bottom I moved through a beaded curtain and found myself in a large lounge. The screaming, hysterical cacophony of the rock music caused a sensation of actual pain in my ears. My eyes were attacked next by tear-provoking layers of thick smoke the nostrils reacting immediately to pungent tobacco.

Suddenly the music quietened. I looked around. To the left and right of the counter were about a dozen tables all of them occupied. A waitress in a red leotard and red high-heeled shoes was swivelling among the tables, taking orders. Behind the counter, a man in a white shirt and black waist coat was drawing a pint. I looked at a thin, ferrety, moustachioed barman and then into his eyes. The irises were blue, the whites latticed by a network of tiny red capillaries.

'What can I get you, love,' he said, at the same time giving me the once over. I knew that I wasn't his usual sort of customer. Geoff had warned me that the pub was one of those sleazy joints where drug deals, dodgy businesses, etc, were conducted. Not a place for a science teacher to be in. I'd deliberately tried to dress appropriately for the occasion, wearing a black mini skirt and a sheer black blouse under a black PVC mac which I'd left unbuttoned. I didn't want to stick out to much in such an establishment.

'An orange ... oh make it a gin and tonic.'

'Ice and lemon?' He continued to scrutinise me. 'You're not one of our regulars.' He didn't smile.

'No...I'm meeting someone.'

'Should I know him?'

'Maybe, he's name's ... Al.'

He smiled then, a great huge beaming smile. 'He's over there sitting at that corner table. Anyone who's a friend of Al's is a friend of mine. And the drink's on the house,' he said as he pushed the G and T towards me.

'Thanks.'

I drifted over to the table wondering what kind of relationship there was between them.

I nodded at Al and appraised him as I sat down. His skin was pale and crenulated as a walnut, and the long white hair was a bird's nest – matted, separated, revealing splotches of pinkish flesh.

'I'm Alex,' I said as I sat down.

'We'll cut to the chase. Geoff has told me you're looking for certain information. It will cost.'

'I know. How much?'

'Well now.' He fingered his chin. 'Should we say a thousand?'

'A thousand. That's too much. Five hundred?' Should you be doing this.

He paused obviously squaring me up. 'Seven fifty. My friend at the bar has to get his cut. He keeps his ear to the ground.'

I hesitated…

'This is a dangerous business. I'm for the high jump if it gets out that I'm passing on this piece of info.'

Alex this is your only chance of finding out who killed Lynda. Go for it. 'Seven fifty it is then.'

'Cash?'

'Of course!' I handed him two envelopes - one containing five hundred quid and the other containing two hundred and fifty quid. I had come prepared. I still had two and a half hundred in my pocket. Just in case.

'Some of this you probably already know from Geoff.'

'Yes, but tell me anyway.' I bit my lip.

Al glanced shiftily behind him and then started to speak.

'Danny had many contacts and, like Bruno Rosso, he acted as a money-lender. The latest is that he helped this baron, Karl Von Lichtenhof with some funding. His wife, Yvonne was a spendthrift and Karl borrowed the money from loan sharks to pay off her debts. The story is that he was being pressurised by a gang to pay off the debt. One of them actually stuck a burning cigar into her face. They then threatened to rough her up if the money and the whopping interest wasn't returned quickly. Karl went to Danny out of desperation.'

'So what happened?' I realized that my teeth were clenched tighter than the jaws of a vice. I tried to relax practicing deep breathing that I had learned at yoga classes.

'Danny lent him money he had received from Nicholas.'

'Really!' Another confirmation - Nicholas was definitely involved in money lending.

'Where did Nicholas get it? Don't tell me. I know. He got it from Rosso.'

'Yes.' Rosso was a moneylender. You know that from the trial. He gave Nicholas fifty grand. Nicholas passed it on to Danny. That paid off the interest. Danny managed to persuade Karl to borrow another fifty from Rosso, via Nicholas of course, and invest in hedge funding. Danny was hoping that the money would double in a short time. This would pay off Rosso. But as you know from Geoff it never happened.'

'Yes.'

'When Danny couldn't return the investment it left Karl high and dry. It was then they first attacked Yvonne.'

'When did all this take place?'

'Just before Nicholas was topped. So fortuitously Danny was able to say to Karl that Nicholas had the money but that he was dead. Karl believed him and figured that you had it.'

'So he persuaded people to keep tabs on me.' My thoughts skittered back to the Gargoyle outside my house. 'And the bag lady was Karl.'

'Yes. The same two men who killed your friend followed you from the tennis club that night.'

'What did they hope to achieve?'

'To locate the money? Stop you on a lonely stretch of the road and scare you into revealing where it was. They messed up big time with Lynda – a pair of amateurs. They were only supposed to get information.' He paused. 'After Lynda's murder the moneylenders started threatening Karl again. But this time he refused to play ball even though they said they'd harm Yvonne. In some way he blamed her for his predicament. When she discovered he was broke she had decided to leave him. So of course when the thugs threatened to harm her he did nothing.'

'Did they harm her?'

'They threw acid into her face.'

'God! Was she badly injured?'

'Yes, horribly. Strangely, she's horrendously deformed down one side of her face. The other side is perfect still.'

'And what has Karl done about it.'

'This is even more bizarre.' They say he likes it this way. Remember she was going to leave him. Now of course she's dependent on him.'

'The police will get him?'

'No, he's fled to Germany.'

'And what of her?'

'She went with him. Now she wears a wig which covers the deformed side of her face. She lives, what some would think is an idyllic existence. Karl looks after her every need and the latest I heard is that she's pregnant and that Karl's father has relented in his attitude. You know he cut Karl off without a penny when he married her.'

'Why?'

'She was a waitress. Not good enough for the son of a Count. Now of course with an heir on the way it has softened him.'

'An heir?'

'Yes, she had a scan and it's a boy. So Karl's over the moon; he has Yvonne with whom he is besotted, and he has managed to pacify his father with news that there's a male heir child on the way.'

'How do you know all of this?'

'As I said, I keep my ear to the ground. It's a lucrative game so long as one is careful. Some of the things I hear I keep to myself. I'd be dead meat if I squealed. Mentioning no names there are some dangerous men out there and I don't even let there names pass my lips.'

I threw a hand grenade. 'Like Foley.'

He wiped a hand over his face in agitation. I could see the terror in his face.

'For God's sake woman put a sock in it.' He glanced around warily and then twisted his face to mine. 'Do you want to end up like your partner?'

'But Luke Foley's in prison.'

'It's not Luke you should fear its ...' He paused. He leant forward and there was steel in his voice. 'You don't want to know.'

'I'll double the money if you give me his name.' I bit my lip nervously. Was I getting in too deep? .Don't go there.

'No one messes with this man, even I know that. No amount of money you could put my way would entice me to open my mouth.' He looked around again and twisting back to me said. 'Leave it there Alex. Let the police sort it out.' His eyes swivelled alarmingly

'But they've closed the case. They've decided they've got their man.'

'Let it be then, take it from me you don't want to know.'

I picked up the tremor in his voice. 'But ...'

'Are you fucking deaf? Do you want to get me slain too?' He had little flecks of spittle at the corner of his mouth and his hollow eyes were manic.

'Fuck off now. I've given you your information.'

He stood up. 'Be gone when I get back from the bog.' His face was now twisted in temper.

A shrinking, anxious fear immobilized me. Who was this man - a man who could put so much terror into those who crossed his black path?

91

WE ALL sat in Ken's office discussing the recent set of events. I leaned against the back of my chair as I listened intently to what Ken was saying.

Peter, reclined in a comfortable armchair, applied a match to the bowl of an old briar pipe and coughed as the smoke caught at the back of his throat. 'Smoking will be the death of me,' he said as he glanced in my direction.

Ken, perched on the side of his desk was, from his body language, making it obvious to everyone that he was in command. He wasn't going to let Peter railroad the meeting.

I began in a quiet voice. 'I met Geoff Baker, a barrister who was very involved with Danny. He told me how Danny managed to persuade clients to invest in hedge funding.' My voice became low and modulated as I fought for the words to come out. 'We now feel we know why Nicholas was murdered and who were responsible.'

'But we know that already,' Peter retorted, unable to keep the sarcasm out of his voice.

'Less of the sarcasm,' Ken replied with steel in his voice. 'You don't know the entire story. So listen to what Alex is saying.' The menace in his voice was clear and I cast Ken a grateful smile.

Quickly I told them the story about Luke Foley, the two million quid and how the middleman had duped Danny.

'You mean to say that Foley was behind Nicholas's murder. But we have no proof surely.' Peter raised an eyebrow.

'We've only Geoff's word.' Ken added.

'And Karl Von Lichtenhof?'

'Yes remember the story you put out in the underworld. Well Karl got to hear about it.'

'We thought it would draw the killers out into the open.'

'Your actions got Lynda killed.' He paused. 'To get back to Karl, he never intended to have Alex slain he only wanted to frighten her, get her to tell where the money was. He sent two men to her house and of course they bungled it. They panicked and ended up killing the wrong woman.'

'Are you going to charge Von Lichtenhof with murder?'

'Can't. First he has diplomatic immunity.' Ken grimaced.

'Surely that can be waived?' Peter said puffing at his pipe.'

'Karl's father is influential and our government doesn't want to upset the apple cart. And we've no proof that Karl was involved. We just have Al's account. Apparently, when they broke into Alex's house and threatened Lynda with a knife she made a lunge at one of them. One ran scared and panicked. He took a shot at her before he ran out the door.'

'But surely you can charge them?'

'We don't know who they are.'

'How did you find all this out then?'

Ken gazed at Alex proudly. 'It's down to Alex. She arranged to meet this Al in a sleazy bar one night. He hangs out in these dives to get his information.'

'Who's Al?'

'Petty larceny. The info' he supplies keeps him out of the nick.'

'So Karl will get off scot free?'

'I'm afraid so.'

'But we've got Luke Foley?'

'Yes, but pinning the murder on him will be difficult. It's one thing hearing that Foley was behind the killing, it's another thing proving it.'

'He's in custody anyhow and he'll go down for Philip William's murder, that's for certain,' Peter said.

'So that's the sum total of it. The muddied water is beginning to clear. Let's see what Foley can give us,' Ken said closing his file.

92

'IT'S HIM, I know.' I said. A day after the meeting I sat in the kitchen chatting to Ken. 'I know the man I saw in my house the night of the murder is Luke Foley. I saw his photo in the paper and I'd know that face anywhere.'

'It's not him.'

'I know it's him, Ken.'

'Luke Foley has a cast iron alibi for the night.'

'He can't Ken I saw him. He must have bribed someone.'

'Alex, I checked him out. On that night he attended a charity function. He and his wife were having dinner at some banquet hall when Nicholas was being murdered.'

I stared wildly at him unable to accept what he was saying.

'It's probably someone who resembles him that you saw. But you're mistaken, it wasn't Luke. I'm a hundred percent satisfied, so as far as I'm concerned the matter is closed.'

I grimaced. I'd leave it for now. But I'd prove to everyone that it was Luke I saw. 'Guess what, Ken. Guess who called to see me the other day.'

'The mind boggles, Alex.'

'Danny.'

'Danny?'

'Yes.'

'What did he want?'

'He said he had vital information. And then something bizarre happened.'

'What?'

'Father O'Malley popped in.'

'Not him again.'

'Danny behaved very strangely. Went deadly pale and ran out the door like a scalded cat.'

'Christ Alex, your bloody priest, why didn't you tell me this before? His face was frozen in pensive rejection at my words. 'Got to go. It may be too late.' And before I had time to reply he was gone.

He left me with my mouth open. How prejudiced can you get. But Ken wasn't into prejudice. I struggled to dismiss it. I had other vital things to think about - namely Luke Foley. Those staring eyes still haunted me. Either that or it was his double. I froze. His double. That's it. It's his twin, I reasoned. Jumping up I reached for my mobile. I'll call Ken and tell him I've solved the mystery. I paused. He'll never wear it. I calmed myself. Was it plausible? Maybe one of the twins was adopted at birth. I'd have to make some discreet inquiries. Who could I contact who would give me information about the syndicate? Maybe I should start with Pat.

I grabbed the phone and dialled.

Pat answered immediately. 'Pat I need to find out about Luke Foley. I think he's got a double working for him or a twin.'

'What the hell do you want raking up facts about Luke Foley? If Foley has an inkling that you're fingering him you're dead. Luke's influence extends beyond prison bars. Anyhow Luke's an only child.'

'How do you know?'

'From Danny. He got it from the Barry's.'

Disappointment enveloped me as I put the receiver down. Was Pat being deliberately evasive or was he weary of all my delving? Racking my brain an idea suddenly came to me. I'll ring Geoff. He might know something.'

'The only one who might have some information is James Quigley, the chief witness against Danny. I'll ask him to give you a call.'

Hours later the 'phone rang. A cultured, sophisticated voice said, 'May I speak to Alex Rowe?'
'Speaking.'
'This is James Quigley. Geoff said you wanted to speak to me.'
Quickly I explained about Luke Foley. Somehow I found myself telling him the whole story.
James agreed to meet with me that evening in a pub.
As I left to meet James I paused. I still haven't managed to tell Pat about the Naza Document. Maybe I should give him a quick ring before I leave. Dialling the number I waited. No answer. Just as I was about to put the receiver down the answering machine kicked in. Should I tell him this? He's my friend after all, I thought. Quickly I gave a brief account of what I'd discovered. Pat's bound to be able to shed some light on it, I thought as I replaced the receiver.

93

I FOLLOWED the noise of the singing, and came to the pub.

Inside, it was surprisingly crowded. Here were the people who lived in these huge blocks of silent council flats that lined the streets.

I pushed my way to the counter, through the noisy bar, and asked for a red wine. I leaned back, against the bar, and stared round. Was he here? Was he that thin man with the drooping eyelids, or that curious creature in sandals, with uncut hair tumbling down his shoulders? Was he that prim little character drinking by himself in a striped suit? Or that man in shirtsleeves, demolishing a meat pie in half a dozen greedy mouth-full? And which pair of eyes was examining me, I wondered. A man at a piano started to play. Some people began singing. I looked at my watch. I'd been here ten minutes and still no sign of him. I'd told him I'd be dressed in red so that he'd recognise me.

Just as I was about to go I felt a light tap on the shoulder. I swung round to find a total stranger staring at me. Was this James or was it a pick up?

'Alex.'

'James.'

'Sorry I'm late,' he said as he led me to a vacant table.

The man who faced me was about forty five, the crisp black hair already greying a little at the sides. Wash faded jeans. Slip-on loafers. White shirt showing just a hint of chest. Sexy. He was perhaps six feet in height and well built. Gazing at him I thought. He's smart, charming and James Bond handsome. But it was the face that interested me, the slight ironic quirk to the mouth of someone who laughed at himself and other people too much or so I thought.

'So you want to know about Luke Foley. Well, I think you probably know as much as I do about him judging by what Geoff told me so I don't think I can add anything else to the jigsaw. All I know is that he's guilty of many acts of violence but he didn't murder Nicholas. His alibi is perfect.'

I remained unfazed. 'I have to know.'

'It's a dead end Alex. There's nothing anyone can pin on Foley as far as Nicholas is concerned.'

'There must be something?'

'I don't know much about Luke and his family except that his mother ran away when he was about two. Luke's father used to beat her up. She was very beautiful and he was insanely jealous. It was the grandmother who helped to rear him.' He paused. His eyes skittered towards me.

'What.'

'Just a random thought like one of those tricks played by the mind as it searches in old, almost forgotten files for a name, a person, a life lived in the shadows. Yes, the grandmother?' James fingered his chin. 'She might be able to tell you something. She's old now and lives in Scotland. I can get her address for you.'

I stared at James. Luke's grandmother! 'I'm going to go there.' I responded vehemently.

'What, are you mad Alex? What do you expect to find out? Clearly Luke had nothing to do with the murder.'

'You're sure of that James?' An idea was forming in my mind and I had difficulty in hiding my excitement. I felt I knew the answer. His mother leaving when he was only two gave me the clue.

'Be careful, Luke's grandmother is very protective.'

'There's something else. It's very puzzling.'

'What.'

'Wait until you hear this.'

'Go on the mind boggles.'

As I related all that I had read about the money exchange I could see James getting steadier paler. 'What's the matter, James?'

'You say what's the matter. Do you know what you have stumbled on?'

'Of course, changing yen into dollars.'

'No you stupid woman.' He frowned.

I obviously looked hurt.

'Sorry Alex. It's just…Oh God … If anyone finds out you have this information…'

My voice trembled. 'James what are you saying?'

'Alex, do you know what you've uncovered?'

'Something in the tone had the hair on the back of my neck prickling. I shook my head.

'This is the biggest case of laundering of money we've encountered this decade.'

'What do you mean?'

'Alex, don't you read the papers.'

'Not if I can help it.'

'The CIA, FBI and MI5 have know for a long time that a syndicate was involved in the laundering of billions of yen into dollars but they were looking to America for those responsible.' James inhaled deeply. 'I can't believe it. All the time the police were sitting on a time bomb. If they know that you have this information you won't last five minutes. I hope to God you didn't mention it to anyone.'

'Of course … not. Do you think I'm daft.'

His gaze skittered to me. 'Are you sure? You were daft enough to tell me.'

'I trust you.'

'You shouldn't trust anyone.'

'That's what Ken said.'

'And he's right. Alex, I'm going now but I'll make some inquiries. I'll be in touch. But Alex, promise me you won't breathe a word of this to a soul.'

'No.' A little voice nagged. You've already opened your big gob. Nevertheless I felt uneasy. Someone else could play the message back.

Better tell Pat and Patrick I'm off to Scotland.

94

TWO DAYS later I was on my way to the north of Scotland after staying overnight in Edinburgh. Why would Luke's grandmother live in such an isolated place? I felt I knew the answer and was getting increasingly excited as I neared my destination.

I had not let the old woman know that I was coming. That would put her on her guard for I knew that she had something to hide. Surprise would be the element.

Eventually I turned off from the main road on to what they would term in Ireland a 'boreen'. Locals in the village I had passed had told me that the place where the old woman lived was about ten miles up a mountain that ran by the north east coast line. It was a cold December morning with the sun shining brilliantly out of a clear blue sky. As I progressed up the steep slope a sense of isolation descended on me as I experienced the black deserted mountainside around me.

Stopping the car I decided to lunch by the side of the road. I'd packed a picnic and began to munch on a chicken leg. Suddenly I was no longer hungry as I surveyed the scene. There was no sign of human life anywhere among the barren reaches of the gorse-covered terrain. In the distance I saw a large rock jutting out like a great giant bear ready to pounce but most of all it was the silence that seemed so menacing. Why would an old woman want to live in such a remote place I asked myself again as I cleared away the remains of my lunch.

Even though the sun was still blazing as I jumped back into my Carmen Ghia a sense of impending doom clutched at my heart. I shook off the feeling of apprehension as I turned the key in the ignition and continued my journey. I couldn't, however get rid of my sense of foreboding. You're just being melodramatic, I told myself. I paused for breath and the ominous silence of the peaks descended on me again. A silence I could almost hear. Not even a bird crying. Next I came to a series of hillocks cutting me off from any distant view. I shivered and then looked up. The view upwards was even less reassuring.

The steep slope had an air of desolation and to my right was a dense copse of miserable firs hanging over rock. The stumps were stunted, bent at an angle away from the sea, their branches twisted into ugly shapes like deformed limbs. Now that I was higher up a wind blowing in off the sea whipped against the car. No wonder the trees were so crippled.

I looked back at the scene, the slanting rays of a low sun turning the streams to threads of gold and glowing on the red heath. The road in front of me grew bleaker and wilder over huge russet and gorse covered slopes. Now and then I passed a moor land cottage, walled and roofed with stone, with no creepers to break its harsh outline. Suddenly I looked down into a bowl like depression, patched with stunted pine and firs that had been twisted and bent by the fury of years of storm. There lay nestled into this vale stood a large cottage. I parked my car quite a distance from the house. I didn't want the old woman to spot my approach.

A brisk walk through an over grown path brought me nearer to the dwelling. An orchard surrounded it, but the trees, like the rest of the area were stunted and nipped, and the effect of the whole place was mean and melancholy. The sun was now low in the sky when I reached the summit of the hill, and the long slopes beneath me were golden-green on one side and shadowed on the other. There was no sound and no movement. One huge white bird, a gull or curlew, soared aloft in the blue heaven. He and I seemed to be the only living things between the huge arch of the sky and the setting beneath me. I descended.

A large gate led to a pebbled pathway between grasses, and beyond was the house. In the dark purple dusk, lights glowed behind the windows. To the right a drive ran up to a large garage.

I pulled the chain that rang a bell inside. Nothing happened for a few seconds; then a shape appeared on the other side of the tiny stained glass panel. I clocked the fact that the door was fitted with a heavy bolt as I heard it been shunted free. There was a pause and the old wooden door swung open.

An old woman with white hair swept back from her forehead opened it. Her dark eyes looked straight at me with a hard, defiant, implacable stare. She had gaunt cheeks, a long chin and thick, sensual, colourless lips. Her figure was thin but sturdy and her manner aggressively self-assured.

'You've come to speak to me about my grandson,' she said before I could utter a word. The tone of her voice was as hard, and as defiant and implacable as the expression of her eyes.

She knows why I'm here. How? The only person I had told was Pat and the priest.

Reluctantly the woman said, 'Come in'.

I entered a neat hall that lead to a large kitchen. As we passed a room on the right of the hall the woman quickly shut the door. In the kitchen there was a large pine table and four chairs around it. The ceiling was low and beamy – menacing.

Straight away I said, 'I'm sorry to trouble you but I'm the partner of Nicholas Murray who was murdered a few years ago. I need to talk to you about your grandson. I believe he might be able to shed some light on the murder.'

'You've come a long way just to ask me a few questions. Luke can't help you so if you've no other motive, I'd like you to leave as I'm busy.' She sat down, picked up some knitting and started to knit with the stoniest and steadiest composure.

I didn't move.

'There's nothing else to say except I wish you good day.'

My skill as an amateur detective was improving. I was taking in every detail of my surroundings. I wondered was there any ulterior motive behind the closing of the door. I would investigate. Trying to soften the old woman I said, 'You've a lovely home here. I bet Luke loves this place?' I was studying her to see if she flinched at the sudden mention of his name.

The woman gazed at me and said, 'He never comes here.'

Not a muscle of her face stirred. 'He never comes here,' she said again.

I didn't believe her, as I knew that the old woman was like a mother to Luke. James had told me this. This woman was hiding something, something she didn't want me to find out.

'Do you mind if I use your bathroom?'

She hesitated. 'It's down the hall, second door on the right,' she said reluctantly. It was obvious that she didn't want me wandering around the cottage but to refuse me such basic hospitality would be too suspicious.

I was ecstatic and flew down the passageway into the bathroom, flushed the loo, ran the tap and quickly dodged out again. Stealthily, I opened the sitting room door. The room was tastefully furnished with antiques, a large sofa, a scatter of armchairs, an ornate cocktail cabinet with an interior illuminated light, and various objects d'art on Victoriana coffee tables.

Glancing around, I took in my surroundings. Nothing untoward here, I thought as I turned to go. Then my eye glimpsed a photograph on the sideboard. It was the photo of a young woman and what I took as a younger version of Luke. He looked about sixteen. I walked over to have a closer look, picked up the frame and turned it over. I gaped and took a closer look. What I saw confirmed my suspicions. An idea began to form. It was born of desperation, but the more I examined it the more sense it made like the moon appearing from behind a thick murky cloud. The pieces had slotted into place, finally making sense - a chilling and horrific kind of sense. I put the frame down.

'What are you doing here?' a voice croaked.

I spun round, nearly jumping out of my skin. In my excitement I'd forgotten the old woman.

'I'm so sorry, I thought this was the bathroom and then I saw the 'photo of Luke and I presume his mother, your daughter.'

'That's not...' There was a momentary flush on her face, a momentary stillness in her hands, which seemed to betoken a coming outburst of anger that might throw her off her guard. But she seemed to master the rising irritation, standing arms akimbo and with a smile of grim sarcasm on her thick lips she looked at me intently and said, 'I begin to understand it all now. You think that Luke had something to do with the murder. And you've come up here to pry and to find things out.' She stopped for a second, her arms tightened over her breasts and she laughed – a hard, harsh, angry laugh.

'I'm sorry,' I said, 'I didn't mean to intrude.' I quickly strode out of the room.

'You left the tap on,' the woman said as she followed me and then entered the bathroom and turned the tap off.

The lie has alerted her. She now knew I'd been prying.

In the kitchen I said, 'Could I have a drink of water before I go. The long drive has made me thirsty.'

333

Reluctantly the old woman filled a glass from the tap. I tried to make small talk as I sat sipping.

'You better be drinking up, it's a long drive back and these roads aren't safe. It's very lonely along here; anything could happen to you.'

Was that a threat? I felt a chill inching up my spine. 'Yes, I must be going.'

Drinking even more slowly for I wished to have a last look around I surreptitiously glanced under my eyelashes studiously taking in my surroundings. My eyes focused on an antique blue jug sitting on the sideboard but what was next to it intrigued me. I had to risk it and investigate further. 'That's a very unusual jug,' I said, jumping up before the old woman had time to stop me. I bounced over to the sideboard. 'The colours are so unique,' I added. 'It's got to be very old?'

'Yes, it was my grandmother's,' the woman said grudgingly.

'May I take a closer look,' I asked timidly. 'I collect old pottery myself.'

All the time I was studying what was in the glass beside the jug. The golden liquid had a sliver of ice floating in it and as I bent and pretended to have a closer look at the jug I sniffed the contents of the tumbler. Yes definitely whiskey and hardly the old woman's; I hadn't smelt whiskey on her breath. Now I sensed there was someone else in the house.

Who was this unknown guest? Couldn't be Luke? He was in custody. Suddenly the truth was here staring me in the face. Now I knew for certain what the whole set up had been.

'It's getting late, you should be going?'

The woman was eager to see me gone. Did she suspect that I'd spotted the glass? 'Oh dear, you're right,' I said looking at my watch. 'I'd better be off.'

As I hurried to the front door the old woman's cruel smile slowly widened her lips as she gazed at me. Was she speculating on what I might have learned or had she something in mind – some sinister plot to do me harm?

I couldn't wait to get out of the cottage. I almost ran out the door. It was then I caught a glint of metal as I detected a slight movement of the garage door. Someone had closed it. That someone was in there and didn't want me to see the vehicle. I wished I'd brought my car nearer; at least then I could make a quick get-a-way. A weeping ash stood close to one of the brick pillars of the front gate, and the branches swished across my path as I passed. The sudden sinister movement made me duck my head, and look back in fear.

I decided to cut through the woods, it would be quicker. The trail between the spruce trees was narrow and steeply twisting. Bracken, dead and partly withered brushed my feet like little furry animals. It was eerily quiet. The dusk falling made the intense silence even scarier. Once I thought I heard heavy footsteps behind me. The brooding silence of late afternoon was such that the smallest twig snapped beneath my shoes with a noise like splintering bone.

It had rained and the mud stuck to my shoes. I cursed myself for wearing high heels. Suddenly something touched my face. I froze. It was just a low branch of a tree.

The sun was low, turning the woods into a kaleidoscope of purples, greens and reds. The track was getting steeper. I started to regret my decision to cut through the wood. I paused and listened. Was anyone following me? I clicked on the small torch I'd attached to my key ring. All I could hear was the gentle swaying of the trees. Was there movement? There among the trees. I spun around and shot a stream of fragile light from tree to tree. I could have sworn a shadow ducked away from the tiny beam. Or was it just my imagination. I strained to see beyond the thick branches. I held my breath and listened. Nothing! Probably just the wind. I listened again and realised there was no wind. Suddenly a force sent me tumbling. I lost my balance and crashed down hard, with my elbows breaking my fall. The lamp flew out of my hand on to the ground beside me. I waited for whoever was near to grab me. I knew I was done for now. Movement - a soft thud. I grabbed at the flashlight and beamed it towards the source of the sound. A deer! Startled the animal disappeared among the trees. Relief, like a tornado, flooded through me.

Then I saw a gap and realised I was near the car. Running the rest of the way I unlocked the car. Quickly I jumped in, turned the ignition and drove at top speed down the boreen. Slow down for God's sakes. But I couldn't wait to put as many miles as possible between the place and me. It held a dark secret and I knew what it was.

A man walked into the kitchen and said, 'Do you think she knows anything?'

The old woman replied. 'Yes. Everything by the looks of it. The way she ran down the path like a demon out of hell she certainty was scared. She's bright.'

'I can't let this one go. I'll have to do something.'

The woman gave him a searching glance and said, 'You must do the necessary.'

They continued to talk in a low voice.

My journey back down the mountain was an ordeal. An icy breeze combined with a drop in temperature had made the twisting road like an endless skating rink. Dusk, continuing to fall made it difficult to see. Inside the Ghia I felt a chill penetrate my body.

To my right there was a cliff wall and to my left a bottomless chasm. Another motorist could force me off the road if he wished. I shivered.

A sinister silence had fallen over the mountain - a heavy ominous silence you could almost hear. The peak seemed to rise up sheer to my left. To the right side of me the abyss, with its white chasm, seemed to beckon to me.

Headlights! Oh no, they're tailing me. The car was gaining on me but I couldn't drive any faster. If I were not careful I'd end up at the bottom of the chasm, dead by my own hands.

The car behind was only a few feet away. What could I do? The perspiration was pouring down me. Suddenly the car started to overtake. Much to my surprise the car gathered speed and disappeared into the dusk. A harmless motorist!

As I got to the bottom and on to a level stretch of the road I stopped and rested my head on the steering wheel. Switching off my engine I wound the window down. Despite the cold air I welcomed it to cool me down. My clothes hung clammily on me. The piercing cry of a seagull made me jump. It sounded like the last lament of a dying soul. Was it a requiem for my death?

I stopped and ate a stale Subway sandwich I had bought two days previously that I found stuck under the seat. I remained still for a few minutes and then drove on until I came to a village with one petrol station. 'I need the loo,' I muttered. I swung into a space near the pumps and dashed inside. Just then my mobile rang. It was the priest.

'Where are you for God's sake? I've been ringing your land line all day.'

'I'm in Scotland.'

'In Scotland? What are you doing there?'

'Didn't you get my message?' I related all that I had found out.

'You're mad Alex. Do you want to get yourself killed?'

His voice held a deep emotion – concern?

'Only a miracle will save me now or a good Samaritan.'

'Good Samaritan?' The question was in his voice.

I paused. 'Yes, you know, in the bible, the parable of the friendly neighbour.'

'Yes, of course.'

Too vague. Too vague. It was happening again. Just like the episode of the wine to water. Cymbals crashed terrifyingly inside my head. A gun fired at my brains eyes.

'Where are you exactly?'

He wants to know my position. How could I have been so slow? How could I have been so slow?

My lips went numb. 'My position? Not sure.' Too vague. Too vague.

'You must know where you are Alex.'

He knows, he knows. He's part of it all. Foley, the priest maybe Pat. No never Pat.' "Ships that pass in the night…. Two souls in one body." Never him. Thank God never Pat -. Nicholas's closest friend. My heart is screaming. My stomach lurches. My mind clicks.

'Where are you Alex? We must protect you.'

'In some village near the border.' Too vague. Too vague.

'What village? Alex. What village? His voice was urgent now. He knows he knows. He knows I'm stalling. He knows I know.'

'I must look at the map. I'll phone you back.' Disconnect

Got to get home, got to get home. I'll ring James. No, can't be sure anymore. Maybe James is in on it too. Oh God who do I turn to.

My terror lessened as four hours later I drove over the border. I was very close to the truth. Maybe James, with his intelligence, might fill in the blanks.

As I drove my mind dwelt on him. I knew by his attentions that he liked me but I was too busy sorting everything out to become distracted by romance. For now I would concentrate on finding Nicholas's killer. And anyhow I could wait. I had learnt not to be needy.

Home at last. I locked the door put the safety catch on and dialled James's number. It was 7.00a.m. I told him bits of the story but kept the bit about the photo back. 'I need to see you James. It's imperative. I can't trust anyone... even you...'

'You can trust me, Alex.'

'How do I know I can?'

'Because...I think I'm falling in love with you.'

He loves me. Oh God he loves me. But the priest -he seemed genuine – a man of God. Perhaps I'm mistaken. 'You could be leading me into a trap.'

'Okay, Alex I understand. Bring Donal with you. You know you can rely on him. I'll meet you at a café of your choice. When you get there phone me with the address. You can have the police stake out the place if you like.'

'Okay. I'll meet you.'

My scientific background had trained me to keep it simple, and so I decided to choose a place somewhere crowded – a small, busy cafe, a place where two people are hard to follow and harder to listen to unless close by. Now I was sitting inside. The place was divided into two sections, separated by several wooden screens. The windows facing the narrow street were draped with heavy lace curtains. I text James and sat, tapping my fingers on the melamine table waiting for him to arrive.

Eventually James arrived. From the door he scanned the outside and when he was satisfied that any invisible watchers had been lost and that no unwanted eyes or ears existed, he walked over to the alcove where I sat.

'Alex,' James said as he sat down, 'no one saw you enter or followed you here?'

'No, I don't think so.'

'I see you didn't bring Donal. He gave a penetrating look. 'You trust me then or maybe the police are outside.'

'No I think I can trust you James.'

The noise of the café flooded the space that separated us. I bit my lower lip, and felt a facial tic scurried across my cheek, and kneaded my hands into a knot of flesh and bone until, finally, I was able to gain some small measure of control. I spoke softly but the fear remained. 'Luke's involved in Nicholas's murder.'

'How, he's got a cast iron alibi?'

'Wait for it...'

'Let's order first,' James, said, 'and then we can talk.'

He ordered two coffees from the hovering waitress and turned to me again.

'So.'

I took a sip of my coffee, drew in a deep breath and began. I told him everything down to the last detail.

The waitress came and took our order for a bowl of the soup de jour. James waited until she was well out of hearing before continuing.

'Alex, what you've found out is even more dangerous then I thought. It all tallies with what we found out about the laundering. Get in touch with Ken as soon as possible.'

Dishes were placed in front of us. We ate in silence.

After eating, James, said, 'I'll go first.' But before he went he bent over and kissed me on the cheek. 'I have a plan but for now we must not be seen together.' With that he made his exit glancing left and right as he closed the door.

Five minutes later I left. Every fibre in my body was tense. Was I being followed? I pulled my heavy overcoat around me to keep out the icy cold. Offering silent thanks for the warm, fur-lined hood, I hurried down the deserted street. Leafless trees waved menacingly in the bitter wind as I anxiously surveyed the blank windows of the houses lining the pavements. For the last few days I'd had a strong feeling that someone close to me was passing information on to the syndicate. The old woman hadn't been surprised to see me; it was as if she'd been forewarned by someone. Who? It had to be the priest. I was almost certain that he was a phoney. But what if I was wrong? What if I was allowing my imagination to run riot? But maybe it wasn't. Maybe it's Ken? Never, he's too forthright, too honest to be on the take. James? Maybe all this friendliness was a scam – a way to get information out of me. And that only left Pat. But Pat – impossible! He was Nicholas's closest friend and now mine. And then there's Cooper – I had already suspected that he could be in league with the killers. That left only the priest. Suddenly he had appeared from nowhere claiming that he knew Nicholas. And then there were Ken's suspicions of him. And then the bible I had given him. He wasn't familiar with the parables in it. But it couldn't be him. There had to be an explanation. He's a priest, a man of God. And his face; it epitomised goodness.

95

NEXT MORNING while I was still in bed I tried to ring Ken but he was away on a conference. I tried his mobile but it was switched off. I dozed off again. The jangle of the phone dragged me from a comatosed sleep. My eyes snapped open. I reached for the phone.

'Alex, it's Pat. I got your message. Listen Alex that document sounds authentic. I'll make some discreet inquiries though and get back to you.'

'It's not all right. It's money laundering.'

'Don't be ridiculous Alex.' His voice sounded irate. 'Danny is certainly not involved in laundering.'

'But James told me.'

'How did you get to know him?'

'I did and what's more I'm inclined to believe him.'

'There's no way James would know anything about Danny's business.'

'He said it's in all the papers – the money laundering.'

'Well it's got nothing to do with our Danny.'

.His signature is on the document, and Nicholas's.'

Should I tell him about my trip to Scotland, my discovery, and about my return journey?

There was a silence on the other end of the phone.

'Are you still there Pat? Listen I've something to tell you. I left a message saying I was going to Scotland. Well this is what I found out.' I related the whole tale to him.

'This is the most incredible story I have ever heard.'

"It's the truth.'

'You must get in touch with Ken.'

'He's away at a conference and his mobile's switched off.'

'When does he return?'

'The day after tomorrow! I'll ring Bill in the morning.'

'I wouldn't trust anyone with this information. Leave a message for Ken to ring you when he gets back. And Alex, don't tell anyone else about this.'

96

'DANNY.'

In the second that Danny recognised the face and the throbbing scar just on the jaw-bone, partly hidden by the white collar, the point of a blade dug in under his ribs, thrusting up into the heart. There wasn't even time to struggle. There was a surprised, pained gasp as the blade went in, then a juddering spasm, as his muscles tensed and his fingernails dug into the material of his assailant's shirt. His face registered incomprehension. Danny let out a long slow release of breath as he relaxed against the priest. He felt a kind of blinding light, no pain, and then only darkness. Frank clasped him close to him while he expired. He placed the body on the ground and grasped the handle of the knife. It made a strange, spluttering sound as he slowly withdrew it. With his left hand he reached into his trousers pocket and produced a piece of tissue paper and wiped the knife carefully with it. He sighed and walked away from the entrance to Danny's office into the darkness. It had begun to rain.

That night in the sacristy of the local church near where Alex lived, Father O'Malley robed for Benediction. Looking into the mirror he stared back at the figure facing him. The deed is done now Father you can go back to being a gangster. Later as he stood in the pulpit, there was genuine passion in his voice as he led the congregation in the rosary, 'And forgive us our trespasses as we forgive those who trespass against us and lead us not into temptation but deliver us from evil.' Who among his congregation would have guessed that he'd just committed a murder?

In the sacristy, afterwards, Frank tossed his white collar into the bin. Having a brother a priest comes in handy. Now to the final phase, the final elimination. He thought about her, thought about her blue eyes, her beautiful smile. She trusted him and needed him. It was a new feeling. He could do without it. He must remember who was paying, must not go all soft. He had a job to do.

97

I SAT watching the TV when the 'phone rang. I snatched up the receiver saying, 'Is that you James?' There was no reply only an eerie, empty silence then what seemed to be a hissing noise. Hearing the person speak a few syllables might prove valuable. Place of origin, age, ethnicity, could be inferred from a voice. Just one clue as to who my stalker is. But nothing. I placed the receiver back and frowned. I began to sweat. Strange? There was no mistaking; there had definitely been someone there.

Midnight! I'd dozed off on the settee in the upstairs living room. I woke with a start from my deep slumber. It was a wild night. The wind was howling outside and the rain was beating against the window. Suddenly amidst all the hullabaloo of the gale, there was a noise from downstairs. Instinctively I sensed danger. My heart began to pound as I heard the stealthy sound again. What was it? It seemed like the creak of the floorboards. There was somebody ascending the stairs? It's only the gate outside in the front garden creaking; I thought and admonished myself for being so jumpy. Yet, in my heart of hearts I knew that something was amiss. Creak ... creak ... the sound was now getting louder and in my imagination it seemed to me that all other sounds were blocked out. By the tone I knew someone was putting an enormous weight on the loose floorboard outside my study ... or judging by the noise, maybe there were two people. Don't be so daft, I thought. The ticking of the grandfather clock seemed to also grow louder. I'm losing it, I told myself but the sound drew nearer and nearer ... then silence. Petrified I waited, huddled on the settee, too terrified to move. The heating had gone off and I could feel an icy chill creeping towards me as if it was an evil presence enveloping me. Maybe I can escape through the front window. No, the drop is too great. I shivered. Has my time run out?

The two men had moved soundlessly down Alex's garden path and took positions on either side of the front door. The smallest of the men gently tried the door. It was locked. He took out a piece of wire and inserted it into the lock. Within seconds, he'd picked it. The tall one nodded to the others. They took out guns with silencers on them and ascended the stairs, revolvers held out in front of them. In the landing, four doors confronted them. One of them was open, the study. The two men moved in, guns sweeping the room. There was nobody there. They moved without haste, knowing that Alex was in the house, somewhere. After all, she'd spoken on the phone earlier. Unhurried, they moved stealthily to the second closed door, the living room. The small one tried the handle. It grated.

I suddenly knew who they were - my killers. From the noise of the creaking there had to be at least two of them. My body went cold with fear.

Life is a very thin strand and it only takes a moment to snap it. It was all becoming a Kafka nightmare. Faceless executioners were condemning me. The door handle moved again.

Fear crackled the hair at the nape of my neck. The grating noise made me twist round and stare at the door handle. Red hot sweat pricked my spine and made my silk shirt stick to my breasts. Panic bordering on hysteria welled up like a flood. Frantically, I grabbed the telephone and dialled 999. It seemed an eternity before there was an answer. Desperately, I whispered down the 'phone. 'Operator, I want the police.

Hurry - it's a matter of life and death. This is Alex Ro ... ' I got no further.

A man's hand reached in front of me and pressed down the receiver. I gave a scream and spun around. I glimpsed a cruel glint there and knew I would be exterminated without a thought. I could see that underneath the rigid stone face was a rage that would explode at any moment.

Two others were present. The taller one moved to one side, and stubbing his cigar out in the ash tray said, in a soft passionless tone, 'Lets go.'

Glancing around the room wildly, I wondered whether I could save myself as I looked for a possible weapon ... a bottle, a crystal decanter, anything. My mouth went dry as the tall one said harshly,

'I wouldn't try anything, if I were you.'

I felt sick with fear as he gave me a push towards the door, and down the stairs, scooping up my car keys from the hall table.

It was dark outside as the two men bundled me into my Carmen Ghia. I wondered why they were using my car. I offered no resistance.

One of the men climbed into the driver's seat. He was a small dark man with a pimply face and sallow complexion, and a deep scar that ran across his face that made him look even more menacing than he might have been. He switched on the engine.

Another man clambered in beside me. The tall one got into a Mercedes parked in front of the Ghia. The driver, who had remained in the car, twisted his head slightly and then took off like a demon out of hell but not before I caught a glimpse of his profile. He looked oddly familiar but his cap was pulled over his face so I couldn't see his features clearly. Nevertheless, a chilling truth hit me. I felt I knew this man and he was with these men.

Pimply face followed close behind.

The man beside me was younger. His eyes were shifty and darted here and there. I could tell that he was nervous. Maybe he'd take pity on me, but as he dug the gun deeper into my side I gave that idea up.

A cold wind blew through the gap in the window. No light relieved the darkness of the night except for the headlights. On each side of the car, great bare branches of trees stretched ominously to the darkened sky and shapeless hedges rustled on the side of the lane. The blackness affected my spirits even more and I felt engulfed by the whole scene around me. I shuddered.

'Take it steady,' the one next to me ordered the driver. 'We don't want to attract the attention of any roving police car at this time of the night. Remember they are looking for drink drivers at this hour.'

The car slowed as the driver lightened his foot on the accelerator. Looking out the window, I wondered where they were taking me. Then my thoughts turned to the driver of the Mercedes again. Suddenly my heart skipped a beat and letting out an agonising scream, I shouted, 'No, no, please God, don't let it be him. Oh God, not him!' My eyes rolled and I felt that I was going to faint but the gun was pushed into my body more and a voice said,

'Try that again and I'll blow your guts out.'

Before I'd time to recover, we came to a large gate with a building barely in outline far back from the entrance. The gate had been opened by someone. We drove in. It was then that I saw the smoke in the sky and smelt the sickly, fetid air. It was the Council Rubbish Facility. Why take me here?

Recalling my first visit to the tip with Nicholas years before, I shuddered as I remembered his words.

'Careful dear, one slip and you are a goner.' Being a man who was fascinated by the unusual he had then proceeded to explain in detail how the process worked: I remembered his ghoulish description:

'The waste is first put into the bunker and then transferred from there to feeder chutes by means of overhead travelling cranes equipped with electro-hydraulic Polyp Graps. These cranes are operated from a control room where closed circuit television provides viewing of the refuse bunker. Then the refuse is moved by the cranes onto a grate in the combustion chamber and is passed down the inclined surface to the burning phase.' Afterwards he had added, 'I read in some paper that in Chicago it's a favourite way to dispose of a body. Only the white bones are left.'

I shivered when I realised what was going to happen.

As though he read my thoughts, pimply face turned and said, 'So you've guessed our little game. You don't think we're going to let you live so that you can identify our man. And this time your friendly detective is not around to protect you.'

As we drove further in, I noticed a group of peculiar-looking constructions that extended almost to the sky - tall red - bricked smokestacks, which looked like chimneys from Auschwitz. Their tortuous silhouettes seemed to rise up out of the earth like giant misshapen mushrooms, as the top of them seemed capped in a fungal architecture. The Ghia rolled up to a complex and came to a stop. The driver jumped out and pimply face held the gun to my temple. 'Get out, and don't try anything. There's no one here to hear you and anyhow one word and I'll blow your pretty face away.'

The reality of the place grabbed me like pincers. Despair glued me to the seat.

The gun was placed hard against my temple and the voice said, 'Move.'

My mouth went dry. In another minute they'll have thrown me into the tip and... I shivered.

Lightening cracked in the clouds above my head as I climbed out of the car and stood facing the men. I was unsure how much the trembling in my knees was due to the sounds coming from the buildings or how much came form the visceral fear of these men who, I sensed, would end my life with as little compunction as one feels when one kills, skins and guts an eel. Another lash of lightening imprinted on my memory the image of the man's face that held the gun. The only distinguishing mark on his slab-like features was a large dark wart by his right nostril.

Drops of rain started to fall. I peered at the rest of captors again and knew I was looking into the countenances of my doom. No mercy showed on their faces only impatience; as if they had tired of it all and wanted to get the job done.

From out of the shadows appeared a figure. His chestnut eyes were cold and piercing and seemed to swell to a size that completely engulfed the eye sockets as they fell on me. 'We've got to make her tell us who knows my secret and where the document is.' Softly he questioned, 'Whom did you tell?'

'No one.'

'You're lying you fucking bitch. We know everything about your movements.' He stared at me with his dead fish eyes now no longer that glassy blue colour that stared out at me the night of the murder. Yes the same retina, the same pupil but the iris had been different then and I now knew why. With blue contact lenses and hair dyed he looked identical to his brother, Luke Foley. I'd found that out on the mountain. And now I was beginning to work out how Michael's existence had remained a secret for so long. Alas to late for me.

He stood before me, radiating a kind of cruel, low menace. I caught a subtle whiff of expensive musk. Growing angry at my silence he dragged me by the hair towards him. The others gathered around.

Again he asked, 'Who knows?'

I whimpered as his hands grasped my arms painfully. I spat into his face. Releasing me he drew a revolver out of his pocket and put it to my head. I waited for the shot.

It didn't come. Instead he threw me to the ground. He laughed, a horrible grotesque laugh as he sat astride me and said, 'Ken can't help you now.' Terror surged through me as his hands fiddled with the zip on his trousers. With one swift movement he tore off my knickers. I felt his hard hands on my breasts and told myself that nothing mattered except staying alive. With one thrust he tore into me.

With my hands clenched and teeth biting my lower lip until it bled, I lay beneath him as he plunged into me. The pain was excruciating like a scorching hot blade lacerating my insides. I was in a nightmare of unspeakable pain – mental and physical. Screeching, howling sounds like a myriad of screaming feral beasts scraped at every nerve ending in my body. Comatosed with shock, I tried to make my mind flee from my body, separating itself from the sensation of what was happening to me. I screamed then. Not a scream of anxiety, or fear or shock or despair but as I heard the shriek echo through the universe it seemed to coalesce all those properties into something so despairing and terrifying that it defied all reason. It was as if all the screams of all the tortured creatures down all the centuries had been rolled into one hideous reverberation. An eerie silence. I twisted my head slightly. Like statues the men stood as if stunned by the atrocity. Even Michael stopped and furtively rose. Through the fog of pain and humiliation I vowed: if I survive this I will stalk you to the edge of the planet.

Electric fear shot through me as the words, 'Use her,' hissed through the air. I was now transported far beyond horror as I waited. Gang rape. But nobody moved except the man with the wart. Before he reached me the tall man shouted, 'Come on for fuck sake, we're wasting time. Let's get the job done.' Perhaps he didn't relish the added violence. He dragged me to my feet.

Still, in some far remote part, my brain was working, trying to think of a way out. The agonising pounding in my head prevented me from focusing on anything except my imminent death. As they surrounded me, I looked at last into the face of the man that had been driving the Mercedes. Incredulity registered first, then shock. I stood powerless, hardly believing that it could be him. Even Judas Iscariot's betrayal could not equal this. With absolute wretchedness, I stared again into his eyes. Memories ... memories of the times we had shared flooded back to me. It had all seemed real then, genuine and now this. This had to be the worst kind of treachery, the ultimate betrayal. I was right about someone spying on me but I'd never have suspected him. Now here I was face to face with the man I had thought of, as one of the dearest men I'd ever known. It was too much. Just the memory of him had made me feel warm and loved. I stared at him, fascinated, wondering what insanity's could have driven him into the obscene world of these men. Whatever the reasons, they had to be powerful. Suddenly, from my throat came a scream - deep and filled with agony.

He looked at me and cast his eyes down.

But I wasn't going to spare him. Tossing my head I looked directly at him and said contemptuously, 'Et Tu. Brute.'

He looked away. I continued to stare until he started to shift uneasily on one foot and then the other. I looked at him. 'My friend just like a Faustian pact you have sold your soul to a prince of darkness ... for what ... to gain the whole world and lose your soul.' My voice broke. My mouth went dry. It was a massive betrayal. Why should I be surprised? 'Ships that pass in the night. Two bodies in one soul.' I turned towards the bunker. One step more and then my final resting place. One thing to pray for - a swift end.

The tall man nodded and made a lunge towards me. He picked me up as if I was a rag doll and slinging me over his shoulder, moved towards the bunker, lifted me into the air, and hurtled me into it. With a thump, I hit the bottom, a distance of about ten metres. As I landed on something hard I could feel the agonising splinter of bones. Every fibre in my body seemed to tingle as if I had touched a 240-volt live wire. The stench hit me first, then the pain. I whimpered and then I lost consciousness.

98

AS I came to I felt the damp mushiness of rotting refuse seep through my dress. Not only was it distressing to breathe from the pain but also the stench of the stuff and the methane gas coming from it made it almost impossible.

Lying there in the darkness, like a disfigured broken toy, useless and discarded, I listened. Silence! The crane wasn't working! Why? Nicholas had said it operated continuously. Gradually the old Alex stirred. There has got to be a way out of this.

Another noise now intruded on my waking hell – a kind of scraping. All of a sudden a furry clingy thing was scrambling over my neck and on to my cheek. Terror struck. Then I felt a movement on my thigh. It palpitated on my flesh. I kicked my leg out. The pulsating ceased. The thing had gone.

What was waiting there? I'd a sense - although I felt it might be my fantasy - of a stealthy movement all round me. A rasping sound? A purring? What? Then a sudden low keening and rustling began.

I shot out my hands and my fingers touched something grizzly. It bit my finger. Sticky blood ran down my hand. Rats!

Oh my God, this is my horror of horrors, my worst nightmare. My fear of been devoured by these creatures was a fate far worse than a merciful burning alive. Only a miracle would save me now. I prayed again, 'Oh Mary Mother of God help me.' My mantra froze on my lips as the shadowy creatures drew closer. Their red eyes stared out at me, waiting.

When one started to chew my ear, I felt that I would die, not with the pain and revulsion of the act but of what I perceived as a sort of cannibalism. Do rats eat you alive? It was painful to move but with a supreme effort, I managed to brandish one arm at them. They retreated. I'd have to find a way out of this hell hole. Fear scuttled up under my hair. I whipped my key ring torch around trying to see with the faint light coming from it.

An idea was forming in my mind but I felt weak and the sweet repose of the tomb seemed to beckon to me. I struggled to retrieve the disposable lighter I had in my pocket for my science experiments. It seemed ages before I managed to grip the cold metal. Success! There was a chance. With shaking hands I tried to flick it on but the pain was intolerable and waves of unconsciousness washed over me. You can't die now. Where's that indomitable spirit of yours.

But an icy mantle of air seems to cover me like some lewd wrapping, caressing my lips with a breath that reeked of death.

With enormous effort; I dragged myself into a sitting position. My fingers trembling, I tried to set fire to the debris. It started to burn, reluctantly, at first, but then something flammable caught hold. The rats retreated. Fire, fire, oh glorious fire, I thought as it burned furiously. My euphoria, however, was short lived. The flames were now almost engulfing me. I was going to be burned alive by my own hands. Oh God this was like a horror movie, one disaster after another. With as much strength as I could muster, I dragged myself over to the side of my prison. Despite the clammy, slimy cold feel of the steel-wall, I crouched against it pressing my body close to it to avoid the inferno. Then another horrifying thought struck me. Perhaps soon the crane would start up and its jaws descend. Panic rose within me and I flung open my mouth, desperately trying to suck in air.

I knelt for a second, wobbling, and my warm, terrified breath coming back at me. The bunker seemed to leap into flickering life around me. Mercifully the rats had vanished. Suddenly, as if my prayers were answered, the falling rain turned into a downpour. I watched as the blaze died down and contemplated my destiny. It became apparent to me that the gang knew exactly what they were doing. They weren't worried about me escaping - if the rats didn't get me the crane would. I must escape. Desperate I pondered my cell. Maybe I could climb up the steel wall. Instinctively, with an almost super human attempt, I stared to pile handfuls of rubbish against it. The exertion was too much and frequently I had to pause for breath. When I had made a pile about a metre high, I dragged myself up on to it and thrust forward with a kind of fury trying to clutch on to some support on the side of the wall. I lurched at it, scrabbling at the sides of the steel walls, gouging my fingertips, my toes tattooing on the steel floor of the bunker in frantic fear.

I felt at that moment that I was on the first rung of the ladder back to life. But there was nothing to cling on to, no second rung. I fell. I lay there; my head sunk into the sodden pile and whimpered. I was exhausted and knowing I couldn't take much more, begged whichever God would listen, 'Let me die, release me from my agony.' It was my last display of extreme anguish before I passed out.

Drifting in and out of consciousness I was aware of how terribly cold I felt. I must stay awake for to drift off again was certain death.

How much longer will it be before I die from cold in this subterranean cosmos of blackness or... put the thought out of your mind?

I heard it then, a sort of rumbling noise first and then a crunching. Giant polyp arms were descending. The end had come. I slumped against the side as it lumbered downwards. A prayer escaped me, 'Oh Mother of God, help me, help me...' but the words died on my lips as the crane moved close its claws digging up the debris. Relief swept through me as I realised it was only operating in the centre of the bunker. If I stayed close to the wall, I'd be safe. The faint ray of hope glimmered for an instant and then became obliterated as the talons hovered directly over my head. Down. Steadily they crept. Relentless! I waited. As the crane came within inches of me, I shrank convulsively as, grotesquely, the brutal limb threatened to immerse me.

99

AT THE central police station D. I. Ken Masterson was in his office chatting to Bill. Suddenly the duty cop Jerry dashed in.

'What's the matter Jerry can't you knock?'

'Sorry chief but you asked me to report anything that concerned Alex Rowe.'

Immediately Ken's eyes glazed over with fear. 'So what do you know?' he said apprehensively.

'Well an operator got a 999 call. The woman who made the call said it was a matter of life or death. She managed to whisper her name.'

'And …?'

'Well all the operator got was Alex Ro … and then the receiver went dead. She checked the number; it's Alex's residence all right.'

Suddenly Ken was all action. 'Let's go. Alex's house!' Ken's features were drawn tight with tension as he picked up the 'phone and dialled zero. 'Alan, I want all squad cars ready. We've something big on.' He slammed down the receiver and said to his Bill. 'Ready.'

'Crosby?'

'Yes, she's in danger.'

Three police cars screamed to a halt outside Alex's house. All the lights were still on. Ken jumped out and ran up the path. Buzzing the doorbell impatiently he waited for a few second. 'Break it down, there's no time to waste.'

Within a jiffy Jerry had put his shoulder to the door and forced it open. Ken raced upstairs first, his heart pounding. Was he going to find her dead? He headed for her bedroom.

The bed hadn't been slept in. His heart skipped a beat as he turned round colliding with Jerry. 'For Christ's sake's get out of the bloody way!' He knew he was panicking. He almost dived into the upstairs living room. Empty! 'They've taken her.' He knew then that time was of the essence or maybe it had already run out.

Somehow he got to the police car. It was then he noticed her car missing. Within seconds a message began to transmit a staccato message giving a description of the car.

But the night was a complete failure. Six o'clock in the morning there was still no sign of Alex or her car. It was then that Ken received the information. A body had been seen in the bunker at the local tip. There was only one body he was interested in. It was his job, a body had been found, some drunk or other destitute. He had to investigate.

100

I HEARD the sound of a voice. I realised I was alive. Lots of lights shone into my eyes. I blinked to stop myself being blinded. At first I couldn't make out the voice so great was my anguish but then I recognised it as being Ken's and as I attempted a groan I heard Ken's voice saying,

'I think she's still alive.'

Something seemed to be lowered down and through the dawn light I could see figures descending down a roped ladder. Suddenly lots of arms gripped me and lifted me gently up. A light was focused on me and I heard someone say, 'Jesus, look at her finger, it's almost half eaten away.'

'I'll kill the bastards.' Ken!

I felt myself slip away, but I forced one puffed eye open and through a narrow blood red slit I stared at Ken. I whispered the word 'Foley.' Ken was staring at me and I realised that I'd only mouthed the words and that no sound had emerged. I lifted myself onto my left elbow and spoke slowly, labouring, in a hoarse broken voice ... 'Foley.' Then I became aware of someone wrapping me in a warm blanket and being placed on a stretcher.

The darkness, stink and horror of it all were over. It was like a resurrection. I could breathe fresh air again. A glorious dawn was just breaking and momentarily I breathed in the silence of a beautiful sunrise in a clear blue sky. I could hear the song of a late bird singing. For a moment I was overwhelmed by this serenity and forgot the terror of what had taken place and my suffering as I became submerged in the peaceful scene. On and on I went until

I was dizzy and the clouds came over and I closed my eyes and let the sky or the wind or the sun lift me up and waft me away. Then I lost consciousness.

101

TWO WEEK later Ken was sitting in his office. Peter Gibson stood against a wall, smoking his pipe. Bill perched on Ken's desk while Alex occupied the armchair. Ken was upset. He'd never seen anyone so changed. Alex was a shadow of her former self. Her face was a sickly grey and her eyes were dead. Her hair hung limply over her shoulders.

He turned away stricken. 'I'll start from the beginning of the night,' Ken said, as he leaned back in his chair. 'When they took Alex to the tip, Foley and his gang knew that the crane would do the rest.'

'Foley but I thought Foley was in prison.' Peter said hesitatingly.

'Wait for it, wait for it,' Ken said as he cast Peter an impatient glance. 'They'd watched the place for days and knew that the operator was sneaking off around midnight to see his lover and returning a couple of hours later. They'd even followed him to discover where he was going and what he was up to. His absence gave them an ideal opportunity to carry out their evil intent.'

'Why the tip,' Peter asked.

'Alex had been dumping garden refuse there. CCTV footage confirmed this. They knew the staff would have noticed her.'

Then, with her car parked there, everyone would assume that with the balance of her mind unhinged by all the events happening in her life she'd committed suicide'.

'So with the operator away they could dispose of her.'

'Yes. They knew that he usually returned around 2.00 a.m. to start the crane. However, fortunately this time he didn't get back 'til 6.00 a.m. By this time Alex had lit a fire in the tip.'

'And of course he noticed the glow.'

'Yes and dialled 999.'

'Lucky for Alex!'

'Yes.'

'What I don't understand is why Luke Foley wanted to kill Alex.'

'Wait for it. In a nutshell this is what happened. Danny Delaney was the lynch pin in all of it. Luke went after Danny for the two million and since he didn't have it Danny fingered Nicholas. It was his only way to escape the fix he was in. He hoped that Luke would believe him.'

'What convinced him?'

'Most people would expect a legal person to hold, on account, such a large sum. Danny and Pat managed to convince Luke that Nicholas had taken the money and that he was going to do a runner. They explained about how desperate Nicholas was to see his daughter and about the vast debts he had accumulated flying over to see her.'

'So they looked to Nicholas?'

'Yes. We know from Rosso that Nicholas had denied having any money from anybody so he probably said the same to the syndicate.'

'So who killed him?'

'Luke's younger brother, Michael.'

'Michael? I didn't know he had a brother.'

'This is where the story becomes bizarre,' Ken said sipping his tea. 'The amazing thing was that no one seemed to know of his existence except of course the immediate family.'

'How come?'

'His mother fled the home when she was two months pregnant. It was a violent marriage and she just disappeared leaving Luke behind with his father. The grandmother helped to rear him. Of course mother and daughter always kept in touch until the daughter died shortly after Luke's eighteenth birthday.'

'Weird,' Peter said shaking his head.

'Luke and Michael were close. When it suited Luke he got his brother to do his dirty work for him thus giving him the perfect alibi - a double. Michael is the image of him.'

'Why this charade in the first place?'

'When a foul deed was committed Luke could claim there was a 'copy cat' carrying out the deeds. It's not the first time the brothers have carried out this double act but that doesn't concern us for here.'

'Strange though, only twins are identical,' Peter said quizzically.

'Disguise; his eyes are brown but with blue contact lenses and hair dyed blonde you'd swear it was Luke. Michael's a bit taller and ten times as hideous.'

'You can say that again,' Alex interjected. Her voice was a dead, flat monotone. 'I'll kill him.'

'Unbelievable,' Peter said, shaking his head.

'When a crime was being committed by Michael, Luke always made sure he had an alibi; like the charity banquet.'

'How did you find out about Michael?' Peter asked in amazement.

'It's down to Alex.' Ken said casting an admiring glance in her direction.

She spoke again. 'I saw Luke's 'photo in the paper when he was extradited from Florida and immediately recognised him as being the man I thought I saw in my hall the night of the murder.'

Ken interjected. 'When she told me about it, I said it was impossible as he'd a cast iron alibi. But she was determined, so of her own bat she went up to the north of Scotland to investigate the grandmother.'

Peter stared. 'How did you know where the old woman lived?'

'James Quigley told me.'

'So what did you find out?'

'When I arrived, the grandmother knew why I was there.'

'How'?

'I'll come to that later. She caught me in the sitting room examining 'photo of Michael and the mother. Michael's name was on the back of the frame. She put two and two together.'

'I'm surprised you managed to get out of there alive.' Peter said.

'Isn't it obvious? They didn't wish to attract undue attention so they decided to get to her nearer home and make her death look like suicide.'

'How did you fill in the pieces so quickly? '

'Pat squealed.'

'He was present when they threw me into the tip.'

'Yes, that was a shocker. I mean Pat being the spy in the camp,' Ken said. 'Shortly before that Alex suspected that someone close was relaying information to the killers. At one stage she even suspected me. She never dreamt it was Pat, Nicholas's closest friend.'

'But how did Pat figure in all of this?'

'After the murder Alex began her own investigations and publicly vowed on TV she'd track the man she'd seen. Foley forced Pat to keep tabs on her. He did so to protect Danny.'

'And what about the two million quid?' Peter asked.

'Dead money as far as Luke was concerned. Nicholas was gone, the only man who'd lead him to the money, or so he thought. Two million was a drop in the ocean for Luke. Once Pat reported her every move he was prepared to wipe the slate clean. Luke and Michael's greatest fear was that she would, somehow, link them to the murder.'

'So all the time Pat was calling on Alex to check out what she knew?'

'Yes, Pat was genuinely fond of Alex. He desperately tried to persuade her to leave well alone and get on with her life. He knew as soon as she'd get too close they'd kill her. He tried to scare her by instigating various ruses. It was he who flicked the fuse in her house and closed the study door. He also trailed her, even went so far as to shout her name out in a crowded street. He even hired a man to watch her and Catherine in the park. When Alex's attention was elsewhere the man took Catherine by the hand and led her. towards a group of trees. Alex of course thought that someone had taken her. Michael's existence had been a closely guarded secret and the Foley's weren't about to let Alex blow the cover,' Ken said.

'It's strange that hardly anyone knew of Michael's existence.'

'Anyone who did was silenced.'

'What do you mean?'

'The old woman who was present at his birth was killed.'

'Jesus.'

'It was the grandmother who ordered her death.'

'What about the priest? Of course we know now that he wasn't one.'

He stared at Peter, looking annoyed. 'Part of Luke's genius was never to leave anything to chance. He didn't trust Pat so he planted his own man in the guise of a man of the cloth.'

'And of course you all fell for it?'

'Alex did but not me.'

'What do you mean?'

'From the beginning I found it rather strange that this priest had never met Zoe and Elizabeth. Being a very catholic family it was only natural to expect the whole family to attend mass together.'

'It could have happened that he mightn't have met them.'

'Yes I knew that so I set a little trap for him and he fell into it.'

'How?'

'I said that I had been to Christ Church and knew St. Mary's church, the one he said he belonged too. I mentioned that it had an unusual spire and he agreed with me.'

'And did it?'

'No, I made it up.'

'So you were on to him?'

'For a while yes.'

'What do you mean?'

'I checked it out.'

'And?'

'There was a St Mary's church but no spire. I was lucky there. However a Father O'Malley fitting the exact description of our priest had been a curate there so I decided that I must have been wrong. But the spire kept bothering me. It couldn't exist because I'd made it up. So I wasn't satisfied and kept a more careful watch on Alex and on the priest.'

'How come you received that information from St. Mary's that Father O'Malley was a priest there?'

'As I said, Luke never left anything to chance. He rigged it. Gave a large donation to the church provided they kept quiet. Being a poor area the parish priest was only too glad to turn a blind eye. Knowing Luke I presume he gave him some plausible excuse.'

'So who was Father O'Malley?'

'One of Foley's henchmen – a man called Frank Moran. Sort of a right hand man.'

'And this brings me to another twist in the tale.'

'Not another one?'

'Danny's dead.'

'Dead!'

'I'm afraid so.'

'How?'

'A stiletto through the heart by Frank's hands.'

'Why?'

'A few days ago Danny called to warn Alex, tell her the truth and our Father O'Malley happened to pop in. He and Luke had paid Danny a visit and killed the dog. Danny recognised him.'

'So of course Frank's cover was blown?'

'Yes, so he took care of Danny.'

'A fitting end.'

'Sad.' Ken stared into space.

'Sad, why?'

'Danny wasn't the worst. Yes, he was a con man but he was a man who got in too deep and couldn't get out.'

'And Pat, what's his reaction?'

'A broken man. I've just come from the prison.' Ken looked in to the distance and recalled his visit.

Pat had sat opposite Ken unshaven, looking as if he hadn't slept for a week.

Ken felt sorry for him. Pat had cooperated fully with the police revealing every last detail. He'd even told him about his deep attachment to Danny. Ken had the unenviable task of telling him about Danny's death.

'I'm sorry to have to be the one to tell you this,' Ken said groping for words that might lessen the blow. 'I'm afraid Danny's... dead, murdered.'

Pat felt his cheeks draw in and his heart seemed hollow. It was as if his whole frame collapsed inwards, unable to support its own mass now that there was only emptiness His grief shuddered through him like a fever. He looked at Ken, a look that would make even the hardest of men weep and then he put his head in his hands and wept, wept uncontrollably, wept until his whole body shook and when he couldn't weep anymore he gazed at Ken with such abject misery that Ken had to look away. The terrible suffering that now ravaged his face was piteous.

'What a high price we pay for love,' Alex whispered, breaking Ken out of his reflections.
'Yes,' Ken replied, 'what a price.'
'So to sum it all up Pat cooperated with the syndicate?' Peter asked
'Yes, they told him that if he didn't keep tabs on Alex they'd kill Danny. Luke knew about Pat's fatal attraction. As I've said Luke never left anything to chance.'
'And Mullins what about him? '
'He really had nothing to do with any of it.'
'What about Rosso? Do you believe he's innocent?'
'We know he was there at the house the night of the murder but as to whether he actually had a part in stabbing Nicholas is something only he and Michael know. He says he doesn't know Michael and still claims that he's innocent.'
'And of course Michael managed to evade capture?' Peter raised an eyebrow.
'Yes, worse luck. He knew the game was up, knew that his secret was out.'

'That wasn't the only reason. I don't believe you know the latest bit.'

'Is there more?' Peter sighed.

'Remember that case in the paper about six months ago? The laundering of billions of yen into dollars?'

'Yes.'

'It was Michael who masterminded it all.'

'Really how do you know all this?'

'Alex told us.'

'What!'

'Remember those six bin bags of papers belonging to Nicholas we gave to your lot to sort through.'

'Yes,' Peter said looking nervous.

'Eventually we returned them to Alex.'

'And?'

'Being the thorough person she is she sifted through the bags.'

'And she found…?' Peter said uneasily.

'A complex contract signed by an M. Foley and Danny and it was acknowledged by Nicholas.'

'Jesus?'

'So she gave it to you?'

'No.'

'Why?'

'Isn't it bloody obvious? How would a schoolteacher recognise that it was a contract to launder money she was looking at? She knew nothing about these things.'

'So how did she find out?'

'James told her.'

'Golly.'

'What sealed her fate was the information she had about the laundering and of course her discovery in Scotland. The document is original and provides all the evidence. It links them all, Michael, Danny, Luke and of course Nicholas.

'How did Michael get into this changing yen into dollars anyway?'

'Through this Oriental he knew, a member of the triads. He has powerful connections. Well, he and Luke were quite close. It was the Oriental who killed Phil. You know already that it was Phil's girlfriend who gave evidence against Luke. If you remember though he didn't actually carry out the deed he condoned it and was there at Phil's execution. The Oriental fled the country at the same time as Luke did. Probably somewhere in South East Asia.'

'Hong Kong no doubt,' Peter said fingering his chin.

'To get back to Michael what about his roll in Nicholas's murder?'

'It's going to be difficult to prove that one. Even Pat sang dumb.'

'Why?'

'Because he knows what Michael will do?'

'So how did you find out about the look- a -like bit?

'When he did a runner we went straight to one of his apartments. It wasn't difficult to get the address from Pat.'

'What did you find?'

'The lot. Blue contact lenses and several bottles of hair bleach.'

'So Michael disguised himself as Luke and murdered Nicholas?'

'Yes.'

'Unbelievable.'

'That's not all. He stalked Alex, knew her every move. We know from Pat that he sent a cryptic note to her - a warning. That was after Danny and Pat managed to convince Luke that Nicholas had the money. So he decided to take action. He thought by putting the frighteners on Alex she'd put pressure on Nicholas and he's return the money. But of course she never mentioned it. And of course Nicholas didn't have it anyway. He's a Psycho you know. Flips from a Dr Jekyll to a Mr Hyde. One minute he's a perfectly charming gentleman and the next he's the devil incarnate.' Ken's eyes rolled.

'So to sum it all up Pat and the priest were working for the Foley's? What about Rosso?'

'My gut reaction is that he was set up.'

'Or maybe he was in it from the start. Or maybe like Danny, he knew Luke.'

'It's hard to tell.' Ken said scratching his head.

'What do you think?'

'Remember the money lending was the common denominator, the thing that linked them all together. Danny borrowed from Rosso through Nicholas. Rosso invested money for many people including Luke and Karl.'

'So Nicholas cleaned the money,' Peter said, his eyebrows raised.

'Yes.' Alex cast her eyes down. 'A tough fact to accept.'

'Do you think he ever had any money?'

'Pat told us that Nicholas passed large sums of money to Danny to invest in hedge funding. So maybe not.'

'Tell me, will we ever know whether they really did intend to kill Nicholas that night?' Peter asked.

'I'm half inclined to believe what Rosso says. It all got out of hand when Nicholas denied having the money.'

'So Michael lost it?'

'Yes, it looks that way. If it was planned they'd have taken him out before he reached the house. No I genuinely think that they went there with the intention of putting the frighteners on him.'

'So Ken, what's your opinion.' Bill suddenly interjected.

Ken fingered his chin and paused. 'I think Luke and Rosso knew each other. Luke knew that Rosso was having difficulty getting monies back from Nicholas. Of course he didn't know that the money had gone to Danny who'd invested it in hedge funding. And we know what went wrong there. It's perfectly plausible that Michael persuaded Rosso to join forces and together pay Nicholas a visit. That way if anything went wrong Rosso would be the fall guy.'

'And he was.' Peter shook his head.

'Precisely! Luke knew that Rosso was an amateur. Dropping his watch and cap at the scene was a dumb thing to do. But he panicked. Rosso was no match for these pros.'

'Who do you think wielded the knife?'

'Michael. It's his modus operandi a knife through the jugular. He's killed before. Of course we didn't know about the set up then. I think Michael was incensed when Nicholas said he hadn't got the money and in a psychotic fury stabbed him.'

'It's amazing, stranger than fiction.'

'There will be an investigation and a trial of course. God knows where Michael is. I'd say by now he's fled the country. His passport was not at the apartment. And his chopper is missing. Probably somewhere in Europe by now.'

'For what it's worth I think Rosso is innocent,' Alex said.

'That's it then.' Ken said as he closed his file. 'We've all had a gruelling time. Let's call it a day.'

102

THEY'D ALL left except for Ken and me. 'We've been through a bit together,' he said casting a concerned glance in my direction.

'Yes, like a cat, I seem to have nine lives.'

'What are you going to do now that it's all over?'

'Get on with my life, for a while.'

'You're determined?'

'Yes.'

'Don't you think you should forget Michael, leave it to us to track him down?'

'Forget Michael; forget what he did to me and to Nicholas? Never, I'll hunt him to the ends of the earth.'

'Alex I wish you'd see some sense. You know now that he's a psycho.

'Yes, I suppose you're right. I'll leave it too you.' If you think I'm going to let this go then you don't know me. 'Look lets change the subject. What will happen to Pat?'

'He's turned Queen's evidence so he'll get a lighter sentence.' He paused and smiled. 'And what about James?'

'How do you know about him?'

Ken smiled conspiratorially.

'Come on Ken tell me.'

'After we found you in the tip and took you to the hospital a very concerned James was on the blower asking about you.'

'Really.'

'Yes, you must know he's fond of you.'

'If he is, he's playing it very close to his chest.'

'I think he's giving you a chance to recover sufficiently from your ordeal before he makes any overtures.'

'Hm.'

'See if I'm right. 'Come on Alex, it's been a long day. I'll drive you home.'

103

SUDDENLY THE darkness was all around me, the sunlight gone instead there were black shapes of irregular foliage beneath the light of iridescent clouds. I had to keep going. To remain immobile was to die. I was on the run trying to evade my pursuers but now they were close behind. As Michael's gang had broken into my house I had slipped out the back door.

I reached the trees at a sprint, branches crunching underfoot as I became obscured by the darkness. I ripped through brambles, ignoring the throbbing as they scratched and clawed at me. I just had to keep running to get as far away from Michael as possible. I scrambled on through the trees threading my way through the dank, dark foliage. Eventually the trees thinned and beyond them was a river with some sort of a pipe embedded in it. As I waded into the water I heard a new sound – dogs barking. Careful not to make the slightest splashing sound I waded into the water until I was up to my waist. I must hide. I cowered down even lower until the water immersed my chin forcing myself to remain calm.

I stretched my arm out until I felt the rim of the pipe. I'd have to crawl inside it. But would the dogs follow me? Somehow, I'd have to throw them of the scent. Cerebral ricochet. Maybe if I put my sweater into the middle of the pipe the dogs would follow the scent. That would give me a chance to make a get a way. Quickly I removed the garment, rolled it into a ball and inserted it in the opening. That done, I crawled in myself, pushing it in about ten metres. Then, abandoning the garment, I inched my way along. The pipe seemed to be getting narrower. Just when I though I would suffocate I emerged at the other end.

Then I heard them. The dogs had picked up my scent again dragging the pursuers to the mouth of the pipe. From a hidden vantage point I watched them yelping and whining hysterically as they lugged the leases from their owners. Rotweilers!

'Let a dog in,' Michael Foley hissed. 'If it chews her up a bit, too God damn bad. This time she'll die.' The dog disappeared. Minutes later it emerged. I breathed a sight of relief. I'd made my way along the side. The water was icy. Ducking below the surface I half crawled along and when I came up for air there was no one around. It had worked. I waded along for 300 metres or more, shivering uncontrollably and almost crying with the cold. Suddenly I heard barking. The dogs had picked up my scent again. I lurched through the water making it surge around me as I'd disturbed some ghastly silver fin. Tears of fear sprang to my eyes as I waded on. I must hide. I bent my legs and sank down until my neck was submerged. Shivering frantically I wondered what to do. Stop to think and you'll die. Impulsively I leapt and hit the bank with a sprint and landed in a load of cow dung. I scrambled on, my eyes watering, ducking as the bare branches whipped against my face. I dived to the ground and whipped round in a crouch, my hands out, ready to dive for cover but there was nothing only trees, dark and mossy. I breathed in and out through my nostrils, my ears straining for any sound. They were there. Very near. I heard a whisper of a dry leaf, a rustle from about three metres away, then the crack of a twig and Michael stepped out from behind the bush.

Part of me wanted to leap up and run but a bigger part told me that it was best to stay hidden. Slowly I inched forward on my stomach, like a serpent pushing myself under a thick bramble bush until I was completely hidden, the thorns tearing my skin. I could hear heavy footsteps drawing nearer. Step by step. Closer! I squeezed my eyes shut to blank out the terror. I remained absolutely still. Hoping.   Waiting. Praying that they wouldn't find me.

Then suddenly someone moved away a few steps the footsteps receding as they got further away from my position. But Michael remained still. He's coming for me, I thought, all the bones in my body turning to jelly. I daren't breathe. Michael would sense it if I did. He seemed so in synch he'd sense even the softest sound: the rush of my blood through my veins, or maybe even the messages jumping from synapse to synapse along my neurones.

He twisted his head first in one direction and then in another and then scanned the trees. After a moments hesitation he continued walking, every now and then stopping to peer around him with great deliberation. Maybe he hadn't heard me. I began to pant with fear, my mouth open like a sheep dog.

Then suddenly I heard a movement behind me. A hand seized me by the arms and dragged me up. It was Frank. Michael was standing beside him. 'Got you,' Michael said.

I caught an expression of diabolical fury, the chestnut eyes glaring savagely. I made an inarticulate little sound and pressed my hand against my mouth. Tears of terror welled in my eyes.

It seemed as if we'd been driving for miles. I lay in the back of a Mercedes my hands tied behind my back and my legs trussed backwards and secured with a thin rope. There was no way I could escape. Frank was driving and pimply face was in the passenger seat.

Eventually we came to ornate iron gates which opened automatically. The driveway was about two hundred metres long. Vast, awesome illuminated gardens receded into obscurity on both sides. We came to a huge manor house. From black tile roofs, red brick walls, windows radiant with gilded light, columns, and terraces, the architect had conjured as much elegance as splendour in this dwelling. Frank jumped out and opened the back door. With a swift swipe of a knife he removed the cord from my legs and hauled me out of the car. I glared at him and he averted his eyes. Some vestige of shame seemed to linger there.

Another car had drawn up outside the house. It was Michael. 'Take her to the greenhouse.' He tossed a quick piercing glare at me letting a nasty snarl creep across his face. My stomach clenched into a ball and the taste in the back of my mouth was acid.

104

A LONG, agonizing scream reverberated through the tops of the palms swaying above in the huge tropical greenhouse.

Michael was trussing me up like a turkey. He restricted himself to a few heavy breaths while he yanked the knot on my wrists until the cord cut hard into the delicate flesh. A pair of hands stuck heavy tape across my eyes and round my head, tugging my long black hair viciously in the process. Then I felt a piece of cloth stuffed into my mouth. More tape was fixed over my lips. With dexterity my wrists were lashed together behind my back. Next my legs were bound, bent behind me and tied to my lower arms, leaving me in a helpless backward arch.

I was lowered onto what seemed a wooden platform. A searing pain ripped through my. Something was piercing my sternum.

Nails?

Thorns?

Spikes?

My heart thumped. A bead of sweat raced down the furrow of my spine. The pain was so ferocious I, momentarily, stopped breathing. Before I could identify the instrument of torture I felt a second stab in my thigh. I squeezed a shriek through the gag. With pain howling around my head I tried to escape from the source of agony but it was impossible. From the texture of the surface beneath me I worked out that I was lying on some sort of a slatted pallet. Clearly the implements were poking up through the slits.

'Bitch,' a voice hissed, coughing. 'You'll die like a pig, and I'm going to savour every minute.' The voice was cold, almost flat, filled with menace.

Footsteps retreat. He's gone. For now! Think, one feeble neuron whimpered. It's Saturday, so no one would miss me until tomorrow.

I waggled my wrists to see if there was any hope of freeing them that way, but they were too well trussed. I attempted to yell but produced only a muffled grunt that might have carried a few yards through the vast interior. Every time I exerted myself, the throbbing in my legs seared into a crescendo of pain.

I lay there and rationalised. It could be days before someone noticed my absence. After all I lived alone. Mental ricochet! The milk will pile up! Hope did a tiny butter-fly flutter in my heart. But then reality zeroed in. The milkman would assume I'd gone to Ireland. He'd stop leaving the milk. Fear shot from synapse to synapse. I'm going to die. I'm going to die.

A blast of white-hot pain shot through my body. The jagged object seemed to be drilling further into my sternum.

Then I heard voices coming from an adjacent room.

'We'll have to leave her for now. The shipment of drugs is due to arrive in another hour. But we'll be back …'

'Why don't you finish her off now? Get it over with. Don't you think this bloody vendetta is gone far enough?'

'What? Because of her meddling she has almost destroyed our operation and every cop in the land is after me. When she finds out what my grand plan is she'll beg me to end her life.'

I went numb with horror. Maybe I could plead for my life. No chance. I remembered what he'd done to me. This man would show no mercy. He had already destroyed all that I held dear. I must untie myself. I knew that whatever I did, I had to do it slowly so that I didn't aggravate the vicious throbbing in my leg. I judged from the angle outside in the murky limbo between dusk and full night.

There was about an hour of daylight left. First I had to release the pressure on my rib cage as the spike, or whatever it was, would eventually bore through and pierce my heart. I arched my head and neck backwards and managed to move my body upwards away from the torture. But only just. With great difficulty I positioned my belt up under my breasts. The effort was too much. I collapsed downwards but this time the metal buckle took all the force.

The next thing to do was to try and free my hands. The only way I could see of doing that petrified me. It meant twisting my body obliquely and as the objects were now embedded in my thighs they'd tear my flesh even further. My trepidation intensified. But I'd no option. I turned sideways as far as I could. Not enough, I thought. Nevertheless, by pushing my arms towards one side, which meant yanking my legs over as well, I succeeded in hooking the cord that bound my wrists over the point of one of them. But the movement led to the sharp tip ripping my quadriceps. A sticky fluid trickled down my skin. Blood! It had now become a manoeuvre way beyond my pain threshold. Still after a pause I took a deep breath and then continued. I used a sawing motion in an attempt to fray the cord. I began to feel it giving way. It had been wound several times round my wrist and when I felt the first strand break, it did not loosen much. All my body ached but I didn't dare take my hands away from the spear. I didn't think I'd ever get them back there. After ten agonising minutes of concerted effort, I felt the bonds coming free. I kept at it. A few moments later, my hands sprang apart and I could straighten my arms. My legs were still tied together but at least I could stretch them out.

Suddenly I sensed a stealthy movement. Someone was coming. He'd see I had freed my hands and removed the tape. Thankfully it was almost dark. Maybe he wouldn't notice that anything was amiss.

Back into the same position again Alex. Head down. Arms and legs back.

More self-coaching.

Calm.

Breathe.

Mantra –hyrng.

Breathe

The pungent smell of 'Diesel' assailed my nostrils. I could feel hot, fetid breath warming my skin. Close now. Very close. Silent shriek. I flinched as though I'd been touched. An awareness, that he was peering at me, crept upon me with dank, scaly fingers. He was there, unseen, slithering through the darkness like the finger of death.

I lay rigid. Then I glimpsed his dark shape on the edge of my vision. He was standing over me.

He chuckled humourlessly - a harsh sound burning with malevolence.

The wind outside battered against the glass panes. A fresh squall of rain threw itself at the window like millions of tiny shrapnel pieces. My terror was almost primal.

105

AFTER ESCAPING from the police dragnet at the tip Michael had gone to his country retreat. The police wouldn't look for him there as only Luke knew of its whereabouts. There he'd planned his move. He'd track her down and kill her but before he did he'd make her suffer. He stared down at her. 'Vengeance will be mine.' As he spoke he felt the hatred start, like a block of ice at the pit of his stomach, spreading through his system like poison, numbing any more complicated emotion that might lurk there. All his frustrations, from being too often thwarted by her were suddenly washed away in the cold, clean balm of hate.

He laughed. His cackle was insidious, a sly creeping snigger. Alex Rowe. The first time he saw her in person he was struck by her looks. High cheekbones. Bold grey eyes that possessed a direct, stare. Long black hair to her shoulders. He had found out a lot about her private personal life. But one thing he'd learned was never to underestimate her. She was clever, determined and fearless and pursued things to the bitter end, like she had him. He chuckled. Now he was the victor, she his victim. He would savour this long slow torture. He smiled as he contemplated his genius - the bamboo canes. But that was only the beginning. He had other things in store for her.

106

MOVEMENT! FOOTSTEPS receding. He hasn't noticed. My lips tried to move in silent prayer.

I lay still, exhausted, trying to control the pain that seemed to be visiting every corner of my being. Having my hands free gave me a kind of hope. I peeled the tape from my mouth and spat out the piece of cloth that had been choking me. I gasped a few breaths.

Then I looked to see what was poking into me. My whole body gridlocked in shock at the macabre outrage below me. A dozen or so bamboo canes, razor sharp, pointed upwards through the gaps between the wooden slats. Some of them were inches away. A further reality struck me as I surveyed the ghastly senario. The canes were actually growing in huge plant containers. Ingenuous! A long slow death he had said. I remembered seeing in some film how it was a form of Japanese torture. The guards would suspend their victims above honed canes. It was the most horrific death imaginable.

Drawing on my scientific knowledge I pondered the situation. A high nitrogen fertilizer encouraged rapid growth of these plants. Being tropical they thrived on a high air temperature and lots of light. I arched my neck upwards and as expected a series of wide spectrum bulbs, unlit, dotted across the roof. I tried to remember the name of the variety that developed the quickest. I knew Phyllostachys bambusoides grew two inches every hour and Phyllostachys nigra took a little longer. How long had I been here? About an hour? Had they grown? As if to confirm my fears I felt the tip penetrate deeper into my leg muscle. Or so it seemed. A tingle in the pit of my stomach coalesced into a cold, hard knot. I calculated. Which variety of bamboo was he using? If it's P. nigra I've a bit longer. If it was prolific I'd be dead before he returned. And after all he'd said he wanted to witness my last agony. It had to be the P. nigra or some other slow growing species. If I didn't escape from here soon I'm a goner. Shout! I took a few deep breaths and bellowed into the large dome. Birds screamed outside, angry at the intrusion. I screeched again and heard my voice fade over the hills.

I listened for any human reaction. None! Five minutes later I was still alone and close to hopelessness. But I filled my lungs and tried screaming once more. Nothing! I lay still and peered through the slats. Some of the shoots were shorter than the others.

Why?

Cognition!

They'd pierce me one by one.

A slow torturous end!

I must free my limbs.

Somehow!

It was then I felt it. Something slithered over me in the twilight, scaly and dry. In that horrific moment I closed my eyes tight and muttered a prayer. 'Holy mother of God not that as well.' Blood hammered in my ears. A hundred beats - a thousand.

I opened one eye. A snake! Terror ripped through me. My dread of reptiles was almost primal. I let out a blood curdling scream.

The animal wriggled and slid over my thigh. The scaly texture sent ripples of nausea through my viscera. A warm sour liquid rose up my oesophagus and into my mouth. Don't puke. I swallowed it. I mustn't scare it. If I remained still perhaps it might slink away. I froze, focusing on the sweet scent of the foliage and the faint gurgle of water coming from somewhere, but all I could dwell on was the harsh hissing of the serpent.

All of a sudden more pain racked my body. The cane, rooted in my right thigh, seemed to be penetrating further. My body convulsed. Startled, the snake flicked out its narrow forked tongue. I felt a tingle in my thigh. I froze. Venom? Paralysis? Was it a poisonous variety? It looked like the harmless black variety from North America. But was it? If not. I shuddered.

Flashing images.

Venom coursing through my veins.

Vampire stakes drilling through my heart.

My lungs.

My brain.

Instead of an eye – flora- blood red sap dripping from it.

Suddenly the thing coiled tighter around my leg constricting my femoral artery. I could not bear it any longer, and my world nearly swirled into darkness.

The creature, flexing back and forth across my back, dragged my mind back from the distant void. I clenched my hands, digging my nails into my palms and tried to stop myself from shrieking by mentally reciting my favourite poem.

"I will arise and go now, and go to Inisfree.

And a small cabin built there,

Of clay and wattles made:

Nine bean rows will I have there,

A hive for the honey bee,

And live alone in the bee-loud glade."

I'm going no where. I'm about to die. Still in some far remote part, my brain was trying to think of a way out, some way of saving myself. But I was burning up. And thirsty! I listed all the symptoms of poison I knew.

Fever.

Nausea.
Faintness.
Pulse racing.
Hot fluid pain
Distinguish the pain.
Flares of red, orange, yellow, green, blue indigo, violet pyrotechnics exploding silently behind my eyes.
Fear in my chest like sludge, like a sledge hammer.
Thirst!
One drop of water to quench it.
Breath stinks.
Mouth soft and putrid.
Numbness.
No numbness!
Hope makes a teeny wriggle in my breast.
Have I earned a place in heaven? I felt the presence of an angel.
Unconsciousness.

I OPENED my eyes.
I could breath.
Alive…
I made the sign of the cross.
Hands were hauling me upwards. Pain seared through me as the spears were wrenched from my thigh. I peered at my saviour and then I lost consciences.

EPILOGUE

'DO YOU think she'll recover?' Ken stood at Alex's bedside speaking to a doctor.

'Until she comes out of a coma - that's assuming she does – we can't say for certain. Her body's taken a battering. One of the canes pierced a kidney. Fortunately we were able to save it. It's a miracle she's alive. Another few hours and she'd be a goner.'

'If she does come out of the coma, how long before she recovers fully.

'Months, maybe longer. Look I've got to go I've other patients to attend to.'

Ken stared down at Alex. She was so thin, just skin and bone. The doctor had administered a glucose drip to strengthen her, put some meat back on her.

He'd been coming in for a week now and still no change. Her family had been in and out every day and had taken a brief respite from it all. But not him. He'd maintained a constant vigil by her bedside. He should have known Michael would do something. He looked down at her again and froze. Alex had opened her eyes and was looking at him. He held his breath. There wasn't a sound in the room. He could hear the whirling of the machines by her bed and the clatter of the crockery as the ancillary staff made their rounds.

He looked down at her again. She had closed her eyes. Perhaps the effort had been too much for her. Then he heard her say. 'I'm thirsty.'

It was late when he left the hospital. He knew that there was a long road ahead for her but she would recover. It was her indomitable spirit. He wondered who it was who had rescued her. Nobody knew - an angel of mercy. He thought of her again. She'd have to be given a new identity, a new life, somewhere far away from Michael Foley.

Months later the Daily Telegraph lay open on the second page. A caption read:

A BODY HAS BEEN FOUND WASHED UP ON THE BEACH NEAR LIVERPOOL THE MAN HAD BEEN SHOT THOUGH THE HEAD. DNA TESTS ESTABLISHED THAT IT WAS FRANK MORAN, A MEMBER OF A LOCAL GANG.

I stared into the distant past and remembered the priest, remembered how he was with me, remembered his kindnesses, even if they had been feigned they had seemed real to me then. Had he risked his life to save me? It was obvious that Michael had killed him. He had to blame someone.

I placed the paper on the table and thought about the priest for a long time. It was time to seek Michael out. Eliminate him. I'd become the hunter. But first I need a rest. I've been living on the edge so long. Suddenly the 'phone rang.

'Alex speaking!'

'It's James.'

'This is a surprise.'

'I told you I'd be in touch. I'm just driving near your place and thought I might drop in. Thought I'd give you a call first.'

'Oh,' I paused. 'That would be nice.' I found my heart beating faster..

'I'll bring a bottle of bubbly. Would you like that Alex?'

'Hmm …yes.' I wasn't sure I could bear for any man to touch me after what Michael had done. But we could always be friends. And maybe in time …

'That's my girl. See you in a jiffy.'

Weeks later I wrote in my diary.

In the beginning the narrative flowers into a love story and then becomes a night mare but ends as something much more profound: a meditation on something triumphant and threnody, and as compassionate as it is cathartic.

'Looking back on my life now I realise that it has not been drama-free, unmarked by tragedy. But perhaps I attracted some of this drama. There is enough pain in everyday living but maybe I had to climb the tall peak, be on the high road to feel that vitality in my veins. Walking a gentle incline was not fulfilling enough for me.

In my suffering, I have at last learned to be happy again. There is lonesomeness for writers that I never experienced when I was a teacher. It is a solitude that you cannot describe.

And love, the highest form of contentment, what about it? There have been so many men for whom I have had a passionate love, but I don't believe I ever experienced what I think was real love except for Nicholas. We had been close. We'd shared private jokes and played silly card games. I could close my eyes and recall the way he sidled up to me and gave me a kiss, the way his fingers combed through his hair in annoyance, the way he smelt after a long walk, the way he took my hand in fingers long enough to enfold the Millennium Dome.

Life is not scaling a cliff and sliding down; it is about pursuing that unfulfilled hunger for that intangible rainbow - love. I hope I will find it again or perhaps it will find me, God willing.

END

About the Author

Veronica St. Clare was born in Kilkenny, Ireland. Her parents made sacrifices to afford her a convent education and, after working for the Civil Service in Dublin, she married in 1964 and set up residence in Coventry, England. She enrolled as a student at the University of Warwick and studied for a degree in Biochemistry whilst bringing up her two young daughters. After graduating with Honours she embarked on a career in teaching both in state and private schools. After a tragic event in her life cut short her teaching career, it was then that she realised that writing could be her salvation. Life took on a new meaning and through writing she saw herself as a woman beginning to succeed, and as a consequence began to alter the course of her existence.

Her goal was to refuse to become that person who is of no interest to anybody and about whom no one will have the slightest curiosity.

Currently she is writing the sequel to 'Stop All The Clocks' where the heroine, Alex pursues her partner's murderer to the edge of the planet.

Now as a Grandmother of three she still lives in Coventry.

In 2008 she appeared as a contestant in the Channel Four reality show – 'Come dine With Me.'

Printed in the United Kingdom by
Lightning Source UK Ltd., Milton Keynes
139900UK00002B/2/P